*Molly thought
she would never trust
another man as long
as she lived.*

*But then again, she'd
never met a man like
Jake Coulter....*

continued . . .

And for her historical novels . . .

Cherish

"Ms. Anderson reaches new heights in *Cherish*. The magnificently drawn emotions and the arresting characterizations give readers another jewel to treasure more than once."
—*Rendezvous*

Simply Love

"*Simply Love* is so beautiful a romance that words cannot do Catherine Anderson justice. . . . This is not a story you'll quickly forget or one that will gather dust on your shelf. Pick up *Simply Love* whenever you need to reaffirm your beliefs or just when you need to feel good."
—*Romantic Times* (4½ stars)

"A delightful comedy of errors. . . . With this latest, Anderson creates a heartwarming page-turner while establishing herself as a major voice in the romance genre."
—*Publishers Weekly* (starred review)

Keegan's Lady

"A story of stunning beauty and great power. Catherine Anderson has a gift for imbuing her characters with dignity, compassion, courage, and strength that inspire readers. The power of *Keegan's Lady* and the lessons within this glorious romance will live on in your heart forever."
—*Romantic Times* (4½ stars)

"Seldom have the themes of trust and forgiveness been so well treated. . . . Ace Keegan, despite his alpha-male persona, is a paragon of patience and understanding, a romantic hero in every way."
—*Publishers Weekly*

continued . . .

Annie's Song

Sweet Nothings

Catherine Anderson

AN ONYX BOOK

ONYX
Published by New American Library, a division of
Penguin Putnam Inc., 375 Hudson Street,
New York, New York 10014, U.S.A.
Penguin Books Ltd, 80 Strand,
London WC2R ORL, England
Penguin Books Australia Ltd, Ringwood,
Victoria, Australia
Penguin Books Canada Ltd, 10 Alcorn Avenue,
Toronto, Ontario, Canada M4V 3B2
Penguin Books (N.Z.) Ltd, 182–190 Wairau Road,
Auckland 10, New Zealand

Penguin Books Ltd, Registered Offices:
Harmondsworth, Middlesex, England

First published by Onyx, an imprint of New American Library,
a division of Penguin Putnam Inc.

First Printing, January 2002
10 9 8 7 6 5 4 3 2 1

To my husband and hero, Sid, who has filled my life with sunshine. When I think back over the years, I realize that love is an ever-changing journey, and I am so very thankful you are the man who has taken that journey with me. When the way has been rough, you have always been there to steady me. When I've grown disheartened, you've given me the courage to keep trying. In the good times, you've laughed with me and shared in my joy. In the sad times, you have cried with me and given me strength.

In short, you have always been and always will be my everything.

Chapter One

Did they still hang horse thieves in Oregon?

No, of *course* they didn't, Molly Sterling Wells assured herself. And she would stop thinking that way immediately. Wasn't that just like her? Always negative and imagining the worst. No wonder she always lost courage before she finished anything.

She had enough problems to deal with at the moment without borrowing trouble. She'd been on the way out the door early that morning when the phone rang, and now she wished she'd just kept walking. As a result of answering that call, she was now over a hundred and fifty miles from home, her stomach was growling with hunger, and, to top it all off, she was hot, tired, thirsty, and hopelessly lost. The next time she got it into her head to play Good Samaritan, she would think twice.

She had taken so many turns on this gravel country road that she had no idea where she was, and there were no street signs to tell her. For as far as she could see, which wasn't far given the hilly terrain, there were only juniper trees, sagebrush, craggy rocks, and straw-colored grass. This was only April. Did they get so little precipitation in Oregon, east of the Cascades?

Accustomed to the lush greenery and cooler temperatures in her rainy hometown of Portland, she puffed at a damp, curly hank of reddish-brown hair that had escaped her French braid. Her red Toyota 4Runner lurched violently just then. She struggled to keep from driving off into the drainage trench, but the pitching weight of the loaded horse trailer made steering nearly impossible. She tromped on the brake before she lost control. Sweat trickled from her armpits as she twisted to look out the dusty rear window.

"*Blast* it!"

Through the front opening of the huge white trailer, she could see Sonora Sunset. Eyes rolling wildly, the black stallion shrieked in terror. Her heart ached for him, but there was a limit to one's patience, and after five hours of fighting the wheel, she had reached hers. She wanted to jump out of the vehicle and scream at him. Didn't he understand that she was trying to save his life?

Curling her trembling hands over the steering wheel, she rested her forehead on the back of her wrists. This would teach her not to put any stock in Hollywood films. In *The Horse Whisperer*, a woman had pulled a frantic horse in a trailer halfway across the country with little difficulty, stopping at roadside cafés to eat, staying overnight at motels. What a departure from reality.

She raised her head to stare at the road. *I'm not really lost,* she assured herself. She'd gotten directions to the Lazy J Ranch from a farmer before leaving the main road. She glanced at the dash to gauge the distance she'd driven, and it was right at ten miles, exactly how far the man had said she would come before reaching the front gate. Jake Coulter, the horse whisperer, couldn't be more than a few minutes away. Before she knew it, she'd be handing Sunset over to a Robert Redford look-alike, and her part in this crazy rescue mission would be finished.

As if to express his displeasure with the delay, Sonora Sunset shrieked again, making the trailer rock from side to side and end to end. The bucking motion of the Toyota brought Molly's teeth together in a grind of frustration. Little wonder she was exhausted. She'd been trying to drive the equivalent of a mechanical bull all morning.

She let her foot off the brake and allowed the vehicle to

roll forward. *No worries.* After all the near misses she'd had on Interstate 5 this morning, navigating a deserted country road should seem easy.

Narrowly missing yet another rut, she executed a sharp curve and spotted an arched entrance up ahead. Made of freshly peeled logs, it fit the description of the gate that the farmer had given her. As she drew closer, Molly could see the name Lazy J on the crossbeam, the letters bracketed by old horseshoes.

Thank God. She'd finally found Robert Redford.

She swung wide to make the turn onto the rutted dirt road. As she nosed the vehicle through the open gate, she heard the muted sound of a motor and leaned her head out the lowered car window to follow the noise. The road forked up ahead. The last thing she wanted was to go the wrong way and run into a dead end. Backing up a trailer wasn't as easy as it looked.

Sunset didn't like the rougher road surface and lodged a loud complaint. *Just a few more minutes, boy.* They were almost there. According to the Portland trainer, if anyone could help this stallion, Jake Coulter could.

Ker-whump. Molly's teeth snapped together as the Toyota bumped over another deep hole. Dust billowed from under the front tires and hit her squarely in the face. She coughed and squinted. Why would anyone in his right mind choose to live out here? Jake Coulter might be a genius with horses, but he was otherwise sorely lacking in brains.

The road suddenly began a steep ascent that made the Toyota's engine lug under the heavy load. Molly tromped the gas. The engine coughed, and the Toyota lurched. She struggled with the floor shift to grab four-wheel low, breathing a sigh of relief when the SUV labored up the last few feet of hill and the overtaxed engine didn't die.

At the top of the incline, she braked to stare at the little valley below. It seemed to have appeared out of nowhere, a lush oasis at the edge of a desert. Broad expanses of shimmering green grass cut swaths through stands of tall pine, and a sparkling stream ribboned its way from one tip of the valley to the other. Off to the right, she saw a sprawling log home with a green metal roof and two rock chimneys, its rustic design perfectly suited to the forest around it. Maybe Jake Coulter wasn't so dumb after all. *What a gorgeous place.*

The road cut right between the house and a green metal pole building she guessed was a stable. Wide doorways along the back opened onto paddocks, which in turn had gates that led to green pastures fenced with split rails. She saw several horses grazing, the sight so picturesque that the ache of worry in her chest eased. It was a perfect place to leave Sonora Sunset.

Her faith in Hollywood films was restored. All that remained to make the scene complete was for Robert Redford to appear. Though she knew it was foolish, Molly watched for him as she drove the remaining way to the house. After passing the stable, she parked near a corral so she wouldn't block traffic. Then she cut the Toyota engine, pushed at the strands of hair that kept falling over her eyes, and went limp with relief.

She'd done it. Sonora Sunset was safely delivered to the horse psychologist.

As she climbed from the vehicle, the breeze felt lovely against her hot skin, carrying with it the country essence of pine, grass, wildflowers, and a faintly pungent odor she suspected was horse manure. Oddly, the last didn't strike her as being unpleasant, merely earthy, which seemed fitting.

The shade cast by the tall pines and the close proximity of the creek made the temperature at least ten degrees lower here than out on the road. *Horse paradise.* It was so peaceful that she wouldn't have minded staying there herself. For the first time since leaving Portland that morning, she felt safe.

The feeling was short-lived. She jumped with a start

when the engine she'd heard earlier roared to life again. Turning, she saw a man off to one side of the house in a stand of tall trees. He was wielding a chainsaw with fluid precision, cutting up a fallen pine. She got a vague impression of tousled sable hair and dark features. Then her gaze dropped, and for the life of her, she couldn't force it back up to his face.

Stripped to the waist, his bare upper torso rippled in a glorious display of rugged strength. Muscle bunched and flattened as he moved, his sun-bronzed skin glistening with sweat. Molly wasn't usually given to gaping at people—she didn't care to be stared at and felt it was rude—but good manners momentarily abandoned her.

He was *beautiful*.

It was an inappropriate description for a man, she knew, but it was the only word that came to mind. His broad shoulders and back angled in a classic wedge to a lean waist, the furrow of his spine forming a shadowy line down to the top of his jeans. Faded denim sheathed powerfully roped legs that seemed to stretch forever. His body was as sculpted and perfect as a carving in seasoned oak. Just looking at him aroused everything within her that was feminine.

The reaction surprised her. Since her divorce, she had sworn off men. Some women enjoyed the game. Others could never quite grasp the rules. She'd learned from hard experience that she fell into the latter category.

As if he sensed her presence, the man suddenly turned to look over his shoulder. When he spotted her, he went stock-still. Even at a distance, his eyes were as blue and searing as laser beams.

A wave of self-consciousness crashed over Molly, and she wished she'd taken the time to dress for a trip to the country. First impressions were important, and Sonora Sunset's life hung in the balance. Her comfortable wedge heels—practical, go-anywhere shoes in the city—were frivolous and inappropriate for this type of terrain. She

brushed at her slacks. Beneath her palms, she felt the network of creases her sweaty body had steam-pressed into
the twill. There was nothing more unflattering to fat thighs
than wrinkled khaki.

The man shifted his gaze to her trendy SUV, then to the
huge horse trailer. Over here in this land of macho four-
wheel drive trucks, a Toyota pulling a two-stall trailer
clearly wasn't a common sight. An expression of incredulity crossed his dark face.

That made them even. She'd been expecting Robert
Redford, and instead she'd got *"I'm too sexy for my shirt."*

Molly assured herself that he couldn't possibly be the
ranch owner. Men that young and good-looking were far
too preoccupied with flexing their biceps to successfully
operate a business.

Using one powerfully muscled arm, he swung up the
saw to turn off its engine. After laying the wicked-looking
piece of equipment beside the log, he grabbed a dark-brown
Stetson and a blue chambray shirt from a nearby stump.

As he walked toward her, he carefully dusted off the hat
and put it on, tipping the brim just so to shade his eyes.
That struck her as odd. If she were nude to the waist, she'd
throw on the shirt first and worry about her head later.

The well-oiled swing of his hips measured off slow,
lazy strides that covered an amazing amount of ground
with an economy of effort. With every movement, his large
silver belt buckle winked at her in the sunlight. She stared
at the triangular furring of dark hair that bisected his flat,
striated abdomen and narrowed to a dusky line just above
his jeans.

As he drew up a few feet away from her, he gave the
shirt a hard shake to rid it of sawdust, then shoved one arm
down a sleeve. His chest muscles rippled with each movement. Tanned deliciously dark, his skin put her in mind of
melted caramel.

"Howdy," he said, his deep, silky voice curling around
her like tendrils of warm smoke. "How can I help you?"

He could start by getting his buttons fastened. Her tongue was stuck to her teeth. "I, um . . . I'm looking for Jake Coulter."

He brushed wood chips from the rolled-back sleeves of his shirt. "You've found him. What can I do for you?"

He couldn't *be Jake Coulter,* she thought stupidly. He looked nothing like Robert Redford.

The sheer idiocy of that thought jerked Molly up short. Naturally he looked nothing like Redford. It was just that he was so *young.* Not that she'd ever met any horse whisperers to know how old most of them were. It just seemed to her that they should be fifty or better, with lots of experience under their belts. She guessed this man to be in his early thirties, only a couple of years her senior.

He searched her gaze, his eyes a blaze of azure that looked too deep and saw too much. Molly groped for her composure.

"Is something wrong?" he asked.

Everything was wrong, the man, the situation, *everything.* "No, nothing. You just aren't what I expected."

His wide, firm mouth twitched at one corner as if he were biting back a smile. "Sounds like you've got an unhappy traveler on your hands."

"Very unhappy." Molly rubbed her damp palms on her slacks. "I, um—I'm Molly Ster—" She caught herself and gulped. If Rodney had the police combing the state to find her, she didn't dare give her real name. "I'm Molly Houston." Where the name Houston had come from, she had no clue. Unless it was because she wished she were in Texas right then. She pressed a hand to her waist. "I—um—"

Um? It was one of her favorite words when she grew tense. At least he was buttoning his shirt. That was good.

Sonora Sunset chose that moment to whinny and kick the doors of the trailer. Molly jumped. Jake Coulter slowly shifted his gaze to the source of the noise. He gave the impression it would take a dynamite detonation to startle him.

When her heart settled back into her chest, Molly swallowed and tried again. "As you can see, I've got horse problems."

He nodded, his eyes filling with questions. "Looks that way."

"A trainer in Port—" She caught herself and cut the word short. The less he knew about her, the better. "A trainer in southern Oregon told me you're a horse whisperer."

His mouth did tip into a smile then—a slow, bone-melting grin that made her insides feel funny.

"I'm sorry," he said. "If it's a horse whisperer you're looking for, I'm not your man. I don't even believe such a thing exists."

Right in the middle of a flutter, her stomach dropped. She'd risked life and limb to get Sonora Sunset here. "But the trainer seemed so *sure* you could help me."

He glanced at the Toyota. His attention came to rest on her hurriedly packed belongings in the back seat and cargo area. A slight frown pleated his thick, sable brows. "I didn't say I couldn't help you, just that I'm no horse whisperer. What seems to be the problem?"

Given the ruckus Sunset was raising, Molly wondered why he would ask. "He, um . . ." She lifted her hands. "He goes berserk when anyone tries to get near him."

Jake Coulter cocked an eyebrow and said, "Ah."

Ah? That didn't strike her as being a suitable response from a man who was supposedly such an expert. "Can you work with a stallion that's totally uncooperative, Mr. Coulter?"

"Could be. Depends on the horse."

Oh, God, she was tired. Down to the bone tired. She wanted him to reassure her and say he'd fix everything. Instead he just stood there, studying her thoughtfully. It was the horse that needed help, not her.

"The trainer says he's dangerous," she went on, "that if something isn't done, he may have to be destroyed."

"How long has he been acting up?" He swung up onto the wheel well with the ease of a man familiar with horse trailers and the gigantic, four-legged critters hauled in them. As he looked in at Sunset through the side slats, he asked, "Did this just start or—?"

Sunset shrieked and lunged so sharply away that the conveyance pitched sideways. Coulter grabbed for hand-holds to keep his footing.

"Holy hell." He directed a smoldering glance at Molly. "Lady, this animal has been whipped."

She wrapped her arms around her waist. "I realize that. I didn't do it, if that's what you're thinking."

"Who did?"

She groped frantically for a safe answer to that question. When one didn't come to mind, she settled for telling the truth. "My ex-husband."

"He should be horsewhipped himself."

Molly thought running Rodney's male pride through a laundry press sounded more satisfying. "This isn't the first time it's happened. It was just never so bad before."

"Lord Almighty, I've seen some mistreated animals in my day, but never anything like this. How could you allow it?"

Molly bristled. "I didn't *allow* it. I had no idea it was happening."

"Your ex has been whipping your horse, and you didn't know it was happening? If this animal is yours, why didn't the trainer notify you?"

She thought quickly. "There were never any marks on Sunset before."

"Even so, the horse must have acted up afterward."

Until this morning, Molly had observed Sunset only from a safe distance. "I never noticed him behaving strangely, and if the trainer did, he never said anything."

He mulled that over for a moment. His gaze still sharp on hers, he finally jumped down from the wheel well. "Does this horse even belong to you, lady?" he asked with lethal softness.

Molly was afraid he'd tell her to hit the road if she admitted the truth. Without his help, Sunset could end up at a glue factory. "Of course he belongs to me. How would I have brought him here otherwise?"

"Good question." The frown creases between his dark brows deepened as he regarded her. "Do you have papers to verify ownership?"

"Papers? Oh, dear. I totally forgot to bring them."

"He looks like a very expensive animal. If he should injure himself while I'm trying to work with him, I could get my ass sued off."

"I'll sign a waiver," she offered, "absolving you of all liability."

"A waiver wouldn't be worth the paper it's written on if you don't own the horse." He rubbed his jaw, his eyes darkening as he searched hers. Then he cut another glance at the trailer and swore under his breath. "I can't afford a bunch of lawyer fees right now."

He was about to send them packing. She just knew it. Molly listened to Sunset's panicked grunts, and her heart nearly broke for him. She couldn't take him back to Portland and let people who cared nothing about him decide his fate. There was also the very real possibility that Rodney might hurt him again. "I just told you I own the horse, Mr. Coulter. Are you accusing me of lying?"

His jaw muscle bunched, and for what seemed an eternity, they engaged in a visual standoff. She held up her hands in supplication. "Do I look like a horse thief?"

She couldn't read his expression, and her nerves screamed as she waited for him to answer. He glanced at the stuff in the back of her Toyota again.

"No," he finally admitted in a gravelly voice, his mobile mouth tipping into a sheepish grin even as he sighed in defeat. "All right. Let's have a look at the poor fellow." He turned toward her vehicle, suddenly all business. "Are your keys in the ignition?"

Before she could answer he was in the Toyota and cranking the engine. She stepped out of the way as he jockeyed the SUV to get the trailer lined up with the gate. He made backing a trailer look so easy she wondered why she found it so difficult.

"You aren't going to turn him loose, are you?" she asked as he climbed back out of the 4Runner.

He was so tall that he'd mashed the top of his Stetson on the roof of her car. "To get a feel for the horse, I have to unload him."

"If you decide you can't work with him, will you be able to put him back? He's being very difficult. This morning it took the trainer and three stable employees to get him up the ramp."

He drew off his hat to reshape the crown, then settled it back on his head. "I think I can manage. If need be, I'll get my brother Hank to help. He's off in the north section, but I can call him in by radio."

Molly closed her eyes in dread as he opened the trailer doors and extended the ramp. She heard his boots thumping on the wood. Then he said, "Easy, boy, easy."

Sunset whinnied and, judging by the noises that followed, started kicking for all he was worth. Molly opened her eyes partway, half expecting to see Jake Coulter come flying out the back end of the conveyance.

"Easy, boy," she heard him say again.

A second later, she glimpsed Sunset's hindquarters. The stallion nearly danced off the ramp, but somehow Coulter managed to get him going in the right direction again. The thunderous tattoo of hooves on wood made Molly hug her waist and clench her teeth.

Sunset had nearly killed his trainer this morning. She had neglected to tell Jake Coulter that for fear he might refuse to work with the horse. Now she wished with all her heart that she'd been honest.

If the fool man got hurt, it would be entirely her fault.

Chapter Two

As it turned out, Jake Coulter proved to be perfectly capable of handling the stallion by himself. When Sunset tried to rear and strike with his front hooves, the well-muscled rancher foiled the attempt, holding fast to the animal's halter and using his weight to keep him from throwing his head. In a flurry of sound and motion, man and beast spilled down the ramp into the corral.

Coulter was incredibly fast on his feet. When he released the horse, he made for the fence with such speed that all Molly saw was a blur. She released a breath she hadn't realized she'd been holding as he vaulted over the barrier, hat still perched jauntily on his head.

He blotted sweat from his brow with the cuff of his sleeve. "Boy, howdy, you're right. He's a handful."

A handful? A two-year-old child was a handful. The horse whinnied and circled the corral. His hooves kicked up clouds of dust that burned Molly's nostrils. Still hugging her waist, she made tight fists on her white cotton blouse. She'd seen Sunset in action this morning and was afraid he might jump the fence.

Coulter didn't seem worried. He shoved up the trailer ramp and drew the corral gate closed. After securing the latch, he rested his folded arms on a fence rail to observe the horse's behavior. At least that was what Molly guessed he was doing. It put her in mind of the way doctors observed patients after they were admitted to a psychiatric ward, a close scrutiny that stripped away layers and missed nothing.

A thick, suffocating feeling came into her throat. She watched Sunset circling the corral, so sad for him that her bones ached. Maybe horses didn't feel the same way people did about having their privacy invaded.

The shift of his shoulders snapping the chambray taut across his chest, Jake began tucking in his shirt with hard stabs of his fingers. Watching him, Molly got a bad feeling. Her trepidation increased when he jumped up to straddle the fence. "Mr. Coulter?"

If he heard, he gave no indication of it. His gaze was riveted on the horse. Molly stared up at his profile, noting the determined set of his jaw. In the sunlight, his bottom lip shimmered like silk, the only hint of softness in a face that might otherwise have been chiseled from granite.

"Mr. Coulter, you aren't thinking about going in there again, are you?"

He flicked her a look. "How else can I decide if I can work with him?"

"But, Mr. Coulter, he's dangerous."

"A thousand pounds of horse with an attitude problem is most always dangerous. That's what keeps me in business."

"At least get something to defend yourself."

"What do you suggest, a club?" He braced his hands on the rail to lift up and get more comfortable. After watching Sunset for a few seconds more, he shook his head. "If I have something in my hands, he'll think I mean to beat him with it."

"I really wish you'd reconsider," she said shakily as he swung his other leg over the rail. "He almost killed his trainer this morning."

If that gave him pause, he concealed it well. He glanced down, his blue eyes twinkling. "Don't worry, I won't get hurt."

Molly clung to the fence rail, watching helplessly as he

lowered himself into the enclosure. Sunset reared and pierced the air with a frantic whinny that held a note of warning.

"Whoa, boy." Coulter set his dusty boots wide apart, his legs slightly bent, the flex of muscle in his thighs visible under the denim of his jeans. "No point in getting worked up."

Sunset was having none of that, not that Molly blamed him. Coulter looked formidable—strong, lightning quick, and prepared for anything. Not even a huge, swift animal like the stallion could hope to escape such an adversary within the confines of a small corral.

Molly knew how it felt to be cornered and helpless. The quivering terror and underlying outrage, the claustrophobic panic that made it nearly impossible to breathe. Oh, yes, she knew.

Sunset wheeled and ran to the opposite end of the corral, then turned to face his tormentor. The whites of his eyes formed crescents over his irises. The muscles in his shoulders quivered with terror.

"You poor, miserable thing." Jake held out his hands so the horse could see they were empty. Tendons and distended veins roped his bronze forearms. "See there? Nothing to be afraid of."

Sunset stood on his rear legs. He screamed wildly and struck at the air, forelegs churning, hooves flashing. When he came down on all fours, his feet hit the earth with such force that Molly could have sworn she felt the vibration.

"Easy." The man was so focused on the horse now that Molly suspected he'd forgotten she was there. "Easy, boy. You're in no shape for this."

Arms still held wide, his lean body tensed to spring if the stallion charged at him, the rancher held his ground while Sunset cut circles around him. He turned to keep an eye on the animal at all times, but beyond that, he didn't move, expending little energy while Sunset exhausted himself.

"You see? I'm not going to hurt you," he said in that same low voice.

Molly dug her nails into her palms and bit down hard on the inside of her cheek, wishing with all her heart that Sunset would stop fighting the inevitable. Why couldn't he understand that Coulter was only trying to help him? Sometimes those who seemed to be your worst enemies in the beginning turned out to be your best friends. Molly had learned that the hard way. Unfortunately, there was no way to impart that bit of wisdom to the horse. He would have to find it out for himself—just as she had.

The horse continued to dart back and forth until he was blowing and stumbling with weariness. His sides looked as if they'd been flecked with shaving cream.

She was dripping with sweat herself by the time the stallion succumbed to exhaustion. Hands locked on the fence, she stared at the horse through a blur of scalding tears. He stood with his rump pressed into a corner of the corral, great head hanging, sides heaving. He was so winded that he looked ready to drop.

She prayed the worst was over, but instead of leaving the corral, Coulter turned slightly sideways to the stallion and bent his head. Keeping his gaze fixed on the ground, he made a slow approach. The horse watched warily but didn't offer to move until the rancher got about five feet from him. Then Sunset grunted and stumbled sideways.

Coulter stopped there. Bewildered, Molly watched him mark the spot with the heel of his boot. Then he backed away, only to approach the line again and again until Sunset showed no reaction whatsoever. Only then did the rancher seem satisfied.

"Good boy," he said, his voice as smooth as warm honey. "We'll get there. But that's enough for today."

He vaulted back over the fence. "I'm sorry about that," he told Molly. "I know it's not easy, letting a stranger do that to your horse."

"What purpose did it serve? You never got close enough to touch him."

Resting an arm on the fence rail, he crossed his booted feet. The breeze kicked back up, molding his light blue shirt to his torso. "It's enough that he knows I could have. On some level, he understands now that I don't mean him any harm." His firm mouth tipped in a grin. "And I learned the same about him."

"You did?"

He nodded. "He's a big old boy and fast as greased lightning. If he had a mean streak, instead of cutting circles around me, he could have tried to run me down. The horse isn't vicious, just damn scared, and who can blame him?"

He walked over to a faucet at the north corner of the corral and began filling a five-gallon bucket. Observing him through the rails, Molly asked, "Does that mean you'll try to help him?"

Instead of answering, he bent to shove the bucket under the fence and then backed away. Sunset eyed him warily. Then he stumbled wearily toward the water. When the horse almost reached the bucket, Jake stepped forward to snatch it away.

Molly clenched her teeth. She watched with growing anger as Jake repeated the process again and again, never allowing the poor horse to drink.

When she could bear it no longer, she cried, "Why are you doing that?"

He flashed her a deadpan look.

"You know he's dying for a drink. Tormenting him that way is cruel."

He moved to the east corner of the corral to slide the bucket under the fence again. "You can't let an overheated horse drink his fill." Once again, he waited until Sunset almost reached the water, then he quickly retrieved the bucket. "When horses get this hot, you have to walk them. Normally I'd lead him around for five minutes and then allow him to have a little water before walking him another five. Since I can't put him on a lead, I'm getting him to move the only way I can."

Molly jerked her gaze back to Sunset. In the heat of the afternoon sunlight, rivers of sweat had begun to crystallize on his lather-flecked black coat. "Oh," she said weakly.

"I'll let him have a little to drink here in another minute." He put the bucket inside the corral again and stepped away so the horse would approach. "Only enough to wet his whistle, though. Then I'll walk him some more. You keep doing that until the horse no longer seems eager to drink. It should be safe then to let him have all the water he wants." He moved forward to reclaim the bucket. "If I let him load up right now, he'll founder or colic. Nine times out of ten, that kills them."

Molly felt foolish, and she hadn't the faintest notion what to say.

A couple of minutes later, Jake finally allowed Sunset to have a bit of water. Then he lured the stallion around the corral again. Molly noticed now that he was checking his watch. When the horse had cooled down, he refilled the bucket and left it inside the corral. He looked thoughtful as he moved to rejoin Molly.

"It appears to me you don't know a hell of a lot about horses," he said conversationally as he rested his arms on a rail. "Can you explain that to me?"

"Just because I've never seen anyone cool a horse off in precisely that way doesn't mean I'm totally ignorant about them." Afraid she might appear tense, she lowered her arms from around her waist. They felt like lengths of stiff hose bracketing her body. "In town, most people board their horses and pay someone for the everyday care." That much wasn't a lie. Rodney and his Yuppie friends boarded their horses, and she knew they seldom did any actual work. "I hired a trainer and was never directly involved in Sunset's daily routine."

In the sunlight, she could see the squint lines that fanned out from the corners of his eyes. His thick, dark lashes cast feathery shadows onto his lean cheeks. "Are you familiar at all with farms and ranches?"

"Farms and ranches?" She sensed her answer was important and that, for reasons beyond her, Jake Coulter might refuse to work with Sunset if her ranch experience was limited. "I've been around them all my life." She thought of the countless times she'd driven past farms and ranches on her way into Portland. That qualified. She'd been around them, right? "Why do you ask?"

He glanced at her wrinkled blouse and slacks. "I'm just trying to get a handle on how much practical experience you have with horses."

Zilch. "I'm no expert, as I said, but I've got enough experience to get by." The trick was in avoiding the beasts entirely, an endeavor she'd been totally successful at until today. "I fall somewhere between beginner and intermediate."

The corners of his mouth twitched. "I see."

Molly was beginning to worry that he really did see, which wouldn't do at all. "Sunset's life is on the line. Without your help, I'm afraid he'll be destroyed."

His gaze moved past her to settle on the Toyota. "It's apparent you need help."

"Well, then? My experience with horses isn't the issue."

"I didn't say it was. It's just that in training like this, owner participation makes all the difference."

"Owner what?"

"Owner participation. I know it may seem like a lot to ask, but one thing I insist upon is that the owners come out to work with their horses several times a week."

Molly felt as if the ground disappeared from under her. She threw an appalled look at the stallion.

Jake raised his dark eyebrows. "Is that a problem? It won't be much help to you if the horse will respond only to me."

For some reason, Molly had likened this situation to dropping her car off with a mechanic. She'd planned to simply leave Sunset here, then come back to pick him up when he was all fixed. "You expect me to—to go *in* there with him?"

"It's a little hard to work with a horse from this side of the fence."

She recalled her vow not to be a quitter this time. But, *oh, God,* she'd never bargained for this.

"I'll take every precaution to make sure you're safe," he assured her. "And I'll always be close at hand in case anything goes wrong. Does that ease your mind any?"

Only marginally. "I, um . . . I live quite a distance away, Mr. Coulter. Driving that far several times a week will be impossible for me."

He glanced at her Toyota again. "Looks to me like you're living out of the back of your car at the moment." He rested his weight more heavily on the fence rail. "It also looks to me like you packed in an all-fired hurry."

She couldn't very well deny the evidence he could see with his own eyes. "I'm sort of—relocating."

"So the distance you'll have to drive won't necessarily be a problem. You can light somewhere nearby."

Her throat had gone so dry that her larynx felt as if it was moving up and down inside a tube of sandpaper. "I suppose that's possible."

He turned to face her, all trace of humor vanishing from his gaze. "That being the case, your working with the horse on a regular basis shouldn't be a problem."

Her courage deserted her, and she almost sold Sunset down the river by blurting out the truth. Just as she parted her lips to speak, she glanced at Sunset. In the slanting sunlight, the blood that beaded his wounds glistened like rubies against black velvet.

Guilt was such a terrible thing, plaguing you every waking moment and then following you into your dreams. Molly remembered the countless nights she'd paced the floors, unable to sleep. Twice in her life, she'd failed people she loved, and they'd both ended up dead. She truly didn't know if she could live with another death on her conscience, even if Sunset was only a horse.

"No, working with him shouldn't be a problem," she said shakily.

"Good." Coulter straightened away from the fence. "I couldn't help but notice that your rig is riding on empty. Can I take that to mean you're short on cash?"

Molly straightened her shoulders. "I'm sorry, but I can't see how my finances are any of your business, Mr. Coulter."

"They'll become my business quick enough when I'm looking to get paid and you don't have the money."

"How much do you charge?"

"Five hundred a week. That covers everything, not just the training, but boarding the horse as well, which can be expensive when you tally up stable wages and feed."

Molly's heart sank. "That seems a little steep."

"You said it best. Horses like that are dangerous, and not just anyone will work with them. I'm damned good at what I do. My services don't come cheap."

"I'm sure you're worth every cent. I don't mean to imply that you aren't." She rubbed her arms, feeling suddenly cold despite the warmth of the day. "How long do you estimate that it may take to get Sunset calmed down?"

"Could take as little as a month, or it may take six. It's impossible to predict. Some horses don't respond at all."

"Oh, *my.*"

"I have a good success rate. Most of the time, a horse will hook on with me, but it's always a gamble. Regardless of the outcome, my fee is the same. I can't see my way clear to work for nothing simply because a horse proves to be beyond help."

Molly didn't blame him for that. He couldn't run a ranch successfully on charity. "Actually, Mr. Coulter, five hundred a week will put me in a bit of a pinch. Would it be possible to work out some kind of payment plan?"

He rubbed his jaw. "I hate to sound mercenary, particularly when an animal has been so cruelly abused, but I can't take any jobs on credit right now. Like I mentioned before, I'm just getting this place on its feet. Things are really tight, and I need to see my money up front. I've got only so many hours a day to devote to horse training, and right now, that's paying my bank loans."

Molly had gone to an ATM before leaving Portland, but the machine had stopped spitting cash after the daily limit, giving her a thousand in her wallet, all totaled. She'd spent some of that on gas to get here. She had another eight hundred in checking, the only account available to her right now, but she didn't dare touch it. All bank and ATM transactions could be traced.

If she gave Jake Coulter a small deposit, she might have enough money left over to survive until she found a job, but there was no way she could afford to cough up five hundred dollars a week. Not unless she meant to sleep in her car and scavenge for food until she found work. *If* she found work. Most employers asked to see an applicant's identification, wanted a list of references, and needed a social security number on file. Just in case the police had an APB out on her, she didn't dare give out that information.

Her head was starting to ache, whether from tension or lack of nourishment, she wasn't sure. Not that it mattered. Pain was pain, and this particular brand was whipping her thoughts into a jumble with the brutal efficiency of a wire whisk.

"Well . . . that pretty much throws a wrench in the fan blades, I guess."

"I accept credit cards," he offered.

That was no help. Crazy, legally incompetent women weren't allowed to carry plastic. Oh, how Molly despised Rodney Wells in that moment. "I'm afraid I don't have a credit card."

He drew off his hat to rake his fingers through his hair, leaving thick furrows in the glistening strands of brown.

After staring at the ground for a long moment, he gouged the dirt with his boot heel.

Molly could see that he was trying to think of a way he might help her. As much as she appreciated his concern, she could think of no way around the money problem and doubted he would, either. Her heart twisting painfully, she kept her gaze carefully averted from Sunset, afraid she might embarrass herself with tears if she let herself contemplate what might be in store for him.

"It looks as if I've troubled you for nothing," she said, forcing out the words around a lump in her throat that seemed to grow larger by the second. "Thank you for—"

He held up a staying hand, cutting her off in midsentence. When his gaze met hers, she saw that the twinkle of amusement had returned to his eyes, only this time she had the impression that he was laughing at himself and not her. "Can I be totally frank with you?"

Molly had a feeling he was about to speak his mind whether she gave him her leave or not. "Certainly."

"I love horses, and I instinctively like you." His voice dipped to a husky timbre. "I'm not sure I'll be able to sleep at night if I turn the two of you away." He hooked a thumb toward her rig. "I have a real bad feeling you're out of work, out of luck, and almost out of money. Am I right about that?"

Molly tried to smile and failed miserably. "That pretty much covers it."

"Do you even have anywhere to stay?"

A flush of shame moved up her neck. Now she knew how homeless people must feel. "Not at present. I'll stay at a motel until I find a job, I guess."

"With a horse in a trailer? You can't keep that stallion locked up indefinitely."

Molly hadn't thought that far ahead yet. She'd left Portland this morning with only one thought driving her, to deliver Sunset to this man.

Thinking quickly, she said, "Maybe I can pasture him somewhere."

"You can't pasture a horse like that just anywhere. He could kill somebody."

She hugged her waist and shifted her feet, trying frantically to think. It was true; Sunset was dangerous, and pasturing him somewhere wouldn't be safe. Only someone like Jake Coulter could deal with a horse that difficult, and the man charged more than she could possibly afford.

She thought of the fortune that her father had left her. All that money, sitting in the bank, and she couldn't get her hands on a single cent of it. *Oh, God . . . oh, God.* Without Coulter's help, Sunset might be destroyed, and she'd be powerless to prevent it.

She couldn't say why she cared so deeply about a horse. She only knew she felt an affinity with the stallion that defied all reason. Maybe her feelings stemmed from the fact that they'd both been nearly destroyed by the same man, albeit in different ways. If she failed to save the horse, would she be able to save herself?

Struggling to hide how devastated she felt, she thrust out her hand to Jake Coulter and forced a smile so stiff it almost hurt her face. "I'll manage somehow. Thank you, Mr. Coulter. If you'll reload Sunset, we'll be on our way. You've been very kind, taking time out of your busy schedule without so much as a phone call in advance. It's time I let you get back to your work."

He took her hand, his long, work-roughened fingers curling warmly over her wrist. He said nothing, just looked at her. Then he smiled slowly. "Can you cook and do housework?"

That was the last thing she had expected him to say. "Can I what?"

His smile deepened. "I've had an ad in the paper for over a month with little response. If you're willing to work, maybe we can strike a bargain."

He still held tightly to her hand. His grip didn't hurt, but she had a feeling it would be as impossible to escape as a manacle. The pain in her temples sharpened, the sun stabbing her eyes like a pick.

"You want me to be a ranch cook and housekeeper?" She might have laughed, but she was afraid the top of her head might blow off.

"It seems like a perfect solution to me. You're down on your luck, your horse needs help, and I'm in sore need of a cook."

His perfect solution was her worst nightmare. She could cook well enough to suit herself, but she was easy to please. Few men were so accommodating. On top of that, it was a risky thing to do. This ranch was miles from town, and Jake Coulter was a total stranger.

"Cooking really isn't my forte. I can't possibly do it for a wage."

"Sure you can." He winked at her. "Any woman who pulled a horse trailer over the Cascades with that glorified roller skate can do damn near anything she sets her mind to."

He made the idea sound so *reasonable*. And, oh, how tempting it was. She might at least buy Sunset some time. If the horse responded quickly, as little as a few days might mean the difference between life and death for him. "It's a very generous offer."

"Then say yes," he urged. "What have you got to lose? Private quarters come with the job." He hooked a thumb over his shoulder at a small log house farther down the creek. "It isn't fancy, but the roof doesn't leak and it's halfway clean. Just a small two-bedroom. I pay four hundred a week, plus board. I usually offer a fairly decent benefit package, but if you'd rather be paid under the table, that's doable as well."

Under the table? That meant she wouldn't have to give him a social security number. It also meant more money because no taxes would be taken from her wages.

"Come on," he cajoled. "This is the only way I can offset the costs to help you."

"Sixteen hundred a month doesn't quite cover your training fees," she pointed out.

"If you're an employee, I can give you a break on my rates. To make up the extra, you can do outside chores. I'm always shorthanded in the stable."

He expected her to work in the stable? Molly remembered telling him she'd been around farms and ranches all her life. He clearly believed she'd be far more useful than she actually would be.

"I'm not very experienced at working in stables."

His eyes warmed on hers. "Somewhere between beginner and intermediate? Don't worry. I'll show you what needs to be done."

He had an answer for everything. She stared wistfully at the little log house. It looked so peaceful, a sanctuary along the stream with a forest at its back. This ranch was tucked away from the world. Even from out on the road, it was invisible. If the police were looking for her, what were the chances that they'd ever find her here?

"We can do it on a thirty-day trial," he offered. "If either of us is unhappy with the arrangement at the end of that time, we can back out, no questions asked. How does that sound?"

It sounded marvelous, like the answer to a prayer. She turned a gaze toward Sunset, feeling numb all over and oddly disconnected from reality. *When the going got rough, the new Molly Sterling Wells got going.* The stallion's life was at stake. If she had cookbooks at her disposal, she might be able to get by for a while in the kitchen, and cleaning was a no-brainer. Didn't a day that had begun so crazily beg for a crowning insanity as its finale?

"Don't think it to death," he advised. "Some of life's best decisions are made on the spur of the moment."

"Eventually, if I can work out some wrinkles, I'll be returning to my job. I'm on a leave of absence of sorts." Sunlight stabbed into her eyes again, blurring his face to little more than a dark silhouette with white spots dancing over his features. "Did I mention that?"

"Not a problem. If you'll agree to give me a month's notice before you quit, I'll have time to find a replacement." He grimaced. "Hopefully I'll have better luck with my ad next time around."

Molly felt as if she were about to take a flying leap off a cliff. *Courage.* Maybe he was right, and she was thinking it to death. Being too hesitant had always been one of her downfalls. *"Life is what's happening while you're trying to decide what to do,"* her father had laughingly told her more times than she could count. This man was offering her a way out, not only a job but a place to live, with lodging and feed for Sunset tossed into the bargain.

"All right," she said a little breathlessly. "I'll give it a try. Why not?"

A slow grin creased his dark face. "We have a deal then?"

"Yes, we have a deal."

His smile broadened. "Welcome to the Lazy J, Molly Stir-Houston."

Stir-Houston? Molly's stomach felt as if it had dropped to the region of her knees. She recalled how she'd nearly blurted out her real last name when she first got here. He had caught the slip, and now he was teasing her about it. That could mean only one thing. He knew she had given him a fake surname.

If he had guessed that much, how much more did he suspect?

Chapter Three

Once Molly accepted Jake Coulter's offer, she got no opportunity to change her mind. Though the man's fastest speed seemed to be a saunter, he covered ground with amazing dispatch, forcing her to step fast to keep up with him. Before she knew quite how it happened, he'd parked her Toyota in front of the small log cabin along the creek and set himself to the task of unloading her belongings. As Molly scurried back and forth carrying bags, her earlier misgivings came back to haunt her, and one question circled endlessly in her thoughts. *Have I lost my mind?*

Savvy women didn't trust strange men. One had only to read the newspaper headlines to understand how foolhardy it was. Now that she was out of the sun, the pain in her head had eased a bit, enabling her to think more clearly. With clarity came a host of concerns. How could she be sure Jake Coulter wasn't a sex offender or serial killer? If she vanished, no one would think to look for her on a cattle ranch in central Oregon.

As if he sensed her nervousness, Jake didn't enter the bedroom with her when he showed her through the house. Instead he stood in the doorway, blocking the only exit with his considerable bulk. *Wonderful.* The man weighed well over two hundred pounds, every inch of him honed to a steely hardness. If he meant her harm, she would have a devil of a time getting past him.

"Are you okay?" he asked, jerking her away from her troubled musings.

Molly blinked and focused on his dark face, studiously ignoring the impressive span of his shoulders. "I'm fine," she assured him, wanting to cringe when her voice came out thin and tremulous. "A bit of a headache is all."

Feeling stiff and graceless, she turned to take in the room, which was small and held only the essential furnishings. She bent to test the mattress. "What a lovely brass bedstead. Have you any idea what they go for now?"

He shifted to brace a muscular shoulder against the doorframe, the crown of his brown Stetson brushing against the crossbeam. "More than they're worth?"

Molly gave a startled laugh. Having haunted antique stores with her adoptive mother Claudia for years, she had a keen appreciation for collectibles. The memories of those shopping expeditions stabbed her with sadness. Not only had she lost her father a year ago, but to all intents and purposes, she'd lost the only mother she'd ever known as well.

"Practically speaking, I suppose brass beds are a little overpriced."

He eyed the mattress. "I'm a nostalgia buff myself, but I draw the line when it interferes with comfort. People back then must have been midgets. When I slept on that sucker, my feet hung over the end, and my ankles banged on the foot rails all night."

Molly could believe it. Jake Coulter wasn't exactly of diminutive stature—a fact that seemed to have taken center stage in her thoughts now that she was alone in the cabin with him. When her therapist, Sam Banks, had encouraged her to let down her guard with men, she felt sure this wasn't the sort of thing he'd had in mind.

She patted the mattress. Then she remembered she'd already done that once and jerked her hand back. If this man was a sex offender, she didn't want to put ideas in his head.

"I'm sure the length will do nicely enough for me. I'm not very tall."

His unnerving blue gaze took a leisurely journey from the tips of her toes to the top of her head. "No, I don't guess you are. If a good wind came up, you'd blow away."

"Hardly." Molly pressed a hand to her stomach. In her early twenties, her rail-thin lower body had filled out, adding an unattractive thickness to her waist and hips and eliciting comments from Rodney that she looked pregnant. Not even the safari shirt she wore hid the flaws. "I'm not what you'd call skinny."

His sable brows drew together as his gaze moved over her again. "Nope. More what I'd call pleasingly plump." He let that hang there, then flashed her a lopsided grin that did strange things to her pulse rate. "With the emphasis on 'pleasingly.' "

He turned away, leaving her to wonder what that meant. In her experience, kindly adults used the phrase "pleasingly plump" to describe chubby children. Not that she cared what he thought. She had long since accepted that her body was far from svelte, and no amount of dieting would change it.

She listened to the rhythmic thump of his boots on the old plank floor as he moved through the small house. Casting a glance toward the comfortable-looking bed, she made her weary body move. She found her new employer in the antiquated kitchen. He'd struck a match and was trying to light the pilot on the propane cooking range, once lime green but now yellowed with age. Never having used such an outdated appliance, she stepped closer to watch.

Just as she bent down to peer at the burner, the gas ignited and flame shot toward her face with a startling *kawhoosh!* She squeaked and leaped away, slapping at her shirt and hair. "Blessed Mother!"

Jake caught her by the shoulders to hold her still. "Are you burned?" He moved a hand over her hair and shoulder. "Molly, answer me."

She clutched her throat and gulped, no longer entirely sure all the heat she felt was due to gas ignition. Everywhere his hand touched, her skin burned. *Red alert.* This man could be dangerous in more ways than one. "I'm fine. I'm sorry. Really, I'm fine." She tried to escape his grasp by wiggling away. "It just went off in my face and startled me. I don't think it actually burned me anywhere."

He gave her hair a final check. "I'm the one who's sorry. I should have warned you. These old gas stoves are bad for that. They even startle me sometimes."

He turned back to test the valves. This time, Molly stood well away, not entirely sure which she most wanted to avoid, the stove or the man. Rings of blue fire leaped to life, making her nerves leap as well. If she had to cook on that horrid old thing, she'd starve.

Apparently satisfied, he turned off the burners and patted the ugly green porcelain with long, sturdy fingers. "She seems to be in fine working order."

He turned on the sink faucets next. The first rush of water was a rusty brown, but it quickly cleared as the flow washed away the pipe sediment. He cupped a hand to collect some water, then bent to taste it. After wiping his mouth, he said, "You'll love the well here. It's artesian."

Molly's gaze was fixed on the old hand pump mounted at one side of the sink. She'd come across a few in antique shops, but she'd never seen one in a house. "Does that still work?" she asked incredulously.

"Like a charm. When I modernized the kitchen, I was going to jerk it out, but my sister Bethany had a conniption fit." He primed the pump with some water from the faucet, then began working the handle. After only a few tries, water gushed from the spout. He stepped to one side. "Try some."

Taking care not to bump against him, Molly cupped both hands under the flow and bent to drink. Maybe she was only thirsty, but never had anything tasted so wonderful. She gulped greedily for a moment and then remembered he was using muscle power to keep up the flow. Embarrassed, she straightened away, wiping her chin. "I'm sorry. That's absolutely *divine*. It's like drinking from a crystal-clear mountain brook."

He stopped working the handle, his gaze falling to the droplets still on her bottom lip. Feeling self-conscious, she scrubbed her hand over her mouth.

The intense blue of his eyes darkened to a stormy blue gray. "No need to apologize. I don't mind pumping, and water's cheap."

"Not in—" Molly broke off, mentally waving her arms to keep from falling into that one. She'd nearly said water wasn't cheap in Portland. She glanced away, wishing, not for the first time, that she were a more practiced liar. "Not in my hometown."

His dark brows lifted. "What town is that?"

She thought of all the communities that lay along Interstate 5. "Grants Pass."

"Ah." He nodded. "Nice place. My college roommate grew up there."

"You went to college?"

He chuckled. "Us country boys need to have some kind of edge."

Molly had meant no offense. She was just surprised. Jake Coulter didn't have the air of any college man she'd ever known. In his Wranglers and blue chambray shirt, he seemed as earthy and elemental as the wilderness bordering his land, and he sometimes spoke with a lazy disregard for proper grammar. "Which university did you attend?"

"Oregon State. That's where a lot of us country boys go. My twin brothers attended the veterinary school there. My brother Zeke went for his MBA. Hank and I focused on ag and animal husbandry."

"Good grief, you've got *four* brothers?"

"And a sister. That's how I got ornery. I was the oldest of six, and the only way to survive was to get mean." He stepped around her to set the temperature controls inside the ancient refrigerator. "What's your alma mater?"

Another wave of memories washed through Molly, this one leaving her cold and feeling oddly empty. "I went to college only for a short time." That was the story of her life; big dreams, no staying power. "Things happened, and I dropped out."

He glanced over the top of the door at her. "Never would have guessed it. You talk like you've got an impressive education under your belt."

She flashed what she hoped was a bright smile. "I read a lot of books."

"A self-made woman, are you? What line of work?"

Her throat felt as if she'd swallowed drain cleaner, and she glanced longingly at the water still dripping from the pump spout. "Finance," she settled for saying. Given her penchant for tripping over her own lies, it seemed wise to stick as close to the truth as possible. "I work at an investment firm."

"When you're not on hiatus?" he inserted.

"Right. If you've got any discretionary dollars to invest, I'm the person to talk to."

He chuckled and ducked back into the refrigerator, his rumbling voice echoing back at her. "Right now, I don't have a discretionary dime. Buying back the ranch has sucked me dry."

Buying it back? Molly wondered what he meant. Had he owned the Lazy J before? She wanted to ask, but it wasn't any of her business, and she squelched the urge.

When he finally emerged from the refrigerator, the old appliance's motor hummed to life, making the floor vibrate. Molly curled her toes. As he closed the thick, rounded door, she noticed the name Gibson scrolled across the white enamel front.

"The old gal's a marvel. Keeps the milk so cold, your teeth ache."

Molly thought of her shiny apartment kitchen in Portland with its 1200-watt microwave and Jenn-Air cooking range. Her appreciation of old things aside, she preferred having modern conveniences for everyday living, and she sincerely hoped the kitchen at the main house was better equipped. If not, she'd be in big trouble.

He plugged in the toaster to make sure the coils worked. The acrid smell of burning dust and stale breadcrumbs rose to her nose. "Looks like everything in here still works well enough," he pronounced, running a broad palm over the countertop to check for dust. "I cleaned thoroughly when we moved out, but you'd never know it."

As he circled her to leave the kitchen, Molly stared worriedly at the stove. Even with the pilot light on, she was afraid it might explode again if she touched it.

When she joined Jake in the small living room, he was crouched before a camelback trunk. She moved closer to peer in. It was just about large enough to hold a dead body.

Not that she still believed he might murder her. He'd been far too concerned about her after the stove mishap to mean her any harm. Her only lingering worry was that his definition of harm might be entirely different than hers. He was far too charming for comfort, a characteristic that might be inherent, but was far more likely to have been acquired with experience and at great cost to the opposite sex.

She eyed the impressive play of muscle across his broad back every time he moved. In Portland, there were plenty of body builders, but they lacked Jake Coulter's hard edges, looking more like overblown rubber sculptures by comparison. Oblivious to her regard, he set aside some wooly blankets.

"Everything in here was laundered after we moved out. I'm pretty sure it's all still clean." He sniffed a pillowcase, seemed satisfied with the smell, and went back to rifling through the bedding. "This trunk should have protected it."

Molly shifted her weight. "I have my own bedding, Mr. Coulter." She glanced at the jumble of bags on the brown-leather sofa. "It really isn't necessary for you to bother yourself like this."

"The name's Jake, and it isn't a bother. You look tired to the bone." He tipped back his hat to glance up. "I'll just help you get settled in, then be out of your way."

He selected a set of white sheets, three blankets, and two embroidered pillowcases before pushing to his feet. Her gaze snagged on the needlework, a telltale sign that there'd once been a woman in his life. Was he divorced? *Probably.* As handsome as he was, he undoubtedly thought monogamous was the name of a prehistoric dinosaur.

Molly followed him to the bedroom. "I can make my own bed," she protested, wishing he'd leave her to it. "I'm sure you've got a ton of other things you should be doing, and I can manage just fine."

He snapped a sheet over the old mattress. As the linen settled, he said, "Nothing I can't do tomorrow and twice as well. Never came across a chore yet that didn't wait until I got to it."

Molly supposed there was wisdom in that. She was also beginning to understand why this ranch was named the Lazy J. Jake Coulter didn't give the impression that he got in a hurry very often. "I hate to disrupt your schedule."

"Don't believe in schedules." He tucked the sheet on his side, forming a corner far tidier than hers, undoubtedly a result of his having such large hands and the strength to pull the linen tight. "Sure as rain is wet, something always happens to screw them up. It's enough to give a man ulcers if he places too much importance on them."

"Well, you're the boss. If you insist on making my bed, have it your way."

"I will." He winked mischievously, making her wonder if he'd practiced that bone-melting grin in front of a mirror. "I generally do."

Disconcerted, Molly bent to tuck the sheet on her side, then moved with him toward the foot of the bed. They worked well as a team, she decided, and then wondered where that thought had come from.

She watched bemusedly as he unfolded all three blankets. "One will surely be enough," she said, recalling the hot day. "I'll roast."

"Better to kick off than get cold." He began tucking in the blankets at the foot of the bed, the thick pads of his hands barely fitting between the mattress and frame. "You'll be glad of the warmth by morning."

Molly doubted it would get that chilly. "It feels like summer out there right now."

"Don't let it fool you. We'll see snow again before spring makes a debut."

"You're kidding."

"Nope. Just a warm snap. Happens in high-desert climates as spring approaches, freezing one day, hotter than Hades the next." He tossed her a pillowcase. "I won't be surprised if we wake up to frost in the morning."

As soon as the bed was made, he was off again with Molly hurrying behind him to keep up. Once back in the living room, he opened a drop-down metal door sunk into the log wall beside the old rock fireplace. "Looks like you need more wood." As he straightened, he added, "Just as a precaution, make sure you always give this door a couple of kicks before you open it."

Her gaze shot to the wall. "Why?" she asked warily.

"Rattlers. Makes for a nasty surprise when you're half asleep."

"Rattlers?" she echoed.

"They're happy enough to leave if you give them some warning. It's probably not even a worry so early in the year, but it can't hurt to be careful."

"Are you talking about *snakes*?" she asked thinly.

He cocked a dark eyebrow at her. "You aren't afraid of them, are you?"

Of course she was afraid of them. "Rattlesnakes get in the *wood box*?" She peered past him at the metal door.

"That doesn't have a latch, does it? Couldn't a snake press against it and come in?"

"Not likely."

When speaking of rattlesnakes, she preferred to deal in absolutes. "But it could happen."

"I suppose."

"Then what stops them from getting in the house?"

"Mostly their good sense. They wind up dead if they get around people. Just give the door a couple of kicks. You'll probably never see one."

She would have a heart attack if she encountered a rattler. She glanced at the tarnished fire tools behind him, wondering if the poker would serve to kill a serpent. When she looked back at Jake, he was tugging on his ear, his expression bemused.

"You've never spent much time in rattlesnake country, I take it."

She pushed at the strand of hair that kept falling in her eyes. "Not really."

"They're reclusive critters. Walk with a heavy tread, make noise. If you go into the woods, find yourself a stick and beat the brush. They'll head for safe ground. I've lived in this country all my life and never known anyone who got bit."

Molly wrapped her arms around herself and glanced worriedly at the wood box again, which prompted him to sigh.

"Would you like me to lay out some rope along the wall?" he asked.

"Why a rope?"

"They think it's another snake and won't cross over it."

"Really? Yes. All right."

He nodded. "I'll have to round some up and bring it over."

"That'll be fine."

His gaze held hers. After what seemed like a very long moment, he smiled. "I honestly didn't mean to give you the willies. Around here, most people take rattlesnakes in stride and don't give them much thought."

"I'll be fine." Molly swallowed, resisting the urge to check behind her for slithering intruders. "Noise. I can make noise. I've never been very light on my feet, anyway. Now my gracelessness will finally serve a purpose."

He continued to search her gaze. She got the oddest feeling he was about to say something and then thought better of it. Finally, he turned and went outside.

Molly stared after him, wishing there were a screen door. With the weather so warm, she'd enjoy a fresh breeze, and she'd be afraid to leave the door open for fear of a snake getting inside. She wasn't sure she could do this.

Rubbing her aching eyes, she once again considered leaving. Only what would become of Sunset? She blinked and stared out the doorway. From where she stood, she could see the stallion in the corral, the bloody stripes on his once beautiful black coat glistening in the sunlight. What kind of person could abandon him?

A loud thump resounded through the cabin. She nearly parted company with her shoes before she determined it was only Jake throwing logs into the wood box.

Exhaustion weighed heavily on her shoulders. She could have collapsed right where she stood. When her employer's looming shape finally filled the doorway, she just stared at him, so depleted of energy that she didn't even feel self-conscious. He brushed back his sagging shirt-sleeve to check his watch. "Supper is at six, sharp. Grab yourself a nap, and I'll see you then. Don't bother to knock. We don't stand on ceremony here."

News bulletin of the century. "I can whip up something to eat here," she said scratchily. "I've a few groceries."

He smiled slightly. "Nevertheless, I'll expect you for supper."

She nearly asked if that was an order, then remembered she worked for the man and bit back the question. Sarcasm had its place, and this wasn't it. She had Sunset to think about. If she tested Jake Coulter's patience, he might tell her to leave.

He touched the brim of his hat. "It'll be canned chili and crackers again tonight with antacid tablets for dessert, but joining us will give you a chance to meet all the men. They'll be rolling in shortly, still hung over and grumpy as bears from Saturday night on the town. It'll cheer them up considerably to know we've finally got a cook."

All the men? He made it sound as if an army was due to arrive. For some reason, she had assumed she'd be cooking for only him and his brother. "How many men are there?"

"Nine full-timers. Eleven, counting me and Hank."

"Will I be expected to cook for all of them?"

"Of course."

Molly had never cooked for more than four people in her life. Rodney had always insisted on having meals catered when they entertained because she was so inept in the kitchen. "I can't possibly prepare food for that many men. I don't even—"

"Sure you can. We're a patient lot. You'll get the hang of it with practice." He backed away from the door. "The hired hands stay in the bunkhouse." He hooked a thumb toward a long log building adjacent to the house. "You won't be responsible for cleaning over there, and they've got their own laundry facilities. Your only worry will be to keep their bellies full. They have weekends off. They generally head for town Saturday morning and roll back in here late Sunday afternoon, hungry for supper. After dinner on Friday nights, you'll be free to leave until Sunday evening if you like. Or you can hang around here, your choice. As long as you're back in time to fix dinner on Sunday, it makes no difference to me. Hank and I are usually here. If one of us leaves, the other one tries to stick around. You should never be alone out here."

"That's good to know." Her mind was stalled on the fact that he expected her to cook for eleven people—twelve, including herself. *Oh, God.* She never should have agreed to this.

"Supper, six sharp," he said with another tip of his hat. "Don't forget. We wait for latecomers like one pig waits on another one. We don't dress for dinner, by the way." His grin hinted that he'd just made a joke and found it amusing. "Just come as you are."

Chapter Four

As Jake walked toward the house, he watched the dust billows that rose around his boots with every step, thinking they resembled miniature mushroom clouds. A fitting comparison. If his suspicions were correct, he had just made a decision that could blow up in his face.

Near the exercise corral, he lifted his gaze to the stallion in the six-foot-high enclosure. Never in all his thirty-two years had he seen a more cruelly abused animal. Those lash marks ran mighty deep. While inside the pen, Jake had visually examined them as best he could, and as near as he could tell, none of them would require stitches, but more than a few would leave scars.

What kind of man could do such a thing?

Resting his elbows on a rail of the pen, Jake rubbed the bridge of his nose, thinking that he needed four ibuprofen chased with whiskey. As a rule, he didn't turn to drink when he felt stressed, but tonight he might make an exception. Sometimes, when a man found answers nowhere else, he could stumble across a few at the bottom of a bottle.

"Holy hell, what happened to that horse?"

Jake jumped at the sound of his younger brother's voice. He whipped around, his thoughts tangling like wet rope as he tried to think how he meant to explain this situation. The prospect was so daunting, he wanted to pull his hat down over his eyes and say he had a headache. It wouldn't really be a lie, given the fact that he had two, one behind his eyes and another taking up residence in the cabin along the creek.

"Howdy, Hank."

"Is that all you've got to say?" Startled by Hank's approach, Sunset reared and shrieked. Hank stopped dead in his tracks. "Ah, Lord, Jake. Where did he come from?"

A tight, choking sensation crawled up Jake's throat. "I'm not real sure where he's from yet. Portland, possibly. Then again, maybe from somewhere down south."

Turning to rest a shoulder against the fence, he watched his brother cautiously close the remaining distance between them. Recently turned twenty-nine, Hank looked enough like their old man to be a clone, his skin tanned as dark as molasses by the sun, his tousled hair lying over his brow like swirls of chocolate. His sweat-dampened T-shirt was smeared with dirt, a result of wrestling with sick calves to give them injections, and the cotton knit clung to his chest like a second skin. His blue eyes fairly snapped as he shoved up the brim of his Stetson to search Jake's expression.

"If you're not sure where he came from, how the hell did he get in our corral?"

"There's a good question."

Hank's jaw muscle ticked. "Looks like somebody whipped the poor bastard."

Jake nodded, noting as he did that Hank had balled his hands into fists.

"Who owns him? Not many things put me in a mood to kick ass, but seeing that sure as hell does."

Jake pointed over his shoulder. "His owner is over at the cabin. Tip your hat before you start kicking ass, or I'll have to kick yours for not minding your manners."

"A lady?"

"Ringer."

Hank's eyes narrowed. "No woman could mark a horse like that, not unless she's built like an Amazon."

"She isn't." Jake almost smiled at the picture of Molly

that flashed through his mind. Amazon definitely wasn't a word to describe her. "I guess her to be about five two. It's hard to judge. She's wearing those newfangled shoes with soles as thick as two-by-fours." He curled a thumb over his belt. "Never have figured out what women see in those damned things. Good way to bust an ankle if you ask me."

Hank frowned. "What does her taste in shoes have to do with anything?"

"Doesn't. I was just making conversation."

Hank started to say something, then pressed his lips closed, his gaze sharp on Jake's face. He folded his arms on the fence rail and hooked a boot heel over the bottom rung, spending the next little while watching the stallion.

The silence gave Jake a chance to gather his thoughts, which undoubtedly was Hank's intent. If anyone understood him, it was his youngest brother.

Jake's voice had gone gravelly when he spoke. "I've done a hell of a thing, Hank. You're going to be royally pissed, and I can't say I'll blame you."

Hank shifted, then resettled in much the same position, one hip cocked, one leg thrust behind him. "I can see your tail's tied in a knot about something."

Jake tried to think of a way to cast the situation in a good light. He was tempted to gloss over a few of the facts. Unfortunately, in his book, that would be lying by omission, and he wasn't a man who dealt in falsehoods, not for any reason. He took a bracing breath, slowly released it, and said, "I think the lady stole the horse."

"You think she *what*?"

Jake winced at the loud pitch of his brother's voice. He felt as if cymbals were crashing in his temples. "Given the fact that she doesn't strike me as the criminal type, my guess is she had no alternative."

"There are always alternatives to breaking the law. Why would anyone do such a harebrained thing as to steal a horse?"

"Beats the hell out of me. I assume she had her reasons.

She seems like an intelligent woman, and you can tell by looking at her that she's got a kind heart." Jake rubbed the bridge of his nose again. "She claims her name's Molly Houston."

"Claims?"

"The first name fits. I think she plucked the last one out of a hat." Jake thought for a moment before he continued. "She's a puzzle, Hank, one of those people who's really hard to read." In his mind's eye, he once again conjured an image of her, soft and well rounded in all the right places, with whiskey-colored hair, huge butterscotch-brown eyes, and a wealth of flawless ivory skin. All his adult life, he'd gone for tall, long-legged women, barely giving the short, generously endowed ones a second look. But there was something different about Molly—an indefinable something that had caught his attention the instant he saw her. He guessed maybe it was her eyes, so wide and wary and dark with suspicion. He couldn't look into them without wanting to hug and reassure her. "She's a pretty little thing, if you like the type and look past all the camouflage."

Hank shot him another sharp glance. "What camouflage?"

Jake tried to think how he might explain. "Have you ever met a woman who does her damnedest to look homely?"

Hank smiled thoughtfully. "A few."

"That's Molly, only she's fighting a losing battle. It'd take a sack over her head to hide that face." Jake thought of the way she wore her hair skinned back in a braid. "She doesn't bother with a lick of makeup, and her clothes are so baggy they'd fit a woman twice her size with room left over for one small girl." He sent his brother a questioning look. "What makes an attractive woman try so hard to downplay her appearance?"

Hank shifted again, then scratched his jaw. "Beats me all to hell. To avoid attention, maybe? Could be she's timid of men."

Jake remembered how nervous she'd seemed around him and decided that explanation had some merit. "Maybe," he conceded. "Overall, she doesn't really strike me as the timid type, though. It took guts to get that horse here. Most people would have gotten spooked and turned back when they reached the first steep grade."

Hank glanced off at the Toyota parked in front of the cabin and then studied the huge trailer. "Where are you going with this, Jake?"

"Well, now, that's the part you're not going to like, so I'm working up to it."

"Just cut to the chase."

Jake took another bracing breath. "I said I'd work with the horse, and I gave her a job so she can pay my rates."

"You *what*?" Hank's dark eyebrows lifted. "Please tell me I didn't hear you right. A job doing what?"

"Housekeeper and cook. We're looking for someone, and she needs a job and a place to stay. It seemed like the perfect solution."

Hank laughed incredulously. "You hired a horse thief? Jake, this is partly a *horse* ranch. What the hell makes you think she won't steal our horses?"

"I'm not claiming it makes sense. I'm just recounting to you what I've done. I couldn't tell her to go." Jake stared at his palms. "I know I should have discussed it with you first. But I just couldn't turn my back on her. She looked so lost, and I couldn't shake the feeling—hell, I don't know—that we were her only hope, I guess."

Hank just shook his head, looking more incredulous with each passing second. "If she stole that horse, the cops are probably looking for her. You could take the rap for horse theft. That's a serious offense." He jabbed a finger at the stallion. "He looks like a racer to me. They don't come cheap. We're talking grand larceny."

"I've thought of all that."

"We could lose the ranch," Hank pointed out. "Have you thought of that? People won't bring their horses to me if my brother's doing time for horse theft. Right now, the training program is all that's keeping us alive."

Jake couldn't think of a single argument in his own defense. "I know," he said hollowly.

"And you're still bent on helping her? Damn, Jake. How do you know the cops aren't looking for her as we speak?"

Jake swallowed and met his brother's gaze. "I have a feeling about her, Hank. I can't explain it, can't rationalize my way past it. I just couldn't turn her away."

Hank puffed air into his cheeks and bent his head. "All right," he finally said. "If it's something you have to do, there's no point arguing about it. It was your money we invested, not mine. What real say do I have?"

"You know better than that. This is Coulter land. We're partners. My money, your money. I've never made a distinction."

"Until now."

Jake bit down hard on his back teeth and met his brother's gaze dead on. "What the hell does that mean?"

"Just what I said. We've sweat blood to get this place back on its feet." He swung his hand to encompass the land. "Maybe I didn't have the money to match you dollar for dollar, but I worked beside you in the bitter cold to rebuild the house, and I waded through mud and snow up to my ass all winter to repair the fences and tend the stock. Now, first crack out of the bag, you put it all at risk without so much as a word to me?"

Jake winced because everything his brother said was true. "I'm sorry," he said gruffly. "You're right, Hank. I'm sorry."

"Sorry won't pay the mortgage if your ass gets tossed in jail." Hank lowered his arm back to the fence rail and bent his head. "*Damn.* I'm all for doing good deeds, but where do we draw the line? This isn't just any piece of land. We were lucky to get it back. Now you're taking a gamble that could end with our losing it again."

Jake sighed and closed his eyes. "You're right. Guilty as charged. I'm sorry, Hank. I'll tell her I've changed my mind and ask her to leave."

Silence. Jake waited for his brother to speak. When no words were forthcoming, he lifted his lashes. Blue eyes stormy with anger, his mouth drawn into a grim line, Hank was staring at the stallion. When he felt Jake's gaze on him, he shot him a glare.

"That's just great. Dump it all on me."

"I'm not dumping anything on you. You've argued a good case, I know you're absolutely right, and there's nothing else to be done. The ranch has to come first. Like you said, we were damned lucky to get it back in the family."

Hank resumed staring at the horse. After a long moment, he shook his head. "What kind of man can turn his back on that? The poor bastard. Just look at him."

Jake had looked his fill already. The sight was testimony to the depravity and mercilessness of humankind, and it made him feel slightly sick. Even worse, he had a bad feeling that the horse hadn't been the only one to suffer. Molly bore no physical scars that he'd been able to see, but not all wounds were inflicted on the flesh. Straightening away from the fence, Jake shoved his hands in the pockets of his jeans.

At his movement, Hank jerked his head around. "Don't go jumping the gun."

Jake smothered a smile. Not quite four years Hank's senior, he'd always felt much older, undoubtedly the result of being firstborn in a family of five rowdy boys who'd looked to him to set an example. He'd watched Hank grow from a gangly, mischievous teenager into a serious-minded college student, but somehow he'd failed to note his brother's final passage into adulthood. This was no boy who frowned at him now, but a fine young man who did their father and the Coulter name proud.

"Sometimes I just get to wondering what it's all about,

is all," Hank said in a low voice. "Other people know where to draw the line. Watching them, it's easy to start thinking that's a smart way to be."

Jake tugged his hands from his pockets and relaxed against the fence again. "If you're bent on it, I'll ask her to leave."

Hank laughed humorlessly. "Nah. I'm as nuts as you are." He looked out over the ranch, his mouth twisting in a sad smile. "When you boil it all down, as much as we love this place, Jake, it's only a patch of dirt."

Jake chuckled in spite of himself. "Coulter dirt. It's special to us in a way no other spread will ever be."

"Only because three generations of Coulters worked it and raised their families here." Hank gazed at the forestland that encroached on all sides. "What do you reckon our great-grandfather would do in this situation?" He slanted an inquiring glance at Jake. "You think he would turn his back on that horse?"

"It's hard to say. I never knew the man."

"We knew Grandpa, and we sure as hell know our father well enough. Remember the time Dad took the quirt away from that cowboy who was beating his horse out at the fairgrounds?"

Jake remembered the incident well.

Hank grinned. "He gave the son of a bitch a taste of his own medicine, and Mom had to bail him out of jail."

"More temper than common sense, that's our dad."

Hank shook his head, his expression growing suddenly solemn again. "Common sense had nothing to do with it. He was setting a wrong right and teaching the bastard a lesson he wouldn't soon forget."

"What's your point, Hank?"

"That we're Coulters, and with the name comes a responsibility to live up to it." He sighed and shrugged. "To hell with the ranch. If we lose it, we can always buy more dirt, but we can't buy back our decency. Comes a time in life when a man can't turn a blind eye, not if he wants to like himself. I reckon this qualifies." He nodded at the horse. "Neither one of us would be worth the powder it'd take to blow us to hell if we could turn our backs on him."

"I know helping her out isn't the smartest decision I've ever made," Jake admitted, "but it was the only thing I could think to do at the time. She was about to leave, and damned if I could just stand there and let her go."

Hank's eyes crinkled at the corners as he studied the stallion. "You know what they say about wise men making it into heaven. It may not be a smart decision, but no matter what happens, it's probably the right one."

Someone screamed. Molly jolted awake and listened. The sound didn't come again, and she decided she had been dreaming. She started to roll over but was so stiff her joints felt frozen. She blinked, tried to see. There was only blackness. Where was she? She felt like a hunk of frozen meat at the bottom of a freezer. She hugged her arms, rubbed her sleeves. She was so chilled that her flesh felt numb.

Another high-pitched scream rent the air. Startled by the sound, she swung off the bed, tripped over her shoes, and landed in a sprawl on what felt like a dusty wood floor. Her chin smacked a plank, and bright spots exploded before her eyes. For a moment, she just lay there, too stunned to move.

When her head cleared a bit, she ran a palm over the floor, trying to place where she was. The awful scream came again, reverberating in the darkness. It came back to her then. The cabin. Jake Coulter. It was Sunset who was screaming.

Something had to be horribly wrong to make the horse scream that way. She needed to go check on him. Her joints protesting with every movement, she pushed to her feet. How long had she been sleeping? Judging by the darkness, the sun had gone down some time ago, which meant she must have been out for hours.

Waving both hands, she groped her way across the bedroom and spilled gracelessly into the living area. Faint but very welcome moonlight shone through the open front door, creating a pale beacon to guide her.

Once outside on the covered front porch, Molly rubbed the sleep from her eyes and squinted through the feeble moonlight, trying to see Sunset. As if on cue, the stallion shrieked again, the sound laced with terror and panic. She was about to move off the porch when a huge, black shape loomed in front of her. Her heart leaped, and she fell back a step.

"Sorry," a deep voice said. "I didn't mean to give you a start."

The breath rushed from her lungs. "Mr. Coulter?" She strained to see, her eyes burning with the effort. "Is that you?"

"Jake," he corrected.

"Oh, thank *God*," she said, so relieved she didn't care that her voice sounded shrill. "I thought you were a bear."

He chuckled, the sound raspy but warm. "I get as cranky as a bear sometimes. Will that work?"

He moved, and his silhouette vanished. Molly narrowed her eyes, trying to find him in the darkness. "Mr. Coulter?"

"Right here," a deep voice, laced with amusement, said near her ear.

She jumped and clamped a hand over her heart. "Good grief."

He laughed softly. "Can't you see?"

Molly missed the city, where thousands of lights illuminated the night sky. "Of course I can't see. It's black as pitch out here."

"It seems bright as day to me."

"I'm happy for you." Realizing she sounded waspish, she tried to lighten her tone. "It's a good thing one of us can see. Something's terribly wrong with Sunset. Didn't you hear him shrieking?"

"He's fine. As fine as can be, anyway. He ate a little

grain earlier, and for the most part, he's settled down. He just got spooked when I walked by his pen."

"Oh. So there's nothing wrong with him?"

"Nothing that time, patience, and a gentle hand won't cure."

She heard paper rustle. Then a clanking sound reached her ears. The next thing she knew, he grasped her by the elbow. "I'll be your eyes until we get some lights turned on." Firming his grip, he set himself to the task of guiding her through the darkness to the doorway. She could have sworn she felt heat radiating from him. "Damn, honey, you feel ice cold," he said, running his thumb lightly over the chilled skin of her arm.

"I got a little cool while I was sleeping."

Once inside the house, he released her to flip on the wall switch. The old floor lamp that stood next to the easy chair by the front window burst to life, bathing the small living area with golden light through its fluted glass globe. Molly blinked, momentarily as blinded by the illumination as she'd been by the darkness.

As her vision adjusted, she saw that he was carrying a quart-sized bowl covered with plastic wrap, a package of what appeared to be Ritz crackers, and a steel thermos tucked under one arm.

"Your supper," he explained. "Can't have you sleeping through meals and losing your strength, not if I mean to work you until you drop."

"Oh. Of course." Molly wanted to kick herself for sounding so humorless and prim. He was kidding around with her, and she should respond in kind. Unfortunately, she never had a clear head when she first woke up, a life-long condition presently worsened by a tumble off the bed and nerves that felt as if they'd been abraded with sandpaper. "And here I thought you were just being thoughtful."

"That, too," he admitted with dry amusement. "Now that I've landed a cook and housekeeper, I don't want her quitting on me." He brandished the chili bowl. "If I never eat another meal out of a can, it'll be too soon."

Standing there in his rancher garb, he looked even more dangerously attractive than he had earlier. His hat was cocked forward to shade his compelling blue eyes, giving her an opportunity to better appreciate the rest of his face. His firm, narrow lips shimmered in the lamplight like wet silk. Shadows delineated his chiseled features, enhancing their masculine ruggedness. He had a slight cleft in his chin, an angular jaw, and a sharply bridged nose thrusting out from between his thick, sable brows like a blade. Along one side, she saw a slight bump, evidence of an old break.

Her gaze dropped to the collar of his wash-worn shirt, the blue chambray faded nearly to white and forming a stark contrast to the burnished umber of his neck. She'd never met anyone like Jake Coulter. Most of the men in her acquaintance wore tailored suits, her beloved late father included. In the business world, successful men dressed the part.

Oddly, though, despite his humble attire, Jake emanated an air of importance and authority. It was in the way he carried himself, she decided, and in the relaxed, self-confident way he interacted with others. He was the kind of man who would always command respect, no matter what he wore.

She tried to picture him in a suit. Somehow the image just didn't gel. He belonged here, in everyday communion with the land and the wilderness at his back door.

When she met his gaze again, she was dismayed to find that he was studying her as intently as she was studying him.

"I didn't realize you were so *tall*," she blurted stupidly.

He flashed her a slow grin. "And I didn't realize you were so short. The heels, I guess. They must tack on a few inches."

"I'm only a little shorter than average."

His grin broadened. "If you stretch? What are you, about five two?"

"Three." Heat gathered in her cheeks. She'd been teased unmercifully in high school about being short, and it had been a sore point with her ever since. She folded her arms at her waist. "If there's a height requirement for the job, Mr. Coulter, just say so, and I'll gather my things."

"No height requirement." He gave her a long look that made her toes curl. "I never take anyone's measure in inches. Your legs reach from your ass to the ground, same as mine. I reckon that'll do."

Once again she had the feeling that he was looking too deeply into her eyes, that there was nothing she could hide from this man. She wanted to break the visual contact but couldn't. Finally he shifted his attention to her mouth, his irises turning a molten blue gray. She glanced nervously away, feeling uncertain and confused. He was looking at her mouth as if—

She cut the thought short. Handsome men like Jake Coulter were never attracted to women like her. It was silly to even entertain the notion. She probably just looked a fright, with her hair all mussed and her eyes bleary with sleep.

"Thanks for bringing me dinner. It was very thoughtful."

She held out her hands to accept the bowl. He smiled and moved past her. After reaching around the wall to turn on the overhead kitchen light, he proceeded to set the food on the round wooden table in the adjoining eating area. "I'll keep you company while you eat. I need to talk with you."

Molly's stomach knotted. What did he need to talk to her about? His tone brooked no argument, but she decided to give it her best shot, anyway. "I'm not at my sharpest when I first wake up. Maybe we should save it for later."

"It's bad for the digestion to eat alone."

During her marriage, Molly had taken most of her

meals alone. Rodney had been far too busy with his many girlfriends to spend much time with his wife. "I'm used to it."

"Is that so?" He set the thermos beside the bowl, then glanced over his shoulder at her. "A pretty lady like you shouldn't be."

Pretty? Her face went hot again. She hated it when men gave her compliments. She knew they didn't sincerely mean them, and that had the perverse effect of making her feel worse about herself instead of better.

She looked at her watch. It was almost eight o'clock.

When he noticed her checking the time, he said, "You won't turn into a pumpkin. Come sit down and eat your supper. This way, I can take the dirty dishes back with me and throw them in the machine."

He turned from the table to catch her shivering and rubbing her arms. His gaze shot past her to the open front door. "While you dig in, I'll start a fire. The night air in this country has quite a bite when you're not used to it."

Molly started toward the kitchen, only to collide with him as he moved toward the door. She came up hard against his chest and was almost knocked off her feet. He caught her by the shoulders.

"Are you all right?"

"I'm fine," she assured him, trying to step away.

"I'd forgotten how small this place is." He maintained his grip on her upper arms. "You can't cuss a cat without getting hair between your teeth. Hank and I were always mowing each other down when we stayed here."

He hadn't mowed her down, exactly, but if he didn't turn her loose, she couldn't say how long her legs would hold her up. Her skin felt electrified where his hands touched, the feeling radiating out to sensitize nerve endings she'd forgotten she had.

"What's this?" he asked, lifting one hand to cup her chin. "Did you take a fall?"

Molly was about to say no when his thumb grazed a

tender spot, calling to mind her headlong plunge to the floor. "I, um—yes, sort of. Nothing serious. I didn't realize I'd hurt myself."

He lightly traced the spot again. "It's only a small scrape, but it may leave a bruise." He moved his thumb up to her mouth. The slight drag on her sensitive flesh made her breath hitch. "Your bottom lip is a little swollen as well."

She couldn't move, couldn't think. Even after he lowered his hand back to her shoulder, his gaze lingered on her mouth as if he were thinking about kissing her. She was afraid she might faint if he did.

Chapter Five

Jake Coulter was a man who knew his business with the ladies. Molly could tell that just by looking at him. When he kissed a woman, he'd take control. No clumsy groping, no hesitance, just masterful hands and lips, taking possession. She balled her hands into fists, appalled by her thoughts. Even worse, what if he saw them in her eyes? This wasn't like her. She barely knew him.

She shivered again, only this time not from the cold. His grip on her upper arms tightened, the strength in his hands compressing her shoulders slightly. He felt capable of lifting her clear off her feet. Molly fleetingly wondered how that might feel.

On her wedding night, Rodney had carried her over the threshold, but that had been ten years and thirty pounds ago, and she could barely remember it now. He'd bumped her head on the doorframe. She did recall that much. And he'd put her down the instant they got inside, more interested in drinking champagne than in making love with his bride.

The memory brought a pang of nearly forgotten hurt. Her honeymoon had ended quickly, mere hours after her wedding. She'd looked forward to an incredible evening— romance, soft music, and passionate lovemaking. Instead, she'd surrendered her virginity to a fumbling drunk who'd collapsed on top of her afterward and snored in her ear. Her marriage had gone downhill from there.

And therein lay her problem with Coulter, she decided.

So many good years were gone, stolen by a man who'd never loved her or even wanted her. Deep down, in a purely feminine corner of her heart, she felt cheated.

She was almost thirty, and though that was still fairly young by many people's standards, she couldn't shake the feeling that time was running out.

What was it like to receive a magical kiss in the moonlight?

How would it feel to be swept off her feet?

She could go to her grave without ever experiencing passion. She could do without the love poems and being serenaded at her bedroom window. If nobody ever climbed the trellis to profess his undying devotion, she could live with that as well.

But, damn it, before her ovaries became atrophied, she wanted someone besides her father to tell her she was beautiful and to give her flowers. Just *once*. Was that so much to ask?

"I guess it depends on what you're asking."

Molly blinked. Jake's face was cast into shadow by the glow of light from the kitchen. "Pardon?" she asked, praying that she hadn't been thinking out loud.

"Is what too much to ask?" he repeated.

She blinked again, clamped her mouth closed. She had mush for brains. "Nothing. My mind must have wandered. I told you, I'm not very clearheaded when I first wake up."

He rubbed his hands up and down her arms. "Let me get that fire started."

He had already started one and just didn't know it.

Molly gulped. *Oh, boy.* This was not good. How could she work for a man when she remembered him without a shirt every time she looked at him?

As if Jake Coulter would ever even give her the time of day. What on *earth* was she thinking? She had pasty white skin, saggy boobs, a thick waist, cottage-cheese thighs, and so many dimples on her buttocks, they resembled oversize golf balls.

She made her way to the table. *Enough.* She was finished with men. Absolutely, totally, forever finished. When she regained control of her money, she'd buy her own darned flowers, thank you very much. A whole bathtubful, if she wanted. The male of her species could take a flying leap.

She sank gratefully onto a battered old chair, her heart racing as she tried to focus on the chili. She was acutely conscious of the sounds Jake made across the room, the clunk of firewood, the crinkle of newspaper. Within seconds, he had a fire laid.

He took a kitchen match from the box on the mantle, and with one quick snap of his wrist, struck it on the side seam of his Wranglers. Molly had never seen anyone light a match on his pants. She tried to picture herself doing it that way and decided she'd either freeze to death for want of heat or set herself on fire.

Fascinated, she observed him while he worked, admiring the way he crouched so comfortably in front of the hearth. Everything about the man, every movement he made, was deliciously masculine.

Deliciously? The word hung in her brain. She was more exhausted than she realized, she decided. Her body was awake, but her brain was still in a partial dream state.

As if he sensed her eyes on him, Jake glanced her way. Molly turned her gaze back to the chili. With trembling hands, she peeled away the plastic wrap. The sharp, hot scent of the spicy beans and ground beef wafted to her nostrils.

At the best of times, she wasn't overly fond of chili. Canned or homemade, it was usually greasy, and fatty foods didn't sit well with her stomach. Neither did she care much for meat. Her mind always conjured images of the poor animals that had died to supply her with sustenance.

Somehow she didn't think that sentiment would be met with enthusiasm on the Lazy J. Raising and selling beeves was a part of Jake Coulter's livelihood.

"Is something wrong with the food?"

Molly threw him a startled look. He was still crouched before the fire. Amber light flickered over his face, limning the hard planes and chiseled sharpness of his features. His eyes gleamed in the dancing illumination like sunwashed silver. In that moment, she decided he had the visage of a wicked angel. She would do well to remember it.

"No, *no,* nothing's wrong with it." She wadded the plastic wrap in her fist and dug in hard with her fingers. "I'm just not quite awake yet."

He chuckled and nodded at the thermos. "There's milk, fresh from the Guernsey this morning and chilled to a turn. Maybe that'll open your eyes."

Oh, it would open her eyes, all right. She'd drunk 2-percent as a child, then switched to skim as an adult because of her weight problem. She'd never tasted raw milk in her life. She doubted she'd like it very well. The pasteurized whole milk she'd sampled in restaurants always left a waxy film in her mouth.

But Jake Coulter was watching, and Molly had learned that it was always best to go with the flow. People who made waves usually got swamped in their own wake.

She unscrewed the little tin cup from the thermos. The light green lining was stained brown from countless servings of coffee. Not really dirty, she assured herself, just stained. She twisted off the stopper and poured some milk. Her stomach lurched. There were little floating particles on top. Cream, more than likely, but that didn't ease her mind. She thought of the high fat content and had to force herself to take a sip.

Just as she expected, the milk left a coating inside her mouth. She swallowed and determinedly took another gulp. Hadn't Jake heard about bad cholesterol? Molly religiously read food labels as she made her grocery selections.

"How is it?" he asked.

"Oh, it's—" She cleared her throat. A string of something slimy dangled from her uvula. "It's lovely. I've never tasted raw milk."

His dark eyebrows lifted. "A dyed-in-the-wool farm girl, huh?"

Too late, Molly realized her mistake. Someone who'd been around farms all her life would have tasted raw milk countless times. "I'm just calorie conscious, is all. Skim milk is only eighty per cup."

He pushed easily to his feet. The firelight threw his shadow across the room, the outline of his Stetson nearly spilling onto her toes. He strode slowly toward her, every tap of his boot heels making her nerves jump. *Oh, God.* She really, really wished he would stop looking at her like that.

"I hope you're not dieting," he said matter-of-factly.

Molly flashed him an incredulous look, which he met with that twinkling gaze she found so unsettling.

"Let me guess. You don't conform to all the weight charts for a woman your height, so you think you're overweight." Without waiting for her answer, he shook his head and added, "Those damned charts are for women with average builds, and trust me, honey, yours isn't average."

Was he toying with her? Maybe that was it. To some men, the thrill of making a conquest was everything, and they'd sleep with just about anyone to stroke their egos. Well, if that was his game, he could count her out.

He kept coming. *Tap, shuffle . . . tap, shuffle.* He had the cowboy saunter perfected to an art, she'd give him that, his long legs lazily marking off strides, his lean hips shifting loosely. She tried to avoid his gaze, but the closer he came, the harder it was. His shadow finally fell over her.

She flicked her gaze to his, couldn't look away. No maybe to it, the man had a gleam in his eyes. Was he *trying* to make her nervous? There was an alarming thought, and now that she came to think of it, that made perfect sense. This afternoon, she'd sensed that he was suspicious of her story. If he'd come over to pump her for information, he would be able to dig more out of her if he kept her rattled.

"You don't warm up to men very easily, do you?" he said, his deep voice laced with humor as he circled the table to take a seat across from her. "Are you this way with everyone, or is it just me? I can't recall ever making a lady so tense."

Maybe all of them had been brain dead, Molly decided. "I'm not nervous. What makes you think that?"

He smiled and nudged his hat back to study her. "You're not afraid of me, are you?"

"Why would I be afraid?"

He rocked the chair back on its hind legs and hooked his thumbs over his belt, which made him look all the broader through the shoulders. "We're a long way from town. It just occurred to me that maybe you're worried. You don't know me from Adam. If I had any meanness in mind, you could be in a peck of trouble."

Molly tried to moisten her lips, struggled to swallow. Her mouth was dry as dirt. "Thank you so much for pointing that out. Now I have something new to worry about."

He laughed sheepishly and bent his head. There was a piece of hay stuck to the crown of his hat. When he glanced back up, his eyes were warm with a mixture of amusement and regret. "I only brought it up because I don't want you feeling uneasy. My mama will vouch for me if you want a character reference."

"Your *mother*?"

"You bet. Nobody knows a man better than his mama. She'll tell you I'm a gentleman, for all my rough edges. If I'm not, just let her know, and she'll snatch me bald-headed."

Molly smiled in spite of herself.

He winked and grinned. "Don't believe anything else she says, however. Like most moms, she keeps a list of my faults, which she's willing to share with almost anyone who'll listen."

"How long a list?"

"Pretty damned long. I think she's been keeping notes since I was about five. I'm one-track minded, bullheaded, quick to lose my temper, and in sore need of some polish, according to her." He winked at her again. "She's fond of saying that I think tact is what the teacher sat on. I keep telling her that being direct is a virtue. I may not have much talent for beating around the bush, but at least people know where they stand with me."

"That's good to know."

"I'm glad you think so, because I don't plan to beat around the bush with you, either."

Molly's heart did a funny little jig at the base of her throat. She felt as if she were about to choke on a lump of vibrating Jell-O. "I'm afraid I'm not following."

"You will be soon enough." He gave her another long, searching look. His jaw muscle started to tick. "I know you stole the horse, Molly."

She was going to have a heart attack. "Why on *earth* do you think that?"

His lashes dipped low over his eyes, but even so she glimpsed a glimmer of impatience. "I don't think, I know. There's no point in trying to snow me. Save yourself the effort."

She had no idea how he'd found out, but there was no doubt that he knew. She could almost hear the key turning in the lock. "H-have you already turned m-me in?" she asked, her voice quivering like a reed whistle.

As quickly as it had come, the impatience left his eyes. "Do I look like the kind of guy who'd turn a lady in?"

"Yes."

He chuckled and scratched his temple. "I have no intention of turning you in. You have my word on that."

Molly's heart was still jumping in her chest. "How did you find out?"

The corners of his mouth twitched. "You're a lousy liar."

"No, really." She glanced nervously toward the door. "I need to know. Have the police been here? Is that how you found out? I *knew* it was a mistake to stop at that rest area. With Sunset kicking up such a fuss, people were bound to notice me."

He sighed and crossed his arms. "No cops have been here, Molly. You're perfectly safe. No one has tracked you down." He paused for emphasis. "Not yet, anyway. But how long will that last, do you think? You can't steal an expensive animal like Sunset and hope to get away with it. This is the electronic age. Law enforcement communication is lightning fast. They're going to find you, the only question being, how soon."

She was going to be sick. What he said was true, and she knew it. If she stayed in one place, they would find her sooner or later. She clamped a trembling hand to her midriff. Bile rose up her throat.

"I suppose you'd like me to leave." She sat straighter on the chair. "That's fine. I understand. You don't want any trouble, and I can't blame you." She dropped the ball of plastic wrap on the floor and grabbed the edge of the table to stand up. "Luckily, I didn't unpack anything. It won't take me long to load my car back—"

He sat forward in the chair, the front legs smacking the floor so sharply that she jerked. He snaked out a hand to capture her wrist. "You're not going anywhere," he said softly. "Get that thought right out of your head."

His grip was like steel, the press of his fingers relentless. Molly stared into his eyes, a dozen horrible thoughts circling through her mind. The one that finally gained front stage was that he meant to keep her there against her will.

"Sit down," he said softly.

She sat. Gaped at him. Struggled to breathe.

He lightened his grip on her wrist, his gaze still locked with hers. As his fingers relaxed, she thought about jerking away and running. But then she remembered how quickly he had moved that day in the corral. He'd be on her before she took two steps.

"Now I've frightened you."

Molly gulped back hysterical laughter. She almost said, "Go to the head of the class."

"I'm not going to harm you, Molly," he said, his voice husky with sincerity. "I only want to help you."

"Oh." Her heart fluttered back down to where it belonged. Sort of, anyway. He wouldn't be the first man to lie to her, and she had no idea if his word could be trusted.

"I don't know what led you to steal the horse," he went on. "I can only guess. But whatever your reasons, they won't matter a whit when the police finally find you. They'll toss you in jail and throw away the key."

Actually, they'd probably take her back to a clinic, but why split hairs? Though she had eventually benefited by her stay at Haven Rest, the place had been a jail of sorts.

She wondered what her therapist, Sam Banks, would say if he could see her now. He wouldn't be pleased. Stealing that horse had not been a smart move.

Molly bent her head, stared numbly at the scarred tabletop. She would *not* have regrets. No matter what happened, she'd made the best decision she could at the time, and it was pointless to start second-guessing herself now.

"I think you desperately need a friend, honey," Jake said, his voice pitched to barely above a whisper. "Won't you trust me?" He slowly trailed a fingertip over her wrist bone. "Tell me what happened. I'll help you get things straightened out."

The starch went out of Molly's spine. She was relieved that he didn't intend to do her any physical harm, but this was almost as bad. She couldn't tell him what had happened. He'd never believe it, for one. It was all so insane, she could scarcely believe it herself.

No. If she told him her story, he'd automatically assume she was crazy, like everyone else. A woman's husband of ten years didn't have her committed unless there was truly something wrong with her. Right?

Wrong. If a man was trying to cover up a murder and gain control of a large inheritance, he'd do almost anything. Only who was going to believe that? Certainly not Jake. It sounded like something straight out of an Alfred Hitchcock thriller. The fact that her own mother had turned against her made it look even worse.

When Molly just sat there, close-lipped, Jake sighed and released her wrist. "All right," he said as he sat back on his chair. "You're not ready to talk yet. I can see that, and I won't press you. But know, even as I say that, Molly, sooner or later you're going to have to. If you wait until the cops are slapping cuffs on you, it may be too late for me to do anything."

"You can't do anything now," she managed to squeeze out. "Nothing."

"There are animal protection agencies I can call. One look at that horse, and they'll be up in arms. If we report this right away, I'm sure they'll intervene on your behalf with the police. Horse theft is against the law, no question about it. But if you did it to protect the poor animal, it's understandable, and they'll go to bat for you. I know they will."

Molly just stared at him.

"Won't you please call them?" he urged. "Or let me call them for you? I realize you're frightened of something, and I'm sure you've got good reason to be. But you can't let that cloud your judgment. You'll only dig yourself a deeper hole by waiting."

"Where were the animal protection agencies this morning?" she wanted to scream. Rodney had threatened to return to the stable with a gun and kill Sonora Sunset, and all the trainer had gotten was a stupid voice mail message when he'd tried to call the Humane Society. The police hadn't been any help, either. They had no facilities to board abused animals, they'd told the trainer. If the owner

of the horse returned with a gun, they would send out an officer, but other than that, there was nothing to be done until the Humane Society returned the trainer's call.

Molly was in up to her neck *because* of the blasted agencies. They'd failed Sonora Sunset when he needed them most. Rodney had flown into a mindless rage because the horse had lost a race. When the trainer called Molly out to the stable and she'd seen how cruelly her ex-husband had whipped the stallion, she hadn't doubted for a minute that he might return with a gun to finish him. What should she have done? Let the horse be shot?

She hadn't been able to *do* that. No matter what the cost to herself, she just hadn't been able to do that.

It was too late for the animal protection agencies to step in now. She was a recently released mental ward patient, still on probation and under a doctor's care, and she'd stolen a sixty-five thousand dollar horse. How would that look? By the time Rodney finished putting his spin on it, Molly knew exactly how it would look.

"Is it your ex?" Jake asked. "Is that who you're afraid of?"

"Yes," she said hollowly.

He sighed and passed a hand over his eyes, then rested his arms loosely on the table. "There's no reason to be afraid of him now."

"You don't know him."

A glint came into his eyes. "I know this. The bastard won't lay a hand on you. He'll have to go through me first. If I can't kick his ass, there'll be ten men standing in line behind me to do the honors."

He thought Rodney might beat her? Molly nearly corrected that misconception, but by doing so, she would be paving the way for him to ask more questions she didn't wish to answer.

The threat from Rodney wasn't physical. It had never been physical. Given Sunset's deplorable condition, Molly could see how Jake might think so, but in actuality, what

Rodney would do to her would be far worse. If he found her, he would strike blows with treachery and lies.

Molly would never underestimate her ex-husband again. *Never.* She had hoped to find temporary sanctuary on the Lazy J, but now she saw that staying here wasn't an option. Jake Coulter knew just enough to be dangerous. She couldn't take a chance that he might take matters into his own hands and call the authorities behind her back, believing that would be best for her in the long run.

She'd saved Sunset from taking a bullet. Now the horse was safely in Jake's possession. That was the best she could do for him.

Chapter Six

Jake was about to plant a boot on the bottom step of his front porch when he hesitated and glanced back through the darkness at the cabin. He couldn't forget the frantic expression he'd seen in Molly's eyes. At times during their conversation, she had put him in mind of a caged animal searching desperately for a way out. Now that he'd left her alone, he was afraid she might run.

What would happen to her then? Jake suspected she was fleeing from an abusive ex-husband who flew into maniacal rages. If Sunset's deplorable condition was any indication, the man was downright dangerous. What might happen to Molly if the bastard caught her off alone? It didn't even bear thinking about.

He shifted his gaze to her Toyota, which was still parked near the porch of the cabin. He smiled thoughtfully and swung back around. Fearing that the horse might raise another ruckus, he kept well away from the corral as he stealthily retraced his steps.

"What the hell is that?" Hank demanded when Jake entered the house later.

Stepping down into the great room, Jake glanced at the object he held in one hand. "What's it look like?"

Hank, who'd been reclining on the couch with a cold beer, sat forward on the cushion and frowned. "It looks like a rotor."

Jake tossed the object in question on the burl coffee

table he'd built a few months back. "If it looks like a rotor, I reckon that's probably what it is."

"Where'd it come from?"

Jake swept off his Stetson and tossed it on the table as well. "The same place most rotors do." He thrust his fingers through his hair, combing away the ring left by his hat. "Out of a distributor."

Hank narrowed an eye. "Whose?"

"Take a wild guess."

Jake struck off for the kitchen. After the day he'd had, that ice-cold beer looked mighty good.

Hank leaped up to follow on his heels. "You *didn't*."

Opening the refrigerator door of the old avocado-green side-by-side he'd borrowed from his parents, Jake said, "I had to do something to be sure she stayed put."

"I thought you gave her a job, that she was going to stay on here and work for us."

"That changed."

"When?"

"When I told her I knew she'd stolen the horse."

An amazed look passed over Hank's dark face.

Jake rushed to add, "I figured she'd feel better if everything was out in the open. Needless to say, it sort of backfired." He plucked a bottle of beer off the top shelf, bumped the door closed with his hip, and tossed the bottle cap into the trash under the sink. "I was afraid she'd try to skedaddle, so I fixed it so she can't."

A slight smile touched Hank's mouth. Jake chugged some beer to wet his throat, then eyed his brother as he wiped his mouth with the back of his hand. "Go ahead and spit it out. I can see you're about to choke on it."

Hank shook his head. After taking a long pull from his beer, he took a seat. The homemade chair he chose was the one that wobbled, compliments of an overlong leg that no one had found time to shorten. He shifted to balance his weight.

"I know tampering with her car was a chicken-shit thing

to do," Jake confessed. "But I couldn't think of any other way to keep her here. Just the thought of letting her leave scares the ever-loving hell out of me."

"I can't say as I blame you there," Hank agreed. "Whoever whipped that horse has a screw loose. I'd hate for him to take after a woman like that." Rocking the chair onto its back legs, he fixed Jake with an inquiring look. "She's going to be royally pissed when she discovers her rig won't start, you know."

"She'll only be pissed if she realizes I'm responsible."

Hank's eyes filled with amusement. "Did you put the distributor cap back on so she can't tell anything's missing?"

Jake's only response was a grin.

"It'll be just your luck that the lady's an ace mechanic."

"Not a chance." Chuckling, Jake straddled a chair to face his brother. "She's probably never even checked her own oil."

Jake no sooner spoke than a loud crash came from the front of the house. It sounded like someone had just thrown open the front door with such force that it smacked the interior wall. He cocked an ear. Hank threw a bewildered look over his shoulder. A fast click of footsteps in the hallway reached their ears.

"Where are you, Jake Coulter!" a high-pitched voice cried.

Hank's eyebrows shot clear to his hairline. "Uh-oh."

Jake was just pushing up from the chair when a small bundle of furious female barreled into his kitchen. Hands doubled into fists, she stopped just inside the archway, braced her feet wide apart, and flashed him a fiery glare.

"Where is my rotor?" she demanded.

"Your what?" Jake tried.

"My *rotor*!" she cried again. "How *dare* you remove it?" She took a threatening step closer. "Tell your mother to add arrogant to that list of faults. You had no right to disable my vehicle. No *right,* do you hear?"

She was shaking. Shaking violently. It occurred to Jake in that moment that she was far more upset than the situation warranted. Granted, he had stepped over the line. But even so, no permanent damage had been done.

He looked deeply into her eyes, and behind the glitter of outrage, he saw panic, the same kind of panic he experienced whenever anyone tried to hold him down. He lost all sense of reason, started to feel as if he couldn't breathe, and fought like a crazy man to get away.

"Molly, keep your perspective," he said, injecting a soothing tone into his voice.

"Perspective?" She grabbed for breath. "You stole my rotor, and now you accuse *me* of losing *my* perspective? You're attempting to hold me here against my will."

"Those are pretty strong words."

She fixed him with a virulent glare. "I want my car part."

"All right." He held up his hands. "Just calm down."

"I'll calm down when you return my rotor, and not before!" She took another step toward him. "I mean it! You hand it over!"

Jake had a bad feeling he was about to be taken apart by a pint-sized whirlwind. She looked ready to put out her claws and go for his eyes. Under other circumstances, he might have thought the situation humorous. But there was nothing funny about that look in Molly's eyes. The lady wasn't merely angry or upset. She was frantic.

He was about to assure her that he would return her rotor posthaste when she spun and started opening drawers. "No one keeps me where I don't want to stay. *No one!*"

She jerked so hard on the junk drawer that the rollers parted company with the runners. With the handle still hooked over her fingers, the drawer dived toward the floor and smacked her across the shins. She cried out in pain. Stuff spilled everywhere.

For a moment, Jake could only stare stupidly at a foil condom package that had landed at his feet. Where in bloody hell had *that* come from? He threw an accusing look at his brother, who shrugged, denial implicit in the gesture. Jake could only conclude that one of the hired hands must have stuck it there. *Fantastic.* Now Molly would think they were a bunch of sex fiends who had olive-oil orgies in the kitchen.

But Molly didn't see the condom. She had eyes only for the rotor, which wasn't there, and she continued to search for it with a single-mindedness that Jake found alarming. She dropped that drawer and jerked open another one.

Hoping to save her shins and his kitchen, Jake stepped forward to grab her arm. At his touch, she turned and planted a knotty little fist directly over his solar plexus. His breath *whooshed* from his chest. For a second, all he could do was hunch his shoulders and gasp like a landed fish while he stared at her in stunned amazement.

"Don't *touch* me!"

Okay, fine, he wanted to say, but the words wouldn't come.

"I want my rotor. You hand it over, or else!"

"I will, Molly," he finally managed to croak. "Just— give me a minute."

"I want it now! Or I swear, I'll steal a truck. Turn me in for that, why don't you?"

Bent forward to hold his belly, he rasped, "We don't leave keys in our vehicles."

"I'll hot-wire one!"

Hank sat back, clearly enjoying the show. "Never checked her own oil, huh?"

Jake shot a glare at his brother. "Shut up, Hank," he said weakly. Grabbing for another breath, he returned his gaze to Molly. "I'll give you the rotor. But first, you've got to calm down."

She thrust her arms down to her sides. "Now! I want it right now!"

Jake cleared his throat, straightened. He started for the archway that led into the great room. En route, he tried to reason with her. "You really shouldn't leave, Molly. At least you'll be safe here. If trouble catches up with you, there are eleven men on the Lazy J to watch out for you."

"I'm sick to death *tired* of being told what to do! And I don't need a bunch of arrogant, overbearing males to watch out for me."

At the back of Jake's mind, he knew he'd be wise to keep his mouth shut, but who had ever accused him of being wise? "Pardon me for pointing it out, but physically, you're no match for a man. If your ex-husband catches you alone, what the hell are you going to do?"

"That's my concern, not yours. Just give me my rotor."

Jake reached the coffee table and stared blankly at its surface. No rotor. He knew damned well he'd put it right there. So where in the hell had it gone? One word circled repeatedly in his brain—*shit*.

"It's gone." He knew before he spoke that she wasn't going to believe he hadn't hidden it. "I put it right here, I swear to God." He bent to look under the table. "Where the hell—?"

"Don't give me that!" she cried.

Jake straightened and held up his hands. "Molly, I swear on all that's holy that I left it right here." He walked around to look under the couch. *Holy hell.* "Hank?" he yelled. "Did you take the damned rotor?"

Hank sauntered into the archway, leaned a shoulder against the frame, and flashed a lazy grin. "Why would I take the damned rotor? I've got my own damned rotor."

"This isn't funny," Jake warned.

His brother crossed his ankles. "Depends on your viewpoint, I guess. I think it's hilarious." Molly turned and let out a hiss so sibilant it sounded venomous. Hank nodded politely. "I'm pleased to make your acquaintance, too. I'm Hank, by the way." His grin broadened. "The arrogant bastard's little brother. And just for the record, arrogance is only one of his many shortcomings. Bad manners rank high on the list, to my way of thinking. He could at least introduce us properly."

"I just want my rotor," she cried.

Hank glanced at the table. "He really did put it right there. I can't think where it went, unless it grew legs." His gaze fell on the Stetson. "You look under your hat, Jake?"

Before Jake could do that, Molly descended on the coffee table. She jerked the hat up by its crown, scrunching the carefully shaped felt with angry fingers. Jake winced. Stetsons didn't come cheap, and he wasn't a rich man.

Sure enough, there lay the rotor.

She dropped the Stetson and grabbed up the engine part. Pressing it to her waist, she hurried from the room as if the hounds of hell were at her heels.

Jake stared after her, feeling ashamed on the one hand, but still very concerned about her on the other. Now that she had her car part, she'd undoubtedly leave as quickly as she could, the only question being where she might go. Earlier that day, she'd told him she had very little money. How long would it last? And what would she do when it was gone, pull off to the side of the road somewhere and sleep in her rig?

The stallion started to scream just then, the shrieks rending the night and drifting faintly into the house. In his mind's eye, Jake saw Molly scurrying past the horse's pen, her footsteps carrying her inexorably toward the cabin and freedom. It would take only a few seconds to put the rotor back in her rig. She could be gone in five minutes.

Still standing in the archway, Hank said, "What're you going to do, Jake?"

At the question, Jake came back to himself, visions of Molly being beaten circling through his head. He grabbed his hat. Without bothering to reshape the crown, he shoved it on his head. "I guess I'll go talk to her. If I can get her calmed down, maybe I can convince her to stay."

"Talking. Hmm." Hank nodded his approval. "There's a

good plan. Too bad you didn't think of it *before* you stole her rotor."

Caught midstride by the dig, Jake stopped and looked back at his brother. "You know, Hank, one of these times someone's going to take exception to that smart mouth."

Hank smiled. "You reckon?"

Jake found Molly sitting on the front porch of the cabin. Arms locked around her bent legs, face pressed to her knees, she was shaking like a leaf. Jake was somewhat encouraged by the fact that the rotor lay beside her on the step. He hoped that meant she was no longer in a big rush to leave, but he thought it more likely that she was simply too upset.

When he stepped close to grab the engine part, she flinched and jerked her head up to stare at him. In the moonlight, her face looked as white as fresh snow and her eyes were huge glistening spheres of amber, reflecting emotions that made his heart twist. She'd been wary of him before; now, thanks to his idiocy, she was downright spooked.

He stood there for a moment, groping for the words to apologize. Unfortunately, he'd never been a glib talker. That was a failing that grew worse when he got upset, and he was plenty upset right then, mainly with himself. Of all the damned fool things for him to do, this latest took the prize.

Words failing him, he strode around to the front of her rig, lifted the hood, and set himself to the task of setting a wrong right. After he finished, he wiped his hands on his jeans and retraced his path to the porch, dreading the conversation yet to come. He owed her a heartfelt apology, and he needed to make it convincing.

When he sat beside her on the step, she inched away and hunched her shoulders. The posture was so defensive he felt a little sick. This was his fault, entirely his fault. The Lazy J was remotely located. Under the best of circumstances, any female with brains would be uneasy, and thanks to him, these were far from the best of circumstances.

He stared off into the darkness, wishing he knew what the hell to say. When nothing brilliant came to mind, he fell back on childlike simplicity. "I'm sorry for what I did."

No answer. She just huddled there, shivering. She looked so small and alone that he wished he could hug her. The yearning came over him so suddenly and with such sharpness that it gave him pause. What was happening here? He'd always liked women and enjoyed their friendship, but this was the first time he'd ever experienced such fierce feelings of protectiveness for a female outside his family.

"I've got a bad habit of acting before I think sometimes," he went on cautiously. "If you want to leave, you're free to go. I'll even help you load back up."

Still no answer.

He sighed and rubbed his eyes. *Damn.* "You're right. It was arrogant of me to think I know what's best for you. If I could take it back, I would."

"Me, too," she said in a quivering voice. "I can't believe I hit you. I've never hit *anyone*. Never! I can't believe I did it."

Jake suppressed a smile, relieved that she was at least willing to talk to him. "No real harm done."

She straightened and extended her arms in front of her, elbows resting on her knees, hands knotted into small fists. "I can't stand to feel trapped. It makes me crazy."

He wished he could coax her into telling him more, but he erred on the side of caution and filed away that tidbit of information for later. "No one likes to feel trapped."

She rubbed her arms, making him wish he had a jacket to give to her. "I was irrational, out of control. I don't know what came over me."

In the moonlight, her eyes were huge splashes of luminous darkness, her pale face framed by a fiery nimbus of rebellious curls that had escaped her braid. Jake ached to cup her chin in his hand and trace the fragile line of her cheekbone with his thumb. Even without makeup, she was lovely, and it saddened him that she didn't seem to know it.

"Only crazy people do crazy things," she said hollowly.

"Well, then, I reckon we're both nuts. Stealing your rotor to keep you here wasn't exactly a rational move."

She flashed him a startled look, her eyes bright with unshed tears. "At least you didn't become physically violent."

On a comparative scale, Jake figured his had been the worse offense. She hadn't really hurt him, after all. "Don't worry about it, Molly. I had a punch or two coming, and I'm none the worse for it."

"I still shouldn't have hit you. You must have thought I'd lost my mind." A haunted look came into her eyes. "Who knows? Maybe I have."

Resting his arms on his knees, he let his hands dangle and listened to an owl hoot into the night. Somewhere out in the darkness, a small rodent was probably scrambling for safety.

"I'll accept your apology if you'll accept mine," he said huskily. "I never meant to upset you like that. I just wanted to help." He waited a beat. "I knew you'd probably take off. I was worried about what could happen to you."

"Nothing will happen if I'm careful not to let anyone find me."

"They're bound to find you eventually, Molly. You can't run long enough or far enough to avoid the cops forever."

"I know that." She rubbed her forehead as if it hurt. "All I need is seven months."

He mentally circled that. "Why seven months?"

"A certain difficulty in my life will be over then," she told him. "After that, I'll still be in big trouble for stealing the horse, but if I act quickly and play my hand right, the consequences won't be too terrible. Unless, of course, he can somehow petition the court for another year."

Jake realized she was talking more to herself than to him and revealing things she didn't intend to in the process. Unfortunately, the information made little sense to him. "Petition the court for another year of what? I'm not following."

She groaned. "I know you're not. I'm sorry. Just take my word for it, all right? I can't contact the authorities about Sunset for seven months. If I do, he'll find me, and if he does, my goose is cooked."

"Then stay here for that period of time," Jake encouraged. "Seven months isn't so terribly long, not in the overall scheme of things."

She threw him an accusing look. "And have you call the Humane Society behind my back, thinking you know what's best?"

Jake knew he had that coming. "I give you my word I won't do that. Not without your knowledge and permission."

"And I'll never give it."

"Why, Molly? Can't you tell me just that much? Getting the animal protection agencies involved and on your side would be a smart move."

She shook her head and shivered again. "Not for me, it wouldn't."

"*Why?* Two heads are better than one. Tell me what's got you so frightened. Maybe together we can find a solution."

A closed look came over her face, and she shook her head again.

Jake puffed air into his cheeks. Calling the Humane Society was the best thing to do. Why the hell couldn't she see that? No court in the land would send her to jail for stealing that horse to protect it.

"At least do this much for me," he said softly. "Stay on

here. Don't take off to parts unknown where you'll have no friends to turn to."

When she started to shake her head again, Jake quickly added, "I won't call the Humane Society, Molly. I swear it. I won't call anyone unless you ask me to. You can stay on, just as you planned. No questions, no pressure. The job is still yours."

She fixed huge, frightened, and very uncertain eyes on him. "How do I know you'll keep your word? That you won't call someone behind my back?"

Jake had always prided himself on being a man of honor, and the question stung for an instant. But the fear he saw in her eyes made it impossible for him to feel offended. She had no way of knowing what kind of man he was, after all. Evidently, she had a great deal to lose if she trusted him, and he stood to lose nothing if he betrayed her. Aside from the Lazy J, which was a family heritage he'd once believed forever lost, Jake had only one possession that he truly treasured.

Straightening one leg to raise his hip, he reached into the front pocket of his Wranglers and drew that possession out. Holding it up by the heavy gold chain, he said, "This is my grandpa's watch. Right before he died, he gave it to me. I've carried it with me ever since." He gazed at it for a moment then smiled ruefully. "It broke some time back. I know I should get it fixed, but I can't bear to let a jewelry shop send it off for repair. I'm afraid it might get lost."

He lifted Molly's hand, lowered the watch onto her palm, and curled her fingers around it.

"What are you doing?" she asked thinly.

"Putting it in your safekeeping," he said huskily. "When you leave the Lazy J, I'll expect you to return it to me. Until then, consider it collateral against my word. If I go in default, it's yours to keep."

She unfurled her fingers, tried to press the watch back on him. "That isn't necessary."

He waved her hand away. "No. You keep it. As insurance. Aside from this ranch and the people I love, there's nothing I value more than that watch. If I go back on my word, it's yours."

Jake pushed to his feet and gazed at the starlit sky for a moment. He thought of that little rodent again, pictured it scurrying madly for safety and possibly making a fatal wrong turn in its panic. The night owl was still calling, ever ready to dive down and seize its prey. The rodent's only hope was to stick tight and keep its head down.

"You can go or stay, Molly. I hope you'll choose to stay. I'm sorry for trying to make that decision for you." He glanced down at her. "If you choose to haul ass, don't forget to leave the watch on the table. If you take it with you, it'll break my heart. When you read the inscription, you'll understand why."

He left it at that, forcing himself to walk away. With every step, the realization was driven home to him that he was leaving a chunk of himself behind, and that it might be gone come morning.

As irrational as he knew it was, he wasn't sure if he was thinking of the heirloom watch or the woman who clutched it in her trembling hand.

Chapter Seven

To stay or not to stay, that was the question. Molly paced a circle around the old leather sofa where her bags of belongings lay in helter-skelter piles. She didn't know whether she should return them to the Toyota or start unpacking. Dust burned in her nostrils, a reminder of the cleaning that would have to be done in the cabin before she could put her things away. If she was going to stay, she needed to get started.

Could she trust Jake Coulter? That was the real question she needed to address, and whether or not she stayed would depend entirely upon the answer.

She gazed down at the old timepiece in her hand. The inscription inside the gold cover read, *"Forever, Matthew, my love, June 6, 1873. Hattie."* By the date, Molly knew the watch was a family heirloom, passed down to Jake's grandfather by his father before him. Little wonder Jake treasured it. If the watch went missing, something truly priceless would be lost to the entire Coulter family.

Molly closed her hand over the gold, now warm and slick from her sweaty palm. Jake had entrusted this into her keeping. If he had that much confidence in her on such short acquaintance, why couldn't she have just a little in him?

She thought of Sam Banks, her therapist, and wished with all her heart that she could phone him without running a risk of her call being traced. During her stay at the clinic and over the last five months since her release, he'd been her sounding board and only steadfast friend, someone she could contact, day or night, if she needed to talk. Though he tried never to pontificate, choosing instead to let her reach her own decisions, he always managed to guide her in the right direction.

What would he say to her now?

Molly closed her eyes, the memory of his mellow voice whispering in her mind. *"We shouldn't stereotype people,"* he'd once told her. *"Give each individual a chance to prove him- or herself before you pass judgment. Giving your guarded trust is never a mistake, Molly, not if you're smart about it."*

Another time, when she had expressed a concern that she was a terrible judge of character, Sam had popped back with, *"Why is that? Because you trusted and believed in people, and they betrayed you?"* Since that was exactly the reason, Molly hadn't been able to think what to say. Not only Rodney had betrayed her, she had reason to believe her father-in-law, Jared Wells, who'd been her dad's partner and best friend, had taken part in the scheme as well. There was even evidence to implicate Claudia, the only mother she'd ever known. What was she supposed to do with that?

Toward the end of that counseling session, Sam had presented her with a question that seemed particularly appropriate to ask herself now. Along with everything else, was she going to let her marriage to Rodney rob her of the ability to trust?

The very thought made Molly tremble with outrage. Her ex-husband had taken so much from her already, so very much—her youth, her peace of mind, her liberty—and, she suspected, even her father. Was she going to let him continue to ruin every aspect of her life? *No, damn it, no.*

Even as determination filled her, she felt a dark cloud of hopelessness move over her. In only seven more months, she would have reached the finish line. Rodney would have lost her power of attorney. She would have been able to walk back into Sterling and Wells to take her rightful place behind her father's desk. She would have then had the financial resources to hire legal representation and stonewall Rodney if he tried to pull any more fast ones in court. She'd been so close, so very close, to regaining her independence. Now, in one fell swoop, she had jeopardized everything, even her plan to avenge her father's death.

Now, thanks to her stupidity, Rodney could get the upper hand again. He would put his spin on the horse-theft incident, holding it up before a judge as irrefutable proof of her emotional instability and legal incompetence. Even Molly had to admit that stealing a sixty-five-thousand-dollar racehorse was a crazy thing to do, and she would have a devil of a time convincing a judge she'd had good reasons.

Sam Banks had warned her. *"Keep your nose clean, Molly,"* he'd cautioned her repeatedly. *"Whether you like it or not, whether it's fair or not, you're living under a microscope right now."*

Since her release from the clinic, she'd lived like a goldfish in a small glass bowl, thinking twice and sometimes thrice before she did anything. Other recently divorced women could quit their jobs, move to exciting new places, go back to school, or start new careers. On a whim, they could bleach their hair, dress like teenagers, go on crash diets, or engage in tawdry affairs. No one cared if their choices were based on sound judgment or if they were even rational. But Molly didn't have that freedom. Before she did anything, she had to think of how it might look to a judge.

In a perfect world, Rodney's power over her personal life should have ended the day her divorce was final, but no world was perfect, least of all hers. The very fact that Sam had helped her obtain a divorce while she was still in the clinic could work against her. Rodney would argue that she'd been incapable of making wise choices, hadn't understood what she was doing, and that her doctor had made a grave error in judgment. He would also claim that she still needed someone, namely him, to look after her and her business interests. Further strengthening his hand was the fact that her adoptive mother, an MD and something of an expert witness in her own right, might testify against her in court.

Molly wasn't sure what motivated Claudia, whether she was involved in the scheme to take over the firm, or if she was merely doing what she honestly believed was best. Molly only knew that her mom had joined ranks with Rodney to have her deemed legally incompetent and had later signed the necessary forms to have her committed. Molly had seen Claudia's signature on the papers herself.

It had been the most heartbreaking revelation of her life.

In the end, it hadn't really mattered what Claudia's intentions had been. The result was that Molly had been stripped of her rights. Individuals who were deemed legally incompetent in a court of law were treated like children in many ways until the mandate was reversed. The court appointed a person to act as their legal guardian. If they had money, they were often denied access to the funds and were allotted only a monthly stipend to cover basic expenses. Their driver's licenses were frequently revoked. They weren't allowed to have charge accounts. If they owned firearms, the weapons were removed from their possession. Their signature on a legal document was worthless unless the court-appointed guardian agreed to co-sign. In many ways, they became nonpeople who could make no decisions for themselves and whose protests went unheard.

In Molly's case, the situation had been even worse because her husband and mother had had her committed, not only calling into question her judgment but casting doubt on her sanity as well. First she'd been stripped of her rights; then she'd been locked up.

At the clinic, Sam Banks, the doctor whom she'd initially seen as her enemy, had turned out to be her knight in shining armor, transforming what might have been a nightmarish imprisonment into a time of healing. He had listened patiently to her outlandish story and had begun to believe her when no one else did. Eventually, he had fought in court to help her get a divorce, telling the judge that it had been her dysfunctional relationship with her overbearing husband that had caused all her problems in the first place.

In a world that had turned viciously against her, he'd been her only ally.

Until this morning, she had followed Sam's advice to the letter, refraining from any behavior that might cast her in a bad light. But now she'd totally blown it, jeopardizing all her plans and putting herself at the mercy of strangers she wasn't sure she could trust.

Unfurling her fingers again, she gazed solemnly at the watch Jake Coulter had given her. In the firelight, the aged gold case seemed to gleam with inner warmth, much like the man who had placed it in her hand. He was a strange one, she thought with a faint smile, forceful and overbearing, yet seemingly gentle and kind as well.

He'd thrown her a lifeline, whether he realized it or not, providing her with a perfect place to lie low for a while. The chances that anyone would think to look for her on a ranch were miniscule. If she stayed on here and took precautions, it was entirely possible that she could ride out the clock until the entire year of probation elapsed, gaining strength each day for the inevitable battles she would face when she returned to Portland, not only to vindicate herself, but to seek justice for her father's death.

In just seven more months, her power of attorney would revert back to her, and she would be legally free of her ex-husband and her mother. If she acted quickly when that day arrived, she could get a good attorney on retainer and reclaim control of the firm before Rodney had time to appeal to the court for an extension. Only seven more months. If Jake Coulter's word was good, she could surely hole up here for that long.

Slipping the timepiece into her pocket, Molly approached the plastic bags that held her belongings. She'd fallen in love with the Lazy J at first sight, thinking it was the perfect place for Sunset to recuperate. Why not remain here herself? It was a beautiful and peaceful setting, so far removed from her usual surroundings that it gave her a sense of separateness and safety. This quaint old cabin was growing on her as well, its air of timelessness soothing her in a way she couldn't define.

Decision made, Molly went to work. Since she'd slept most of the evening, she could afford to stay up late. Thanks to Rodney, she didn't have much by way of household goods to put away. If she got right to it, she'd be finished unpacking inside of two hours.

As she washed out kitchen drawers and set herself to the task of putting her cooking utensils away, Molly recalled her rampaging attack on Jake's house. She still couldn't believe she had behaved so badly, and then, horror of horrors, she'd capped it all off by slugging the poor man.

An unbidden grin tugged at her mouth. The look on his face had been priceless, and for just a moment, she'd felt so *free*. Though she wished now that she could undo the incident, she had to admit that a perverse part of her had enjoyed being wildly out of control for a few minutes. What did that tell her?

Sam would probably say she'd been releasing long suppressed rage, and Jake Coulter had just been standing in her line of fire. He would then advise her to find healthier, less objectionable ways to vent her feelings in the future.

Well, punching a pillow had never given her a rush like she'd felt this evening, and there had never been a sense of closure, either. She had experienced that with Jake. He had apologized and so had she. That felt nice. Instead of trembling with helpless anger when she thought of him, she actually wanted to smile. *"I'm sorry for what I did."* Such simple words, uttered with husky regret. In ten years of marriage, a sincere apology had never passed Rodney's lips.

Satisfied with the order of the kitchen drawers, Molly turned her attention to wiping out the cupboards. Tomorrow she would begin cleaning Jake's house. She had gotten off to a rocky start, but she would make it up to him.

Though she'd taken no time to admire it, he had a lovely home with an impressive, log-wall interior, beautiful oak floors, and an eclectic collection of handmade furniture, fashioned from logs. She would sweep and scrub and polish until the place shone. She'd also do her best to put tasty, wholesome meals on his table. He'd not be regretting his decision to hire her.

She just hoped he had some cookbooks.

Finished in the kitchen, she moved to the bedroom. As she hung her slacks and tops in the closet, Molly worried her bottom lip. Her wardrobe wasn't exactly suitable for ranch life, but she'd have to make do.

She turned to grab another sack, thinking it contained only underclothes. The corner of something hard poked through the bag and touched her leg. She thrust in a hand and drew out a folding picture frame. Sadness clutched at her even before she looked at the two photographs, one of her best friend Sarah, the other of her father. Molly studied their faces, her feelings of regret and shame still sharp. It had been well over ten years since Sarah's death and eleven months since her father's, but the hurting never stopped.

She set the frame on the nightstand, turning the pictures toward the bed so they would be the last thing she saw when she went to sleep. Reminders of grave mistakes helped a person never to make the same ones again. Seeing her father's smiling likeness also reminded her that she had a far more important mission to accomplish than merely getting her affairs back in order. Her father was dead, and if her suspicions were correct, Rodney Wells had pulled the trigger of the gun that killed him.

She couldn't let that slide, she thought, knotting her hands into aching fists. If it was the last thing she ever did, she would make Rodney pay. Only then would she be able to lay her father to rest and move on with her life.

From outside, she heard Sunset whinny, the sound forlorn. She stepped to the window and swept aside the lace curtains to push up the bottom sash. Crisp night air, redolent with the scents of nearby forest and rolling grasslands, flowed in around her, the chill a sharp contrast to the fire's warmth that caressed her back. Down along the creek, frogs raised their voices to the moonlight, the melodic cacophony underscored by the rhythmic hiss of irrigation sprinklers in the fields.

Molly dragged in a deep breath, marveling at how different it smelled here. Off in the distance, she heard a coyote baying at the moon. From up near the main house, a dog barked in response. The unharmonious duet prompted Sunset to neigh again.

Though Molly squinted to see through the darkness, she couldn't make out the horse. Nevertheless she leaned out the window, hoping Sunset might be able to see her.

"I'm here, boy. You're not all alone. I'll leave my window partway open so I can hear if you need me. No one's going to hurt you ever again. I promise."

The stallion grunted and whinnied softly, almost as if he was comforted by the sound of her voice.

I did the right thing, she thought. *No matter what happens to me, I did what had to be done, and that's the end of it.*

"*Molly?*"

The masculine voice slipped into Molly's dreams. "*Molly, can you hear me?*" She struggled to wake up, afraid if she didn't that they'd give her another injection.

No more. Please, no more. She had to talk to them, make them believe her. She couldn't do that when her head was muzzy. She wasn't crazy. Had to tell them. Not crazy. No more shots.

"Molly!"

Molly jerked awake. For a moment, she stared blankly at the knotty pine ceiling, uncertain where she was. Then the events of yesterday slammed into her brain.

Rap—tat—tat. The sharp, rhythmic report sat her up straight. She rubbed her eyes, squinted against a shaft of blinding morning sunlight, and groaned. Someone was knocking on the door. *Jake Coulter? What time was it, anyway?*

Blearily, she glanced at her watch, decided it had to be wrong, and stumbled from the bedroom.

"Coming!" she yelled. Once in the living room, it occurred to her that she shouldn't assume it was her new employer at the door. There was still a very real possibility that the police might find her. She stopped dead in her tracks. "Who is it?"

"Jake."

Recognizing his deep voice, she fumbled with the deadbolt. The apparatus rattled like a bunch of aluminum pots as it disengaged.

A tall blur of blue stood on the doorstep. Even half asleep, she felt her stomach tighten at the sight of him. "What time is it?" she managed to croak.

"Six," he informed her in that deep, silky voice she remembered so well, "and we're running late."

Molly pushed at her hair. *"Late?"*

He gave a low chuckle. "Yes, late."

She looked at her watch again. "How can we be running late when it's only six in the morning?"

He chuckled and stepped inside, thrusting a large mug of coffee under her nose. "I brought you some morning wake-me-up."

She took the proffered cup with undisguised eagerness.

Not even six-feet-plus of well-muscled male was enough to wake her up without the help of a strong jolt of caffeine. She slurped a little into her mouth and swallowed before saying, "God bless you."

He gave another low laugh. "I wasn't sure if you had the makings for coffee over here. I can't get my eyes open without it."

Molly's eyes were coming open with record speed. "My goodness, it's certainly *strong*."

"I usually have time for only one cup, so I try to make it count."

A spoon would have stood straight in the stuff.

She took another sip, then cradled the mug in her hands. Jake moved inside and closed the door. Without considering how it might look, Molly retreated a step, then wanted to kick herself for acting like an idiot. She wasn't sure why this man unsettled her so. She only knew that he did.

This morning he wore clothes identical to those of yesterday, the only difference being that the blue chambray shirt and jeans looked freshly laundered. Beneath the brim of his Stetson, his sable hair was a shade darker with dampness from his shower, and he was freshly shaven, his jaw shiny and red from scrubbing, the woodsy scent of his cologne mixing nicely with the earthy smells he brought in with him from outdoors.

He smiled as he gave her a head-to-toe once-over. "Do you always sleep fully dressed?"

She glanced down at her wrinkled attire. Heat rose to her cheeks as she forced her gaze back to his. "Only when I'm so tired that I fall asleep before I realize what hit me." Feeling painfully self-conscious under his unwavering regard, she switched the mug to one hand and pushed at her hair again. Her braid had come partially undone, and a rippled shank of brownish red hung forward over one eye. "I'm sorry. I must look a fright. I stayed up late unpacking."

"You look fine." His warm gaze trailed slowly over her

face. He had a way of looking at a woman that made her feel beautiful, a talent she felt sure had served him well over the years. "A little sleep rumpled and tired, but you had a rough day yesterday."

Determined to remain immune to his well-practiced brand of charm, she tried to blink the bleariness from her eyes. A yawn tried to crawl up her throat. She swallowed it back.

He shoved back his sleeve to check his watch. "I apologize for rousting you out at this hour, but here on the Lazy J we get up with the chickens. I was hoping to give you a walk-through over at the house and discuss your job duties before I start my day. I usually head out pretty early."

Molly lost her battle with the yawn and blinked again. "Don't apologize. It's my own fault for staying up so late. Can you give me a few minutes? I need to grab a quick shower and get my eyes open. Then I'll be over."

He nodded. "Not a problem. I have milking to do and eggs to gather. How does thirty minutes strike you?"

She stifled another yawn. "Make it thirty-five, and you've got a deal."

He grinned, the flash of his white teeth almost blinding. "Thirty-five, it is."

He started to leave, then turned back, his hand coming to rest on a length of rope tucked over his belt. "I almost forgot." He tugged the hemp free and dangled it before her nose. "I promised you a snake deterrent." He stepped around her to advance on the wood box. After arranging the rope in a half circle on the floor, each end touching the log wall, he made his way back to her. "That should do it."

Molly glanced dubiously at the rope. "That really works?"

"No snakes will get in the house and crawl over that rope, guaranteed."

A short length of rope seemed pitifully inadequate to her, but he had to know a lot more about it than she did. "Thank you. Having it there will ease my mind."

"That's the whole idea, easing your mind." He opened the door. "Sorry to run, but I've got chores. I'd best get to them."

Sleepy-eyed, she watched as he stepped back out onto the porch. After the door crashed closed, she dropped onto the old leather easy chair to finish gulping down the coffee. Thirty minutes? That was barely enough time to prop one eyelid open. She groaned and rubbed her face. It had been too long since she'd had to get up early for work. Her body was in shock. For the last five months, she'd been restricted from taking a job, so she'd staved off boredom by volunteering at the hospital pediatric ward in the afternoons. Reading *Winnie the Pooh* aloud and bending flexible straws into imaginative shapes hadn't kept her in shape for the rigors of real employment.

Getting up with the chickens was really going to suck.

Thirty minutes later, Molly knocked on the front door of the house. With every breath she exhaled, foggy puffs of steam formed. She glanced at a big, clock-faced thermometer mounted on a railing beam to her right. *Thirty-five degrees?* She shuddered, wishing she'd had the good sense to grab her parka. The sleeves of her loose cotton top clung to her skin where she'd failed to get completely dry after her shower, and she'd braided her hair while it was still wet. She felt like a human icicle.

From inside, she heard voices. Then came the sharp tap of boots on the interior oak floor. She expected to see Jake. Instead, a wiry older man with thinning gray hair and friendly green eyes opened the door. "Howdy!" he said warmly. "I reckon you must be Molly." He thrust out a gnarled hand that looked none too clean. "I'm Levi."

Molly grasped his extended fingers, expecting the usual polite shake. "I'm pleased to meet you, Levi."

"Not as pleased as I am." He proceeded to raise and lower her arm as if it were a pump handle. "I understand you're one hell of a shade-tree grease monkey."

"One hell of a—?" Molly broke off, swallowed, and revised that by saying, "You understand I'm a what?"

"A mechanic." Instead of stepping back so she might enter the house, Levi joined her on the porch and shut the door. "My Mandy has a perplexin' hitch in her get-along."

Molly was beginning to wonder if they spoke the same language.

He grasped her elbow and turned her about-face. "Runnin' rough as a cob, like as if there's water in her gas tank. No crack in the block, though, and the fuel checks out fine. I changed all the plugs, and that didn't help." He led her down the steps. "Threw in a new fuel pump, and that didn't help, either. Jake, now, he's a fine mechanic. Most times, he can fix what's broke. But he hasn't had time to spare all week."

With Molly firmly in tow, Levi walked to a battered brown Ford pickup with rusted rims and a bumper wired on with coat hangers. He slapped the front fender. "She don't look like much, but we're old friends. Can you tell me what's ailin' her?"

This was her first day on the job, and she didn't want to be late meeting Jake. But when she looked into Levi's worried green eyes, she couldn't tell him no. "Well," she said hesitantly. "I suppose I can take a look."

She stood back as he climbed into the pickup and started the engine. The resultant roar nearly split her eardrums. Black smoke puffed from the rattling tailpipe. After the initial explosion of noise, the engine settled into an erratic pattern of sputters, coughs, and vibrations. Molly tipped her head. "That sounds like a timing problem."

"No kidding? Can you fix her?"

Molly stared at him incredulously. Most men smirked at her mechanic skills. Women had their place, and under the hood of a vehicle definitely wasn't it. "I, um . . ." She knew she should put him off until later, but his expression was so imploring she didn't have the heart to do it. "I suppose I can try. Do you have a timing light?"

Levi spilled back out of the cab, amazingly spry for a man who looked to be well past sixty. His red cotton work shirt was spotlessly clean, the sleeves rolled back to a precise three-quarter length. "Honey, there's not much by way of mechanic tools we don't got. Mainly we're lackin' in know-how." He flashed her a smile. "It's glad we'll be to have another decent mechanic on the place."

How long could it possibly take for a woman to shower and dress?

Jake sighed and stepped to the stove to pour a third cup of coffee, a rarity for him. Here it was, seven fifteen, and he hadn't even started his day yet. When Molly finally showed up, they would have to come to a clear understanding, namely that he expected her to be prompt.

"What's got you in such a grump?" Hank asked when he stepped in from outside. "You look like you could chew bolts and spit out buckshot."

"Molly's forty-five minutes late. I told her yesterday that we aren't much on schedules around here, and I guess she took it to heart."

Hank chuckled. "She got waylaid."

"By whom?"

"Levi. He's got her working on his pickup."

"You're not serious."

Hank grabbed some crackers from a plate. "If you want to chew her ass, now's a fine time. She's head down under the hood, with nothing but cute fanny poking out."

Hank's description titillated Jake's imagination. He set his mug on the counter and strode through the house to the front door. When he stepped onto the porch, he saw that Hank had called it right. Molly's body was angled head down over the battered grill of Levi's pickup, the seat of her denim jeans pointing skyward. There was more of her than just fanny showing, but that was the part of her that caught and held the male eye.

Nice. As he ran his gaze over those sweetly plump contours, Jake wished, not for the first time, that the lady would wear some clothes that came close to fitting her.

Molly chose that moment to wiggle her butt, providing a display of feminine roundness that resulted in a swift arch of Jake's eyebrows. On second thought, he wasn't sure snugger britches would be a good thing. As it was, Benny was lingering in the doorway of the stable, his blue eyes fixed on Molly's upturned posterior, a vacuous expression on his craggy face. Standing behind him was Jake's youngest hand, Danno, a redheaded twenty-year-old with more testosterone and freckles than brains.

As Jake descended the front steps and started across the yard, he shot both hired hands a warning look that jerked them to attention. Benny, the older of the two at thirty-six, ran a finger under the red bandana at his throat, collected himself, and swung around to return to the stable, only to collide with Danno, who suddenly decided to head out. In a tangle of arms and legs, they looked as though they were doing the tango for a moment.

Jake released a sigh. Nope. Snug britches on Molly would not be conducive to labor output. As he made his way across the remainder of the barnyard, he assumed a scowl, which he felt was deserved under the circumstances. Just because the lady had a world-class ass and more curves than a road atlas didn't mean she could keep him waiting for forty-five minutes without hearing about it.

As he drew up at the fender of the truck, Jake cast a grinning Levi a narrow-eyed glance. Raising his voice to be heard over the now smooth purr of the engine, he said, "I hired this woman to cook and clean, not work on trucks." He glanced at his watch. "We had an appointment forty-five minutes ago."

At the sound of Jake's voice, Molly gave such a start she dropped the timing light, rapped her head on the raised pickup hood, and almost fell off the bumper. Levi caught her from toppling with a hand on her rump, which made her jump as if he had goosed her. In a borrowed denim jacket that was several sizes too large, she looked too cute by half as she teetered on her dented chrome perch and grabbed for balance.

"Mr. Coulter!" She fixed huge, butterscotch-brown eyes on him. "Has it really been forty-five minutes?"

He struggled not to smile. It was a little hard to stay mad when she looked so horrified. "It certainly has, and I have work to do."

She clamped a greasy hand over the smarting spot on her head. "I didn't think I'd been out here that long. I knocked on the door precisely at six-thirty. Honestly."

Since it was her first day and he knew Levi, Jake decided to go easy. He assured himself that his decision to be lenient had nothing to do with the worried, apprehensive look in her big brown eyes. What in God's name had happened in her life to give her such a low estimation of men? He wasn't going to fire her for being a few minutes late.

Softening his tone, he said, "Hank told me you got waylaid." He glanced at his hired hand. "Levi tends to come on like a high wind sometimes." He took the sting out of what he said next by giving her a teasing wink. "I'll let it go this time. Just don't let it happen again, all right?"

She gave the crown of her head another rub, then grimaced as she lowered her hand and saw the grease on her fingers.

"You about finished up?" Jake asked. "Sounds like she's running better."

She reached for a grease cloth lying over the radiator cap. As she wiped her hands, she said, "It was only the timing." She flashed a sweet smile at Levi. "She needs a lot of other work done, though. The points should be replaced, and that liquid weld you put in the radiator won't last. You might call around to some junkyards, Levi. If you can find a radiator, I'll be happy to help you put it in when I have a day off."

"You're an angel, Miss Molly. I'll get right on finding one."

The elderly cowboy offered her a hand down. Jake observed the interaction between the two, Molly hesitant and uncertain, the old man oblivious to her shyness. Levi Trump had never met a stranger. Though she still seemed tense, it appeared to Jake that his housekeeper was already well on her way to making friends with the old codger. Unless he missed his guess, Molly needed a friend, and for all his rough edges, Levi would be a fine one. He was old enough to be safe, yet young enough to remember being on the shy side of thirty with more problems than solutions.

Jake glanced at his watch again. Molly's cheeks went pink. "I'm ready."

"I certainly hope. The day's half over." Glancing at Levi, Jake said, "I thought you and Shorty were supposed to be changing hand lines."

"We're headin' out straightaway." Levi plucked the grease rag from Molly's fingers. "I thank you kindly for fixin' Mandy, honey."

"It wasn't any big deal." Molly's cheeks turned a deeper pink as she peeled off the jacket and returned it to the hired hand. "I was glad to do it."

Hooking the jacket over his shoulder by a thumb, Levi nodded and winked at Jake. "Thanks for the loan of your cook, boss. Though I gotta point out, maybe you hired her for the wrong job."

Jake listened to the purr of the engine for a moment. "Maybe so."

He swung a hand, indicating that Molly should precede him to the house. She set off, affording him a pleasing view of her backside as she walked. The breeze picked up, molding the loose folds of her cotton top to her body, showcasing a slender waist and full hips that could easily make a man go cross-eyed if he admired the action for too long.

"I really was at the door by six-thirty, just as agreed,"

she said over her shoulder, "but Levi caught me before I got inside."

"At least Mandy's fixed. He's been pestering me all week to have a look at her, and I haven't had time." Lengthening his stride, Jake drew abreast of her as they reached the porch. "So tell me, how did a pretty girl like you become an ace mechanic?"

She rolled her eyes, whether at the compliment or the question, Jake wasn't sure. "I can thank my father for what little skill I have. He was into antique cars and did all the refurbishing himself."

Jake took her arm as they went up the steps. Her hip bumped against his thigh, and he felt her stiffen. "So you developed an interest in old cars and learned a lot about engines in the process?"

"Actually, I didn't enjoy working on cars all that much. I think I knew, even as a teenager, that I might end up single, and just in case, I wanted to have rudimentary mechanic skills."

Jake shot her a sharp look. "Why was that?"

"It can be tough for a single woman if she knows nothing about cars."

Jake released her arm as they gained the porch. "No, I mean why did you think you'd end up single?"

"Do you think that I suddenly woke up a plain Jane yesterday morning?"

Jake looked deeply into her beautiful eyes, and his heart caught at what he didn't see there. No laughter, no hint that she was joking. She honestly believed she was plain.

Try as he might, he could make no sense of that. Granted, she wasn't Jake's usual type, but there was no denying that she was pretty. How could she possibly look at that face and not see what everyone else did?

Had someone told her she was unattractive? All too often, one's self-image was formed by the cruel remarks of others. If Molly had been told she was plain, she would see a plain woman when she looked in the mirror. It was as simple and as heartbreaking as that.

He absolutely could not tell this woman she was pretty again. This was her first day on the job, and she was the only female on the ranch. If he paid her too many compliments, she might think he was coming on to her. A man in a position of authority had to be careful what he said and did when dealing with a female employee.

There would be no misunderstandings of that nature, not if he could help it. After showing her through the house and explaining her duties, he would give her the list of groceries they needed, write a check for the purchases, supply her with a vehicle, and leave her to manage the rest on her own.

Chapter Eight

Eight hours later, Molly entered the pantry and stared at a collection of small coolers on the top shelves. They were a variety of colors, none large enough to hold much more than a six-pack of soda pop and all sporting ground-in dirt. Why on earth were they taking up kitchen storage?

She didn't have time to worry about it. Going into town for groceries had taken up most of her morning. She'd spent the afternoon cleaning and doing laundry. Now it was almost five. She didn't want to be late getting dinner on the table.

Throat constricted with nerves, she went to get the vegetables. The amount needed to fix a stir-fry for twelve people was amazing. Feeding so many, she would have to go shopping for fresh produce every few days.

She was pleased that there was an industrial range with a nice grill and a gigantic oven. There was also plenty of commercial-size cookware. She wouldn't have the added headache of having to use three or four pots to fix enough of one thing.

She worried her bottom lip as she began peeling carrots. She'd never been a blue ribbon cook. This teriyaki dish was one of her personal favorites, and she was adding chicken because she figured they'd all like meat. She wanted to start out with a meal that everyone enjoyed. First impressions were important.

Oh, *God*. Why had she agreed to take this job? Rodney

had hated her cooking. Now, here she was, trying to feed eleven men. *Hello, Molly. Are you out of your mind?*

As soon as she got the vegetables rinsed, she had to get the rice on the stove. She glanced at the wall clock. Yet another of Jake's creations, its case was a four-leaf clover made of horseshoes, the hands fashioned with antique nails. It was unique and suited the rustic log house perfectly, as did the old Jack Daniel's barrel that served as a sink vanity in the downstairs bath. Molly had never seen a home built by its owner from the foundation up. The plank doors and rudimentary detailing in every room created a delightful pioneer simplicity that made her feel as if she'd stepped into the past.

The clock said ten after five, leaving only fifty minutes if she meant to serve dinner at six. Looking at that silly clock soothed her frazzled nerves. Jake Coulter seemed to be a simple man with simple tastes. He would be happy with anything she cooked as long as it was edible. It was dumb to get in a dither.

Jake was starving and figured his hired hands were as well. They'd been out of bread for sandwiches that morning, so they'd all worked straight through with only crackers and peanut butter for lunch. When men did hard physical work, they needed plenty of grub to keep their strength up.

The house smelled divine when he stepped inside, the mix of scents sharp, rich, and mouthwatering. Not wanting to mess up the clean floors, he wiped his boots on the entry rug. As he made his way through the great room, he was pleased to see that the burl tables had been polished. Envisioning the buildup of grime that had accumulated throughout the house, he felt as if a thousand pounds had been lifted from his shoulders.

Man, this was terrific. To have a woman waiting when he came in after a hard day, to have his home all spiffed up and shiny, to know he probably had clean socks and shorts for tomorrow. It was enough to make him think about getting married. Not that he believed a woman's place was in the home, or that her sole purpose in life was to see to his needs. But it sure was nice for a change. Ordinarily he dragged in, so tired he could barely blink, and it was his responsibility to cook or heat something up.

Just outside the kitchen, he stopped to hook his Stetson over one of the dowels he had sunk into a log to create a coat rack. Then he followed his nose toward all those fantastic smells. *Food*—the hot, tasty, homemade variety.

"I've died and gone to heaven," he said as he stepped through the archway. "Something sure smells good."

Molly jumped at the sound of his voice and whirled from the stove, making him wish he'd thought to holler out a warning as he entered the house. Startled while stirring the contents of a pot, she'd slopped what looked like broth over the front of her blouse. She plucked at the cotton, trying to tug the searing wetness away from her skin.

"Damn." Jake hurried across the kitchen to grab the dishcloth. Anchoring her with one hand on her shoulder, he dabbed at her blouse. "Are you scalded?"

"No, no. It just stung a little."

She caught his wrist, her cheeks flooding with color as she met his gaze. Without fail, her eyes always reminded him of butterscotch, his favorite flavor on earth. He wanted to think that he was only hungry, but deep down, he knew that wasn't the problem. There was something about this lady that appealed to him in a way he couldn't define, let alone understand.

Tossing the rag back in the sink, he retreated a step. "I didn't mean to startle you. Working outside all day, I get in the habit of talking loud, and I forget to turn down my volume when I come indoors."

"No worries." The smile that touched her lips didn't reach her eyes. "I knew you'd be coming in to eat soon. I don't know why I reacted that way. Being in a new place, I guess."

Jake had a feeling it didn't take much to startle her. Even the way she stood suggested brittle tension, her softly rounded shoulders rigid, her body taut. Whenever he looked at her, she had trouble keeping her hands still, her nervous fingers tugging at her blouse or toying with the buttons.

Normally, Jake might have wondered if she was afraid of men, but after their confrontation last night over the rotor, he found that difficult to believe. She'd stood toe to toe with him, ready to do battle. He'd known very few women with the courage to take on a full-grown man.

She was a puzzle, this lady, anxious and painfully unsure of herself in many ways, yet at the same time displaying strength and courage that a lot of people lacked. The contrasts fascinated him—and tugged at his heart.

She splayed a hand at the base of her throat, her fingertips doing a fluttery little dance over her collar. Tendrils of curly hair had escaped her braid to frame her face with wisps of amber. To his delight, he saw that she'd tied a kitchen towel around her middle to serve as an apron, cinching in her smock-like top to show off her figure. And what a figure it was. The lady was stacked. She had delightfully generous breasts, a proportionately slender waist, and ample hips that made him contemplate the pleasures to be found with a woman who was soft all over.

If she were actually his wife, he'd sample her first and save supper for later. Much later.

Uncomfortable with that train of thought, he turned his gaze to the long plank table. It was a patio-style affair with cross-buck legs that he'd thrown together with scrap lumber and shined up with several coats of polyurethane. Nevertheless, she had set it all fancy with water glasses and wine goblets at every place. At the center of each plate, paper towels, folded into pretty, pleated fans, stood at attention. Jake stared, wondering how long she'd worked to make all those itty-bitty creases.

"I know." She waved a hand. "It probably looks silly. I

didn't realize there were no napkins until I was already back from town."

Jake had never seen paper towels look prettier. "When you work with horses and cows from dawn 'til dark, a little bit of fancy at the end of the day is kind of nice."

"Not very fancy, I'm afraid. Next time I'm in town, I'll buy some napkins. Rings as well. A meal tastes so much better if it's pleasing to the eye."

Jake couldn't afford linen napkins or rings. At present, he was still operating in the red. "Paper towels are fine. Are we having wine?" He wondered how much she'd spent on that.

"Just some inexpensive white zin."

He cued in on "inexpensive" and gave her marks for being perceptive. "That'll be a treat." Afraid she might grace the table with wine he couldn't afford every night, he quickly added, "Just don't make it a habit."

"Oh, no. I just—" Her fingertips flitted down the line of buttons on her blouse. His quick reaction with the dishrag had saved the cotton from staining, he noticed. "This is the first dinner I've fixed here, and I want it to be special."

Just having her there made it special. Her smile was so sweet and hesitant, the appeal for approval difficult to resist. It seemed to him that the kitchen seemed cheerier with her in it—brighter, somehow. He panned the room, taking in the shine she'd put on everything. He could see his reflection on the front of the old side-by-side.

"Just getting a home-cooked meal will be special." He glanced at the large pot on the stove. "What's cooking?"

"It's a surprise."

"Well, I'm hungry enough to eat the south end of a northbound jackass." He stepped over to the sink to wash up. "Don't keep me in suspense too long."

Molly spent the next few minutes dishing up the rice and stir-fry. While she worked, several more men filed in. When she turned to serve the meal, all but one place at the end of the long table had been taken. The men all sat straighter as she advanced on them with the huge bowl of rice in her hands.

"This is Molly," Jake said by way of introduction. "Starting at my left"—he pointed a finger—"that's Skeeter, Preach, Shorty, Benny, Danno, Tex, Bill, and Nate. You've already met Levi and my brother Hank."

Molly scanned their faces, which ranged from young to very old. Except for Levi, who wore a red shirt, they were all dressed in chambray and denim. In the sea of variegated blue, their features blurred, and she promptly forgot their names. The only person who stood out, aside from Hank and Levi, was the redheaded youth named Danno, who had so many freckles she could barely make out his hazel eyes.

"I'm pleased to meet all of you." She turned to fetch the serving bowl of vegetables and chicken. "I hope you enjoy. This is one of my favorite dishes." When no one moved to dig in, she added, "I'll pour milk for those who want it, and wine for those who'd like that. Meanwhile, feel free to dish up."

"Where's the bread?" Danno asked.

Molly glanced at the table. "I, um . . . didn't plan to serve bread, Danno. We have rice."

"Rice?" Danno squinted into the bowl. "It's funny looking. What did you do, douse it with soy when you cooked it?"

"It's brown rice." Jake began dishing food onto his plate. "They say it's healthier than white. Try some, Danno. It's a great substitute for potatoes."

"Even with potatoes, we always get bread," Danno complained.

Molly could see the young man wouldn't feel fed until she gave him bread, so she hurried into the pantry. "I haven't any dinner rolls. Will this do?"

Danno's eyes brightened as he grabbed the end of the loaf bag. "This'll do fine." He drew out four slices then scanned the table. "Where's the butter?"

Molly stepped to the refrigerator and plucked out the butter spray, which was a flavorful substitute, calorie free, and contained no fat. "Here you go."

Danno took the spray bottle, stared at it for a long moment, and then said, "What the flipping hell?"

Every head at the table swiveled to stare. *Silence.* Molly licked her lips. "It's, um, butter spray. It's very good. You can't believe it's not the real thing."

Danno frowned. "What happened to the regular butter?"

"I didn't buy any."

Danno flashed a glance at Jake. "When did we start buying butter?"

Jake spooned out some vegetables and chicken onto his rice. "This is Molly's first day, Danno. I didn't have time to show her how to make butter."

Molly threw a startled look at her boss. He expected her to *make* butter?

Jake glanced up. "We have an electric churn. It's no big deal."

Molly wasn't particularly interested in learning how to make butter. She liked her unclogged arteries and wanted to keep them that way. There were also a few older men at her table who needed to watch their cholesterol. No one was having a heart attack on her watch, not if she could prevent it.

Brave thoughts. In reality, she knew she would make butter until it came out their ears. Anything to please them. She needed to keep this job.

As she made her way around the table to pour the wine, Danno sprayed his bread, scowling gloomily. When he finally took a bite, he snarled a lip and asked, "Do we have any jelly?"

"Oh, yes." Though she couldn't imagine anyone's wanting jelly with zesty stir-fry, Molly hurried back to the fridge. She was starting to feel as if she were in a footrace. When she handed Danno the small jar of Simply Fruit, he studied the label before removing the lid and then scooped out nearly all the jar's contents onto his bread. He folded one slice lengthwise over the oozing preserves and stuffed the whole works into his mouth. "Mmm."

Molly decided then and there that she'd better buy less expensive jam from now on. If Danno was any indication, these men were into quantity, not quality.

By the time she took her place at the foot of the table, she had begun to suspect that her first meal at the Lazy J had fallen short of expectations. She unfolded her napkin, noting that Jake was the only other person who'd bothered to spread his over his lap. The other men had set their paper towels beside their plates. She waited expectantly for someone besides Danno to sample the food. Just as expectantly, her diners stared back at her.

It struck Molly then that they were waiting for her to take the first bite. "Oh, please, don't wait on me," she said, feeling more nervous by the second. "I'll be up and down all during the meal." Determining that no one at her end was going to pass her the rice, she came up from her chair to reach for the bowl herself. The contents were nearly gone. "Just enjoy your food."

Waiting in an agony of suspense to see their expressions when they tasted the stir-fry, Molly forgot all about the rice bowl she held in her hands.

Jake finally took a bite, glanced pointedly at his men so they would follow suit, and said, "Mmm, this is delicious, Molly." He flashed her a smile as he lifted his goblet. "The white zinfandel will set it off perfectly."

Following his older brother's example, Hank started shoveling food in his mouth. When he tried his wine, he graced her with a broad grin. "First time we've used the crystal. It was a housewarming gift. Our sister Bethany and her husband Ryan got Jake a whole set."

"It's lovely." Molly had been pleasantly surprised to find the fine glassware in one of the cupboards, and she'd wondered about it at the time. Jake didn't strike her as a man who spared much coin for anything that wasn't essential.

As though he read her mind, Hank grinned and added, "It's impractical as hell." He winked and extended his pinky as he took another sip of wine from the fluted goblet. "Ryan's a rich boy. I feel downright highfalutin."

Molly searched Jake's dark face. His expression as he applied himself to his meal was unreadable. Despite his seemingly sincere compliment on the food, she couldn't shake the feeling that he wasn't entirely happy with what she had served. A knot of dread formed at the pit of her stomach. If she lost this job, Sunset was doomed and so was she. Just thinking of the possibilities made her stomach tighten with anxiety.

"This wine *is* good," the sandy-haired man called Shorty said. He settled questioning blue eyes on Molly. "My partner is waiting on the porch. His name's Bartholomew, Bart for every day. If you've got any leftovers tonight, he'd surely appreciate them."

"Your partner is out on the porch?" About to dish herself some rice, Molly set the bowl aside and pushed up from her chair. "There's no need for him to wait out there, Shorty. We'll make room at the table. He can have my place."

Jake's head snapped up. "Bart's a dog, Molly. I asked Shorty to keep him outside from now on. I didn't think you'd appreciate him tracking up the clean floors."

Shorty bent his head, but not before Molly glimpsed the resentment in his eyes. Clearly, Bart had been allowed to come inside until now.

Though she'd never been around dogs very much because her father had been allergic, Molly didn't want to make any unnecessary changes in the usual ranch routine. She stepped over to open the back door. There on the steps lay the ugliest, shaggiest, dirtiest creature she'd ever clapped eyes on. His right flank was partially bald. One blue eye shone up at her with suspicious curiosity, the other clouded with white and angled off in the wrong direction.

"Hello, Bart." The greeting was all the invitation the dog needed. He rose and moved over the threshold into the kitchen. As she watched the canine make his way toward Shorty, Molly saw that he was carrying a front foot. "Oh, no, he's hurt!"

All the men turned to look as Shorty bent to examine the dog's paw. "Another damned foxtail," the old hired hand pronounced.

"Where in hell did he pick up a foxtail?" Levi asked. "Kindee early in the year for 'em, ain't it?"

Shorty patted the dog's head and softly told him to lie down. As he turned to resume his meal, he said, "Leave it to Bart. If there's a foxtail within a hundred miles, he'll find the dad-blamed thing."

Molly returned to her place, her attention fixed on the dog. Bart whined softly and began licking his paw, clearly in discomfort from the sticker lodged between his toes. Her already nervous stomach knotted with sympathy.

"Shouldn't someone pull out the foxtail and disinfect the sore?" she asked.

Shorty nodded. "I'll get right on it, soon as supper's done."

It seemed to Molly that the dog's foot should come first, eating later, but she refrained from saying as much. It was important that she get along with everyone, and offering her opinion where it wasn't wanted was no way to gain popularity. "Is Bart accustomed to having his dinner while everyone else is eating theirs?"

Shorty raised his gaze and nodded. "Yes, ma'am. Nothing special. Just whatever the rest of us are having."

Molly glanced incredulously at the dog. "Surely he won't like stir-fry."

"Neither do we," Danno inserted, "but we're eatin' it."

"Danno," Jake said warningly. He smiled at Molly.

"Don't pay this young whippersnapper any attention. The rest of us think your stir-fry is wonderful."

Levi seconded that. "Yes, ma'am. Damned good grub."

The dark-haired, craggy-faced man named Preach lowered his wine glass to say, "It's got my vote."

At the rate the rice and vegetables had already disappeared, Molly doubted there would be anything left for poor Bart, so rather than resume her seat, she went to put on more rice. She could scramble some eggs to mix in with it. That would do as Bart's dinner for tonight.

"What are you doing now, Molly?" Jake asked. "You haven't even filled your plate yet."

"First, I want to put on a little extra rice for Bart. We can't have Shorty's partner going hungry."

Behind her, Molly heard a chair scrape the floor and the ensuing thump of boot heels. She glanced around to see Jake at her end of the table, scooping what remained of the rice onto her plate.

"I can do that."

"Not if it's all gone, you can't." He flicked her an amused glance. "It would seem that your stir-fry is a hit."

Molly looked away, afraid her expression might reveal how pleased she was. Aside from Danno, everyone else seemed to like the food. That wasn't a bad success ratio.

After putting the rice on to cook, she reclaimed her chair, fully intending to partake of the meal even though she had little appetite. She'd taken only one bite when Bart whined. She glanced down to see the dog chewing on his paw. Her heart caught with pity. It seemed cruel to just sit there, ignoring the animal's distress.

Gazing the length of the table at her employer, Molly cautioned herself not to interfere in what was clearly the established order of things. Shorty would see to the dog in good time, and Bart would survive until then, she assured herself. It wasn't her place to say anything.

She had nearly convinced herself when Bart whined

again. That did it. She couldn't just sit there, pretending not to notice.

"Please, excuse me for a moment," she said politely, as she left the table to go to the downstairs bathroom.

Jake sighed as he watched Molly leave the room. At last count, she'd taken only one bite of food. Never in all his days had he seen anyone so tense. As if her life hung in the balance, she'd watched the men's faces while they ate, and she'd grown downright pale when Danno criticized the meal. Jake ached to tell her that he had no intention of firing her. Cooking for so many was no easy task, and he fully expected her to make a few blunders while she was learning the ropes.

He was relieved when she returned to the kitchen only seconds later. His feeling of relief was quickly replaced by apprehension when he saw that she carried a bottle of hydrogen peroxide, cotton balls, and tweezers. She clearly intended to remove the foxtail from Bart's paw.

Jake glanced worriedly at Shorty, wondering how the old man would react. It was an unspoken law with many cattlemen that a man's dog was to be touched, fed, and given commands only by its owner. Those individuals believed that a canine's loyalty to its master was diminished by outside influence. Though Jake disagreed with that school of thought, he respected Shorty's right to believe whatever he chose. The old hired hand loved Bart and treated him kindly. That was all Jake really cared about, that the dog never suffered for his master's eccentricities.

Unaware that Shorty allowed no one else to mess with his dog, Molly knelt beside Bart and began cooing softly. The canine, as unaccustomed to women as he was to friendly overtures from strangers, responded with low, warning growls. Instead of seeming alarmed, Molly only cooed more sympathetically.

Warning signals jangled in Jake's brain. He had a very bad feeling that his cook knew very little about dogs. Ordinarily that wouldn't have posed a problem—but Bart was no ordinary canine. Cattle dogs were as different from their domestic cousins as night was from day.

"I don't blame you a bit for feeling grumpy," Molly murmured consolingly to the disgruntled blue heeler. "There's nothing worse than having a hurt foot, is there? Well, don't worry. I'll have that nasty old foxtail out in two seconds, and you'll feel better."

Shorty stopped chewing, pocketed the food in his cheek, and bugged his eyes at Jake. Hank threw his brother an anxious look as well.

"Careful, Molly," Jake warned. "Bart is surly, and he snaps sometimes."

"Oh, surely not," she replied. "He seems like such a sweetheart."

The dog's growls didn't sound very sweet to Jake.

Shorty turned on his chair to fix Molly with a disapproving scowl. "Just what're you up to, missy? He's my dog. I'll take care of him."

Soothing Bart with gentle strokes of her slender hands, Molly glanced up and smiled, her big brown eyes shimmering in the overhead light. "I thought I'd get this foxtail out for you, Shorty. Go ahead and enjoy your meal while it's hot. I'm not all that hungry, and I don't mind the interruption."

The elderly man's shoulders stiffened. "Bart don't take kindly to bein' pestered by strangers. Don't you hear him snarlin'?"

"Oh, those aren't snarls." Molly bent to cluck her tongue at the growling dog. "He's just talking to me. Aren't you, Bart? Yes. You're telling me all about it, aren't you? Poor baby. I know how it must hurt." She ran a fingertip along the dog's muzzle, apparently heedless of his sharp incisors. In a singsong, baby-talk voice, she said, "I'd be grumpy, too. Yes, I would. Your little paw is all swollen. I'll bet that foxtail has been in there all day. *Ouch.*"

By no estimation was Bart's paw little. The blue heeler was large for his breed, a variation from standard that had made Jake question his bloodlines more than once. More alarmingly, the dog's bared teeth weren't small. Molly could be badly hurt if Bart decided to bite her. "Molly, maybe you'd better let Shorty take care of that," he tried.

"Really, I don't mind," she insisted. "It'll only take me a few seconds."

Shorty had completely reversed his direction on the chair to stare at their new cook. The old man was clearly amazed that Bart hadn't already tried to take her arm off. "I'd listen to the boss and back off if I was you, missy. Bart's been known to bite on occasion."

Molly gave the dog a measuring look. Then her mouth curved into a beatific smile. Jake had known a lot of women who pretended to be sweet and caring, only to discover later that they were hell on wheels. With Molly, however, he didn't believe it was an act. As hokey as it sounded, even in his mind, she fairly glowed with goodness. You simply couldn't look at her and doubt that she had a kind heart.

"He won't bite me," she assured Shorty. "He's just feeling out of sorts. And who wouldn't?"

With that pronouncement, she proceeded to lift Bart's paw onto her knee and go fishing with the tweezers. Shorty gaped. The dog growled more ferociously, but to no avail. Molly ignored the warnings. Jake pushed up from his chair and moved closer.

Instead of sinking his sharp teeth into Molly's tender flesh, the dog only whined, cast a resigned look at his master, and licked Molly's wrist. Jake relaxed and winked at Shorty, who looked as if he'd just swallowed a sock.

"I don't gen'rally let strangers touch my dog," the hired hand said.

"That's very wise," Molly observed, flashing the old man a quick but understanding smile. "You just never know who might do something despicable. I read in the paper just last month about some man who went around poisoning dogs at the city park. Isn't that terrible? He put arsenic in bits of ground beef. I can't imagine anyone's doing such a heartless thing, but there you are. For Bart's sake, you need to be cautious."

Shorty looked helplessly at Jake. Then he sighed and slid off his chair to crouch at Molly's elbow. After watching her gently probe for the foxtail, he grinned and said, "He's taken a shine to you, no question." After watching her work a minute longer, Shorty added, "I've always heard tell dogs can sense things about people that we can't—like as if they can smell the goodness or evil in a person. My mother was a firm believer in that. Had herself an old coon dog that didn't take up much with strangers. When that old hound liked a man, my ma trusted him with her life." Shorty reached to scratch behind his dog's ears. "I reckon old Bart is givin' you a real high recommend, Miss Molly. A real high recommend, indeed."

Molly's cheeks went pink. She glanced wonderingly at Bart. "I like you, too, punkin. If you had a bath, you'd be a very handsome fellow." She touched the bald patch on the dog's flank. Then she resumed probing for the sticker. "What caused him to lose his hair there, Shorty? Was he injured somehow?"

Shorty sighed. "One time while I was inside paying the tab at a gas station, I left him in the back of my truck. When the attendant tried to put fuel in the tank, Bart took exception and raised a ruckus. By the time I got back out there, the dad-blamed fellow had doused him with gas. I didn't know it happened until I saw him shiverin' and bitin' at himself later. By then, he was burnt pretty bad, and the hair never grew back."

Molly's eyes darkened with shadows. "Oh, how *awful*. Why would anyone do something so mean?"

Shorty shook his head. "Like I said, Bart can be ornery sometimes. Maybe he snapped at the fellow."

"That's no excuse, and Bart isn't ornery," Molly

protested. "He's a doll." She made kissing sounds near the dog's nose. Moments before, Jake would have worried for her face, but the bedraggled canine clearly recognized a bona fide sweetheart when he met one. "There!" she finally cried triumphantly. "I got it, Bart." She held up the tweezers for the canine's inspection. "Now, doesn't that feel better, sweetie?"

Bart bypassed the tweezers to lick Molly's face, which made her sputter and laugh. "Oh, dear, you have bad breath. The next time I'm in town, I'll get you a toothbrush and some dog toothpaste. We'll take care of that little problem."

Shorty's eyebrows arched toward his balding pate. "Dog toothpaste? I've never heard of such."

Molly set aside the tweezers and peeled Bart's lip back to examine his teeth. "Just *look* at that tartar buildup. No question about it, he needs better oral hygiene, or he'll get cavities soon." The men at the table exchanged amazed glances as she went on to say, "The toothpaste comes in doggy flavors. I've seen it advertised on television. Bart will love it."

Shorty looked none too certain about that. "Hmm. Well, I'll be. I never knew there was folks who brushed their dogs' teeth."

"We brush ours," Molly pointed out.

"Seems like a lot of fuss for nothin' when a good bone'll do the job."

"I'll get him some bones, too." Molly dabbed between Bart's toes with the disinfectant. Then she glanced up at Jake. "I'll pay for everything. No worries."

For once, the farthest thing from Jake's mind had been his concerns about money. He was far too fascinated, watching Molly interact with Shorty and the dog. On a good day, it was a toss-up who was the more difficult to get along with, the canine or the old man. Yet she had won them both over without half trying.

"I can brush his teeth for him every day if you'd rather

not be bothered, Shorty," she offered. "I know you're busy, and I won't mind taking the time to do it."

Shorty thought about it for a moment and then nodded. "I reckon it can't hurt. I'd hate like heck if his teeth went bad. False chompers for a dog would cost dearly."

Molly gave a startled laugh. "I bet they would, at that." A fond warmth crept into her eyes as she regarded the old man. "If such a thing existed, you'd get him some, though. Don't tell me you wouldn't. When it comes to this dog, you're a softie. I can tell."

"I reckon I would," Shorty agreed. "He's gotta be able to eat, don't he?"

Jake resumed his seat to finish his meager meal, incredulous but pleased that Molly was already making friends with his men. There was something about the lady that made a man go a little soft in the head the instant he looked into her big brown eyes.

His grin broadened when he glanced at Bart. Whatever that indefinable quality was, it seemed to have the same effect on canines as it did on men.

Chapter Nine

When the meal was over, Jake rolled up his sleeves to help Molly clean the kitchen. The instant she realized his intent, she got all flustered, her cheeks turned a pretty pink, and she tried to take the rice bowl out of his hands.

"I can do this, Mr. Coulter. You worked hard all day, and cleaning the kitchen is my job."

Just once and of her own accord, Jake wanted to hear her address him by his first name. Keeping a firm grip on the serving bowl, he said, "You worked hard today, too. The house looks wonderful. Did I mention that?"

Her eyes went all sparkly with pleasure. "I barely skimmed the surface. I'll do some deep cleaning tomorrow."

"Nevertheless, I know you put in a hard day, and I really don't mind helping you clean up. That way, the work will be over more quickly for all of us."

She finally relinquished the bowl. "It has been a long day. Everything being new, I've been slow. I'll get a routine worked out soon, I'm sure."

Jake could hope. She'd bounced up and down so much during supper that she'd eaten hardly anything. Not that there had been much food left to put on her plate. He and his men had taken only a small portion each, but there had been barely enough to go around, even then.

How could he tell her that she needed to cook in much larger quantities? She'd done her best, and she was obviously so worried about her performance that he was afraid any criticism, no matter how kindly intended, might do more harm than good. Given the fact that gentle deliveries weren't his specialty, that presented one hell of a problem.

He had enjoyed the meal, such as it was. But he worked long and hard, and so did his men. They burned off calories almost as fast as the food went into their mouths. Stir-fries were fine as an occasional main dish, but she needed to add more protein, fix several rich side dishes as well, and make sure there was a lot of bread and fresh butter on the table. Otherwise he and his men were going to be hungry all the time.

At least no one but the dog had been rude enough to lick his plate.

Mulling over the problem, Jake set himself to the task of rinsing dishes and putting them in the dishwater. While he worked, Molly flitted around him, clearing the table, washing the counter, polishing the stove, and putting things away. Jake had always been a stickler on kitchen tidiness, but he'd never cleaned up quite as thoroughly as Molly did.

She was so tense she seemed to have trouble staying focused. She kept forgetting where she had laid the dishcloth. She wandered around, opening cupboard doors to stare blankly into them while she muttered under her breath. Jake could only hope she started to relax around him soon, or they were both going to have a nervous breakdown.

When the kitchen was spotless enough to suit her, he glanced out the window, saw that night had fallen, and offered to see her home. He hoped he might find an opening during the walk to tell her she had to start fixing more food.

"Oh, you don't need to walk me," she protested. "I know the way."

"It's dark out there. With your poor night vision, you could take a wrong turn and get lost."

She laughed. "My night vision isn't *that* poor."

Acutely aware that she felt uneasy with him, Jake might have let her go home unescorted if he hadn't recalled her reference to bears last night. She was clearly out of her element in this rural setting, and he didn't want her to grow frightened out there, alone in the dark. He led the way from the kitchen, stopping just beyond the archway to collect his hat. "I'll rest easier if I see you to your doorstep."

Hank, crouched before the wide rock fireplace, glanced up from rumpling newspaper. "Best let him walk you, Molly. I spotted cougar track along the creek last week. It's a worry when they come in so close to the house."

Molly paled. "Cougar track? Oh, dear."

Jake wished that Hank had kept his mouth shut. The actual danger of a cougar attack anywhere on the ranch was fairly miniscule. "Don't listen to him, Molly. Cougars seldom bother humans."

"Bull. Wasn't that long ago a cougar attacked a little boy standing in line at a municipal swimming pool."

"That wasn't in Oregon," Jake reminded him.

"Like cougars know what state they're in? What about the cat outside Lakeview that attacked the mail truck? That was in Oregon."

"That happened quite some while back, and for all we know, it was nothing but a story. I never saw mention of it in the newspaper."

Molly fixed Jake with a worried look. "If there's a danger, please don't keep it from me. I'd rather be a little nervous and take precautions."

Jake didn't want her jumping at shadows. "Cougars rarely attack people."

"That poor lady jogger in northern California probably told herself the same thing," Hank inserted. "All they found were pieces of her jogging outfit."

"Oh, how *awful!*" Molly shivered and rubbed her arms. "What a terrible way to die."

"Not so bad, actually. The cougar probably snapped her

spine upon impact." Hank nodded sagely. "That's how they make a kill." He snapped his fingers. "Just like that. They tracked the cat down. She only weighed eighty pounds, just a young female with cubs. The cougar along our creek is a big old fellow. I could tell that by the prints."

Jake glared at his brother over the top of Molly's head. "Are you finished having your fun, Hank? You've frightened Molly. Now she'll be nervous every time she steps outside."

Hank angled a mischievous look at Molly. "Have I scared you, Molly?"

"No. Not really. I just—" She rubbed her arms again. "My goodness! Where I live, cougars aren't a problem."

Jake could believe that. He had a hunch she came from Portland, and the only cougars in the downtown areas were probably stuffed. "They aren't a problem here, either."

"Yes, they are, and growing to be more so each passing year," Hank protested. "They're way overpopulated and easily habituated to humans, so they get bold."

Jake was going to kill his brother before any cougar got a chance. While Hank was still spouting alarming facts about cougars, he hurried Molly from the great room.

"Have a nice walk, you two," Hank called, a twinkle in his eye.

The instant they stepped onto the front porch, Molly came to a dead stop and pressed closer to Jake. Darkness and the chill night air curled around them. He felt her shiver. When he glanced down, he saw that she was peering owlishly toward the steps. Her wariness of him had apparently been shoved from her mind by a greater fear, namely big-toothed predators.

"Can cougars really jump from heights of sixty feet?"

Even as she spoke, she tucked herself more snugly against his side. Jake slipped an arm around her. "Don't listen to Hank. He's twenty-nine, going on sixteen. Telling spooky stories to a pretty lady makes him feel macho."

She laughed nervously. "You didn't answer my question. Can they?"

Jake sighed. "Yes. According to the statistics I read, they can. I've never seen it myself. You have to remember that those statistics are the most impressive ever documented, the feats of supercougars, in other words. Around here, the cougars are all wimps."

An owl hooted, and she nearly jumped out of her skin. She nudged her shoulder into his ribs, getting as close as she could without joining him inside his Wranglers. He tightened his arm around her. She stiffened slightly but made no offer to pull away.

As they started down the steps into the deeper darkness, she craned her neck to see through the shadows. She felt so good, snuggled up against him, all feminine softness and intriguing curves. Every time he flexed his splayed fingers on her side, he felt her flank muscles quiver, creating images in his mind of how she might quiver if he touched her in other places.

When she moved just right, one of those places grazed the knuckle of his thumb. Never in his recollection had the weight and heat of a woman's breast felt so tempting. He wanted so badly to cup that generous softness, to learn the shape of her, to capture her nipple and give it a tug, to hear her breath catch.

Holy hell. He was going to murder Hank when he got back.

He'd been too long out of a relationship. That was the problem. Since starting up the ranch, he'd had no time for a social life, and now his body was telling him about it. That was all it was, he felt sure. He liked tall, leggy females with figures his mother likened to Barbie dolls, not short, sweetly plump women who could kiss his navel without having to bend much at the knees.

Now there was an interesting possibility.

One he had no intention of exploring, of course.

This was not good. Molly, with her big, vulnerable

brown eyes, wasn't his type. She had hips. And, hey, the women he dated *always* wore acrylic nails—long, wicked, blood-red claws. He hated them, but that was beside the point.

So, what was the point?

With Molly pressed so temptingly against him, Jake honestly didn't know. He only knew she reminded him of his mother in little ways. Jake loved his mother as much as the next guy. She was one of the dearest people on earth and still beautiful even in her late fifties. It was just one of those things that only men understood, he guessed. When it came to carnal pursuits, anything that put you in mind of your mom was to be avoided.

Molly definitely reminded Jake of Mary Coulter. They each had big, guileless eyes and smiles to light up a room. They also had similar builds, both of them short, curvaceous, and soft. They were the kind of women who were made to cuddle children close.

They were also the kind of women who bore lots of children because their husbands couldn't keep their hands off them.

What was he *thinking*?

Suddenly narrow-hipped, long-legged, big-busted women no longer seemed very appealing. He wanted short and soft and—*don't go there, Jake.*

With some women, acting on an instant attraction was fine, but Molly wasn't one of them. He could see her heart in her eyes, and a bruised, wounded heart it was. He would never forgive himself if he hurt her, and he'd never been a staying kind of man. He liked to think that was because he hadn't met the right lady yet, but what if he was wrong? And what was to say Molly was the right lady?

"Thank you for walking with me." She glanced worriedly upward as they passed under a tree at the edge of his yard. "I really appreciate it."

Jake was so damned tempted to play this up, but he

wasn't a hormonal teenager, and fear had long since ceased to be a tool of seduction.

"Molly, no cougar is going to attack you around here. Do you really think I would neglect to tell you if I thought it was a possibility?"

She fixed a big, worried gaze on him, her eyes luminous in the moonlight. "Hank seems to think it's a possibility."

"Hank is an idiot." Jake winced. "Not an idiot, exactly. An opportunist might be a better description. He played the cougar thing up because he knew I was walking you home. He thought he was doing me a favor." He remembered his vow not to pay her too many compliments. So much for that plan. "You're a very pretty lady, and just look at you now, melting over me like a pat of butter on a biscuit."

She snapped erect. The worried look in her eyes vanished. "He was matchmaking?"

Jake mourned the loss of her softness pressed against him, but he relinquished his hold on her waist. "He didn't mean any harm. He's a big tease and doesn't take much of anything too seriously."

Molly folded her arms. "You and me? If that isn't beyond silly."

And what was so silly about it?

He could kiss her silly. What would she have to say about that?

She picked up her pace, leaving him to step fancy in order to catch up with her. Ahead of them, a knee-high shrub grew at the edge of the patchy lawn, and Molly was headed straight for it. He grabbed her elbow just before she ran over the top of it.

"Bush dead ahead," he said as he steered her around it. "How do you navigate at night, girl? Bats are blind, but they have radar."

"I wish I did. Is it always so dark in the country?"

Jake switched hands on her elbow and slipped his right arm around her waist again. This time she jerked as if he'd stuck her with a pin. He almost released her. When she wasn't afraid, the lady obviously didn't appreciate being touched. No matter. He didn't want her to trip over something in the dark and get hurt, which was exactly what might happen if he turned her loose.

She stiffened away from him as they walked, trying without success to keep distance between their bodies. Jake firmed his hold on her and set an even pace, measuring his strides to accommodate her much shorter legs. She fit nicely against him, her soft fullness molding to the hard planes of his body. He liked the way she felt and, once again, he found himself wishing he could explore all those plump places.

He looked up at the sky and said, "Will you just look at that?"

It was a corny, shopworn line, but it worked. She glanced up, sighed in appreciation, and relaxed against him. "Isn't that *incredible*? I never realized there were so many stars."

"Out here, you can see them better, is all. No city lights to dim their sparkle." Jake didn't add that he was far more captivated by the sparkle in her eyes.

Sunset whinnied at their approach, the sound less panicky than yesterday, but not exactly a herald of welcome yet. "Did you stop to visit with him today?" Jake asked.

Molly laughed, the trill decidedly edgy. "I said hello before I went grocery shopping and again when I got back, but I wouldn't say we had a visit. He goes the other way when I get close and stays in the corner until I leave."

Steering her with a slight pressure of his hand, Jake detoured toward the corral. Sunset shrieked and reared. Moonlight glanced off the shiny sections of his black coat where he'd sustained no injuries, and his mane lifted in the breeze, flashing around his arched neck like tarnished silver.

"Did he act up like this?"

She shook her head. "No. He just grunted at me and

danced around a little. I think he was afraid I might go inside with him."

Jake wondered if she saw the significance of that. If the horse didn't shriek and rear at her approach, it was a very good sign. After watching Molly with Bart earlier, he wasn't surprised to discover that the stallion instinctively trusted her. Some people had a natural gift with animals.

Jake had a way with animals himself. It was a talent that had served him well, enabling him to make good money training horses. Sunset hadn't warmed up to him yet, but it was early on, Jake was a man, and the memory of the whipping was still fresh in Sunset's mind. Jake had every confidence that he would begin to make headway in a few days. He just had to be consistent and patient.

Once at the fence, he opted to keep his arm around Molly. She was shivering slightly, whether from his touch or the chill air, he couldn't say. Just in case she was cold, it seemed only gentlemanly to share his body heat, since he hadn't thought to bring a jacket.

He smiled to himself. The truth was, he liked having her close. She felt so right, which made no sense at all. He was a lofty man. The top of her head didn't quite clear his shoulder even when she was wearing three-inch heels. In sneakers, she was definitely what he would term vertically challenged.

He'd never seen so many curves packed into sixty-three inches.

Beneath his palm, he could feel the ladder of her ribs, the generous overlay of soft flesh and silky skin supple and warm. As near as he could tell, there wasn't much unneeded padding there, only enough to make her feel lush.

Why in the hell was she on a diet?

"What is it?" she suddenly asked. She peered through the gloom at Sunset. "Is something wrong with him?"

Realizing that he'd betrayed his thoughts by tensing his body, Jake forced himself to relax and turn his mind to safer things. "He's fine." He glanced down. "Can't you see him?"

"I can see him—sort of. Not very clearly, though."

Jake stooped down, making a show of getting at her eye level. "Is the light worse down here or something?"

She laughed and inched her face back from his. "I doubt it's any worse down here than anywhere else."

Jake thought the view was a hell of a lot prettier down there. Her lips were only inches from his. Never in his memory had he wanted so badly to steal a kiss. That mouth. Naked of any lipstick, it was a natural pink and shimmered in the moonlight, the pout of her bottom lip begging him to take a taste.

If she'd been any other woman, Jake would have acted on the urge. At thirty-two, almost thirty-three, he'd been around the block more times than he could count, and with maturity, he'd lost any hesitance with the ladies that he might have once had. A friendly kiss meant nothing. If it led to more, that didn't usually mean much, either. He dated women who knew the score. As long as he gave as much pleasure as he took, he owed them nothing more than that, and they expected nothing more.

Molly was different, though. He'd sensed that the first time he saw her, and his feeling hadn't changed since, except to grow stronger. She was well past the blush of girlhood. In her eyes, he saw wisdom that had been hard earned through painful experience. But, for all of that, she was vulnerable. When he kissed her—if he kissed her—nothing about it would be simple.

He straightened and spoke to the stallion. Sunset whinnied and pranced nervously at the louder pitch of Jake's voice.

"When will you start working with him?" Molly asked.

Jake glanced down, wondering if she could see his face clearly. "I'm working with him already." He resettled his hand on her side, noting as he did that she didn't jerk or stiffen this time. "Several times today, I got in the corral, sat in one corner, and stayed until he stopped feeling nervous."

"That's what you call working with him?"

"It can't happen overnight, Molly. And, yes, the way I train, that's working with him, maybe the most important part. I don't like to force my will on an animal. It can be done. Easily, I might add. But what's gained? Sunset already knows he's at a disadvantage, that I could use hobbles and twitches and do anything I wanted to him. Shall I drive the point home to him yet again?"

Her expression softened as she studied the horse. "So instead you're letting him get used to you slowly."

"Exactly. He's been terrorized enough. This time, we'll do it the easy way, in small increments, until he isn't so afraid of me. That can only be accomplished by repeated exposure. By hanging around his corral, I'm desensitizing him to my presence. When I can approach without setting him off, it'll be time to move on to the next step."

"What will that be?"

Jake searched her eyes, which glistened up at him like twin measures of expensive Scotch shot through with moonlight. "The first step will be to move in closer yet. When he accepts that, closer still, until he gets used to me and welcomes the touch of my hands."

"And then?"

"I'll doctor him, even if he no longer has any open wounds."

"Why will you do that?"

Jake thought a moment, trying to come up with the words to explain what he did instinctively. "Because, healed or not, the wounds will still be there."

She made a slight sound at the base of her throat and nodded. Her sadness for the horse rolled off her in waves, filling Jake with a melancholy that made him ache.

"With a person, you can accomplish quite a lot with words, but all a horse understands are a few basic commands and tone of voice. You have to communicate with him in other ways, mostly by your actions. I need to tell Sunset that I'm sorry about what happened to him, that I know all the pain he suffered, and that I want to make him better."

Tears glistened in her lovely eyes. "I wish I could tell him that, too."

Jake tightened his hand over her side. "You already have, honey. By bringing him here, you told him. Somewhere in all his confused thoughts right now, I think he understands that you're the one who saved him. When he's ready, I won't be surprised if he trusts you more than anyone else."

"What makes you think that?" she asked tautly, sounding none too pleased by the prospect.

Jake bit back a smile. "You say he didn't shriek and act up when you stopped to visit him today? That he just grunted and danced around a little?"

"Yes."

"That means he's not as afraid of you as he is of me, that on some level he already trusts you. He probably senses that you care about him. At least, that's my guess."

"Oh, do you really think so?"

Her expression was such a mixture of hope and dread that Jake couldn't help smiling again. "I really do. To be gifted with that kind of trust is a very special thing. I hope you'll appreciate what an honor it is, and that you'll use it to help in every way that you can."

"How can I do that?"

"You can start by spending time with him every day. Just hang around his pen for a half hour or so and talk to him. It doesn't really matter what you say. Your tone of voice will convey your feelings. Let him know you care about him and that you're here for him. He's very frightened right now."

"Yes," she agreed faintly. She straightened her shoulders and stared through the darkness at the nervous stallion. "He sort of scares me."

Sort of? Jake thought that fell short.

"He's so big, and he gets so violent when he's frightened," she added. "I'm not sure I'm the right person to help him."

"In time, that'll change. You'll feel more comfortable with him soon."

"Oh, I don't know. I'd much rather just watch you work with him."

"And accomplish what? Every time that whip cut into him, his pride and dignity took a blow, and the hurt of that will never heal until it's acknowledged and an attempt is made to soothe it away. As his trainer, I can get him partway there, but someone who loves him will have to take him the rest of the way."

Her uplifted gaze went suspiciously bright again. After taking a shuddering breath, she swallowed, looked away, and said, "I don't love him. Not really. I just feel sorry for him."

Jake didn't believe that for a minute. The very fact that she'd stolen the stallion to protect him told Jake her feelings ran deep and strong, that she felt far more than just pity, even if she hadn't realized it herself yet.

"We'll see how it goes. One peculiarity about horses and most other animals is that they choose their masters. We buy them and claim ownership, but the heart of a creature can't be owned. Sunset will choose who he'll love, and if that turns out to be you, you won't have a hell of a lot to say about it."

"In other words, he'll be my horse whether I want him or not?"

"I'm afraid so."

Jake studied her profile, thinking to himself that Sunset might not be her only conquest. Something was happening inside him. He felt it every time he looked at her. He had the strangest feeling that this was absolutely right—that he'd been waiting for her all his adult life. It was a feeling that grew stronger each time he was with her.

"I'm so glad I brought Sunset here."

"I'm glad you came," he said huskily.

"I'll do my best with him," she promised hesitantly. "Even though I'm nervous with him, I'll try."

Jake already knew that. The lady wasn't lacking in backbone. In fact, he'd venture to say that she had no idea how strong she actually was.

"It'll be a long, hard haul," he warned. "But nothing worth doing comes easily."

"Sunset is worth it." A distant look came into her eyes. "I wish you could have seen him the way he used to be. He was magnificent." She smiled sadly. "He had a dauntless spirit, and you could tell just by looking at him that he'd been born to race. He ran his heart out for Rodney. Literally ran his heart out."

Rodney. Finally, the bastard had a name.

"It's so sad, seeing Sunset the way he is now," she whispered. "He loved Rodney so much, and he tried so desperately to please him, but nothing he did was ever good enough." She rested clenched fists on the fence rail. "When you try that hard, when you give someone your very best and it's never good enough, it does something to you. Way deep inside, it does something, and you're never the same again."

Jake's heart caught. He knew she wasn't speaking only of the horse. There was too much pain in her voice.

"Rodney was never satisfied with anything. I think that broke poor Sunset's spirit long before the whippings did."

Jake wanted to put his arms around her, gather her close. She looked so sad, and so very, very lost.

With the echo of her words still circling in his mind, he knew he couldn't possibly criticize her performance in the kitchen. She'd tried her best, giving him all she had. He would be damned if he would tell her that, once again, her best hadn't been good enough.

*   *   *

A few minutes later, Molly slid home the bolt on the cabin door. From outside, she could hear the tap of Jake's boots on the planks as he crossed the porch and descended the steps. When the sounds faded away to silence, she turned to lean against the door. *Exhaustion.* It seemed as if an eternity had passed since six that morning, and she'd spent every second in high gear.

Passing a hand over her eyes, she went into the bathroom to prepare for bed, her weary joints protesting with every step. In the harsh light cast by the ceiling fixture, her reflection in the mirror looked pale and haggard. She avoided looking at her face as she loosened her long hair from the braid and began her nightly brushing ritual. Not that shiny hair mattered to her anymore. She'd long since stopped wearing hers loose. It was so wildly curly and uncontrollable that it overwhelmed her features.

Five strokes into the brushing ritual, Molly heard a knock at the door. Laying the brush aside, she moved back into the tiny living room. It hadn't been far from her mind all day that the police might still find her here. "Who is it?" she called, her nerves jangling.

"Jake."

There was no mistaking that deep voice. Molly hurried over to unfasten the deadbolt, wondering why on earth he was back. As she opened the door, she voiced her first concern. "Has something gone wrong with Sunset?"

"No, no, he's fine. I just—" A looming silhouette in the darkness beyond the threshold, he broke off from speaking to stare at her.

Molly peered up at his shadowy face, trying without success to read his expression. "Yes?" she prompted.

"I'm sorry. Your hair. I've never seen it down."

Her hand flew to the cloud of curls over her right shoulder. "Now you know why."

"I almost didn't recognize you."

She pushed at a thick hank. "Probably because you can't see me."

"I can see you fine." He leaned a shoulder against the jamb, bringing his face into the spill of light from the old floor lamp by the front window. His blue eyes moved slowly over her hair, then came to rest on her face. "My God. Do you have any idea how beautiful you are?"

Molly had to resist the urge to look over her shoulder to see if someone else was in the room.

He nudged up his hat, his gaze still fixed on her face. "Being your boss and all, I promised myself not to do this. But, *damn*. Talk about hiding your light under a bushel. All that glorious hair, and you keep it in a braid? I could get drunk just looking at you."

Molly gave a nervous laugh.

"Your hair is the exact color of Scotch whiskey." He continued to study her. "Very expensive Scotch whiskey," he added.

Molly touched a hand to the side of her head. Some people had the occasional bad-hair day; she'd had a bad-hair life. In the early years of her marriage, she'd made the mistake of getting it cut short, and she had looked like an overweight, female version of Bozo the Clown. Rodney had threatened to divorce her if she ever went near a beauty shop again.

Jake whistled softly. "Damn. I do have eyes in my head, and I realized you had fine features. But I had no idea you were so pretty."

Molly wondered if she'd fallen asleep on her feet and was having a crazy dream. "Um . . . what do you want, Mr. Coulter?"

"Damned if I can remember."

He didn't seem in any great hurry to regain his memory. He just continued to lean against the jamb, studying her.

"I hope it wasn't important."

"I'm sure it was or I wouldn't have come all the way back over here." He smiled suddenly and shook his head. "It'll come to me in a minute." He pushed erect and moved into the house, closing the door behind him. "I'm sorry for gaping. The transformation is just so startling."

Molly pushed at her hair again. "It's startling, all right. Needless to say, I never wear pink. Can you imagine the clash?"

He smiled slightly as his gaze moved slowly over her. "You'd look fabulous in pink. You really hate your hair, don't you?"

"Hate is too mild a word. I detest it. You're very kind to say it's the color of whiskey. I've always likened it to red mud."

He chuckled. "I think you're your own worst critic, Stir-Houston, and wouldn't believe you were pretty if they crowned you Miss America."

"You'll never see me in a bathing suit contest. All those spotlights, glaring on my white thighs? The judges would go blind."

He shook his head again. Then he snapped his fingers. "I remember why I came back. Do you have an alarm clock? I can lend you one of ours."

"I have one."

"Good, good." He hooked his thumbs over his belt, his gaze still moving over her as if he couldn't quite believe the change. "Well . . ." He took a backward step toward the door. "I'd better make tracks so you can get some sleep."

"Morning will come early. Up with the chickens, and all that."

A moment later, he was gone, and Molly was left to stare at the closed door again. Bewildered, she touched a hand to her hair. Then she threw the deadbolt and returned to the bathroom to finish her nightly ablutions.

When she resumed her position in front of the mirror, she couldn't resist taking a long, hard look at herself in the glass, something she seldom did since her divorce. *Beautiful?* She trailed a fingertip down the bridge of her nose, then traced her cheekbone. It was the same old face staring back at her.

As she studied her reflection, Molly got the oddest feeling she didn't know the woman who stared back. It happened to her a lot lately, which was why she seldom gazed at her reflection overlong these days.

Her features seemed to blur, their definition becoming less distinct with every beat of her heart. She stared, and kept staring, her pulse slamming in her temples. Mud red and serpentlike, the strands of her hair seemed to undulate and slither, curling ever tighter over her face.

No more, Molly.

She flattened a hand against the glass, her breathing ragged, her body filmed with sweat. A singsong voice in her head whispered, *"Molly, Molly, where have you gone?"*

The horror of it was, she no longer really knew. "Beautiful," Jake Coulter had called her. *Lies, all lies.* Molly Sterling Wells was not beautiful. She had it on good authority that she was, in fact, ugly, so ugly that her husband had found her repulsive and turned to other women in the early days of their marriage.

Molly cupped her hands over her face, hating Jake Coulter for doing this to her. Was he only being kind? Or was he amusing himself with her?

She had no idea what his game was, but she did know one thing.

She didn't want to play.

Sleep didn't come easily to Molly that night. She slugged her pillow into a lump and then slapped it flat, unable to get comfortable. She tossed, turned, and lay on her back in a sprawl. Then she tossed and turned some more. The sheets caught around her legs, confining her lower body like a straightjacket. She detested the feeling and kicked free, only to shiver when the cool air washed over her.

When at last she drifted into a restless slumber, she

began to dream, the images coming in confusing, disjointed cameos.

It was late evening, and Rodney, sitting at the edge of the bed, drew open the nightstand drawer. He took out a magazine and opened it to stare, glassy-eyed, at pictures of nude women.

"Why do you do that?" Molly asked tautly. She glanced at the glossy photographs. The women were beautiful, and their bodies were perfect. "Aren't I enough for you?"

"I need visual stimulation, is all. A guy has to charge his batteries somehow." While he continued to look at those other women, he began touching himself. When he was sufficiently aroused, he turned off the light and took her into his arms. "Unfasten your gown and give me some sugar, darling," he whispered. "Push the tops up with your hands. I like sweet little firm ones."

He drew her into his mouth and made loud, wet sucking sounds. Molly wanted to die because she knew he was pretending she was someone else. That was why he turned out the lights, so he wouldn't have to look at her. It went on and on. With each pull of his mouth, she shuddered and felt as if she might vomit. Her skin felt as if it was turning inside out.

He suddenly caught her nipple between his teeth, biting down hard enough to make it hurt. Then he spit her out, as if the taste of her was vile. "It's like sucking on a cow teat."

Molly tossed in the bed. *Dreaming.* This wasn't real. She was free of him now. It wasn't real. She needed to wake up. Only she couldn't, and the dream changed.

She was dressing for work, and Rodney came into the bedroom.

"If you don't do something soon, your tits will be hanging to your knees. I'll pay for the surgery. Don't mention it to your folks, and just get it done. Don't you love me? Don't you want to please me?"

She had done nothing but try to please him. She walked

the way he wanted, dressed the way he wanted, talked the way he wanted, laughed the way he wanted, even thought the way he wanted, all to save a marriage that hadn't been worth saving. She didn't know who she was anymore, except that she was Rodney's wife. Now he wanted her to let some surgeon hack away at her body. Breast augmentation, a tummy tuck, thigh liposuction. The list of his complaints went on and on. The thought of doing it made her feel frantic. Her body was all she had left—the only thing about her that was still Molly. And now he wanted her to change that, too.

Maybe she wasn't beautiful. Maybe she wasn't desirable. Maybe she was just plain ugly. But it was her body, not his. If she had surgery, he would own her. She'd be the object that Rodney Wells had created.

"I'm not having surgery, Rodney."

His eyes glittered. "Yeah? Well, maybe I don't want to spend the rest of my life married to a fat cow. I love you, Molly. But that's too much to ask of any man. You could have it all fixed. If you refuse, it's the same as telling me to hit the road."

She deliberately chose a dress she knew he despised and drew it off the hanger. "So what's keeping you? Go, Rodney. I no longer really care."

"You don't mean that. No other man will ever want you. Then what'll you do?"

"Die a happy woman."

The scene changed.

She was lying in bed, and she was sick, so horribly sick. "No more pills, Rodney. They make me so dizzy and nauseated. Please, no more pills."

He gently lifted her head. "Darling, don't be difficult. I'm trying to help you. Swallow them down. There's a good girl."

In a dizzying swirl of blacks and grays, she felt herself falling.

Then Rodney was there, kneeling beside her on the

floor, his face drawn with worry. "Oh, darling. Oh, dear God. How long have you been lying here? Molly? Molly, can you hear me?"

She tried to answer, wanted to answer. But her tongue seemed disconnected from her brain. The pills. They were making her sick. She knew that for sure now. But she was too doped to tell him.

He carried her to bed. Vaguely she was aware of him shaking out medication onto his palm. She clenched her teeth, determined not to swallow the pills this time. No, no, no. They were the problem. Why couldn't he see what they were doing to her? Yes, they helped her sleep. But she woke up violently ill, and she couldn't think clearly.

The shadows swirled again.

Rodney was sitting on the mattress beside her.

"Darling, I have some papers I need you to sign from the firm," he told her as he propped her up in bed. He put a pen into her hand. "Hold on to it, love. There you go. There's my good girl."

She tried to see the documents. Her vision was so blurred it was impossible. She could barely bring Rodney's face into focus. Her father had told her never to sign anything until she read it. Now he was dead, and he'd left her his half of the firm. She had to be responsible—a good businesswoman, as he'd raised her to be. She could remember telling Rodney that. She wasn't sure when, but she distinctly remembered telling him. So why did he persist in trying to get her to sign these papers?

"Sign the damned things!" he raged. "I'm your husband, goddamn you. I've had it with this absurdity. Sign the fucking papers!"

Molly thought he was going to hit her. Never in all the ten years of their marriage had Rodney lifted a hand to her. But now he stood over her with a raised fist. She tried frantically to focus, but she saw two of him, then three. Which of those upraised fists would strike her? Looking up at him and struggling to clear her vision, she no longer be-

lieved she knew her husband. The veil of kindness had slipped, revealing a monster underneath.

"If you can't trust your own goddamned husband, who can you trust?" he raged.

Fear turned Molly's blood to ice. She could trust no one, absolutely no one. She realized that now.

Now, when it was too late.

Chapter Ten

Jake Coulter wasn't an easy man to avoid. The next morning, after cleaning up the breakfast mess, Molly went into the utility room to familiarize herself with the milk separator. She'd barely had time to look it over when she heard a floorboard creak behind her. She turned to see her new boss in the doorway. Dressed in what she was quickly coming to think of as rancher garb, chambray and faded denim, he looked absurdly handsome, his sun-darkened skin and sturdy shoulders showcased to best advantage by the wash-worn blue cloth.

"Need some help with that?" he asked lazily.

Just the deep timbre of his voice made her nerves hum. "I think I can figure it out."

He moved to stand beside her. "You pour the milk in this reservoir, and then you just flip the switch. The machine does the rest, filtering the separated milk into that reservoir and funneling the cream out here. It beats skimming it off with a ladle."

"That sounds easy enough." Molly hefted the five-gallon bucket. It was heavier than she expected it to be. "My goodness, the poor cow, carrying all this around."

Jake chuckled and helped to steady the bucket. "I've thought the same thing myself a time or two."

Acutely aware of his nearness and the fact that his left hand grazed her side, she concentrated on getting the milk poured so she could move away. She put the empty bucket in the deep utility sink to wash later. "Thank you for showing me how to run this thing. I know you're busy."

"Not a problem. I'll show you how to use the churn as well. It'll be nice not having the cream go to waste. I haven't had time to make butter in days."

"Are you sure you have time right now? I honestly do think I can manage by myself."

"No point in that when I can show you how it works in two minutes flat."

Two minutes stretched into an hour, and Jake was still there, helping Molly wash up and sterilize the equipment. He talked almost nonstop the entire time they worked, revealing an amazing talent for carrying on a one-sided conversation. Molly wondered if that was due to his having worked alone so much. She imagined most ranchers spent much of the day with only animals for company.

"How did you learn to separate milk and make butter?" she asked.

"I grew up out here. Not in the same house, of course. The family place burned to the ground about five years ago, so I had to rebuild. But the remoteness of the location hasn't changed. Imagine having to drive clear to town to keep milk in the fridge for six kids. My folks got a milk cow, and the rest just followed."

"I thought—" Molly glanced wonderingly out the window over the sink at the forestland that bordered the yard. "I thought you were just starting up this ranch. You said something once about getting it back, but I figured I misunderstood."

"No misunderstanding. My father went bankrupt and lost the Lazy J about nine years ago. The man who bought it didn't insure the dwellings, and when the house burned, he couldn't afford to rebuild. His family of five had to live in the cabin, which was tough. The price had bottomed out on beef as well, and he never really recovered financially. When I made him an offer late last summer, he jumped at the chance to sell."

His eyes darkened as he spoke, telling Molly far more than he probably realized, that he loved this piece of land. It was more than just a ranch to him; it was his heritage. She glanced back out at the trees, scarcely able to imagine the history that must exist for him in every blade of grass. "You played in that yard as a little boy?"

He grinned. "I was born out here, so, yeah, that was my playground."

Molly threw him a questioning look. "Born out here. Your folks were living here at the time, you mean?"

"No, I mean I was actually born here. My dad was out working cattle, and he didn't get word that my mom was in labor in time to take her to town. He had to deliver me."

Molly pressed a hand to her waist. "Oh, my."

He shrugged. "My great-great-grandfather started the ranch, and four generations of Coulters, including my own, were born on this land. After surviving my debut into the world, my mom decided hospitals were for the birds, and for the next five kids, my dad and a midwife attended the births."

Molly could not imagine having a baby at home. Not that she'd ever have the chance to make the choice. Rodney had promised her babies, but, as with everything else, he'd never carried through. Raised as an only child, she'd always yearned to have a large family. Accepting that she would never have even one child, let alone a half dozen, was one of the heartbreaks of her life, right up there with the grief of losing her father.

"What?" Jake asked softly.

Molly realized her expression had turned glum. She forced a bright smile and shook her head. "Nothing."

He searched her gaze for a long moment. Then he returned his attention to the dish washing. "It'll happen. You're young yet."

Molly gaped at him. She couldn't believe he'd guessed her thoughts. He flicked her an amused look. "One kindred soul recognizing another," he said by way of explanation.

"I want children, too. Being the oldest of six kids, with all of us boys so close in age that our mom barely had time to take a breath in between, I've always wanted a large family." A dreamy look came into his eyes. "My little sis gave birth just last week. A little boy. I can't tell you how I felt the first time I held him. It made me want one of my own so bad, I damned near got tears in my eyes."

"You?" she asked incredulously.

He threw back his dark head and laughed. When his mirth subsided, he said, "Yes, me. Why does that surprise you? Don't most people want kids someday?"

"Most men don't. Not really. I think they only say they do because it's what women like to hear."

That prompted him to laugh again. "I'm not touching that with a well-charged cattle prod. I'll only say that I must be an exception. I want kids. I can't tell you how much."

Molly had heard that refrain before. Suddenly tense, she busied herself reassembling the churn. The scattered parts were a puzzle, and when she grew stumped, he reached over to help. Her throat going tight with emotions she couldn't and didn't want to name, she stared at his forearm, watching the play of tendon each time he flexed his wrist, fascinated by the way the light glistened on the silky dark hair that furred his wet, sun-bronzed skin.

"See?" he said softly after reassembling the churn. "Right when everything seems hopelessly jumbled, something happens and it all falls into place." He winked at her. "After a divorce, lots of people feel defeated and finished, Molly. It's natural, and in time, you'll heal." With a damp fingertip, he touched the tip of her nose. "Right when you least expect it, some fellow is going to come along. He'll take one look at you, and he'll be a goner."

Molly no longer believed in true love and forever after. Aching in places she had refused to acknowledge for years, she stared up at his dark face. *Wishing . . . wishing.*

The rumbling timbre of his voice suffused her with warmth, and the feeling frightened her half to death.

Dipping her chin to break eye contact, she summoned a chirpy voice to say, "Well, this is done. I suppose I'd better get to work. I haven't had time to make out a list of things to do yet, but I think it may be taller than I am when I'm finished."

"Forgive me for pointing it out, but that's not saying much."

"It isn't nice to tease people about their shortcomings."

"Lack of height in a woman isn't a shortcoming. A lot of men think it's attractive. I think it's attractive."

He pulled the sink stopper. The water made a gurgling sound as it spiraled down the drain. Molly struggled to focus on that noise. It was real. Jake Coulter wasn't. He was just a wish in her foolish female heart that could never come true.

"Before you get started on cleaning, we need to go over how we do lunches." He led the way to the pantry, stepping aside at the doorway so she might enter first. Waving a hand at the small coolers on the top shelves, he said, "On a ranch, it's not always possible to come in for lunch at a specific time. It's more practical to pack the midday meal in coolers so we can eat in the field—or wherever else we happen to be. We keep small packs of blue ice in the freezer. It keeps the food cool, even on a hot day. I know it'll be a pain, fixing both lunch and breakfast so early, but on the plus side, it'll free you up during the day to do household chores and get in some extra work outdoors."

"Ah. I wondered what all the coolers were for. I thought someone here on the ranch owned shares in Coleman."

He laughed. "They make handy lunchboxes. You can toss them in the back of a pickup or strap them on a horse, no fuss, no muss."

That explained why all the coolers sported ground-in dirt. Molly decided she would scrub them down with abrasive cleanser and do her best to keep them clean from now on.

"What sort of things do you like for lunch?"

"Sandwiches, chips, snack cakes. Nothing fancy. Just make sure you give each man plenty. They work their tails off."

Molly made a mental note to pack two sandwiches in each cooler. Believing that their conversation was concluded, she started to leave, but he blocked her way with his considerable bulk, bracing one arm against an adjacent shelf and leaning slightly toward her. It seemed to Molly that the log walls moved in closer and the air went thin.

"Was there something more you wanted to tell me?" she asked.

His unnerving blue eyes trailed to her hair. "You're wearing a braid again."

"Yes. Is that a problem?"

"No. It's a nice, tidy style for the kitchen." A mischievous twinkle slipped into his eyes. "But when you're not cooking, I hate to see you hide something so beautiful." He reached over her shoulder to grasp her braid and draw it forward, his strong fingers sliding to its end, which lay over her breast. Moving his thumb back and forth over the elastic band, he smiled slowly. "I keep thinking how you look with it down."

The brush of his knuckles over the crest of her nipple made her stiffen. Uncertain if the contact was intentional, she pushed his hand away and made a fist over the braid herself. "Long hair worn loose in the kitchen is unsanitary."

He shrugged and trailed a fingertip lightly along her jaw. "Maybe, but you'd sure be a glory to look at."

Before she could think of a response, he turned and exited the pantry. Molly stared after him, still clutching her braid. When she felt sure he was gone, she touched a hand to her cheek, feeling oddly off balance, much as she had as a child after jumping off the merry-go-round. *"A glory to look at?"* On the one hand, she wanted to laugh, but on the other, oh, how she wanted to believe him.

Jake. Over the next few days, it seemed to Molly that he was there nearly every time she turned around. When she arrived at the main house each morning, he was waiting for her in the kitchen and insisted that she join him for a cup of coffee before they began their respective chores.

During those impromptu coffee klatches, he plied her with friendly questions in an obvious attempt to become better acquainted with her. Given the fact that he was true to his word and never pressed her for damning information about her past, Molly didn't really mind. She worked in the man's home, after all, and it was understandable that he wanted to learn all he could about her.

"Do you enjoy any sports, Molly?" he inquired one morning.

"I used to love golf and played nearly every Saturday with my dad," she replied easily. "I was never very good, I'm afraid. But we had a lot of fun."

"There's nothing wrong with being mediocre if you enjoy the game."

Mediocre had not been good enough for Rodney. Golf was a wealthy man's game, he believed, and one's skill was a reflection of one's breeding. Her amateur performance on the course had been an embarrassment to him.

"Yes, well, I wasn't that passionate about it, I guess. When I grew older, I lost interest and didn't care to play anymore."

"When you grew older? After you were married, you mean?"

A cold, empty feeling filled Molly's chest. "Yes, after I was married."

Another morning, he said, "So, tell me, Molly, what's your favorite time of year?"

"I'd have to say autumn."

"Ah." He smiled and nodded. "That is a gorgeous season."

"I *loved* the brilliant colors on the hillsides and the crisp chill in the air." She felt a little embarrassed, but added, "Most of all, though, I loved the holidays—the anticipation, the get-togethers, and all the decorations."

He smiled as though he shared that sentiment. "Which holiday season is your favorite?"

"Hmm, that's a tough one. I enjoyed Halloween and Thanksgiving a lot, but I think Christmas was always most special."

"We usually have snow here by Christmas. There's nothing more beautiful than cheery lights reflecting off the snowdrifts."

A picture flashed in her mind of his house, twinkling cheerfully inside and out with Christmas lights. She saw Jake at center stage, crouched before a gigantic tree with a dark-haired little boy at his side. In that moment, it was all too easy to imagine herself as a part of that homey scene. She quickly shoved the image from her mind.

Another morning he was sitting at the kitchen table reading a novel when Molly walked in. "Good book?" she asked as she peeled off her green parka.

He tossed down the paperback. "A whodunit. Nothing spectacular. The plot is pretty thin."

"Ah, a mystery buff, are you?"

He nodded. "Do you like to read?"

"I used to have my nose in a book all the time."

He grinned. "What was your genre?"

Her cheeks went hot. She hung her coat on a dowel and moved into the kitchen. "I was crazy about historical romance in my younger days."

"Ah." A mischievous glint warmed his eyes. "Romance is what brought us all to the dance. What made you stop reading it?"

She wrinkled her nose. "Rodney felt that my reading

love stories gave me unrealistic expectations of our relationship."

The amusement in his eyes became more pronounced.
"Sounds to me like good old Rodney was afraid he
wouldn't measure up."

That was an understatement. Uncomfortable with the
conversation, Molly bypassed having coffee and dove into
the breakfast preparations. As she began peeling apples for
the bowl of fresh fruit that she served without fail each
morning, Jake came to lean his hips against the counter.

"Can I ask you something?"

Molly had become accustomed to this question-and-
answer game. "Sure. Fire away."

"Why do you always refer to yourself in the past
tense?"

She stared at him, bewildered, an awful, cold feeling
clawing at her chest. The kitchen had gone unnaturally
bright, the overhead lights glaring, the bits of chrome on
the appliances flashing with blinding brilliance.

His voice sounded far away as he added, "I really enjoy
hearing about the things you used to enjoy. Don't misunder-
stand me. But I'd also like to know who you are right now."

"Who I am now?" she repeated stupidly.

"Yes, now. I know that you used to love to read and enjoyed playing golf. But what interests you now?"

"I'm the same person. I haven't changed."

"How long has it been since you read a romance?" he
asked softly.

It had been nine years, but Molly couldn't bring herself
to admit that. "A while," she settled for saying.

"How long has it been since you played golf?"

Her only answer was a shrug.

His expression grew concerned. "How long were you
married, Molly?"

Pain lanced through her skull, and the cold feeling in
her chest moved through her whole body. *Where are you,
Molly? Where have you gone?* That frightening little voice

that had taunted her so many times when she looked in the mirror was now a singsong in her mind as she looked into Jake Coulter's eyes. In those blue depths, she glimpsed dead dreams, and she wanted to run from him. Big problem. His ranch had become her only sanctuary.

"Why are you asking me all this?"

He searched her gaze. "Because I want to know you better." He folded his arms loosely across his chest. "Not who you used to be, but who you are right now."

She shook her head. "That's silly." Her voice sounded hollow even to her. "I'm the same person."

"Are you?" He let that hang there for a moment. Then he whispered, "Molly?" He said her name softly and reached over to cup her chin in his hand. Jerked from her confused thoughts, she stared up at him with growing dread, unable to shake the feeling that he was parting curtains in her mind that she might never again be able to close. "I'm sorry, honey," he said huskily. "I don't mean to upset you."

How could he hope not to upset her when he was asking such disturbing questions? *Who are you, Molly?* She no longer really knew. It was as if something inside her—a very vital something—had been obliterated. A few mornings ago, he had told her that everyone felt this way after a divorce and she would get over it in time. But she didn't think so. There were no bleeding wounds within her to heal. There was only emptiness—an awful emptiness.

He trailed his thumb over her cheek. "I'm sorry," he whispered. "Forget I said anything."

He pushed erect and glanced at the clock. "I'd better get cracking, I guess. The cow won't milk herself."

Listening to the sharp tap of his boot heels on the oak floor, Molly let the partially peeled apple slip from her numb fingers. The fruit fell into the bowl with a soft plunk and rolled onto its side. In the time that she'd stood there holding it, the ripe pulp had already begun to turn brown in places. Intellectually, she knew that the discoloration was a chemical reaction of some kind that occurred when the fructose was exposed to the air. Emotionally, she likened it to the first stages of rot. If left exposed for too long, all that was good and sweet and wholesome within the apple would turn sour.

Jake paused at the back door to turn on the radio. When the reception came in, he tuned in to a station that played popular oldies. As it happened, that morning they were doing an 1980s top-hit countdown. The very first song was an almost-forgotten favorite of Molly's from her high school days.

When she heard Jake step out and close the door, she stared woodenly at nothing, her eyes filling with tears. It had been eight years since she had listened to that song.

That afternoon when Molly went out to spend her obligatory hour with Sunset, she saw Jake in the adjoining pasture, working with a baby horse. Over the course of her stay so far, she'd noticed that he rarely worked with the cattle, choosing instead to devote the majority of his time to the training program.

A smile touched her mouth as she watched him rub a saddle blanket over the young animal's body. Most people would have done it a couple of times and been done with it. Not Jake. He repeated the process again and again, flapping the blanket near the foal's head occasionally, which startled the little fellow.

Some fifteen minutes later, Jake vaulted over the split-rail fence and came striding toward her, the thick wool hooked over his thumb to ride his shoulder.

"What was that all about?" she called.

He grinned. Even at a distance, his eyes were a blaze of blue. "That was blanket flapping 101."

She laughed. "I see."

Drawing ever closer with those long, seemingly lazy strides of his, he said, "Having a man chase you with a blanket can be a pretty scary proposition."

Molly could well imagine that it might be, especially if that man could move as swiftly as Jake Coulter could. She turned her gaze back to the foal, which was now romping in the grass, delighted to be free again. "So you're teaching that little guy not to be afraid?"

"You got it." He joined her at the fence and drew off his hat. His dark hair was depressed where the band had rested. He raked his long, sturdy fingers through the chocolate-colored strands, then resettled the Stetson on his head. "All creatures are instinctively afraid of some things." He turned a thoughtful gaze on her. "The only way to overcome fear is to face it repeatedly until the thing that frightens you no longer seems scary."

Molly averted her gaze. Though she knew him better now, she still couldn't shake the feeling that he read more in her eyes than she wished him to sometimes. "That's an interesting thought."

"A true one."

She nibbled the inside of her lip. "Fear isn't always unfounded. Sometimes the things we fear will do us great harm if we don't avoid them." She immediately wanted to call the words back. That feeling intensified when she met his gaze again. He was studying her with a thoughtful frown.

"And sometimes," he said softly, "there's nothing to fear at all. If you're afraid of something and don't face it at least once, how can you ever know if your fears are real or only imagined?"

Molly straightened away from the fence. "Good question." She hugged her waist and stared hard at Sunset. Hoping to change the subject, she said, "He's growing more at ease with us. Have you noticed?"

A hint of a smile played at the edge of his hard mouth as he joined her in regarding the stallion. "He still gets antsy when I enter the pen. The courtship period isn't over yet."

"The courtship period? Is that what you call it?"

His twinkling gaze met and held hers. "Moving in, backing off. Much of horse training is a courtship of sorts, slowly overcoming shyness and fear to build a relationship of trust. Sunset would just as soon pass, but he's cornered and doesn't have a choice. In time, he'll come to realize I'm more stubborn than he is and accept the inevitable."

Molly felt cornered as well, and she quite often got the feeling that he was playing the same game with her. *Moving in, backing off.* Only to what end? He was a handsome, virile man who could have his pick of beautiful women. Why would he waste his energy on someone like her?

She wanted to tell him that her situation was nothing like Sunset's, that she was free to leave anytime she chose, but even as the thought slipped into her mind, she knew it wasn't true. She was trapped here for now, held fast by the velvet manacles of safety that she could find nowhere else.

She glanced at her watch. "My goodness. I didn't realize the time. I need to get dinner started."

"And I've got two more horses to put through their paces before I quit for the day."

"I guess we'd both better get back to work."

As she struck off for the house, Molly could feel the heat of his gaze on her. Her back tingled, her butt tingled. She wanted to whirl around and tell him to stop staring. Instead she hurried up the steps, anxious to escape into the house. At the doorway, she threw a searing look over her shoulder, only to find that her target had vanished.

He hadn't been watching her at all. It was only her imagination.

As she let herself inside, Molly wondered if everything else was her imagination as well. Maybe she was making mountains out of molehills, reading hidden meanings into things he said and did that he never meant to convey.

That was it, she decided with some relief. That *had* to be it. Jake Coulter was so far out of her league, it was ludicrous to think he would ever even give her a second look, let alone plot ways to seduce her.

* * *

Of an evening, when Molly finished her work for the day, Jake always walked her home. That night, Molly vowed to walk at a fast clip. Whether it was all her imagination or not, this man did things that made her nervous. He seemed to look too deep and see too much. She was a woman with secrets she didn't dare reveal. She needed to be careful, and the most surefire way to do that was to keep her distance.

To her dismay, he veered right toward the creek instead of walking her directly home. "Where are we going?" she asked.

His teeth gleamed blue white in the moonlight when he smiled. "I thought it might be relaxing to take a little stroll."

That was the last thing she wanted to do, but his firm grip on her elbow brooked no argument. "I hope you don't plan to stroll too far. I'm tired tonight."

"You'll rest better for the dose of fresh air."

Once at the stream, Molly was so charmed by the tenebrous beauty that she forgot to feel tense. A breeze whispered in the lofty pines, the sound surreal and melodic. Moonlight shone through the swaying boughs in misty beams, making the water look like molten silver spilling over the rocks. Near them, the frogs, frightened by their presence, had grown quiet, but farther downstream, their voices were still raised in a raucous cacophony.

"Why do you reckon frogs croak?" Jake suddenly asked.

Molly suppressed a smile, wondering how it was that this man could so easily work his way past her defenses. She'd been so determined not to talk with him tonight, and now here she was, about to engage in a conversation about frogs, of all things. "I have no idea. Maybe they're conversing with each other."

He listened. "You think the ones with shrill voices are lady frogs?"

Resisting the urge to laugh, she cocked her head to listen. "Maybe."

"Could be the fellas are whispering sweet nothings in their ears, and that's a lady frog's way of tittering."

She giggled. She couldn't help herself. "Sweet nothings? That croaking doesn't sound very romantic to me."

"Maybe it all depends on who's talking and who's listening."

Molly sighed and hugged her parka closer. He glanced down. "You cold, honey?"

"Only a little."

He startled her by slipping an arm around her waist. "I've got plenty of heat to share."

He did, at that. The warmth radiating from his big body curled around her. Molly's pulse accelerated. Try as she might, she couldn't relax against him. He was too—*everything*—too big, too strong, too handsome, too charming. From the first, he'd sparked her imagination and made her want things she had no business wanting.

"What are you thinking?" he asked.

"Nothing, really."

He glanced down at her, his eyes glistening in the moonlight. "Nothing, Molly? Or just nothing you want to share with me?"

She drew away from him and cupped a hand over her mouth, pretending to yawn. "Excuse me. I must be more exhausted than I realized. Do you mind if we head for the cabin now?"

He smiled slightly, his indulgent expression conveying that he saw right through her. "Not at all." He grasped her elbow to guide her up the bank. "Watch your step going over these rocks."

Molly was about to say she could see just fine when she caught her toe and stumbled. He stopped her from falling with an arm around her waist, his big hand splayed over her midriff. Her breath trapped at the base of her throat, and she jerked her head up to look at him. He slowly drew his arm from around her, his expression, concealed by the shadow of his hat, unreadable.

Unsettled by his touch, which had come perilously close to the underside of her breast, Molly gathered her composure and struck off again, acutely aware of his grasp on her arm. Her hip occasionally bumped against his thigh as she hurried along.

"You racing to put out a fire?" he asked.

They reached the front porch of the cabin just then, saving her the need to reply. She pulled away from him and moved hastily up the steps. At the top, she turned, thinking to thank him for walking her home. She nearly jumped out of her skin when she found him standing right behind her.

"Oh!" She pressed a hand over her heart. "You startled me."

He chuckled. "It doesn't take much. Correct me if I'm wrong, but I think I make you uneasy."

"Don't be silly, Mr. Coulter. Why would you make me uneasy?"

"The name is Jake."

"I know what your given name is."

"Then why won't you use it?"

"You're my employer."

His dark face creased in another grin, the lines that lashed his lean cheeks looking as black as ink in the eerie light. The smell of leather, hay, and man surrounded her. She shivered and rubbed her arms.

"My other employees call me Jake."

"That's their choice. I prefer to keep things more businesslike."

"Because it makes you feel safe?"

Molly couldn't think what to say, which elicited another smile from him. "No question about it, I definitely make you uneasy." He ran his gaze slowly over her face as though searching for answers in her expression. Molly could only hope he found none. "Why is that, Molly?"

She moistened her lips and swallowed. "I'm not sure. Post-divorce jitters, I guess."

He toed a board of the porch, then settled his hands at his hips. "Was Rodney ornery with you?"

She just stared at him.

"Behind closed doors, I mean." He cupped her chin in his hand. "Is that why I make you nervous, because you never knew what to expect from him?"

"Rodney was never physically abusive to me. As for why you make me nervous, it has nothing at all to do with that. I don't even think of you that way."

He rubbed his thumb over her bottom lip, his mouth tipping into a thoughtful grin. "You don't, huh?"

"No, of course not."

He lightened the graze of his thumb, treating her to a soft caress that set her lip to tingling. "Maybe you'd better start," he said huskily.

Speechless, Molly gazed after him as he loped down the steps and struck off into the darkness. Her night vision being what it was, he was a shadow one moment, then gone the next.

Taking a deep breath and exhaling slowly, she closed her eyes and chafed her arms again, feeling cold in a way that went deeper than the flesh. The night wind gusted in under the porch overhang, its whisper seeming to say, *"Molly . . . Molly . . ."* She curled an arm around the support beam at the top of the steps and pressed her forehead against the wood. *"Molly . . . where are you?"* She shuddered and clenched her teeth. Maybe Rodney had been right all along, and she was crazy. Normal people didn't hear voices in the wind.

She pressed closer to the beam, needing the support and finding comfort in the solidness. It made her think of Jake, of how sturdy his big, lean body felt when he drew her against him. A tight, suffocating feeling welled in her throat. She wrapped both arms around the log and clung to it, wishing with all her heart it could hug her back.

Chapter Eleven

"Is any of that rice and eggs that Molly made for the dog left over?"

His mouth filled with crackers, Jake whipped around to locate his brother in the gloom. It was four o'clock in the morning, and he hadn't expected anyone to be up and about yet. They usually got off to a slow start Monday morning. The hired hands were never completely recovered from their Saturday night festivities, and he and Hank were usually exhausted after doing all the work themselves over the weekend.

"What are you doing up so early?" Jake asked. "I figured you'd sleep in."

Padding on bare feet, his brother came into view, his dark hair rumpled, his chest bare. His jeans were zipped, but he'd left them unbuttoned. "Who slept? Supper last night was deserving of Levi's cowboy blessing."

Jake hated to bite on that one. "What's Levi's cowboy blessing?"

" 'Three beans for four of us, thank God there ain't no more of us.' "

Jake chuckled. "It wasn't *that* skimpy."

"Pretty skimpy. If God had meant peppers to be stuffed, He'd have made them that way. And what the hell kind of soup was that she fixed?"

"Minestrone."

"It was so thin, I could've drunk it with a straw. I'm starving. I tossed and turned all night."

Jake shoved the jar of peanut butter along the counter so his brother could help himself. "She's trying. Did you notice Bart last night? Yesterday afternoon she gave him a bath and doused him with aftershave. He smelled so pretty I damned near kissed him."

Hank chuckled. "I happened by the house while she was bathing him. The bathroom looked like a hurricane had struck, and she was wet from head to toe."

"She sure is a sweetheart."

"No argument there," Hank agreed. "But her being sweet doesn't put food in our bellies, Jake. You have to talk to her. In all your life, I've never known you to pull your verbal punches." He grabbed the table knife and piled peanut butter onto a cracker. After popping it into his mouth and chewing a couple of times, he swallowed and said, "Now, suddenly, you're Mr. Tact. You've picked a hell of a time to become a diplomat."

"It's not easy, learning to cook for so many. She'll get the hang of it soon."

His expression thoughtful, Hank popped another cracker into his mouth. "You really like her a lot, don't you?"

Jake considered the question. "Yeah. Yeah, I do."

"Are you getting serious?"

Again Jake took a moment to consider before answering. "As serious as I've ever felt," he said softly. "She grows on a fellow. You know? With some women, the better you get to know them, the more unappealing they are. But Molly is sweet all the way through. Her brushing Bart's teeth, for instance. He isn't exactly cooperative, but she does it anyway. And she's always doing other little things, just to be nice. Sewing on buttons, mending jeans, putting little surprises in our lunch pails. I've never asked her to do any of that stuff. She takes it upon herself."

"The carob-coated raisins were a surprise, all right."

Jake sighed. "It's the thought that counts. She wants us to eat healthy. You can't fault her for that."

"I'm not faulting her. I'm just hungry." Hank grabbed another cracker. "Hot cereal and fruit for breakfast just doesn't cut it." He glanced over his shoulder. "Is that why you haven't turned on the lights, because you're afraid she might see and realize you're up, raiding the kitchen?"

"I don't want to hurt her feelings. Being a little hungry for a few more days won't kill us."

Hank shoved another cracker in his mouth. "Speak for yourself. I wonder where she's from?"

"My guess is she's from Portland."

"Portland?" Hank had been up that way a few months ago. "Oh, man, I hope she doesn't serve us any of that field-green salad shit."

"What is field-green salad?"

"Just like it sounds, greens out of a field. Dandelion leaves and stuff."

"You're kidding."

"It's all the rage in the nice restaurants up there. City people. There's just no figuring 'em." Hank shuddered and shook his head. "They charged me eight bucks for that crap. I'm telling you, we could make a fortune. Just turn them out to graze and charge by the head."

"Eight bucks for field greens?"

"Everything on the menu cost separately."

"À la carte," Jake inserted.

"À la highway robbery, more like. My supper cost me over thirty dollars, and all I got was a tiny piece of prime rib and a bunch of what cows eat. No bread, no spuds. I damned near starved to death."

Jake chuckled. "Now you're sounding like Danno."

The back door opened just then, and both men gave a guilty start, afraid the new arrival might be Molly. Instead, Levi poked his head in. "Howdy." He stepped over the threshold and softly closed the door. "What're we havin' here, a convention?"

Jake sighed and shoved the jar of peanut butter along

the counter to his hired hand. "We're just filling our empty spots, Levi. If that's why you're up early, help yourself."

Later that morning, Jake gathered his men in the stable to line them out for the coming week. Usually they sat around the kitchen table on Monday morning, and he assigned each man his chores over coffee, but he'd been anxious to get them out of the house today. Judging by their disgruntled expressions, their time off hadn't sweetened their dispositions any. Jake feared they were about to mutiny, and he didn't want Molly to see the fireworks.

"What the hell were those things she fed us for breakfast?" the gangly, ever-hungry Danno asked.

"Crêpes," Hank supplied. "Fancy French pancakes."

"The French can have 'em."

Jake sighed, took off his hat to stare blankly at the inside of the crown, and then returned it to his head. "Gentlemen, let's all practice a little patience. That was a real pretty breakfast she served. Just think how hard she worked, cutting all those strawberries into flower shapes."

"Those pancakes were so thin, you could read the newspaper through them, and each of us only got four." Preach, the quiet one of the bunch, scowled at his boss. "I'm so hungry, I could eat frogs while they're still hopping. Pretty doesn't fill a man's gut."

Nate, a nice-looking twenty-five-year-old with a winning smile and a penchant for teasing, laughed and inserted, "If pretty filled a man's gut, Preach, we'd just toss Molly on the table and forget about food."

Just that fast and Jake was mad. He fixed Nate with a glare. "Any man who lays a finger on the lady will answer to me. Is that understood?"

Nate raised his eyebrows. "I guess that's plain enough."

"You keep a civil tongue in your head when you speak to her, and do it with your goddamned hat in your hand."

Hank touched his brother's sleeve. "Hey, Jake, he was just joking."

Jake shook his arm free. "There are lines we don't cross on this spread, and that's one of them. She's a lady, not some Saturday-night bar floozy, and she'll be treated with respect by every last one of you, or I'll know the reason why."

Nate's brows arched higher. "Kinda touchy this morning, aren't we, boss? I'd never get out of line with a lady, and you know it."

"Make damned sure you don't."

Even as the anger roiled within him, Jake knew he was overreacting. Nate's remark had been a little off-color, but he'd meant no real harm. He took a deep, calming breath, wondered what the hell was wrong with him, and tried to soften his expression. "Molly is pretty, and we wouldn't be men if we failed to notice that." He scanned the group, offering no quarter with his gaze. "Just mind your manners when you're around her, and you'll have no problem with me."

All the men nodded.

Jake grabbed his clipboard, gave his notes a quick scan, and began assigning the men their jobs for the week. When the last hired hand had sauntered away, Hank gave him a pointed look and said, "Pardon me for pointing it out, but no matter how much you like Molly, you did hire her to do a job. If she's not cutting the mustard, you either have to get her straightened out or can her ass. The men have to eat."

Jake bit down hard on his back teeth. "I'll handle it."

"When? We're all starving."

"You won't waste away."

"Maybe not, but my work has been off, and it will be again today. After a breakfast of see-through pancakes, you can bet she packed us piddly-ass lunches again, only two sandwiches each, and those with fat-free mayo." Hank made a face. "Where does she buy all that whole wheat crap? Those chips taste like sawdust."

"I think she gets them at a health food store."

"Well, I hate them. We all do. Even Bart won't eat 'em."

"I *said* I'll handle it."

Jake heard the front door of the house open and close just then. He leaned around to look out the stable doorway and saw Molly coming down the front steps. Once she gained the ground, she fetched a huge, gnarled limb she'd evidently left leaning against the porch. As she cut across the yard toward the creek, Jake gazed curiously after her.

"Great," Hank whispered. "See-through pancakes for breakfast, and now she's taking a morning stroll. If she's going out to pick field greens, I quit."

"You can't quit. You're part owner."

"I haven't kicked in any money. All I'll be out is sweat."

Jake sighed, his gaze still fixed on their cook. Dressed in baggy jeans and a loose, white cotton blouse, she looked adorable in spite of herself. She tiptoed daintily over some stones to get across the stream, then set off toward the woods, swinging the tree limb at the brush as if it was her aim to flatten it.

"What the hell is she doing?" Hank asked.

Jake watched Molly for another few seconds. "I have no idea."

"Whatever she's doing, she's going at it like she's killing snakes."

Snakes? Jake remembered the conversation they'd had about rattlers that first day. He groaned. "Oh, *damn*."

"What?" Hank glanced back at him.

"I think she's beating the brush for rattlers."

"What?" Hank stepped to the doorway to get a better look. His shoulders jerked with laughter. "Who in God's name told her to do that?"

"I did."

"You're joking."

"I didn't mean for her to do it that way." Jake watched Molly whack a sage bush. He chuckled and shook his head. "But I did tell her to beat the brush." He observed her a second longer. "Well, hell. After putting the rope in front

of the wood box, I kind of hoped the snake issue was put
to rest."

"You put a rope in front of her wood box? What for?"

"As a snake deterrent."

Hank narrowed an eye. "That's an old wives' tale. It
doesn't work."

"I know that, and you know that, but she doesn't. It
eased her mind, mission accomplished."

Hank resumed watching Molly. His dark face creased in
a mischievous grin. "You reckon we'll have any brush left
when she's done?"

Jake slapped his brother's gut with the clipboard.
Hank's breath rushed from his chest as he grabbed hold of
the notes. "Where you going?"

Never breaking stride, Jake called back, "To show her
how to beat the brush and have a talk with her about her
cooking."

"Tell her we like spuds, and lots of 'em!" Hank yelled
after him.

Jake groaned and nodded. This was one chore he was
not looking forward to. Just as he reached the creek, he
heard Hank holler, "Homemade biscuits, too!"

Sunlight streamed through the boughs of the ponderosa
pines, the shafts of light filled with motes that shimmered
like pearl dust in the morning glow. The vanilla scent of
tree bark, the musk of sage, and the moldiness of the forest floor, carpeted with countless layers of decaying needles, filled Molly's nostrils. She hauled in a deep breath,
thinking how absolutely glorious the morning was and
how blessed she was to have a moment to enjoy it.

As she moved deeper into the woods, she felt as if she'd
stepped off into a fairy tale or traveled back through time
to the pioneer days. Indulging in a rare moment of fancy,
she recalled the countless Indian romances she'd read during her first and only year of college. This was just the sort
of setting she'd always imagined when she read about a

beautiful, fair-skinned heroine coming face-to-face with a dark and dangerous half-breed warrior.

She grinned and was about to whack another bush in her path when a branch snapped behind her. Her heart shot into her throat, and she whirled around with the limb raised high.

"You gonna thump me with that thing, or is it safe to come closer?" a deep voice, laced with amusement, inquired.

When Molly recognized Jake moving through the trees, she released a pent-up breath, touched a hand to her throat, and let the limb sink to the ground. "Mr. Coulter, you frightened me half to death. I thought you were a cougar."

His twinkling blue eyes narrowed on her face. "I told you it's fairly safe to take walks during the day."

"The key word being '*fairly.*'" She glided her fingertips down between her collarbones as her heart slid back into its proper place.

"The way you're swinging that club, no cougar in its right mind would dare take you on. You look downright fearsome."

He was the one who looked fearsome, so tall and dark, his shirt stretched taut over his broad shoulders, the faded denim of his Wranglers sheathing his long, powerfully muscled legs. Molly tried to imagine him in nothing but a loincloth and moccasins. The picture that leaped to mind was enough to give her arrhythmia.

It was silly in the extreme for her to think about him in that way, of course. But for some reason, she couldn't seem to help it.

"What?" Jake asked, his gaze still searching hers.

She realized she'd been staring. "Nothing. I'm just surprised to see you out here. I thought you were working."

"I'm never too busy to take a walk with a pretty lady."

That was a big part of her problem with him, she decided. He not only acted as if he thought she was pretty, but he said so, making it difficult for her to keep her perspective.

Molly wondered why he had followed her. "If you're upset because I'm taking a break, I only meant to be gone for a few minutes." She glanced at her watch. "I started work before five, and it's half past eight. I thought I'd take a short walk. I guess I should have checked with you first to make sure that's allowed."

For what seemed to her an interminably long while, he looked deeply into her eyes. Then his hard mouth tipped up at one corner in a smile.

"I'm not here to jump you about taking a break, Molly."

"Oh." She fiddled nervously with the buttons of her top, then pressed a hand to her waist. She really, really wished he'd stop looking at her that way. "Why, then?" She thought quickly. "I know the crêpes were a little tough. I'll do better next time."

He nudged up the brim of his hat. The better to stare at her, she guessed. A shaft of sunlight filtered down through the tree boughs, playing over his burnished face.

"Why do you immediately assume that I came out here to chew your ass about something?" he asked softly.

Molly considered the question. "Because I can't think of any other reason you might have followed me."

He shook his head, his smile broadening, yet not seeming to reach his eyes, which she could have sworn looked sad just before he glanced away. He spent a moment gazing off into the woods, his expression thoughtful.

"Maybe I came out here to tell you those were the best damned crêpes I ever ate. Did you think of that?"

"I thought they were a little tough."

"They were delicious," he corrected. "Everyone cleaned his plate."

"They were probably just being polite." Nervous beyond measure, she dug the sharp end of the tree limb into the ground. "If you didn't follow me to complain about the crêpes or chew me out for taking a break, why are you here?"

"I came out to take a walk with a pretty lady." The slashes at each corner of his mouth deepened as he smiled this time. "You don't mind having some company, do you?"

"Oh, no, I don't suppose I—"

She broke off when he stepped forward, grabbed the limb from her hand, and tossed it into the brush.

"That's my snake stick."

"How big do you think the snakes are hereabouts, the size of pythons? Beating the brush with a limb that large will wear you to a frazzle." He bent to pick up a skinny branch. "This is more the thing."

"That isn't big enough to kill a snake."

"Killing a snake isn't your aim. You just want to warn them away." He grabbed her by the hand and set off at a much faster pace than she'd been going. His palm and fingers felt incredibly hard and warm, wrapped around hers. As they walked, he tapped the bushes, rather like a blind person might a cane. "That's all you need to do," he said as he handed her the branch. "Every rattler for a mile will feel the vibrations and clear out. If you're walking through really thick brush, you can get a little more ambitious and occasionally whack a bush. Keep an ear cocked for any buzzing sounds and watch where you step. You'll probably never see a snake."

Molly cast him a dubious look. He laughed and chucked her under the chin. "Trust me, all right? There's no need to bludgeon every bush you see."

"Hmm."

He rubbed his thumb over her knuckles, sending zings up her arm. Molly whacked a sage bush, using a little more force than he claimed was necessary.

"Just in case," she said by way of explanation.

"Go ahead. Wear yourself out. You'll never want to come walking again. Your arms will be sore for days."

She decided her arms *were* getting tired. She followed his example and began tapping the bushes. "Are you sure this is enough?"

"Positive. Rattlesnakes aren't deadly, you know. If you're unable to get antivenin, their bite just makes you all-fired sick. Occasionally, someone has secondary complications and dies, but a healthy adult usually doesn't."

"If the bite doesn't kill me, the heart attack will."

He chuckled. "You're really afraid of them, aren't you?"

"I'm the biggest chicken you've ever seen when it comes to snakes. Even the garden variety makes me hyperventilate. I'm not at all afraid of spiders, though, and when I was small, I caught a mouse and made a pet of it, so they don't frighten me, either. Just keep snakes and all things slithery away from me."

He gave her fingers a squeeze. A friendly gesture, nothing more, Molly assured herself. If tingles raced up her arm, that was her problem. She wished he'd let loose of her hand so she could think straight.

"You know how to tell a ponderosa pine from a lodge-pole?" he suddenly asked.

Molly stopped thumping the dirt to glance at the trees around them. "The bark of a ponderosa is the color of cinnamon, and the bark on a lodgepole isn't?"

"Not all ponderosas turn cinnamon. A lot of them are plain old brown."

"How do you tell then?"

"The needles." He reached up to grab a cluster and held it before her nose. "A ponderosa has three per cluster, a lodge pole only two."

"Ah."

He flashed her a grin that sent electrical heat ribboning through her. "You know how to tell a juniper with your eyes closed?"

She thought for a moment. "No, I can't say as I do. By its smell?"

He nodded.

"What do they smell like?"

"Cat piss."

Molly burst out laughing. "Not really."

His dancing gaze met hers. "Honey, would I lie to you?"

Molly was still trying to think of a response when he launched into another spiel about wildlife, telling her a host of different things about the golden-mantled squirrels they saw, then moving on to skunks, mule deer, and lastly, black bears.

"If I see a bear, I should raise my arms and talk to it?" she asked incredulously. "Is there any particular topic of conversation they favor?"

He narrowed an eye at her. "You want to learn this stuff or not?"

"Yes, absolutely."

"Then stop with the sarcasm." He squeezed her hand again. This time, she assured herself he only did it to let her know he was kidding. "Bears have very poor eyesight," he went on, "and if you're downwind of them, you need to let them know you're not another bear. Lifting your arms makes you look larger, and talking helps to distinguish you from other animals. Hold your ground, make eye contact, and say, 'Yo, bear! How you doin' today?' "

"And that'll make it go away?"

"Most of the time. There's the rare fruitcake black bear, of course, but they're few and far between. Grizzlies are another story, but we don't have any of those around here."

"For future reference, what should I do if I ever meet a grizzly?"

"Be extremely polite."

The reply caught Molly off guard, and a startled giggle lodged crosswise in her throat, making her snort. Heat seared her face. "Excuse me. I haven't done that in *years*."

His gaze was warm when it came to rest on her face.

"Don't apologize. I think that's the first time I've ever heard you cut loose and really laugh."

"That was a *snort,* not a laugh. I used to do it a lot until I broke myself of the habit."

"Why did you break yourself of it?"

"Because it's—" Molly was about to say it was unlady-like, but as the words formed in her mind, she heard the echo of Rodney's voice. *"Don't ever laugh like that in front of my friends again. It's humiliating to have your wife snort in public like some fat, old sow."* "My husband found it annoying, and I just broke myself of it, is all."

He frowned slightly. Then he shrugged. "Each to his own, I reckon. I happen to think it's a very cute laugh."

"You think the way I snort when I laugh is *cute?*"

"It's more a feminine snicker than a snort."

He drew her between two trees, then around a thatch of sage. Watching him from the corner of her eye, she admired the easy way he moved, his shoulders shifting slightly with each swing of his lean hips. He was sure-footed, the heels of his boots connecting solidly with the ground each time he stepped.

"What really bugs me is phony-sounding laughter," he said, picking up the thread of their conversation. "I hate it when women shriek really loud when they laugh. The sound sends shudders up my spine after a few minutes."

Molly had heard women laugh that way and knew exactly what he meant. "Well, rest easy. I never shriek."

He slid her a sidelong glance. "Never? Some men might take that as a challenge."

She flashed him a startled look. The suggestive gleam in his eyes turned her brains to mush. Unable to come up with a response, she decided to pretend the comment had gone straight over her head. She sighed and glanced around them. "Oh, *look*! What lovely flowers."

He led her to the deep pink blooms. "These are early maiden pinks," he said as he bent to snap a stem. When he straightened, he tugged on her hand to pull her closer and held the blossom to her cheek. "Just as I thought," he said huskily. "Pink doesn't clash with your hair." He tucked the flower stem behind her ear. "You'd look beautiful in it."

"I've found that neutral shades go better with my complexion."

"Neutral meaning shades of white, brown, and beige?" He drew her back into a walk. "You have a complexion like cream, lady. You could wear any color. I think you've got the prettiest skin I've ever laid eyes on."

Molly decided it was time to put a stop to this compliment business before she did something totally stupid, like start believing him. "Jake, I really think—"

"I'll be damned. Let me clean my ears out. Did you just call me Jake?"

She released another sigh. "About the 'pretty' business."

"What about it?"

"You're very kind, but I don't feel comfortable with your paying me compliments constantly."

"I haven't done it constantly. A few times, at most."

"It's just that I'd rather you didn't."

"Why? If it's because I'm your boss, that's really not fair. I do have eyes in my head, and it's a little hard not to notice what's right in front of my nose. It's not as if I've let it interfere with our working relationship."

"I never meant to imply that you had."

"Then what's wrong with me saying you're pretty?"

Molly pressed her lips together, trying to think how she might explain. "It has nothing to do with your being my employer. *Nothing.* It's just that I know you're only being nice, and I find it more embarrassing than flattering."

Silence. They covered several more feet of ground before he finally spoke. "You think I'm only being nice?"

She wished now that she hadn't said anything.

In a gravelly voice, he asked, "Who told you that you aren't pretty, Molly?"

"It wasn't necessary for anyone to tell me. I look in the mirror on a daily basis."

"You must not look very hard. You're a beautiful woman, and I'm not the only man on this ranch who thinks so."

She rolled her eyes. "Oh, please."

"You don't believe me."

"Of course I don't. You're either very kind or very blind. I know I'm not much in the looks department."

"Not *much*?"

He suddenly stopped walking. With her hand enfolded in his, Molly was jerked to a stop when she reached the length of her arm. Startled, she swung around to look at him, her snake stick held aloft in her free hand.

"You going to hit me with that?" he asked softly.

"Good grief, no." She lowered the branch. "Why would I do that?"

"Because I'm going to do this."

He tugged hard on her hand. Molly wasn't expecting to be jerked off balance, and she tumbled against his chest. He locked his strong arms around her and dipped his head. The next instant, he was kissing her. He didn't ask; he just took, his wonderfully firm, mobile mouth staking claim.

It was—*oh, God*—it was—she couldn't think clearly. Her heart turned a somersault, her nerves leaped, and her legs went watery.

His mouth was hard and moist and hot and hungry. He grasped the underside of her jaw, pressed in at the joints, and forced her teeth apart. Then he plunged deeply with his tongue, tasting her as if she were a culinary delight and he was a starving man.

Molly tried to breathe, couldn't. Tried again to collect her thoughts, and had no luck with that, either. His chest grazed her breasts, and her nipples went instantly achy and taut, eliciting a moan from deep within her.

"Sweet Christ," he whispered when he dragged his mouth from hers to grab for air. His eyes were molten on hers, his breath, scented with coffee, wafting over her face. "Where's your stick? I think you better whack me with it before I take this any further."

Molly had no idea where her stick had gotten off to. As for taking this any further, it was complete and utter madness. She intended to tell him exactly that, but all she managed to get out was a bleep before his lips settled over hers again. This time, he closed his hand over her braid to tip her head back and hold her still. Then, with a deft twist of his fingers, he stripped the elastic band from her hair, loosening the tresses and gathering them in his fist.

"You're *beautiful*," he whispered fiercely against her lips. After kissing her until every rational thought in her head went flying again, he intensified the assault by bending his knees to bring his pelvis hard against hers.

She moaned into his mouth. Her legs would no longer hold her up. He angled an arm under her rump and drew her hard against him. She could feel his arousal, pressing in where she was most sensitive, the upward drag of denim and man sending jolts of pure pleasure zigzagging through her.

In all her life, she'd never wanted anything like he made her want him. It came over Molly like a landslide, crushing the breath from her, making her mind spiral wildly. She wanted his hands on her, his mouth at her breasts with the same hungry urgency with which he now took her lips. Oh, how she *wanted*.

She ran her hands over his shoulders, glorying in the pads of vibrant muscle and flesh that rippled under his shirt. She dug in hard with her fingers to resist her urge to tear at the chambray to feel his bare skin. *Jake, with the laser-blue eyes.* She couldn't believe he was kissing her. Things like this never happened to Molly Sterling Wells.

No man had ever jerked her into his arms and devoured her mouth.

No man had ever run his hands over her back and up her sides to feverishly touch her breasts.

When he thumbed her nipples through the layers of her clothing, the shock of each pass made her whimper.

He abandoned her mouth to trail kisses down the column of her throat, his teeth and tongue doing wonderful things to her skin, making it go hot and cold at once. Between her legs, she was wet, the folds of her flesh throbbing, her opening quivering in grasping spasms for the hardness that ground against her.

She *wanted* him.

As if the sheer force of her yearning was transmitted to him through the pores of her skin, he suddenly tightened his arms and lifted her off her feet. Startled, Molly cried out and clung to him as he moved to a tree. Pressing her back to the trunk, he sandwiched her between his hard body and the rough bark, his hungry, persuasive mouth trailing kisses down her neck.

"Molly," he whispered, "put your legs around my hips."

She sobbed, driven by a tidal wave of yearning to do as he told her. When she locked her thighs around him, he pushed her higher against the tree. Dimly Molly realized that he was supporting her weight with the press of his lower body. He put his now unencumbered hands to quick use, cupping her breasts in his hard palms and shoving upward until her tight nipples thrust turgidly against her clothing, becoming easy targets for his mouth.

He caught one hard tip between his teeth, nipping lightly and tugging. A shock of sheer delight zigzagged through her, and she cried out, her clutching hands knocking aside his hat and threading through his thick hair. He responded by drawing her nipple, clothing and all, into his hot mouth.

The sharp pull shattered Molly, the sensations making her muscles quiver and jerk as though she were a marionette on strings. She tightened her fists in his hair and felt as if she were melting in the rush. "Jake?"

He moved up to kiss her eyes closed, his deep voice pitched to a soothing whisper, his silken lips tracing the arch of her brows. "Dear God, you are so beautiful, Molly. If you ask me to stop, I will. But please don't. Please don't."

She felt his clever hands unfastening the buttons of her top, felt his work-roughened fingertips separating the placket.

Dapples of sunshine played warmly over her face and upper chest, a sharp contrast to the cool caress of the morning air. She stiffened, feeling suddenly self-conscious because she knew he was about to bare her breasts and would be able to see every flaw in the unforgiving brightness.

"Cow teats," Rodney had called them.

Even now, the memory made Molly cringe. Her eyes snapped open, her blood running cold as she stared at Jake. Sunlight glanced off his thick, sable hair and played over his strong jaw. He was so handsome, far better looking than Rodney in every way. *Oh, God.* What was she thinking? If she wasn't good enough for Rodney, how could she hope to measure up to Jake's expectations?

She imagined the look that would come over his dark face when he saw her saggy breasts and white, flabby thighs. An awful, chilling shame swept through her, and she knew she couldn't go through with this.

Couldn't, absolutely couldn't.

Just as he was about to tug her breasts free from the cups of the bra, she grabbed the front plackets of her top and jerked them together. Startled by her sudden resistance, he flicked a passion-hot gaze to hers, his features taut.

"What is it?" he whispered.

Holding tightly to her blouse, Molly let her head fall back. "I—I don't—want to do this. I don't know what came over me. I really don't want to do this."

She could feel his gaze on her face and knew he expected more of an explanation. What was she supposed to say, that she was embarrassed for him to see her, afraid he would turn away in disgust as Rodney had countless times?

Scalding tears burned at the backs of her eyes. "I'm sorry, Jake. So sorry. If you think I'm a tease and hate me, I won't blame you. But I—just can't do this. I'm sorry."

She felt the tension go out of him. She half expected him to step back from the tree and let her fall. If he had, she wouldn't have blamed him. A mature woman didn't lead a man on and then, for no apparent reason, turn him off cold. It was cruel and inexcusable.

Instead of jerking away and letting her fall, Jake continued to hold her against the tree trunk with the press of his hips. She heard him grab a deep, ragged breath, then *whoosh* like a blowing whale.

"I'm sorry," she repeated shakily.

He took several more breaths. Then he cupped her face in his hands and forced her to look at him. His eyes were the color of molten steel, their usual clear blue now cloudy with turbulence. He looked furiously angry, but Molly knew by the gentle press of his fingers on her skin that, for reasons beyond her, his rage wasn't directed at her.

"Don't apologize," he whispered, his voice gravelly. "What have you done to be sorry for?"

"I shouldn't have let things go this far."

He chuckled and pressed his forehead against hers, his eyes and dark features blurring in her vision. "I don't think you were entirely responsible for that." He straightened to let her slide down the tree. When her feet connected with the ground, the heels of her canvas sneakers were angled up onto the gnarl of a root, giving her added height and putting her face closer to his. "As I recall," he went on, "I was the one who jumped you, not the other way around."

Molly tried to return his smile, but her trembling mouth refused to cooperate. He murmured something unintelligible and dipped his head to nibble lightly at her bottom lip, his thumbs tracing her cheekbones. With the first brush of his firm, silken lips over hers, she lost her ability to think clearly again and abandoned her hold on her blouse to make tight fists on his shirt.

"Dear God," he whispered. "I've never felt like this. What's going on here?"

Molly didn't know what was going on with him, but she felt fairly sure she had lost her mind. When he drew away, the smoldering heat in his eyes left her in no doubt that he felt the same way, which struck her as being even more incredible. He *wanted* her? She was so tempted to ask him why. What could a man as handsome as Jake Coulter possibly see in someone like her?

"I think I'd better walk you back now," he informed her huskily as he bent to retrieve his hat. "Otherwise I may break my own cardinal rule."

"What's that?"

He dusted the Stetson on his pant leg, then positioned it just so on his dark head, his eyes twinkling as he regarded her. "Thinking no means maybe."

He moved back to her, his gaze dropping to her still unbuttoned blouse. When he reached toward her, Molly pushed his hands away. "I can do it," she insisted.

He watched her fumble with the buttons for a moment, then he reached to lend assistance. "I undid them. I guess I can help put you back together."

Molly was trembling so badly that she finally gave up and allowed him to finish the job. Her nerves leaped with every brush of his knuckles against her chest, and her breasts ached for him to touch them again. She swallowed, hard, doing her best to avoid looking at him.

His hands stilled on the last button. "Molly?"

He said her name softly, but his tone was no less compelling for all that. She glanced up. The instant their gazes met, she knew she couldn't have looked away if her life depended on it. The tenderness she saw in his eyes nearly brought tears to her own.

"You're beautiful," he told her softly. "From the top of your head, to the tips of your toes, you are absolutely beautiful, and if anyone ever told you differently, he was a damned liar."

Chapter Twelve

Hank was still in the stable when Jake returned from the woods. A quarter horse mare was about to foal, and Hank had volunteered to stay close all day to watch her.

"How's White Star doing?" Jake asked.

"Pretty good." Hank closed the gate of the foaling stall farther up the aisle, then came to join Jake at the front doors. "She's dropped a little more. To be on the safe side, I just rewrapped her tail. She hasn't passed the cervical plug yet, though. My guess is, it'll be another day or so."

"Is she feeling pretty restless?"

Hank nodded.

"That's always a sign. We'd best continue to keep an eye on her. We don't want her to surprise us."

"How'd it go with Molly?" Hank asked.

"It didn't."

"What do you mean, it didn't? You talked to her, right?"

"No." Jake hooked his arms over the gate of a front stall and gazed somberly at the buckskin mare within the enclosure. "I just couldn't do it, Hank."

Hank came to stand by him. After getting settled, he asked, "What happened?"

Jake rubbed a hand over his face and blinked. More had happened out there than he'd ever intended. "The minute she saw me, she started trying to guess what I'd come out there to jump her about." He glanced at his brother. "I think her ex-husband did a four-deck shuffle with her self-esteem. It's damned near nonexistent. I couldn't bring myself to deal it another blow."

Hank's mouth tightened.

"What am I going to do? I know I need to talk to her, but when I try, I think of the paper towels, folded all pretty, and about her chasing Bart around the kitchen with the toothbrush."

Hank smiled ruefully. "I was more impressed with the strawberry flowers on my see-through pancakes. *Those* took time and effort."

"You're a big help."

Hank chuckled. "I was just trying to commiserate." His amusement faded, and he chafed his palms. "I know what you're saying, Jake. She may not be hitting the mark, but she's no slacker. She's worked her fanny off. Have you found little sacks of perfume stuff in any of your drawers yet?"

Jake tugged up the neck of his T-shirt to give it a sniff. "No wonder I smell like a French whore. I thought it was the laundry soap or something."

"Nope. Bart's not her only victim. She's making us all smell pretty."

"I don't guess that'll kill us." Jake's voice went oddly thick and scratchy. "To criticize her performance when she's trying so hard—I don't know—when I look into those big brown eyes, I just can't do it."

Hank rotated his shoulders and then resettled his weight against the gate. "Maybe you need to try a totally different tack."

"Like what?"

"Instead of criticizing her cooking, how's about if we just pitch in and show her how we'd like it done?"

"That'd be the same as saying she can't cook for shit."

"No, it wouldn't. We like most of what she fixes. There's just not enough of it. The trick here is to be subtle. Just go in before mealtimes and say you want to show her how to fix some ranch-style dishes that all of us particularly like. She's a quick study. She'll notice how much more you cook. One problem solved. And she'll learn how to fix a few new things, like pan gravy and country biscuits." Hank warmed to his subject. "I can catch her before she fixes lunches a couple of mornings. Say I've got some slack time and want to help."

"Slack time at five in the morning?"

"She may be a little suspicious, but that's better than openly criticizing her."

"Do you really think helping her in the kitchen is the way to go?"

Hank nodded. "She hasn't been packing us nearly enough lunch. I'll just grab the real mayonnaise and make each of us four sandwiches instead of two. She'll notice the increase, and when the coolers come back empty, she'll realize we need more food. It'd also help if you could take her grocery shopping at least once. If I have to eat another health-food corn chip, I'm going to barf."

Jake considered the suggestion for a moment. "You know, it just might work."

"It *will* work if you handle it right," Hank assured him.

Jake passed a hand over his eyes. Then he nodded. "All right. I'll try it. It'll mean taking time out of my day to work in the kitchen with her, though."

"Like anybody will bitch? We can all take on some extra chores for a few days and cover for you. Anything to get more food."

Jake felt as if a thousand pounds had been lifted off his shoulders. At least one of his problems with Molly was on its way to being solved.

Hank shifted his stance to look Jake full in the face. "Something else is worrying you. You going to tell me what?"

Jake tensed. "What makes you think something else is wrong?"

Hank searched Jake's eyes. "Come on, Jake. We're brothers. You can't bullshit me."

Jake glanced away. "It's personal."

"You're downright sick about something. If you can't talk to me, who the hell can you talk to?"

"No one," Jake replied gruffly.

"Ah, so it's about Molly. Never let it be said that you're a man to kiss and tell. Is that it?"

Jake shot his brother a warning glare and straightened away from the gate. Without another word, he turned and left the stable. There were some things he simply couldn't share, not even with his brother. Secrets of the heart were personal things, and Molly's belief that she was ugly was exactly that, a secret of the heart.

Jake decided to put the problem with Molly on a back burner and just let it simmer for a few days. He needed time to think. She needed time to get over their encounter in the woods. It seemed best, all the way around, to back off and see how things cooked up when he wasn't stirring the pot.

Good plan, bad situation. The minute he stepped into the kitchen that evening, Jake knew it wouldn't work. Molly took one look at him and turned an alarming shade of vermilion.

Jake hoped it was a passing thing. He sat down to eat, doing what he thought was a credible job of pretending nothing was wrong. Molly took her usual place at the opposite end of the table and proceeded to ignore him in a very *loud* way.

"So, boss, how'd it go today?" someone asked to dispel the tension.

"Pretty good. How'd it go for you?"

Silence. Expecting a reply, Jake glanced up to find every head at the table turned toward Molly. Following the gazes of his men, he saw that his cook-cum-housekeeper was dishing a veritable mountain of rice onto her plate.

She suddenly froze, staring at the spoon in her hand as if she wasn't quite sure how it had gotten there. Then she shifted her gaze to the amount of rice she'd served herself, and her cheeks went pink again. She glanced up and saw everyone staring at her. The flush spread over her whole face, deepening by degrees to a brighter pink.

"I'm sorry. I was woolgathering," she explained in a taut, hushed voice. She started scooping rice off her plate back into the serving bowl. "My goodness. What on earth was I thinking?"

Jake knew exactly what she'd been thinking. Evidently his men realized something untoward had happened between him and Molly as well. Nine pairs of accusing eyes turned toward him. Despite the fact that they complained loudly behind Molly's back about the amount of food she prepared, they had all clearly come to care about her and were almost as protective of her as Jake was.

Not that he blamed them. She fussed over everyone like a little mother hen, a fact that was driven home to him as he glanced around the table. The sleeve of Shorty's shirt sported a neat line of stitches where she'd mended a rip. At her insistence, Levi wore a Band-Aid over one eyebrow to cover a small scratch he'd gotten while working with barbed wire. Tex smelled strongly of the wintergreen she rubbed on his shoulder each evening to ease the pain of his bursitis. Bill, who could rarely afford a barber because he paid so much in child support, had a tidy new haircut. In short, there wasn't a man in the group who hadn't been a recipient of her kindness in some way. Even the dog's life had improved since her arrival.

His mouth full of gooey rice, Jake struggled to swallow. After a moment, he chanced another glance at Molly. Head bowed over her plate again, she was hacking at a piece of chicken. Since she seldom ate meat, that was, in and of itself, an indication of how upset she was.

So much for putting the problem on a back burner.

He knew he had to talk to her. Some things could be let go, some things couldn't, and this obviously fell into the latter category.

Avoiding Jake's gaze, Molly flitted busily around him as they cleared the table and rinsed the dishes to put them in the machine. When addressed, she murmured a clipped reply, but no unnecessary exchanges took place.

"I can see myself home tonight," she informed him when the kitchen was in order. She stepped over to grab a flashlight lying on top of the side-by-side. Then, without so much as a backward glance, she left the kitchen, pausing just beyond the archway to fetch her parka. "It's really not that far, and I'm not worried about cougars anymore."

Jake guessed cougars had taken second seat to a greater danger, namely him. Following her to the coat rack, he got his Wrangler jacket. He left his Stetson hanging there. Some maneuvers were best executed while a man wasn't wearing a hat.

Molly gave him a startled look when she saw him donning his jacket. "I said I can see myself home."

"I heard you." Jake stepped over to help her with her parka. He felt her flinch when he ran his fingers under the collar to tug out her braid. "What you can do and what you're *going* to do are two different things."

Before Jake could say more, she was off, making a beeline through the great room for the front door. Once on the porch with the door closed behind them, she turned to confront him. Lifting her small chin to a defiant angle, she fixed him with big eyes that shimmered in the moonlight that slanted in under the porch overhang.

"Molly, I know you're very upset with me," he tried. "Can we talk?"

"I'm not upset with you," she said, her voice quivering. "I'm upset with myself. There's a big difference."

"Why are you upset with yourself?"

She flipped on the flashlight. "I really don't want to discuss it, Jake. I'd like to pretend this morning never happened."

He thought he glimpsed tears in her eyes just before she whirled away to descend the steps. Jake gazed after her for a moment. If the erratic bob of her flashlight beam was any indication, this was going to get worse before it got better. He sighed, shoved his hands into his pockets, and went down the steps three at a time. When he hit level ground, he kicked into high gear, lengthening his strides to catch up with her.

When she heard his footsteps coming up behind her, she spun around. This time, when she spoke, her voice went from quivery to downright tremulous, every intonation shrill. Jake knew by the sound that she was trying to hold back tears and going to lose the battle.

"Would you leave me *alone*?" she cried.

"I think we need to talk."

"We do not need to talk. To what end? So you can try to convince me I'm beautiful and make me feel less ridiculous?"

"Ridiculous? *Why?* I'm the one who started it, not you. If anyone should feel ridiculous, it's me."

The flashlight beam cut a wide arc around her feet as she swung her arm back and forth against her leg. "I don't want to talk about this. Right now, I don't even want you *near* me. Can't you see that?"

He could see it, all right. The question was, why? The panic in her eyes told him that flight might be her next course of action. They had to get this settled between them. If he left it until morning, she might be gone.

"Why don't you want me near you?" he asked. "Can you tell me that?"

"It's obvious, isn't it?"

"Ah, Molly," he said hoarsely, "what in God's name has he done to you?"

Her chin came back up, only a slight quiver of her lower lip giving her away. Her eyes were huge splotches of moon-touched amber in her face, and all Jake could see in their depths now was pain. Pain that ran so deep, it went beyond tears.

He took a step toward her, wanting nothing more than to gather her up in his arms.

"Don't!" she said.

"Don't what?"

"Just *don't*," she said again. "I know you feel badly, and it's very sweet of you to want to make me feel better. But that will only make it worse."

"What?"

She made a low sound of frustration and squeezed her eyes closed. "What's your game, Jake? Whatever it is, I don't want to play."

"I'm not playing a game, Molly. Why would you even think that I am?"

She fixed him with an accusing glare. "Because this doesn't make an iota of sense, that's why. We're both mature adults. Can't we simply move past this and forget it happened?"

"But it did happen."

"Yes, unfortunately." She sighed and tipped her head back to stare at the sky. "You know what I think the problem is? You're too nice for your own good, and mine as well."

"Thank you for that much, at least."

She laughed softly, the sound totally lacking in humor and laced with bitterness. "Misguided, but nice."

"Ouch."

She sighed and met his gaze. "I'm sorry, but it's true. You shouldn't go around kissing women to make them feel good. It's dangerous."

"Ah, I see. I should kiss women to make them feel bad?"

She rolled her eyes. "Don't be deliberately obtuse."

"Ouch, again." Jake bent his head and rubbed his jaw. "Molly, I think we need to back up and clarify why I kissed you to start with."

"What's to clarify? You paid me a compliment, I didn't believe you, and in some misguided desire to make me feel pretty, you kissed me to drive home the point. Unfortunately for you—and for me—it backfired. You found yourself being attacked by a horny divorcee, you didn't want to hurt my feelings by pulling away, and things got out of hand." She sighed and drew an arm from around her waist to push at a tendril of hair that had escaped her braid. "Thank God I came to my senses."

Jake was beginning to wish now that she hadn't. They might have avoided this if only she had let passion run its course. She wouldn't be hunching her shoulders to hide those gorgeous breasts right now, that was for damned sure.

"For the record," she went on, "I don't blame you for any of it. I know men are easily aroused, especially if they've been working hard like you have for months on end and neglecting their physical needs. I was all over you. There was friction between our bodies. You couldn't control your physical response to that, and it went downhill from there. It was just—" She broke off and shrugged. "It was an unfortunate mess, is what it was. I'm very sorry it happened, and now I just want to forget that it did."

"So you have it all figured out, do you?"

She avoided looking at him. "Mostly. Your following me out here is a little baffling. I'm afraid you've got some harebrained notion that you can kiss me again and make it all better. Not a good plan."

"Why not?"

"Because you're—" She sighed and waved a hand as if to erase the bad start. "Never mind."

"Because I'm what?" he pressed. "I hate half-finished sentences."

"Too attractive," she muttered.

"Pardon?"

"You heard me."

"You find me attractive, Molly?"

She narrowed her eyes. "No, I think you're a real dog.

What exactly do you think this morning was about? Do you think I react like that to every man who kisses me?"

Jake folded his arms to keep from touching her. "I hope to God not. I'm the possessive type."

She rolled her eyes again. Then she turned and struck off, calling, "I'm going home now, end of discussion."

Jake set off after her. As he drew abreast, he said, "I've let you have your say. It's only fair that you let me have mine."

"Talk fast. When I reach my door, I'm going inside, and you're not invited."

Jake reached out to grasp her arm and slow her pace. "First of all, I don't kiss women to be nice. I never have, I never will, and I didn't today. I kissed you because I've been wanting to ever since I first met you."

"Oh, *brother.*"

"I didn't interrupt you with sarcastic asides. Don't interrupt me." He drew her to a stop and turned to study her pinched face. "Secondly, I resent the implication that I am so easily aroused and so sexually deprived that any warm body will do."

She threw him a startled look. "I never meant it like that."

"It's a damned good thing because I don't sleep with just anyone."

"Oh."

"Contrary to the belief of some, not all men's decisions are made for them by what's behind their fly. Good Christ." He hooked a thumb toward the woods. "I don't know what the hell happened out there. Spontaneous combustion might best describe it. I only meant to kiss you, and the first thing I knew, I had you up against a tree."

"Don't remind me."

"How do you think that makes me feel? I generally try to treat women with respect. I've only known you for a little over a week, and there I was, going for it. And in broad daylight, no less."

"Must you give me a blow-by-blow replay? It wasn't one of my finer moments, either."

He ignored that. "I have nothing against nature and daylight. Don't get me wrong. But we were no more than a stone's throw from the house."

She cupped a hand over her eyes. "Oh, *God*."

"Anybody could have come along, and there we would have been."

She groaned again.

"I totally lost it."

"Me, too," she said faintly. "I'm so sorry. It was my fault."

"Your fault?" He nudged her hand from her eyes, caught her by the shoulders, and leaned down to put his face before hers. "It wasn't anybody's fault, Molly. It just *happened*. You're a beautiful lady, and you're one sweet armful. I've never been hit so hard and so fast by a kiss in my life."

"There you go again."

"There I go with what again?"

"Saying I'm pretty. You really need to stop doing that."

"Why? You afraid you may start believing me? Why not? You believed Rodney."

"Let's leave Rodney out of this."

"We can't leave him out of this. It's his lies that are causing us problems right now." She started to speak, and Jake laid a finger across her mouth to silence her. "Molly, do you trust me?"

She wrinkled her nose.

"Forget about what happened this morning," he urged. "Before then, did you trust me?"

"I'm here, aren't I?" she said against his fingertip. "If I didn't trust you, I'd be long gone."

"Good. Then will you give me fifteen minutes?"

She blinked and peered up at him owlishly. "To do what?"

"I want to introduce you to someone."

"To whom?"

"It's a surprise. Will you give me the fifteen minutes?"

"I suppose," she said hesitantly. "But only if you promise to behave yourself."

Jake turned her toward the cabin, taking a firm grasp on her arm to draw her along. Flashlight beam bobbing in front of her, she cast him a bewildered look. "I thought you were going to introduce me to someone."

"I am."

They reached the porch, and Jake hustled her up the steps as fast as her shorter legs would allow. He shouldered open the door, reached inside to flip on the lamp, and nudged her into the cabin ahead of him. After closing the door, he glanced at his watch and then shoved it under her nose so she could see the time.

"Fifteen minutes," he repeated, "and your complete trust. I promise you won't regret this."

"I'm already regretting it," she said when he grabbed her arm again to guide her toward the bathroom. "What are you doing? There's no one in there for me to meet."

He pushed her ahead of him into the dark enclosure. "There is now." He flipped on the overhead light. Blinded by the brightness, she narrowed her eyes to see. Before her vision completely cleared, he had her standing before the mirror and was unfastening her braid. When she reached to stop him, he stiffened his arms against her and said, "Trust. Remember?" After loosening her plaited tresses, he said, "Stand right there. Don't move."

"You're making me very nervous."

Jake jerked open the door of the small linen closet. Inside were towels that he'd left at the cabin for guests. He bypassed all those at the top to tug a pink one from the bottom of the stack. Next he fished through the toiletries lying on the shelf above, locating a brush with strands of whiskey-colored hair caught in the stiff bristles.

As he stepped up behind her, he smiled at her in the mirror. "I don't mean to make you nervous. Just bear with me a second. All right?"

Setting the towel on the edge of the sink, he dispensed with the flashlight, then drew off her parka and tossed it aside. That accomplished, he began brushing her hair. It felt like silk as it ran through his fingers, the curls clinging to his hands, exhibiting far more friendliness than their owner ever had. He caught her bewildered expression in the glass.

"There's a method to my madness."

Her eyes darkened as she stared at her reflection. "I can't do this," she said shakily. "I really can't do this."

Jake heard the note of panic in her voice. He sharpened his gaze on her face, which had drained of color. Perspiration glistened on her forehead.

Then he looked into her eyes. Never in his life had he seen anyone who looked so hopelessly lost. His hands stilled. Where his wrists rested against her shoulders, he felt the shallow, rapid pace of her breathing. "Molly?" he whispered. He glanced down and saw that she was gripping the edge of the sink with such force that her knuckles had gone white. "Sweetheart? What's wrong?"

He felt a shudder move through her body. Her frightened gaze sought his in the mirror. "I can't do this. I know it's stupid, but—" She broke off and squeezed her eyes closed. "I just can't, is all."

Jake set the brush aside and gripped her firmly by the shoulders. "What's stupid?"

"Nothing," she said faintly.

"Molly, tell me," he urged.

"You'll think I'm crazy."

He ran his thumbs in a circular massage over the knotted muscles in her shoulders. "No, I won't. I swear. Tell me."

"It's just—" Her face twisted, and she dragged in a shaky breath. "When I look in the mirror, I can't find myself anymore. The person in the glass—she's someone I don't know."

Jake rested his cheek atop her head. Pain twisted through his chest, hurting so much it almost took his breath. "Is that all?" He forced himself to chuckle. "Honey, we all feel that way sometimes. It's natural."

"This is different," she insisted. "I'm empty inside. The person I used to be isn't there anymore."

Jake sighed and slipped his arms around her waist. The fact that she didn't try to pull away told him how very upset she was. "That isn't so," he assured her. "You're in there, honey. Trust me on that. You're just feeling lost and confused right now." He studied her pale reflection, smiling slightly as he took in each lovely angle of her face. In that moment, he realized that every feature had been indelibly engraved on his heart. "I see who you are all the time, in countless little ways, and so does everyone else. You've got the kindest heart of anyone I know. If you don't believe me, just ask Bart. He's never had it so good. Or get Sunset's opinion. He can tell you a few things about yourself, namely that you've got more courage in your little finger than most people do in their entire body."

Her lashes lifted, and she fixed him with a question-filled gaze. "I'm not courageous."

"You rescued that stallion and broke the law to do it. Trust me, honey, that's courageous."

"I had no choice. Sunset could have ended up dead."

"A lot of people wouldn't have cared, not so much they would have been willing to put their bacon on the plate. No matter how you circle it, that took guts."

Faint touches of color rose to her cheeks. Jake smiled at her in the glass. Bending down to put his face beside hers, he whispered, "All your fine inner qualities aside, I'd like you to see the Molly I do. I don't think you've really looked at her before. Or it's been a very long time since you did." He caught her chin on the crook of his finger and lifted her face to the light. "Feature by feature, I want you to really look, Molly. Forget everything anyone else ever said to you and really *look*."

Her gaze shifted to her own face.

"You have the most beautiful hair I've ever seen." He lifted a mass of curls on his palm and turned them to catch the light. "Just look at how they shimmer. Have you ever held a glass of Scotch up to a flame? Your hair is like that—the color of whiskey shot through with firelight." He kept turning his wrist until she joined him in staring at the play of light on her hair. "*That* is beautiful, Molly. Don't you agree?"

Her throat worked as she swallowed. "The way you're moving it in the light makes it look pretty," she conceded.

"This is nothing compared to how it catches the light when you wear it loose and you move your head. It's like looking at swirls of liquid fire."

He let her hair slip from his palm and resumed studying her face. "Now your eyes," he said with a grin. "Just look at those eyes."

She did as he suggested.

"They're almost exactly the color of your hair, and they sparkle so pretty. From the moment we met, they captivated me. That was the first thing I noticed about you, your beautiful eyes."

Those eyes filled with bewilderment now. "You noticed my eyes?"

"I definitely noticed. Even with no liner or shadow to make them stand out, they're heart grabbers."

A flush touched her cheeks. "This is silly."

Jake glanced at his watch. "I've got ten minutes left to be silly." He turned her face slightly. "Now the nose." He couldn't help but smile when he looked at it. "It's small and perfectly straight, except for right at the tip where it turns up just slightly. How could anyone find fault with a nose like that? Mine is twice that large and crooked to boot."

"It isn't crooked."

He grinned and narrowed an eye at her. "We'll argue that point later. For now, we'll move on from that perfect nose to those sculpted cheekbones." He ran a finger along the hollow of her cheek. "I've heard that movie stars get their back molars yanked out to achieve that look."

"You're kidding."

"Would I lie to you?" He ran his thumb over her bottom lip. "And look at that mouth, would you? Not a trace of lipstick, and it's such a pretty pink. That second night after I met you, I wanted to steal a kiss so damned bad I ached."

"You did?"

He chuckled. "I'm damned glad now that I didn't. I got myself in enough trouble this morning."

She bent her head, her dark lashes feathering over her cheeks like spider etchings. "It's not just my face, Jake. It's the rest of me."

"I'm getting to that."

She threw him an appalled look. "Oh, no, you're not."

He winked at her. "No bare body parts, I swear. I just want to show you something."

"What?"

He reached around her to unbutton her blouse. She grabbed his wrists. "You said no bare parts."

"And I'm a man of my word. Relax." He unfastened the second button, then a third and fourth. "I just want to tuck your collar under and open the front."

"That's baring parts."

"Then I see bare parts downtown all the time," he challenged. "Women wear tops cut this low every day."

"They aren't me."

"No, but they probably wish they were." He directed a pointed glance at the bountiful display of cleavage above the V of her blouse. "Your breasts are beautiful, Molly."

"They're big and floppy," she informed him in a faint voice.

"Flop them my way and see what happens." He draped

the towel over her chest to form a scoop neckline. "There,"
he whispered. "Get a load of that."

She looked up and went still. Jake smiled. "Where's the
clash?" he asked. "Pink is your color, lady. Just look at
how it makes your skin glow." He trailed a fingertip along
the edge of the towel, acutely aware of the way she shivered at his touch. "If that isn't flawless, nothing is," he said
huskily. "And the pink strikes a perfect contrast—putting
me in mind of raspberries and cream."

He drew away the towel and let it drop into the sink.
Then he settled his hands at her waist. Smiling at her over
the top of her curly head, he said, "Molly, meet Molly, one
of the prettiest ladies I've ever clapped eyes on."

Another flush crept up her neck to pool in her cheeks.
Jake met her gaze in the mirror. "There isn't an unmarried
man in my acquaintance who could have resisted kissing
you this morning. I guess maybe I should apologize for letting it get out of hand, but I'm not going to. I'll do it again
if I get half a chance, so consider yourself warned."

She lowered her gaze to stare at the faucet.

Jake checked his watch. "I've got seven minutes left.
Since I asked you to trust me, I'll behave myself, and I
won't kiss you again tonight. I am going to take liberty
with words, though, and tell you a couple of things that are
probably going to embarrass you and make you hate me
just a little. But they're things you need to hear, so I'll take
my chances."

He braced his hands on the edge of the vanity and
leaned down to smell her hair. The scent of shampoo and
soap and Molly filled his head, making him feel a little
dizzy.

"You have *gorgeous* breasts." He felt her stiffen. "I'll
say that again. You have gorgeous, perfect breasts."

"You haven't seen them," she whispered tautly and
tried to slip out from between his body and the vanity.

Jake blocked her way with his braced arm. "You're not
going anywhere, Molly. Not until I've finished."

Her expression pinched, she met his gaze in the mirror. "Don't do this."

"Don't do what? I'm only telling you the truth. Granted, maybe it's not a subject for polite conversation, but we went beyond polite when I had you pressed up against that tree this morning. At which point, I might add, I held your breasts in my hands and kissed them through your blouse." He winked at her again. "You can tell yourself that I really don't know what's under the clothing. I beg to correct you. I have the touch."

"The what?"

"The touch." He lifted his hand to rub his fingers and thumb together. "These hands know gorgeous breasts when they feel them." He studied her face for a moment. "I'd venture a guess that it was good old Rodney who told you that your body is less than perfect."

She glanced quickly away.

"I thought so." Jake gripped down hard on the edge of the vanity. "I've never met the man. But I've only to look at what he did to his horse and wife to know that he's a pissant."

She threw him another startled look, which he answered with a grin.

"A *lying* pissant," he revised. "You're a short, sweetly rounded lady. You want to know my take on Rodney? I think he's a limp-dick excuse for a man, an even poorer excuse for a husband, and an all around lying bastard, if you'll excuse my French. He didn't want his wife to read historical romances because it might give her unrealistic expectations. *Hello?* That screams inferiority complex to me. I think he did his damnedest to make you feel ugly because it gave him more control. He was probably afraid you'd discover what a loser you were married to and trade him in for a better model."

Jake pushed erect.

"If I had been him, I would have been reading your books every time you laid them down to see how I could improve my skills and please you. Second warning of the night." He moved to the doorway. "I bought a couple."

She turned from the sink. "You bought a couple of what?"

Jake looked her dead in the eye. "Historical romances. I'm three-quarters through the first one." He flashed her a slow grin. "All I can say is, I like the way your mind works."

Chapter Thirteen

After Jake left, Molly turned back to regard her reflection in the mirror. Touching a hand to her hair, she stared at the masses of uncontrollable curls, which she'd never liked and had grown to hate after she married Rodney. Now, after listening to Jake wax poetic about how glorious her hair was, she wondered if she should start wearing it loose. Maybe he was right, and it was one of her best features, not one of her worst.

Gathering up the towel he'd dropped in the sink, she draped it across her chest again and studied herself critically. Could it be that she really had been hiding her light under a bushel for a decade? She'd always loved the color pink, but Rodney had convinced her it made her complexion look ruddy. Holding the terry close to her face, she leaned toward the glass and trailed a fingertip over her cheek. As hard as she tried, she could detect no increased reddish tones in her skin. Maybe Rodney had lied to her all those years, just as Jake insisted.

According to him, pink was her color. Though he hadn't come right out and said as much, she knew he wished she would stop wearing only neutral shades and become a bit more daring in her dress. A vision of herself in tight jeans and a figure-hugging, outrageous pink knit top spun through her mind. Just the *thought* of exposing her shape that way brought an embarrassed blush to her cheeks.

Reddish tones, she thought as she took in her heightened color. She had always flushed very easily—from ex-

ertion, heat, or embarrassment. Maybe her tendency to turn
red at the drop of a hat was what Rodney had been talking
about. She pressed even closer to the mirror to stare hard
at her skin. The pink in her cheeks didn't seem to clash or
look particularly ruddy against the towel. Did it? Jake had
likened the contrast to raspberries and cream.

Rodney—Jake. Jake—Rodney. Whom was she supposed to believe? Who was right, and who was wrong? As
she pondered the questions, an ache took up throbbing residence in her temples. She didn't know what to believe
anymore. Should she listen to Jake or continue as she had
been, dressing and wearing her hair the way Rodney had
suggested?

At the thought, the pain in her head became knifelike.
Dear God. It was absolutely true; she was still living her
life according to the guidelines Rodney had set down.
Every stitch of clothing in her closet had been selected
with his advice in mind. *"Loose, concealing garments and
neutral colors,"* he'd always preached. *"You don't have
the figure or the complexion to carry anything else off."*
Because of him, she wore no makeup, afraid of looking
like a trollop. Because of him, most of the time she wore
platform-soled shoes that she detested in an attempt to
look taller. She no longer even *laughed* naturally because
of him.

Was it any wonder she couldn't find herself when she
looked in a mirror? Molly pressed a hand to her throat as
an even more alarming revelation came to her. Now, instead of following Rodney's rules, she was seriously thinking about complying with Jake's.

Shaken, she sank down on the toilet, not knowing what
to think anymore. Only one thing seemed clear to her in
that moment. Ten years ago, she'd bent over backward,
trying to please Rodney, wearing the kinds of clothes that
he preferred, doing her hair the way he liked. Now, after
surviving a hellish marriage and coming out on the other

side, she was listening to another man and about to do the same thing all over again.

She knotted her hands into fists and pressed them hard against her knees. She was so tired, so sick to death *tired,* of being told what to do. If she wanted to shave her head and wear a bodysuit of bright purple spandex, it was nobody's business but hers. It no longer mattered what Rodney thought. And she wasn't about to start living her life according to Jake Coulter's dictates. She was single, almost thirty, and this was a free country. No one was going to tell her what to do, how to behave, or how to look.

From this moment forward, she was going to do what *she* wanted, to hell with everyone else.

Leaping to her feet, Molly spun to take in her reflection. *Hair.* That was all she saw. She had a small face, and it was barely visible in the cloud.

Trembling violently, she threw open the cupboard door and searched frantically for the scissors. When she found them, she whirled back to the sink, grabbed a hank of hair, and whacked it off about two inches from her scalp. *Snip, snip, snip.* As she sheared off the hated curls, she refused to assess the damage she was doing. She didn't care. *Snip, snip.* Take *that,* Jake Coulter. *Snip, snip.* She wasn't a stupid sheep, to be pushed and prodded and led around. Maybe she'd start wearing fire-engine red lipstick and gaudy earrings that dangled down past her shoulders. Why not?

When she ran out of curls to whack off, she felt limp with exhaustion. She let the scissors slip from her fingers and clatter into the sink with the towel and all her shorn locks. Almost afraid to look at herself, she forced her gaze to the mirror. The instant she saw her reflection, tears flooded her eyes.

Rodney hadn't lied. He'd been telling the absolute truth. She looked like Bozo the Clown.

*   *   *

"Molly's running late," Hank said grumpily.

Jake merely smiled as he poured himself a second cup of coffee. "Yeah, she is."

"She's never late," Hank pointed out. "Aren't you worried something's wrong?"

Jake chuckled. "She'll be along any time now."

"I was going to help her fix sandwiches."

Jake turned from the coffeepot. Lifting his steaming mug to his lips, he took a slow sip of brew, eyeing his brother over the porcelain rim. "We don't want to overwhelm her with too much the first morning. Why don't you go ahead with milking and gathering the eggs?"

"You going to help her fix breakfast?"

Jake nodded.

"What are you going to make?"

"A country-style breakfast with all the trimmings," Jake said.

"Biscuits from scratch?"

"Yes."

"Fried potatoes and pan gravy?"

Jake grinned. "Yes."

"Bacon and sausage and eggs?"

"Maybe even some ham as well," Jake assured him.

Hank looked as if he were about to drool. He went to the utility room for the egg basket and milk bucket.

As Molly left the cabin, her gaze was caught by something lying just over the threshold on the porch. She looked down and focused bewilderedly on a paperback novel and a nosegay of maiden pinks. She crouched down to stare. The delicate flowers were bound together at the stems with an old strip of leather.

Jake.

Tears stung Molly's eyes. Aside from her father, no man had ever given her flowers, not even her husband of ten years. Hand trembling, she picked up the nosegay and touched the blossoms to her nose, inhaling their delicate

scent. How *sweet*. She imagined Jake traipsing through the
woods in the predawn gloom to pick her a bouquet, and the
sting of tears in her eyes became a flood.

With her free hand, she swiped at her cheeks, disgusted
with herself for being so emotional. It was only a nosegay,
after all, and had cost him nothing. Women received gorgeous hothouse roses all the time and didn't weep all over
them.

Only somehow this nosegay with its smashed stems
held fast by a leather thong seemed far more special than a
delivery from a florist. Jake had invested a good chunk of
his time in the endeavor. Then he'd bound the stems and
made the delivery himself.

She'd never been the weepy type. Now, all of sudden,
her tear ducts seemed to be turning off and on at will. Fresh
tears sprang to her eyes, and no matter how fast she
blinked, she couldn't dispel them.

It was just so sweet of him. *Flowers*. Finding them here
brought back so many wonderful memories of her father.
He'd always left her surprises. *"Little I-love-yous,"* he'd
called them, and they'd often been flowers he'd picked
from the garden. Nothing expensive, really. She'd wake up
in the morning to find roses in a drinking glass on her
nightstand or a nosegay of pansies next to her cheek on the
pillow. It had been a lovely way to wake up and an even
lovelier way to start her day, knowing her dad cared about
her in a special way.

After she married, there had been no more sweet surprises on her pillow, only tear stains from where she'd lain
awake crying while she waited for her husband to come
home to her from the arms of another woman. She'd
yearned for Rodney to give her flowers, just once, but he
never had.

Remembering those times now, Molly knew that was
nine-tenths why she'd tried so hard to please him. She'd
been constantly competing with faceless rivals for his love,
and she'd fallen into the trap of thinking she was the one

at fault, that if she just tried hard enough, she might win his affection. She'd changed her appearance and altered her behavior in order to seem more sophisticated. Though it had happened slowly, she'd eventually changed herself so much that she could no longer recognize the person she had become.

Smiling sadly through her tears, Molly sniffed the maiden pinks again and then picked up the paperback. She wasn't surprised to see that it was a historical romance. She'd mentioned in passing that she'd once loved them, and in a very subtle way, Jake was calling her back to that, not to be the woman he wanted her to be, but to simply be herself again.

"Who are you now, Molly?" he'd asked her. At the time, she'd been so disturbed by the question that she'd resented him for asking it. In the days since, she'd often felt cornered and believed he was playing some vicious game, trying to seduce her, not because he really wanted her, but simply because she was there.

Now this.

She sighed and hugged the book to her heart, accepting now what she should have realized from the start. Jake Coulter was nothing like Rodney Wells. He was his antithesis in practically every way, the only similarity being that he was male.

Touching a hand to her hair, Molly wished now that she'd thought twice before cutting it. After ten endless years, a man had told her she was pretty, and instead of taking the compliment, she'd thrown it back in his face.

He was going to *hate* what she'd done to herself, and he'd probably be furious. By cutting off her hair, she'd told him she didn't value his opinion, plain and simple. He wasn't a stupid man. He'd get the message. Big problem. After finding the flowers and book, she wasn't sure that was the message she wanted to send.

* * *

Jake was wondering if Molly would be wearing her hair in that dreadful braid again this morning. On the one hand, he was reluctant to influence her too much. He had a feeling she'd gotten enough of that from her ex-husband to last her a lifetime. But another big part of him yearned to see her cut loose and be a free spirit for a change—to literally let her hair down and thumb her nose at the world.

He was imagining how she might look with all those fabulous curls falling in a riotous cascade to her shoulders when he heard her enter the house. He smiled smugly, keeping his back to the archway. The last thing he wanted was for her to think he was expecting her hair to be down. If by chance it was, the trick would be to act surprised. Then, after he collected himself, he'd shower her with compliments, pretending it had been all her idea.

"Hi," she said from behind him.

Her voice was shaky and faint. His smile deepened. He'd been around females enough to know when a woman was waiting on tenterhooks for a man's reaction to her appearance. Taking a last sip of coffee, he slowly turned, determined not to disappoint her.

The instant he saw her, he choked. Coffee went up his nose and down his windpipe. A harsh whistling sound erupted from his mouth. Molly's eyes went huge. She touched a hand to her hair, looking stricken.

"Jesus H. *Christ*," Jake rasped when he finally got his breath. "What the *hell* did you *do*?"

All the color drained from her face. Plucking at a short tendril of hair, she just stared at him, offering no explanation. Not that he needed one. He'd gone out of his way last night to tell her how gorgeous he thought her hair was, and now it was—*gone*. He'd been told to shove it a few times, but this took the prize.

Anger was his first reaction. Deep hurt quickly followed. And then he just felt stunned. She looked—*beautiful*. The short cap of amber curls feathered forward over her temples and cheeks, creating a perfect showcase for her delicate features. The cut was shaggy, and on someone else, it might have been unattractive, but the tousled, carefree style suited Molly perfectly, giving her a sassy look that was adorable.

Collecting himself, Jake set his mug of coffee on the counter and walked slowly toward her, barely able to take his eyes off her face. She shifted her feet, pushed self-consciously at her hair, and then dropped her chin as if she were ashamed to let him look at her.

"I'm sorry," she said faintly. "I know it was a dumb thing to do and that I look awful."

Jake slowly circled her. He really hated to be wrong, and he hated having to admit it even more. "Don't be silly. I think it's cute." He no sooner spoke than he wished he'd thought to use another word. Cute was sort of lukewarm. Gorgeous, on the other hand, would probably be suspect. What was a guy supposed to say? That it was darling? That was a feminine word, and he'd feel ridiculous. "I, um . . . " He came to stand in front of her. "It's perfect on you. Really. As pretty as I thought it was long, I like it this way even more."

She shoved at her hair again. The light glanced off the disturbed wisps of amber, making him want to touch them himself. "Right," she said. "There's no need to lie to save my feelings. I know it looks *awful.* Maybe I can go to a shop and get it evened up."

Jake liked it wispy and tousled. "Don't even think about it. No beautician on earth can improve on it."

She flashed him a miserable look. "It grows pretty fast. It'll be long again before I know it."

Jake laughed and caught her face between his hands. "I didn't mean that it's beyond repair, Molly. I meant that it's not possible to improve on perfection."

An incredulous expression slipped into her lovely eyes. "You mean you really like it?"

"I really, really do. I thought it was beautiful long, but this is even better." Crooking a finger under her chin, he lifted her face to the light. "I'm no expert on hairstyles, but wearing it short brings out your eyes and draws attention to your face."

"Oh."

He couldn't help but smile. "With fine features like yours, that's a plus."

She lifted a dubious gaze to his. "Do you really think so?"

Still holding her face between his hands, Jake thought he'd never seen anyone so sweetly beautiful. Looking down at her, he could only wonder what he'd ever found attractive about tall, leggy blondes and redheads who wore gobs of makeup. Molly was what he'd wanted all along, but he'd been too dumb to realize it.

"I really think so," he whispered huskily.

For the remainder of the day, Jake grinned every time he recalled Molly's new hairstyle. She was turning out to be the most unpredictable female he'd ever met. What would come next, spike heels and black net stockings? He hoped not. Molly was more the Madonna type, and he hated to see her change that.

On the other hand, he'd been wrong about the hair. She'd probably knock his eyes out in black fishnet. Maybe the best thing for him to do was butt out entirely and let her create her own look.

The thought no sooner entered his brain than Jake knew he'd just experienced a rare moment of genius. *Of course* he needed to butt out. Molly had been pushed around too much already. *"I can't find myself anymore,"* she'd whispered to him last night. He had a very bad feeling that was because she'd buried herself to please her husband. Jake didn't want to make the same mistake.

It was high time that she should discover who she really was, and she didn't need his help to do that. When all was said and done, he'd take her in a heartbeat, be she in fishnet or a nun's habit. He wasn't sure when it had happened—or even exactly how—but he'd fallen head over heels in love with her. Done deal, no turning back.

Rationally, Jake knew it had happened way too fast and probably made little sense. Love and marriage weren't things an intelligent man jumped into. It was only smart to wait, to test the waters. Only somehow that didn't seem smart at all with Molly. She was running from the law. He couldn't shake the feeling that time was short and might soon run out, that he might forever lose his chance with her if he didn't move quickly.

He couldn't let her slip through his fingers. He was damned near thirty-three. He'd been waiting for the right lady to come along ever since he'd grown mature enough to realize that love and sex were two entirely different things. If he didn't snatch her up while he had the chance, what were the odds that he'd ever meet anyone like her again?

That night, after cooking a meal under Jake's direction that was, in Molly's opinion, large enough to feed and clog the arteries of half the population of Crystal Falls, she set herself to the task of cleaning the kitchen. As always, Jake rolled up his sleeves to help. He took his usual position at the sink to wash while she dried.

"I've gotten the impression that the men you've known weren't much for helping with domestic tasks," he said.

She put a dinner plate in the cupboard. "My dad always helped in the kitchen on Cook's night off."

"Ah, so you had a cook, did you?"

Molly shot him a wary look. She glimpsed a twinkle in his eyes before he returned his attention to the pot he was scrubbing. "You have a cook," she pointed out.

"I also have a ranch and a lot of extra mouths to feed, which makes it a necessity rather than a luxury. We both know your father didn't own a cattle ranch. I'll venture a guess you've never been on a ranch or farm before in your life."

Molly's cheeks burned with embarrassment over all the lies and half-truths she'd told him. Now that he was calling her on it, she couldn't think what to say. "I'm sorry, Jake," she murmured.

"For what?"

"For lying to you. I can only say I don't make a habit of it."

He smiled. "You've only done what you felt you had to."

Molly couldn't think what to say. She drew a skillet from the drainer.

"So," he mused aloud, "if you had a cook while you were growing up, your father must have been wealthy then?"

"Well off. He wasn't a billionaire or anything."

"That leaves a lot of room for supposition. A millionaire, then?"

Molly's pulse escalated, and her fingers grew stiff and clumsy. She tightened her grip on the skillet handle. If she answered that question, Jake would be one step closer to learning her true identity. There weren't that many millionaires in Oregon, and she'd narrowed the search down considerably by telling him that she'd worked at an investment firm. She cast him an uneasy glance. She guessed it all boiled down to whether or not she trusted him.

Only it wasn't that simple. While she had come to trust that Jake would never deliberately hurt her, he was operating under a cloud of ignorance she didn't dare dispel. Her freedom and Sunset's future hung in the balance. So did her need to seek justice for her father's death. How might he react if she told him she was recently released from a mental ward and was still supposed to be under a doctor's care?

Under other circumstances, she might have taken a calculated risk and told him everything. But she wasn't like other women. Until a judge rapped his gavel and said otherwise, she was vulnerable in a way that terrified her.

She'd been married to Rodney when she'd been deemed legally incompetent, and he had been appointed her guardian by the court. Because of the firm and all the related business entanglements, Rodney's attorney had been able to keep much of the arrangement status quo after the divorce, arguing that Rodney and Molly's financial future and all their marital assets hung in the balance. She'd still been at the clinic then. What judge worth his salt granted a mental ward patient the right to handle her own affairs when millions of dollars and the future of a financial empire were at stake?

As a result, Rodney might no longer be her husband, but he still had power over her. It was Rodney who had doled out money to her each month from the firm's coffers, Rodney who still had access to all those accounts, Rodney who could hire all the big-shot attorneys. She couldn't even scrape up a retainer fee, and if she managed, what lawyer in his right mind would take her on? There were the liability factors no attorney in his right mind could ignore. Representing a legally incompetent individual gave rise to a host of difficulties and possible legal infractions they preferred to avoid.

What had happened once could happen again, and if Molly forgot that, even for an instant, her fate would be sealed. The very thought filled her with cold fear. Rodney hated Sam Banks, the doctor who'd become her champion. If her ex-husband and mother had her committed again, it was highly unlikely that they would put her back in a clinic where she already had an ally. Oh, no. She'd be handed over to strangers, individuals who'd be predisposed to disbelieve everything she said.

After her release from the clinic, she'd tried once to get a restraining order against Rodney, and all she'd earned for her trouble was a pat on the arm. In short, crazy people weren't taken seriously, and nothing she'd said had carried any weight with the police. Harrassment? Stalking? Legally, she didn't have a leg to stand on.

Jake had no idea what a tangle her life was in. All it would take was for him to grow curious and make a few phone calls to the wrong people. If word of his inquiries filtered back to Rodney, she might be tracked down. It was anyone's guess what might happen then. It certainly wouldn't be pleasant.

"Okay," he said with a laugh when her reluctance to answer became obvious. "I guess that wasn't a fair question. Let's move on from there. So your dad helped in the kitchen on Cook's night off. Is that what you called her, Cook?"

"How do you know Cook wasn't a man?"

He laughed again and flicked suds at her. "I'm a redneck cowboy. I think the ERA is a real estate company. Don't burst my bubble."

She smiled in spite of herself. Jake was as far from being a male chauvinist as any man could get. "Yes, we called her Cook."

"How was Rodney for helping in the kitchen?"

"He didn't."

"Never?"

"Never. That was woman's work, amen."

Jake grinned and winked at her. "Like I said, a pissant."

A few minutes later, Jake was walking her home. As he'd taken to doing quite frequently, he detoured toward the creek. Molly almost gave in to the urge to simply follow along. Then she thought better of it and drew to a stop.

"I think I'll forgo the walk tonight."

He swung around to look at her questioningly. In the moonlight, he looked so tall and sturdy and handsome that Molly stood her ground with some regret. It was so tempting to bid common sense good-bye and grab this opportunity with both hands.

"Coward," he said softy.

She didn't prevaricate. "Yes, I'm afraid so." She scrunched her shoulders and hugged her parka closer, feeling suddenly cold. "I told you last night, Jake. I'm very attracted to you. In return, you issued a warning, if you'll recall. I'm just heeding it."

The brim of his hat cast a shadow over his face. It was testimony to the brilliance of his blue eyes that they gleamed at her through the gloom. "You afraid I'll kiss you?"

"And more."

He stood on a slight slope, one boot at a slightly higher level than the other, his long, denim-sheathed leg bent. Placing his hands on his hips, he regarded her as though she were a complicated puzzle. "Molly, nothing will ever happen between us that you don't want to happen. You do know that, I hope."

"Yes, well, that's the problem, isn't it? We don't always want what's good for us." She bent her head. "I've done a lot of thinking today, Jake. I'm not confident in my ability to tell you no a second time."

"That's good to hear."

She laughed and then groaned, her gaze returning to his dark face. "I'm not interested in a steamy interlude. I'm sorry. I know it's not a contemporary attitude. But I'm not the type to engage in casual sex and emerge from the experience whole."

"I never thought you were, and casual sex isn't what I have in mind. There's nothing casual about my feelings for you."

She had to smile. "I suppose it all boils down to one's definition of casual. I understand that a lot of people nowadays have what they call meaningful relationships outside of marriage with individuals they care about, but that's just not how I'm made." She shrugged and swallowed. "I'm not real sure about a lot of things right now, but I do know that much about myself. I'm an all or nothing kind of person. If I give my body to a man, my heart will be part of the package. I suppose it's a silly way to think, but we can't change our stripes."

"Do you see me laughing? I think it's a charming way to be."

"Yes, well, women who take these things less seriously have a lot more fun, I'm sure. I wish I were more like that." She dragged in a bracing breath. "If I thought for a minute that I could have an affair with you and watch you walk away later without it breaking my heart, I'd do it in a blink. But I'd get hurt, sure as the world, because I'd fall in love with you. I know I would. That being the case, I'm going to be a smart girl and say good night."

She turned to walk away. She only got two steps when his softly spoken, "Molly," jerked her to a halt. She looked back at him over her shoulder.

"Don't go." He hadn't moved, but even in the semidarkness, she could feel the pull of his gaze. "Are you wanting a ring and promises? Is that it? If so, I'll happily give them to you."

"Oh, Jake," she whispered, so touched by the offer she wanted to weep.

"I'm falling in love with you. I'd marry you in a heartbeat. If you think I'm bluffing, try me."

She sighed and shook her head. "Marriage isn't the answer for me, either. Aren't I a mess?" She dug her heel in the dirt. "Lucky for you. You haven't known me long enough to make a commitment like that."

"I know you as well as I need to." Absolute certainty rang in his voice. "You're a wonderful person, Molly. I knew that the second I saw you."

She rolled her eyes.

"Seriously. There you stood, no bigger than a minute, with that horse trailer rocking behind you and lifting the tires of your Toyota off the ground. I thought, 'There's a lady with a heart twice as big as she is.' And guess what? You haven't proved me wrong since. There isn't a male on the ranch who isn't a little bit in love with you, poor old Bart included. I'm just a whole lot more in love with you than the others."

She fixed her gaze on the tree line at the far side of the creek where pine boughs were etched in silhouette against a dark-blue velvet sky. She fancied them to be dancers, poised in a graceful ballet, the stars forming the diamonds in their delicate coronets. "I don't want any more entanglements. I'm free for the first time in ten years, Jake, and I'd like to stay that way. There are so many things I want to do. You know?" She thought of her stalled career and lost dreams. Some of those dreams could never be recaptured, she knew, but others might still be possible. More important, she needed to seek justice for her father's death so she could finally lay him to rest. "There are things I have to do. I know you don't understand. I wish I were free to explain. Just know that there are unresolved issues in my life, and I'll never be able to make a commitment to you or anyone until they're settled to my satisfaction."

"Let me help you then. Marriage is a partnership, honey, not a prison."

"Maybe not for a man, maybe not for most women, but it was for me."

"It won't be that way again."

"Yes. At least it could. Down deep, parts of the Molly I used to be still exist. I was a devout Catholic. I'll bet you never guessed that."

"I've got nothing against Catholics."

"You're missing the point. I didn't believe in divorce. I was trapped in a marriage that was a nightmare with a man who took advantage of my sacramental bondage at every turn. I'll never sucker in for that again."

"Sacramental bondage," he repeated. "That's heavy."

Molly doubted he had any idea just how heavy. "Like being buried alive under a thousand pounds of ice."

He moved slowly up the bank. "I'd never infringe on your personal freedoms, Molly."

"You'll never get a chance," she said lightly.

They fell into a slow walk together. He shoved his

hands deeply into his jeans pockets. "So where does this leave us?"

"With friendship. If you touch me again with anything more than that in mind, I won't be here when you wake up the next morning. I'll leave your watch on the table, and as soon as I find work of some kind, I'll send you all the money I can to cover Sunset's expenses. But you'll never see me again."

"You don't leave a man much negotiating room," he said with a dry laugh.

"I don't intend to. This isn't negotiable."

"I don't want you to go away, Molly."

"You've heard my terms."

He drew to a stop, tugged his hands from his pockets to rest them at his hips, and leveled a look at her that made her heart do a funny little skip inside her chest. "And here are mine," he said softly. "I'll honor your stipulations—for a time. There's not a damned thing wrong with being good friends before we become lovers. I've got no quarrel with that. Just understand that I want more, and the day will come when I'll press you for more."

"When you do, I'll leave."

He flashed her a slow grin that turned the skip of her heart into leaps and somersaults. "We'll see."

"I'll never give another man control over my life."

He shrugged, looking totally unruffled by the proclamation. "Fine by me. I don't want control. I see marriage as a fifty-fifty proposition. My wife will be my partner, not a possession."

"That's what they all say until the ink dries on the marriage certificate."

He chuckled. "Now *that* is an archaic outlook. Have you checked the calendar lately?"

Molly shoved her hands into her jacket pockets and made tight fists. "Once burned, twice shy."

"I can see I've got my work cut out for me."

Molly sighed. "Have you heard anything I've said? All I'm interested in is friendship."

His teeth gleamed in the moonlight as he flashed her another grin. "As long as that's all you're interested in, that's all you'll get. That doesn't stop me from trying to convince you otherwise." As if he read her feelings in her expression, he quickly added, "In a completely hands-off way, of course. I'll never touch you unless you want me to."

Molly relaxed slightly. She could keep her head around him as long as he didn't kiss her or anything. No matter how much she might sometimes wish he would, that would be her secret. "Fine. Then we have a clear understanding?"

His eyes twinkled mischievously. "Crystal clear."

Why was it she had a feeling he found this entire situation vastly amusing?

He thrust out his hand to her. "That said, how about if we shake on it to seal our agreement?"

Molly was no longer totally sure what their agreement was. Nevertheless, she drew one hand from her pocket to place it across his broad palm. His long fingers closed around hers. His thumb traced light circles over the back of her wrist, sending little shocks of awareness up her arm.

"Fine, then," she said stupidly.

His grin broadened. "Now that we have that settled, will you come for a walk with me?"

He was still caressing her wrist. That didn't exactly strike her as being a good omen. Did he know how his touch tied her insides into knots? She had an awful feeling he did.

"Come on," he cajoled huskily. "Take a walk with me. You still trust me, don't you?"

Molly swallowed, her throat feeling suddenly dry and sticky. She did trust him. Excluding her father, she trusted him more than she'd ever trusted any man. On the other hand . . .

"I just agreed to your terms," he reminded her. "Friendship only. What can possibly happen?"

"Nothing, I don't suppose." She dragged in a breath for courage and nodded. "All right. Sure. Why not?"

Never releasing her hand, he turned and tucked it over the bend of his other arm. Then he began leading her back toward the creek. As Molly walked beside him, she found herself remembering a nursery rhyme from childhood.

Welcome to my parlor said the spider to the fly.

Chapter Fourteen

Over the next few days, Molly began to feel as if Jake were spinning a magical web and luring her ever deeper into its silken bonds. It was as if he sensed the emptiness within her and had set himself to the task of filling her up with a daily measure of beauty.

Practically every morning as she left the cabin, she found a gift lying on her doorstep. One morning, it might be a pretty rock or a feather from a wild bird. Another, she would find flowers. One morning, he left her a posy of spring clover blossoms, and for some reason, that was her favorite surprise of all, representative of all Jake Coulter was and everything he stood for, a man as earthy and elemental as this land from which he had sprung.

His habit of leaving her silly gifts reminded her so much of her father, leading her to begin assessing him in other ways and measuring him against Marshal Sterling. Jake looked nothing like her dad. As far as their mannerisms went, the two men were light years apart. But there were other similarities Molly couldn't deny, traits that ran deep and true, making them stand apart from all the rest of the men she knew.

When White Star had her foal, Jake insisted that Molly attend the birthing. It turned out to be the most amazing event she'd ever witnessed, followed by a bonding ritual called imprinting that she would never forget.

Over the first hour of the foal's life, she helped Jake desensitize the newborn to a host of stimuli that might otherwise frighten him later in life. They performed a mock shoeing and handled every part of the foal's body. When he was finally allowed to stand, Molly had the honor of introducing him to his first halter. "Surely he won't remember all this," she commented.

"Precocious newborns are programmed by nature to bond over the first hour of life with their mothers and any creatures hovering nearby, thus the herd instinct. It's necessary to their survival in the wild. So, yes, on some level, he'll remember everything he experiences today, and he'll be far more inclined to trust people." Jake ran the back of a vibrating clipper over the foal's hip. "Over the next few weeks, we'll repeat all this a few times to better imprint the lessons. At three months, this little guy will stand calmly for his first hoof trimming, he won't be frightened by a halter, rope, or slight weight on his back, and he'll come when he sees us, anxious for a scratch behind his ears. When he's old enough to ride, it will be an uneventful transition that he's been prepared to accept all his life."

Taking in Jake's lean, muscular body, Molly said, "You could break a horse the old-fashioned way. That would take much less time, wouldn't it? Why imprint?"

He frowned as he considered his reply. " 'Break' is the key word in your question, and it means just what it implies, that the horse's spirit or will is broken. Sometimes it's done gently, sometimes not. I've trained horses that way, and I've trained them this way. You can end up with a fine horse using old-fashioned methods, but what's to say that the same horse couldn't have been extraordinary?" He shrugged. "Have you ever seen a twitch, Molly?"

She shook her head, prompting him to lead her from the birthing stall to a spot midway up the central aisle of the stable. "That is a twitch," he said, pointing to an apparatus hanging on the wall that reminded Molly of a huge nutcracker. Indicating the circular end, he explained, "This part is clamped over the horse's nose. The resultant pain becomes the focus of his attention, enabling his handler to do pretty much whatever he likes to some other part of his body."

Molly shivered. "How awful."

Jake chuckled. "Not really. Necessary is the word when you're trying to work with a powerful animal that could make mincemeat out of you." He took the twitch from the wall. "Sometimes, for the horse's own good, we have to use a twitch." He pressed the circular end close to her face. "It's usually safer than a sedative." His voice dipped low. "So we pinch the tender flesh midway between upper lip and nose, do what's necessary, and then release the pressure."

"Your point?"

He smiled slowly. "A question, not a point. Bearing in mind that twitching is extremely uncomfortable, if not downright painful, if you were one of my horses, would you want me to use a twitch routinely when I had to work on you?"

"Definitely not."

He chuckled and hung the twitch back on its hook. "Point made. If imprinting makes a horse easier to handle and doctor, eliminating the use of a twitch in many situations, it's worth all the time and effort I put into it."

"You really love your animals, don't you?" she said softly.

"Yeah, I really do. I'd much rather befriend than conquer."

Molly had never met anyone like Jake Coulter, and she doubted she ever would again. He was the extraordinary one, in her estimation, a rare individual with such a depth of caring that he amazed her with some new revelation every time she spent time with him.

"Walk with me," he said at least once a day. It sounded like such a harmless pastime, a simple matter of placing one foot in front of the other and carrying on a friendly conversation. But Molly soon discovered that nothing about Jake was simple—and while in his company, things

that seemed harmlessly mundane could suddenly become treacherously complicated.

"We've discussed what colors you feel you look best in," he said one evening, "but as I recall, you've never said what your favorite color is."

As a girl, she'd done her bedroom in varying shades of mauve with all four walls papered in roses. Practically every article of clothing she'd worn back then had been pink or sported touches of the color somewhere. For her eighteenth birthday, her dad had even bought her a pink car, and he'd presented her with the keys on a resin key ring that encased a miniature rosebud.

"I don't have a strong preference for any particular color anymore," she said.

"Aw, come on."

How could she explain that she'd stopped thinking in terms of what she liked years ago? "I used to love pink," she confessed.

"Past tense again," he chided. "Do you *still* like pink, Molly?"

"I tend to go overboard with things I like. Pink can be a very gaudy color if you overdo it, and I never had any restraint."

He chuckled. "Is that what life is about, restraint? What's wrong with gaudy if you like gaudy?"

Her limbs went tense. "Nothing, I suppose. But with a brilliant color like pink, one runs a risk of appearing gauche."

"Gauche?" He assumed an expression of mock horror. "God forbid."

Molly's cheeks burned. "Rodney hated me in pink. Now you're laughing because I've learned moderation. *Men.* Why not just leave me alone?"

He smiled thoughtfully. "I'm not laughing at you, Molly, and I'll be happy to see you wear whatever color or style you like. I'm just concerned because it seems to me you're still hanging back."

"Hanging back from what?"

"Being yourself." He reached over to ruffle her curls. "I *love* what you've done with your hair. You know what that tells me?"

"No, what?"

"That you should go with your instincts. You say you've learned moderation, but it seems to me you're practicing self-denial instead. I don't want to influence you. I think you need to make your own choices. But you aren't doing that. Where's the moderate amount of pink in your life? Even if it were true that you don't look good in it, what would be wrong with decorating your world in that color?"

"I'll paint the cabin pink tomorrow."

He laughed and shook his head. "Fine. Make jokes. Pink logs might be a bit much. Even I have to concede that point. But you could use pink to dress the place up."

"Pink doesn't lend itself well to quiet dignity."

"The world according to Rodney?"

Molly set her jaw and stared straight ahead. She wished he would just drop the subject. Discussing Rodney made her stomach upset. But Jake never backed off from subjects that disturbed her. He just kept digging and pressing until she forgot herself and said too much.

This time, he suddenly broke stride to step behind her and grasp her shoulders. "Look at that," he said in an oddly fierce tone.

"At what?" Molly asked, her gaze darting to the tree line, her nerves jangling. She half expected to see a bear or cougar lurking in the forest.

"At the *sky*," he whispered near her ear. When she glanced up, he tightened his hold on her shoulders. "Just *look* at that sunset, Molly. Have you ever seen such incredible shades of pink in all your life?"

Molly could scarcely believe she hadn't noticed the sunset on her own. Jake was right; it was absolutely breathtaking. "Oh, how lovely," she whispered.

"Is God gauche?"

The question took her off guard, and she snorted with laughter. "No, of course not."

"Would you say He practices restraint?"

The sky was a veritable pallet of rose shades, so beautiful, so perfect, that she could scarcely believe it was real. "No, He hasn't practiced restraint," she replied tautly.

"Would you say He lacks dignity?"

She laughed in spite of herself. "*No.*"

"Well then?" He rested his jaw against her hair to study the sky with her. "It appears to me that Rodney, the pissant, was wrong. *Dead* wrong. Pink is a beautiful, very dignified color, and the bastard wouldn't recognize gauche if it ran up and bit him on the ass." He massaged her shoulders, forcing the last bit of tension from her muscles. "Forget being restrained. Forget moderation. Forget self-denial. Celebrate life and drown yourself in pink if you want. It's perfectly okay."

On another evening, Molly confessed to Jake that she had no fashion sense and had always deferred to her husband's impeccable taste in clothing.

"Who said you have no fashion sense?" Jake asked.

Molly thought back, and as she did, her head started to ache, the pain sharp and centered directly behind her eyes. "Rodney," she admitted tautly.

"Ah," Jake chuckled dryly. "Who elected him fashion guru of the century?"

"Rodney," she whispered.

"Hmm," was all Jake said, but that one word conveyed such disgust, it was unnecessary for him to say more.

Two days later, Molly was in town to go grocery shopping and pick up some fluorescent tubes for Jake. As she hurried along the sidewalk toward the electric supply, she passed a ladies' apparel shop. There in the window was a gorgeous pink top.

Molly stopped dead in her tracks and stared at it. Never

in her recollection had she wanted anything quite so much. She wasn't sure why, but in that top, she saw freedom. It was *her*, the Molly she'd lost, exactly the sort of thing she would have loved back in high school.

Of course, she'd weighed thirty pounds less back then, a spindly girl with an oversized bust. In her twenties, she'd grown thick at the waist and hippy. Something like that probably wouldn't look good on her anymore.

Even as she told herself that, Molly entered the shop. A pretty blonde clerk came from behind the register. She wore a navy blue dress with red piping and sassy red sandals. Her shoulder-length hair was salon-conditioned perfect. Molly felt dowdy and plain by comparison.

"Hello," she managed to say. Gesturing at the window display, she added, "I noticed that pink top as I was walking by. Now that I'm closer, I can see it's not my color or style."

The blonde smiled. "You think not?" She stepped to a rack and pulled out a pink top like the one in the window. Holding it up against Molly, she grinned mischievously. "Wrong. It's perfect on you."

Molly glimpsed the price tag and nearly fainted. It was almost forty dollars. She'd spent less than two hundred of the thousand dollars she'd brought with her from Portland, but even so, blowing forty bucks on something so frivolous wasn't wise. Fingering the knit, she thought of a time in the not-so-distant past when she'd have spent three times more without blinking. She had Rodney to thank for her present financial straits.

Oh, how that burned. And suddenly she wanted that pink top beyond all reason.

"It's a little expensive," she said.

The clerk laughed. "Not at the prices these days. Live a little. At least try it on."

Molly couldn't resist. She grinned and stripped off her parka. When the other woman saw her clothes, she raised her eyebrows. "Have you lost weight?"

For a moment, Molly couldn't think why she asked. Then she glanced down. Her khaki slacks hung from her hips like tent canvas, and her blouse could have served as a maternity smock. "Yeah, I have," she lied. "Nothing fits right anymore."

"We have a huge sale going," the clerk said with a mischievous wink. Before Molly could protest, she was descending on a rack of jeans. "Aren't these darling?" she said as she turned to assess Molly's size. She drew out a pair of pants. "These are half off."

A fifty-percent discount was a really great deal if one had the money to take advantage of it. Molly didn't. She kept telling herself that as the clerk herded her to a dressing room. Leaving the door ajar while Molly changed, the woman kept bringing different outfits for her to try on.

"*This* would look marvelous on you," she said. Or, "This is so *you*!"

"I really can't afford a new wardrobe right now," Molly kept insisting, not sure who she was trying to convince, the clerk or herself.

"Any woman who loses that much weight owes herself a whole new look!" was the clerk's retort.

Molly knew she should leave, but trying on the clothes was so much fun she couldn't bring herself to run. The blonde had no idea of Molly's history. She didn't rave about how nice Molly looked just to bolster her confidence. Best of all, she had a flair for fashion. Anyone with eyes could see that by the way she was dressed. She might have stepped off the cover of a magazine.

Before Molly knew quite how it happened, she'd selected tons of clothes. The large discounts aside, she knew the total would be astronomical. She had to be out of her mind to even consider blowing so much money when she had absolutely no way of replacing it. All her wages at the ranch went toward Sunset's care and training.

"I really, *really* can't afford all this," she confessed.

The blonde winked. "Come on up front. Let's run it up on the calculator and see what we're looking at."

The total was over six hundred dollars, including the large sale discounts. Molly glanced down at the outfit she was wearing, a pair of snug jeans and a snappy red sweater. It was so totally outlandish, something she never would have considered wearing less than an hour ago, but she liked the way it made her look, transforming her in some magical way from dowdy old Molly into someone colorful, daring, and maybe even a little sexy in a plump sort of way.

"I really shouldn't."

The clerk winked at her. "I don't offer to do this for just anyone, but for you, I'll make an exception. I get a twenty-five-percent discount, working here. I'll take that off the total as well. Does that make the cost a little more manageable?"

Molly could scarcely believe she'd offered. "Don't you work on commission?"

"Yes. But I've done well this week with the clearance sale. And, hey, what's the use in having a job like this if I can't have fun once in a while? It's not every day that I can totally make someone over." She leaned closer and grinned conspiratorially. "I haven't used my discount all winter. The old battle-ax who owns this place is getting off cheap." She straightened and ran her gaze over Molly. "You look *so* great in that outfit. That's all the commission I need."

Molly left the store with so many outfits the bags were difficult to carry, forcing her to return to the truck before she went on to the parts store. She'd changed back into her old clothes, and when she saw herself in the store windows as she hurried along the sidewalk, she cringed. The new Molly was in Jake's truck, and she couldn't wait to get home to try her back on.

*   *   *

When Jake walked into the kitchen that night, his eyes nearly popped from his head. Molly stood at the stove, only she looked nothing like the Molly he knew. She wore a pair of snug jeans and a bright red sweater that clung to her ample breasts. Jake's blood pressure shot clear off the chart before he knew what hit him.

When she turned fully toward him, he could only gawk. *Holy hell.* If he had this much trouble keeping his mouth closed, how were his men going to react? She was mouth-watering. Every delicious curve of her body was show-cased.

He'd known she was sumptuously built, but he'd never in his wildest dreams imagined her to be this curvaceous. Ample didn't describe her breasts. A little bit of her cleavage was showing, and with breasts as generous as hers, a little bit of cleavage went a hell of a long way.

His gaze shot from there to her slender waist, which flowed gently into delightfully round hips and full thighs. Until now, he'd never realized the stretching properties of denim.

"You can't wear that."

The words no sooner popped from Jake's mouth than he wanted to call them back. It was just—sweet Lord above, didn't she realize how she looked? She had a body that made a man think about hot sex on silk sheets. He'd sug-gested a little more color in her wardrobe, not formfitting brilliance.

Didn't she understand that she was a lone female, work-ing on a ranch with a bunch of horny men? Even the older ones still had some fire in their ovens. The younger fellows might get ideas, and if they did, a pass at Molly wouldn't be long in following. Jake would kill the first man who so much as made an off-color remark to her.

Jake saw that she'd gone as pale as a moonbeam. For a long moment, she just stood there looking at him with her heart in her eyes. Then, glancing down, she murmured, "I guess it is a little much." She plucked at the front of the sweater. "You're right, Jake. I'm sorry. I don't know what I was thinking. Can you, um, watch dinner while I run over to change?"

Jake wanted to kick himself. Only he couldn't until he removed his size twelve boot from his mouth. "Molly, I didn't mean that you don't look nice."

Her stricken expression remained.

"You look *fantastic*," he rushed to add. *Too* fantastic. *Shit*. She didn't believe him. He could tell that by her pallor and the injured look in her eyes. He hadn't meant to hurt her feelings. "I was, um, just—startled when I first saw you, is all."

"Yes, well." Her eyes went all shiny, giving him reason to suspect she was about to cry. Instead she laughed and flashed an over-bright smile. "Startling people wasn't my aim when I got the outfit." She shrugged. "I never should have listened to that clerk. I told you my taste in clothes is atrocious."

Before Jake could collect himself and think of something else to say, she rushed from the room, so upset she didn't even stop at the coat rack to grab her parka.

Jake was at the stove, turning the chicken and cursing to turn the air blue, when Hank walked in the back door. "What's wrong?"

"Everything!" Jake handed his brother the fork. "Watch the chicken, would you? I have some fences to go mend."

"We just rode fence line yesterday. Everything looked pretty good."

"Not *that* kind of fence. Damn, Hank, I've really screwed up this time. Molly finally got up the courage to get some new clothes, and I ruined it for her."

"Why'd you do that? If anybody needs some new clothes, she does."

Jake passed a hand over his eyes. "She was wearing a sweater and jeans."

"Nothing wrong with that."

"There is with Molly packed into them. Bright red."

Jake gestured helplessly at his chest. "Holy hell. I can't have her looking like that out here on the ranch. The men won't be able to keep their eyes off her."

"No harm in looking as long as they don't touch."

"And what if one of them decides he isn't satisfied with just looking?" Jake shot back. "I'd kill him. I don't need the hassle."

Hank lifted the lid off the skillet to check the chicken. "Hmm. Sounds like a bad case of the green monster to me. Molly's perfectly capable of deflecting any unwanted advances. Trust her to handle it."

Jake ground his teeth. Molly was *not* capable of handling unwanted advances. She was too sweet to tell a man where to get off, for one thing, and too unsure of herself for another.

"You afraid somebody'll trespass on your turf, bro?" Hank asked softly.

"That's a cheap shot. I've never had a jealous bone in my body, and you know it."

"You've never cared enough about a woman before to get jealous," Hank pointed out. "What about all the gals you've dated who paraded around out here in halter tops and shorts that left little to the imagination? You never got bent out of shape when the men looked at them."

"That was different. They knew the score."

"And Molly doesn't? Give me a break. She's been married. I'm sure she's got a pretty good understanding of the birds and the bees, which is undoubtedly why she chose to wear jeans and a sweater, which are pretty modest compared to the two patches of material held together by strings that I've seen a few of your bimbos wear."

"I never dated any bimbos."

Hank grinned. "Exhibitionists, then. Remember that blond gal—Veronica, I think her name was—who teetered around out in the yard in spike heels and short shorts last September? When she bent over, it wasn't only her hairdresser who knew for sure. When the guys came on to her, you never so much as blinked."

Jake's blood pressure was rising again. "Where are you going with this?"

"I'm just trying to point out that jeans and a sweater can't be that risqué by comparison, even if they are skintight. We're all big boys. If we can't handle ourselves any better than that, we deserve a good ass kicking, and it sure as hell won't be Molly's fault."

Jake had heard enough. Hank had never been in love. He didn't understand anything about anything. He grabbed Molly's parka from the coat rack. Though spring was making its debut, it still got freezing cold after the sun went down, and he didn't want her taking a chill. "I'll be back in a bit."

Once outside, Jake sat on the porch. Clutching Molly's parka in his fists, he pressed the nylon shell to his face and breathed in the sweet scent of her that lingered on the cloth. Her smell made him think of wildflowers and sunshine, an essence as fresh and unpretentious as she was. *Jealous?* Damn Hank for saying that. Jake had never been the possessive type. If a woman wanted to be with him, then she wanted to be with him, end of story. If someone else caught her eye, he was perfectly willing to say adios without a hassle, no skin off his nose. He was *not* jealous.

He pressed the jacket harder against his face, repeating the refrain to assure himself it was so. He just didn't want Molly to get herself into a sticky situation. She was on her own out here, and he was her employer. That made him responsible for her, right?

Wrong. Jake knew he was bullshitting himself. As much as he hated to admit it, Hank was right. He was green with jealousy, and he felt possessive as hell. Just the thought of other men ogling Molly's body made him do a slow burn. Even worse, deep down, there was a part of him that was afraid she might find someone else. That was a scary thought.

He *loved* her, damn it. He didn't want to lose her to some jerk who wouldn't appreciate her or treat her the way she deserved to be treated.

Sighing, Jake pushed to his feet. He needed to go talk to her. What he meant to say, he had no idea. But somehow he had to fix the mess he'd made of things.

She didn't answer when he knocked on the cabin door. He knocked again. Again no answer. Since he figured he couldn't screw up any worse than he had already, Jake walked right in.

"Molly?"

He heard a gasp and a rush of movement in the bedroom. Clenching his teeth, he tossed her parka on the couch and made a beeline for the open doorway. She stood before the closet, holding the red sweater to her chest. He'd caught her changing.

Jake almost turned away. Instead he bent his head and stared at the floor. "Can you slip that sweater back on so we can talk?"

"There's nothing that needs saying. Give me a minute. I'll be right out."

"There's a lot that needs saying."

Jake lifted his gaze. The wad of red knit pressed to her breasts brought out the flawlessness of her skin. Her short-cropped curls shone in the overhead light like molten brass. And her eyes—oh, *God*—those eyes. They were dark with shadows that he knew he'd put there. Ever since meeting her, he had reviled Rodney. Now who was the bastard?

"I owe you an apology," he said hoarsely. "You look beautiful in that outfit, Molly, and I need my butt kicked for making you think otherwise."

She dipped her chin. The way her fingertips caressed the soft knit told Jake how very important the sweater was to her. He recalled telling her once that marriage to him wouldn't be a prison, that he'd never dream of infringing on her personal rights.

If choosing her clothing wasn't a personal right, what the hell was?

"Ah, Molly, sweetheart, I'm sorry."

She shook her head. "I'm afraid you don't understand." She met his gaze again. "I'm changing into something else for one reason and only one reason, because you're my employer and I'm still on shift." Her quivering chin came up. "In my free time, I'll dress however I like." She clutched the sweater more tightly to her chest. "If you don't approve, that's your problem."

Looking into her eyes, Jake realized that he'd misread her. That wasn't only hurt there but a strong dose of anger as well. He wanted to smile. Her outrage was a very good sign, and it told him more than she could possibly know, namely that she was finally starting to heal and find herself again.

"I see," he said carefully.

"No, you don't, and you probably never will. How could you?" Her larynx bobbed as she struggled to swallow. "No one's ever owned you."

Jake's heart caught at her choice of words. Was that really what her marriage had been like?

"Before my divorce, I couldn't even *vote* the way I wanted," she rushed to add. "Not unless I was prepared to lie about it afterward, and as I'm sure you've noticed, I'm a rotten liar. If Rodney found out I'd gone against him, he made my life hell for days, sometimes weeks, depending upon the seriousness of my transgression."

"Oh, Molly," he whispered.

"You have no idea what that was like," she continued in a taut, tremulous voice. "No idea at *all*. For ten years, I did everything I could to please him." She knotted her fist and pressed it hard against her chest. "I was only eighteen when we married. He was older and seemed so sophisticated. Whenever he wasn't happy, about anything, it was always my fault. *I* was the problem. Therefore I was the one who had to change. After a while, it becomes a mind-set. You fall into a trap without even realizing it, and pretty soon you don't even think about what you're doing."

Jake had no clue what to say.

"Maybe I don't look good in this outfit. Maybe I look *awful* in it. But you know what, Jake?"

He wanted to refute those last two statements, but see-ing that she needed to get this off her chest, he merely said, "No, what?"

"How I look doesn't matter. What counts is how I feel."

He couldn't have agreed more.

"From this point forward," she went on, "things are going to change." With one hand, she released her hold on the sweater to jab her chest. "I'm going to do what *I* want from now on. If you don't like my clothes, that's too bad. If I don't look good in them, tough. When I'm not work-ing, I'm going to dress however I like." She flashed him a defiant glare. "When it's on your dime, I'll respect your wishes, but after hours, how I look is nobody else's busi-ness."

Jake only nodded. She was fighting for her freedom, trying desperately to be an individual again and find defi-nition. If she fell into the trap of trying to please him as she once had Rodney, she was afraid she'd end up in the same situation all over again.

The insight enabled Jake to understand her in a way he hadn't before. Little wonder she was reluctant to make an-other emotional commitment. She was only recently di-vorced. He was a direct, straight-shooting man with a forceful personality. It was only natural that she might dread the thought of his having any control over her.

Jake had no intention of trying to control her. He'd tried to tell her that. Now he guessed it was time to put his money where his mouth was. He rubbed his jaw, acutely conscious of the faint rasping sound his fingers made on the stubble of whiskers.

"Dress however you like after hours, Molly. I think that's only fair."

"I will," she said stubbornly.

Jake couldn't help but smile. "May I make one suggestion?"

"Of course. I won't necessarily follow it, but feel free."

"If I were you, I'd wear the outfit now."

She flashed him a wary look.

"It's not as if there's a dress code. You're you. Dress however you want."

"But you don't like—"

"I never said that," he cut in. "I think that's a great outfit, and you look beautiful in it. *Too* beautiful."

Her delicate brows drew together in a scowl.

He cleared his throat and searched for words. "I didn't object to the outfit because I don't like it. The truth is, I like it a lot, and I'm afraid all the other men will as well. In short, I'm feeling a little jealous." He swallowed. "Strike that. I'm feeling a lot jealous."

"Of whom?"

"Anybody, everybody." Glimpsing the bewilderment in her eyes, he added, "I know it's stupid, but there it is. I don't want other men looking at you." That sounded so absurd that he felt heat crawling up his neck. He scratched his temple, groping for some way he might better explain. He came up blank. There was no rational explanation for the way he was feeling. "I know it's wrong of me, and I'm sorry for reacting before I took time to recognize my feelings for what they are. My only excuse is that I've never felt this way before. Given time, I'm sure I'll get a handle on it."

The bewilderment in her eyes had turned to incredulity.

"It's true," he said gruffly. He inclined his head at the sweater. "You looked so beautiful, Molly. You about knocked my eyes out. I knew if I felt that way, some of the other men would, too. As much as it pains me to admit it, I felt threatened."

"Oh, please."

"I'm not lying, I swear. Deep down, I'm afraid I'll lose out if a bunch of other men start coming on to you. It's not as if I'm any grand prize."

He scuffed the sole of his boot over the floor, noticing how clean the boards were. After working all the hours she did at the house, he had no idea how she found time to tidy up here. But then, he didn't know how she found time to brush Bart's teeth and give him baths, mend clothes, and fuss over all of them like she did, either. All and all, she was an amazing lady, her finest quality being that she always thought of others before she thought of herself.

He noticed some plastic shopping bags lying on the bed just then. The sleeve of a pretty yellow top protruded from one of them. He realized that she'd been on a shopping spree, that the jeans and sweater weren't all she'd bought. He remembered how her eyes had sparkled when she turned to face him in the kitchen, how she'd stood with her chin high and her shoulders straight. For the first time in a very long while, she had felt pretty, and in two seconds flat, he had crushed her.

He would never make that mistake again.

A few minutes later, Molly stood on the porch, rubbing her clammy palms on the legs of her new jeans. From inside, she heard voices, the deep timbre of a familiar one in particular. *Jake.* He'd convinced her to wear the sweater, not because she believed for a minute that he really thought she looked good in it, but simply because she wanted to.

The girl who had married Rodney Wells had been too young to know who she really was. For ten endless years, she'd drifted along, never fighting the changes because she hadn't realized her loss. She'd been Mrs. Rodney Wells, and in that role, she'd found definition, which had seemed enough.

Now the marriage was over, and she was faced with making choices for herself. She was supposed to be someone in her own right. Only she wasn't. Without Rodney to give her direction, she had to think for herself, and that was frightening.

Now she'd come to a crossroads, all because of an impulsive shopping spree and a silly red sweater. Only it wasn't just a sweater, not to her. She'd committed mutiny in that ladies' apparel shop today, breaking all of Rodney's rules and spending nearly her last dime to do it. She couldn't chicken out now. If she did, Rodney won.

As she opened Jake's front door and moved into the entryway, Molly had an awful feeling of impending doom. She placed one foot before the other, heading for the kitchen. She could tell by all the voices that most of the men had come in from the fields. She'd forgotten her coat at the cabin, and when she entered the room, they would see her.

She imagined startled gasps and raised eyebrows. Her insides shriveled in a tight knot of humiliation. Her face went red hot. Her skin felt as if it were shrinking and was suddenly a size too small for her body.

At the archway, she paused. Jake was turning from the stove and saw her first. He flashed a welcoming smile. As much as she appreciated that, it was the look in his eyes that lent her courage, a twinkling challenge that seemed to say, *"You've come this far. Don't stop now."*

Holding her arms rigid at her sides, she took another step. Then another. Sitting at the table, Danno glanced up. His red eyebrows lifted as his hazel eyes moved slowly over her. Following his gaze, Nate turned to look at her as well.

"Wow!" Nate said. "What happened to you?"

Molly gulped. "I, um . . . went shopping."

Nate gave her a slow, head-to-toe assessment, his

laughing blue eyes warm with appreciation. "A paycheck has never been better spent. You look great!"

Levi followed that with, "You sure do, darlin'. Red is your color."

Shorty chimed in next. "Well, ain't you pretty as a speckled pup."

Given the fact that Shorty loved dogs, Molly decided to take that as a compliment. The other men nodded to her and smiled, but no one offered further comment. That was it? No gasps of shock, no derogatory remarks? She moved to help with the final meal preparations, feeling stiff and self-conscious. The conversation quickly shifted to a discussion about horse training, and her new outfit was forgotten.

As she began dishing up the mashed potatoes, Jake came to help hold the large pot. When she glanced up, he looked deeply into her eyes. Then he moved his gaze slowly downward. When he had finished his assessment, in a husky whisper for her ears alone, he said, "I don't know what that outfit cost, but it was worth every cent. You look absolutely beautiful."

Chapter Fifteen

The following morning, it was already half past six by the time Jake grabbed a shower, a quarter to seven before he'd gathered his clothes to get dressed. Still half asleep and groggy as hell because he'd been up half the night tending a gelding with a spasm of the diaphragm, called the "thumps," he yawned and tried to blink himself awake as he dragged on a clean pair of Wranglers.

What the Sam Hill? There was something in the right front pocket of his clean pants. He dived his hand inside and closed his fingers over a familiar shape, his grandfather's watch. His blood ran cold. Molly had promised to return it to him if she ever decided to leave. Now it had mysteriously appeared in a clean pair of his jeans where he would be sure to find it.

Jake swore under his breath and tugged on his boots. He grabbed a shirt, not bothering to put it on before he dashed from the bedroom. As he sprinted down the stairs, he imagined her out on the highway, driving aimlessly. He knew for a fact that she had only a little money and nowhere to go. Even worse, she'd been afraid the police might have an APB out on her car. What was she thinking? *Damn.* He had to find her before she drove too far, had to convince her it wasn't necessary for her to go at all. Had he spooked her with his references to jealousy? Maybe his autocratic, "You can't wear that," had been too reminiscent of Rodney. *Sweet Lord.* If the son of a bitch caught her off alone—Jake cut the thought short, unable to bear thinking about it.

His pickup keys were kept on a hook in the kitchen. He raced through the house, trying to dress as he ran, and had one arm shoved down a sleeve by the time he reached the archway.

"Jake? My goodness, where's the fire?"

He braked to a stop so suddenly that his boots skidded on the floor. Molly stood at the stove, scrubbing a burner plate. As he said her name, a piece of bread popped up from the toaster, making her jump. She flapped her hand. "My breakfast. Yours is warming in the oven. Shorty and Levi told me about the sick gelding. Bless their hearts, they volunteered their services and helped me in the kitchen this morning." She reassembled the burner. "I saved you some eggs, bacon, and pancakes. They were like kids in a candy store, and I was their short order cook." She smiled. "Not that I minded. They helped a lot."

All the starch went out of Jake's spine. He'd never been so glad to see anyone in all his life. This morning, she was wearing that pretty yellow top he'd glimpsed last night and the same pair of jeans. The yellow cotton knit skimmed her figure like sunshine. The scoop neckline dipped low, revealing the tantalizing swell of her breasts. She looked young and beautiful and so sweet she made his heart catch.

He shoved his other arm into the sleeve of his shirt. "I thought you were gone."

A bewildered look came into her eyes. "Gone where?"

Jake couldn't help himself. He was across the kitchen in three strides. "Don't even think about leaving. Do you hear me, Molly?" He grabbed her up into his arms. "You scared the sand right out of me."

She gave a startled squeak as her feet cleared the floor. Jake felt the wet rag flop against his nape as she grabbed hold of his neck.

"My watch. You put it in my jeans. I thought you'd left." Jake hugged her close, so relieved to know she was still there and safe that he wanted to squeeze the breath right out of her. "You're not going anywhere, lady. Get that thought straight out of your head."

"But, Jake, I—"

"I mean it. I'll dismantle the whole damned Toyota and scatter the parts from hell to breakfast. You're staying put." He pressed his face to the curve of her neck, loving the smell of her, a blend of lotion, talc, and feminine essence that was exclusively her own. Sunshine and wildflowers. God, how he loved her. With each passing day, the feeling grew more intense. It was almost frightening to care so much about someone. "No arguments."

"I'm not arguing." She laughed shakily. "I didn't return the watch because I plan to leave. Not any time soon, anyway."

Jake went still. "You didn't?"

She leaned her head back, trying to see his face. "No. I just don't need to keep it anymore, and I figured you'd feel better if you had it back. A family heirloom like that is irreplaceable."

Jake straightened to search her eyes. "It was your only guarantee that I'd keep my word and not contact the authorities. Your collateral, remember? If you aren't planning to leave, why don't you need it anymore?"

Steadying herself by gripping his shoulders, she arched her spine to put distance between their chests. The rag, still in her right hand, trailed wetly down his sleeve. Jake didn't care. All that mattered was that she was there, that he could hold her like this and protect her if it became necessary.

She was everything he'd ever wanted. Absolutely everything.

"I don't need collateral anymore. Your word alone is enough." A suspicious shimmer came into her eyes. "I realize that now. You aren't the kind of man who breaks his promises."

Her expression told him more than she could know. He wasn't the only one who'd fallen in love.

"Thank you. That's one of the nicest things anyone's ever said to me."

He wanted so badly to kiss her then. Memories of that day in the woods hurtled through his mind—how sweetly she had responded to him, how she had melted against him, offering no resistance. Not three feet away, the kitchen counter beckoned, offering a perfect stage for another seduction. The other men were already out working. They were alone in the house. He could deposit her on the edge of the counter, kiss her until she went boneless, and then peel away all those clothes. He yearned to kiss her beautiful breasts, this time without two layers of cotton to shield her nipples, and hear her gasp with pleasure. And, oh, God, how he wished he could curl his hands over her bare bottom. He could feel the sweet warmth of her skin even through her jeans.

"I thought maybe—I don't know—that something I said yesterday had upset you, and you'd decided to leave."

"Nothing upset me *that* much."

He was beginning to feel a little foolish, but he was loath to release her now that he had her in his arms again. "Promise me something?"

"What?"

"That you'll never leave without telling me, no matter what happens."

"I won't," she said solemnly.

"Do you promise?"

"I promise. I'll at least tell you I'm going first."

In which case, he would do everything in his power to stop her, he thought fiercely.

"I'm sorry I frightened you," she said. "I couldn't think how to explain about the watch, so yesterday morning when I did laundry, I just slipped it into your clean jeans where I knew you'd be sure to find it."

She had explained herself quite eloquently. *"Your word alone is enough."* That she had come to trust him so much meant more to him than he could say. He threw a last, yearning look at the counter, then loosened his hold on her, letting her slide down his body until her feet touched the floor. The feeling of all her ample softness abrading his hardness almost snapped his control.

Ah, but he was a patient man, and some things were better if you waited. When he made love to this lady, he wanted everything to be perfectly right.

After cleaning the kitchen and doing her household chores, which took her until well past noon, Molly started washing the windows, a task she'd been putting off in favor of more pressing jobs. She had moved outside and completed about half of the lower story panes when she heard Jake saying, "Whoa. Easy boy." Her heart caught, for she knew the instant she heard his voice that he was working with Sunset.

Molly descended the ladder and sneaked around the corner of the house to watch. Man and horse stood stock still, facing each other, like two pugilists waiting for the bell to ring. Until now, Jake had always sat quietly in one corner of the pen. Since that first day, he hadn't tried to approach the stallion again.

Fascinated, she climbed the steps and leaned against the porch post to watch. On the afternoon breeze, she could hear the rise and fall of Jake's voice but couldn't make out all he said. Sunset cocked his ears, then snorted and shook his head. Jake only smiled and kept talking.

After a moment, Molly gave up trying to hear exactly what he said. The words themselves didn't matter. The unthreatening way he stood was eloquent, his tone of voice conveying everything.

Sunset was nervous. The muscles in his flanks quivered, and he lowered his head, a sign of equine subservience, according to what Jake had told her. Glancing at the man, Molly decided she would surrender, too, if she were Sunset. Jake looked tall, strong, and ready for anything, a fearful opponent, indeed.

Keeping up a steady stream of assurances, Jake slowly sidled up to the horse. It was a beautiful, warm afternoon that made the thought of lazing about in the sunshine sound far more appealing than window washing. Molly considered the half-finished pane she'd so abruptly abandoned and told herself she really should go back to work. Fascination with the man, the horse, and the bonding that was about to take place had her sinking down onto a step instead.

After watching Jake for a moment, she knew he meant to touch Sunset today. Gaze fixed, heart pounding, she hugged her knees. He stood with his head bent, his face slightly averted, his arms spread. As he raised his hand toward Sunset's neck, the stallion quivered from chest to rump, and his snorts turned to a plaintive nickering.

"I know," she heard Jake say.

And then he was touching the horse's neck, his palm barely grazing the glistening black coat. Molly held her breath.

"I know," Jake said again. "But it's okay, Sunset. That's all over. No one is going to hurt you again."

Sunset whickered and shifted. Slipping his hand under the stallion's neck, Jake stepped in closer until they stood shoulder to shoulder. As if the contact were simply too much, Sunset wheeled away. Jake let him go, turning to keep the horse in sight. After circling the corral several times, Sunset stopped and turned to face him again.

And Jake began the entire process over.

An hour later, Molly still huddled on the step, watching. She had long since lost count of how many times Jake had approached the stallion, touched him, and then lost him again. She'd never seen anyone with such patience. One tiny step forward, a gigantic step back. He'd told her once that horse training was very like a courtship, and she saw now that it was true. Jake didn't seem to mind that he was making no progress. He was content to repeat the same steps as many times as Sunset needed him to repeat them.

Tears filled Molly's eyes. *Jake.* She thought of all the nosegays and other little surprises he'd left on her doorstep. Her fireplace mantel was cluttered with pretty stones, colorful feathers, and parched blossoms. *"Sweet nothings,"* he always said with a shrug when she thanked him. Molly disagreed. Those silly sweet nothings meant the world to her.

He was like no other individual she'd ever known. Horse whisperer or ordinary man, it no longer mattered. As he approached Sunset, she could almost feel his gentleness and concern. He had a very special gift, an air about him that worked past barriers and touched in a way that even a terrified horse couldn't resist.

"Come down here, Molly," he suddenly called.

She snapped erect. She hadn't realized he knew she was there.

"Come on," he called again.

Her legs had grown stiff. She pushed slowly up from the step. By the time she reached the corral, Jake had scaled the fence and stood outside. He smiled when she walked up to him.

"You've seen how it's done. Now you try it."

"Oh, no, I—"

He caught her chin on the edge of his hand, his gaze locking with hers. "You said this morning that you trust my word. Do you?"

"Yes, of course, but—"

"He won't hurt you. You've got my word on it."

"How can you know?"

Jake released her chin and turned his gaze toward the horse. "I feel it."

"You *feel* it?" Molly was tempted to laugh, only then she recalled the many times she'd seen him out in the fields, working with other horses. A silent communication seemed to take place between him and a horse that couldn't be explained by everyday standards, but was no less real.

Molly searched his gaze, all her senses suddenly acute. *Trust.* She'd sworn to never give hers blindly again.

"The whole time I've been working with him, I've caught him looking your way. That horse worships you, honey."

Molly gulped. She had come to trust Jake Coulter in a way she hadn't imagined might be possible when she first arrived, but she wasn't sure she trusted him so much she was willing to put her life on the line.

Molly was trembling so badly, she could barely climb over the fence. Sunset didn't help matters any. The moment she invaded his pen, he began grunting and sidestepping. Molly hung halfway down the inside rails, looking over her shoulder at the stallion, convinced he would trample her the instant her feet touched the ground.

"He's only talking to you," Jake assured her.

"What's he saying?" she asked shrilly.

Jake came to rest his arms on a rail and gazed over the fence at the horse. "He's saying it's about time you came in to visit him. He's been waiting and waiting. Isn't it just like a woman to drag her feet?"

Molly didn't believe for a minute that Jake knew what the horse was thinking, but she drew strength from the twinkling amusement in his eyes. If she knew nothing else about him, she believed he was a good and kind man. He wouldn't be laughing if he thought she were about to get hurt.

Trust. It kept coming back to that. Where men were involved, it didn't come easily to her. When she had awakened from a drug-induced stupor to find herself in a clinic for the emotionally ill, she'd lost her faith in the benevolent nature of the male of her species.

Now, here she was, at another crossroads. Jake was asking her to trust him with her safety, possibly even her life. If he was wrong—oh, God, if he was wrong—she would never be fleet enough of foot to escape before the stallion did her serious injury.

Her feet connected with the dirt. Molly gulped. It was all she could do to relax her grip on the fence rail. On legs that threatened to buckle, she turned to face the horse.

"His h-head is up," she said in a wobbly voice. "He's not subservient."

"No," Jake agreed softly. "Would you just look at that?"

Molly was looking, and she almost wet her pants. The stallion whickered, threw his massive head, and pawed the dirt with a front hoof. "Oh, God!"

"Sweetheart, he isn't afraid of you. *Look* at him. That's a welcome sight, if ever I saw one. He's just telling you hello."

"Oh." Molly struggled to swallow. "Hello, Sunset."

The stallion grunted and high-stepped in a figure eight at his end of the pen, his tail lifted high. When he wheeled to a stop, he whickered and threw his head again.

"Ah, Molly," Jake murmured. "Go to him."

She groped behind her for the fence rail. . . . *Nothing.* "I, um . . . maybe it'd be better if I wait for him to come to me."

"Just take it slow. You watched me. You know how to do it."

"Sort of sideways?"

"If you like. I'm not sure that's necessary. That's my signal to him that I mean him no harm. I think he already knows that you don't."

Molly figured the stallion probably wasn't afraid of her because she was so pathetically unthreatening, a plump woman of diminutive stature who tripped over her own feet.

"One slow step at a time," Jake whispered. "Go to him."

Molly took one step. Sunset blew through his nose and scared her half to death. "What's that mean?"

"Nothing. He's just talking to you."

"What's he saying this time?" She took another step. "I'm really not cut out for this, you know. What'll I do when I reach him?"

"Just pet him."

"Don't horses bite?"

"He won't bite you."

Molly prayed not. Sunset had gigantic teeth. She took another step, then another. The horse stopped prancing and stood stock still, his head still lifted high, his ears cocked forward.

"Talk to him," Jake instructed. "Reassure him."

"Hello, Sunset," Molly called in a quivery trill. "Don't kill me. Okay?" She took another step. "I, um . . . don't know anything about horses, you know. Make my first experience a pleasant one." She took several more steps and ran out of courage. "I can't, Jake. I just can't. He's so *big*."

"You're better than halfway. You can do it."

"No. I think maybe . . . " The horse took a step toward her. "Oh, dear. *Jake?*"

"I'll be damned," he said when the horse took another step. "Will you just look at that. Stand tight, Molly. He's as wary as you are. Don't frighten him by making any sudden movements."

Molly seriously doubted the horse was as wary as she was. He outweighed her by a goodly amount, and he had hooves and teeth.

Step by hesitant step, Sunset closed the remaining distance. When he reached Molly, he sniffed her chest. Then he simply stood there with his great head hanging.

Molly was no expert on horses, but even she could interpret this body language. Inexpressible weariness rolled off the stallion in waves. Her gaze shifted to his poor, abused body. From close range, she could see where the whip had sliced deeply into his flesh. Some of the wounds would leave vicious scars, and she knew the deep ones that hadn't yet healed must still hurt terribly.

"Oh, Sunset," she whispered. "I'm so sorry he did this. I'm so sorry."

The horse grunted and nudged her hand. His nose felt as soft as velvet. Molly turned her wrist to touch his muzzle with her fingertips. Sunset wiggled his lip, tickling her skin.

Just like that, the fear left Molly. Sunset wanted her as his friend. Not Jake, but *her*. Trembling, she ran her fingers up the center of his nose. She hadn't realized until now that horses had eyelashes. Sunset had long, sooty ones, and soulful brown eyes that pleaded with her. She touched the silky tufts at the base of his ears, then fingered his mane, which was coarse and heavy, the texture of the strands reminding her of raw silk.

"You're beautiful," she whispered in awe. "You're so beautiful, Sunset." Growing braver, Molly stretched out a hand to touch his neck, then she stepped closer to gently stroke his shoulder, taking care to avoid his lacerations. "Good boy. You're such a love."

From behind her, Jake said, "You've got your work cut out for you today. Those cuts need disinfectant and salve. The ones that haven't healed are starting to ooze puss."

Molly could see that they were, a sign that mild infection had set in. "He needs antibiotics."

"I have some penicillin in the stable fridge. Maybe later, when you're feeling more at ease, you can give him an injection. For now, it'll be a step forward just to clean them."

"You want *me* to do it?" she asked incredulously.

"No one else can touch him," was Jake's reply. "His vote carries the day, honey, and he's chosen you."

Molly had never been chosen for much of anything. In grade school, she'd been thin and undersized. None of the other kids had ever called her name when they were teaming up for sports. As she'd grown older, she'd become a bookworm, exacerbating the problem.

Warmth spread through her—a wonderful, uplifting feeling of warmth. Sunset had chosen *her*. Jake was far more qualified. He knew how to doctor horses, how to give injections. He was an all around expert, while she knew absolutely nothing. But Sunset had chosen *her*.

"I'm going to run and get you some disinfectant and

cotton. Two things for you to remember. Don't step behind
him, ever. Horses can't see behind them, and they sometimes kick out. Another thing to bear in mind, always, is
that he's got binocular vision in front, monocular to the
side. When you stand near his rump, it's hard for him to
see you unless he turns his head. Keep a hand on him so he
knows where you are and talk to him a lot so he can keep
track of your voice. A large percentage of the time when
horses injure humans, it's because the humans do something stupid."

That sounded reasonable. "Are you sure it's safe to
leave me then? I'm a master at stupidity."

He chuckled. "I'll only be gone a couple of minutes.
Just continue as you are, Molly. Pet him, talk to him.
That's the best medicine for what ails him right now, what
he needs the very most."

"What do I say?"

Jake hesitated before replying. "What would you want
someone to say to you?"

Keeping her voice pitched low so as not to be overheard,
Molly spent the next few minutes speaking from her heart
to Sunset, saying all the things she felt he needed to hear
because she needed to hear them herself.

"It wasn't your fault," she whispered. "You gave him all
you had and tried your hardest. That was never enough for
him. He just kept pressing you for more, and then for
more, pitting you against older, faster horses, wanting the
fatter purse. It was never your fault, Sunset."

Sunset whinnied softly and thrust his nose in Molly's
armpit. She stiffened, uncertain what to do, but when the
horse only stood there, keeping his muzzle pressed against
her, she realized he was only frightened and wanted to be
as close to her as possible. A dog might have crawled on
her lap. Being too large for that, Sunset sought comfort in
the only way he could, by surrounding himself with her
smell.

Taking care not to hurt him, she rested her other arm over the crest of his neck and pressed her cheek to his forehead. "Oh, Sunset, life is so unfair. I wish I could have stopped this. If only I had known, I would have stolen you sooner."

Jake returned with the medication just then. He waited with it at the opposite side of the fence, hesitant to enter for fear he might frighten the horse. "This stuff doesn't sting, and it has anesthetic properties to ease his discomfort," he said as she came to the fence for the bottle. "All you do is soak the cotton balls with it, then gently swab the lacerations, cleaning them as thoroughly as you can. Afterward you can apply salve, which will keep dirt out of the cuts and help them heal."

Molly nodded. Jake held her gaze, his dark face creasing in a smile. "You're doing great so far," he told her warmly.

"I'm not so scared now." She blinked and glanced quickly away. "Oh, Jake, he's so—broken. I remember how proud he used to look whenever I saw him, and now he's so broken."

"Nothing is irreversible," he assured her.

"I pray you're right. It would be such a shame if he never got over it."

"He will. If you love him enough, he will."

Molly met his gaze again, no longer caring if he saw the tears in her eyes.

"The pride is still there in him," he said. "That's why this has been so hard on him, because he's got pride and an inner strength that Rodney couldn't beat out of him. You know that saying, 'The bigger they are, the harder they fall.' Sunset took a painful tumble, Molly, but he's got it in him to get back up."

"I don't know," Molly said, remembering how the stallion had thrust his nose under her arm. "I really don't know if he has that kind of strength left."

Jake gazed solemnly at the horse. When at last he

spoke, his voice had gone thick. "You have to believe in him, honey. Right now, he's so lost, and his world has been turned topsy-turvy. You have to help him believe in himself again." His mouth tipped into a sad smile. "You're his mirror. How you see him is how he'll eventually come to see himself. Do you understand what I'm saying?"

A lump came to Molly's throat. "That we see ourselves as others do?"

He reached through the fence to cup her cheek. After regarding each of her features as if to commit them to memory, he said, "Exactly. We see ourselves as others do."

When he turned and walked away, Molly gazed after him, unable to shake the feeling that he'd been referring to far more than just the horse.

We see ourselves as others do. Over the next two hours, as Molly worked with Sunset, those words circled endlessly in her mind.

Arms resting on a fence rail, Jake listened to Molly reassure the horse. In the not so distant past, she'd questioned her ability to be Sunset's mistress, claiming that her feelings for the stallion ran closer to pity than to love.

That wasn't what he heard now. Every word, every inflection of her voice, rang deep with caring. Jake relaxed slightly, confident that he'd done the right thing. He could easily have hooked on with Sunset himself, but when he'd felt Molly watching him, he'd started pulling back. She needed this, maybe even more than Sunset did. As she talked to the horse, she was talking to herself as well, whether she realized it or not.

"It wasn't your fault, Sunset. Never yours."

Nor had it ever been Molly's fault. Jake was absolutely sure of that.

"He's a vicious, cruel *monster* for doing this to you."

Rodney had been just as cruel to Molly, and it was only a matter of time before she began to realize it.

"He made you lose faith in yourself."

Molly's faith in herself had been destroyed as well.

"You're so beautiful, Sunset. So very, very beautiful."

Jake looked at Molly and thought how very beautiful she was. The sassy haircut and new clothes had transformed her. More important, he had completely lost his heart to the person she was within. All his life he'd been told that beauty was only skin deep, but he'd never really understood what that meant until now. He was going to love this woman forever, not just while she was young and pretty but when she grew old. Fifty years from now, when he looked at her, he would love every gray hair on her head and every wrinkle on her sweet face.

We see ourselves as others do.

Now that she'd said the words, how long would it be before the truth of them was driven home? How long would it be before she looked in the mirror and saw herself instead of the distorted image that Rodney had created in her mind?

Sweet, beautiful Molly, who believed she was plain.

Sweet, beautiful Molly, who constantly dieted in a futile attempt to alter the glorious figure that nature had bestowed on her.

Sweet, beautiful Molly, who looked but couldn't see.

"I'll never forgive him for what he's done to you," she whispered to the horse.

Jake heard the words and closed his eyes, thinking that he, too, would never forgive. He didn't know exactly what Rodney had done to her, but the results had been devastating, and, like the horse, she had a very long journey still ahead of her to reach wellness.

It was Jake's hope that woman and horse would make the journey together.

Chapter Sixteen

Molly dreamed that night of Sarah and her father. Their faces haunted her in slumber as she never allowed them to during the day. *"Molly, help us!"* they cried, imploring her, reaching out to her.

Molly met with countless obstacles as she struggled to reach them. The world went dark with shifting shadows that drifted like sooty smoke, the tendrils seeming almost alive as they curled around her. She didn't know where she was, and nothing looked familiar.

She came to a deep, yawning chasm spanned by a rickety footbridge. When she looked across the fissure, she saw Sarah and her father standing on the other side, both of them reaching out to her. Molly called out that she was coming and hurried onto the bridge. Running, running . . . *No matter how she tried, she seemed to get nowhere. With growing terror, she saw that the footbridge was becoming narrower and narrower until she was balanced on a quivering strip of wood little wider than a ruler. Afraid of falling, she turned back to find another way across, only the bridge behind her had vanished.*

She fell then, head over heels and endlessly, plunging ever downward, the echoes of Sarah's and her father's screams becoming so faint they were barely whispers in her mind. When she hit bottom, she sank into a fathomless blackness as thick as crude oil. Drowning in it and frantic to breathe, she struggled upward. When at last she broke the surface, she treaded in place, searching the edge of the chasm for her father and friend.

Finally she spotted them, arms thrown wide as they pleaded with her to save them. When she tried to swim, the thick coldness nearly sucked her under. She pressed onward, gasping for air, her heart slamming. I'm coming, *she thought.* I hear you this time, and I'm coming.

One minute it seemed to be Sarah's voice calling to her, the next her father's. Molly struggled onward, frantic to reach them. She couldn't let them die. Not this time. She wouldn't fail them again.

At last she saw Sarah just ahead. Her friend seemed to be standing under a spotlight, its harsh brilliance illuminating every detail of her person. Dressed in an oversized nightshirt, she looked frightened and confused, much as she had in the days before her death. In her right hand, she held a razor blade. "Help me," *she cried, and then with a sob, she slashed her wrists.*

"No!" *Molly screamed.* "Please, no! Wait for me, Sarah. I'm almost there! Don't, please, don't!"

Only it was too late. Sarah sank to her knees, crimson splashing over her white nightshirt and down her legs. Horrified, Molly realized the black slime all around her had turned to blood. Sarah began to scream, long, high-pitched cries of agony—and still Molly couldn't reach her. Not again. It couldn't happen like this again.

Molly jerked awake.

For a frozen instant, she stared blankly upward, her body rigid. Then she sat bolt upright in bed, her skin beaded with sweat, her legs tangled in the sheets. She covered her face with her hands, unable to get the screams out of her head. Shrill and piercing, they seemed so real.

Molly dropped her hands to listen, her horror growing as she realized the screaming wasn't part of a dream. She leaped from the bed and dashed to the open window. Flickering orange light played over the upper panes of glass. Grabbing the sill, Molly thrust her head out the opening and looked through the trees. *Fire*. The stable. Oh, dear God, the *stable*.

She never gave a thought to a robe as she raced from the bedroom. Once at the front door, she stumbled to a stop, bewildered to find it standing ajar. She would have sworn she locked it before going to bed.

The screams jerked the thought from her mind. The horses. All those poor horses. Was Jake already out there? Did he even realize that the stable was on fire?

Light from the flames reached into the darkness, enabling Molly to see. As she ran, she barely felt the pricks and jabs to the bottoms of her feet. She thought of White Star's brand new baby, then of the mare herself and all the other horses. What a horrible way to die, trapped in a raging inferno. If Jake wasn't already awake, she had to raise an alarm.

When Molly drew near the burning building, she heard shouts and saw the dark silhouettes of men rushing about, some manning water hoses, others trying to calm the panicked animals they'd led from the building. The commotion was confusing. Horses shrieked and fought their leads, trying desperately to escape both the men and the fire. She saw Shorty and Tex struggling to free a hose from beneath the animals' churning hooves. Then she spotted Hank and Bill, tending to White Star's new foal, which looked more frightened than hurt.

Relieved not to be the first person on the scene, Molly ran to check on Sunset. The stallion stood at the far end of his pen, rump pressed to the rails, his attention riveted to the flames. When he saw Molly, he grunted nervously and swung his head. She skirted the corral and reached through the rails to pet him.

"It's okay, boy. You're safe here."

Almost as if he understood, the stallion nodded his massive head and pawed the dirt.

Convinced Sunset would be fine, Molly left him to go find Jake. Later she never knew how she managed to pick him out of the melee, but she spotted him almost instantly. Wielding a flashlight, he was moving from horse to horse, checking them for injuries. As Molly drew closer, she glanced at the burning stable, thinking that Jake's time might be better spent trying to help put out the blaze. A few of his hired hands were trying, but it looked as if they were losing the battle.

"Are all the horses okay?" she asked as she reached him.

He glanced up, then snaked out a hand to grab her wrist and draw her to his side. "Never do that, Molly! You'll get the shit kicked out of you."

Molly realized she'd run up behind the gelding. The long fingers of flickering amber that played over them suddenly flared more brightly, followed by a crashing sound and a burst of fiery orange against the night sky. Molly jumped with a start. The gelding wheeled and whinnied, panicked by the blast of heat.

Still holding Molly's wrist, Jake sprang erect and shoved hard against the animal's rump to keep it from side-stepping onto her feet. Glancing past his shoulder, she saw that the stable roof had just caved in.

"Oh, God," she cried, raising her voice to be heard over the din. "The stable, Jake. How did this start? Are all the horses out?"

"The horses are all fine." He jerked her hard against him, releasing her hand to slip an arm around her. "Damn, Molly, what are you doing out here half dressed and barefoot?"

Without waiting for an answer, he thrust the flashlight under his belt and shouldered his way through the milling horses and men, protecting her with his bulk as he drew her along. Only at the edge of the stable yard did he allow her to escape his embrace.

"What the hell were you thinking?" he asked sharply. "You don't come around panicked horses without shoes. Do you have any idea the damage their hooves can do?"

Molly hugged her waist, suddenly and acutely aware that she wore only an oversized T-shirt and a pair of white lace panties. Jake skimmed her with a glittering gaze, his attention lingering for a split second on her bare legs. "Go get some clothes on," he bit out.

She retreated a step. "I'm sorry. I just—" She broke off, the words to explain eluding her. "I wasn't sure if you knew. About the fire, I mean. So I just ran out here without thinking."

She turned to walk away. She took only two steps before he checked her flight with a steely hand on her shoulder.

"Molly."

Just that. *Molly.* Yet the way he said her name told her everything. She stopped to look back at him. In the play of firelight, she could see streaks of soot on his face. For the first time since she'd known him, his broad shoulders were slumped. He looked so defeated.

"I'm sorry," he ground out. Still grasping her shoulder, he glanced back toward the fire. "I shouldn't have snapped at you like that."

A horse screamed, and his grip on her shoulder tightened. Molly reached up to pry his fingers away. "Go, Jake. They need you, and I'm fine."

"I'm sorry," he said again. "I was just afraid you'd get hurt, and I—" He broke off and swallowed. "I'm sorry."

Molly managed a smile. "I'll get dressed and come back."

He gave her shoulder a gentle squeeze. "Stay away from the horses until they've calmed down. I've lost enough for one night."

Molly gazed after him, admiring the easy, sure strength of his movements as he broke into a run. When he reached the horses, he slipped the flashlight from his belt and resumed his task of checking them for burns.

Molly stood there for a time, observing him. He seemed totally focused on the animals. The shouts of the men fighting the fire didn't seem to penetrate his consciousness. When more timbers inside the burning building collapsed, he barely glanced in that direction, more concerned with the welfare of the horses than with the loss of his property. Seeing that tugged at Molly's heart. She had already come to admire Jake Coulter, but never more so than now.

The collapse of the timbers spooked a mare that had been tethered to an outside front corner of Sunset's pen. She reared and fought the rope, her front hooves slashing wildly at the fence rails. Jake hurried over to grab her halter.

"Whoa, whoa," Molly heard him say. Using his strength and weight, he hauled down hard on the frantic horse's head to prevent her from rearing again. She whinnied and trembled, sidestepping nervously. Jake ran a hand over her withers and leaned close to whisper something. The mare made plaintive grunting sounds, but she quieted under his touch. Jake untied her rope and led her to the opposite end of the corral where she would be away from the fire.

Molly smiled, remembering how he had denied being a horse whisperer. Far be it from her to argue the point, but she could testify to one thing. He had a way about him that soothed horses and gained their trust.

Her smile deepened. He had a way with women as well.

A few minutes later, as Molly ascended the porch steps to the cabin, she recalled the front door being ajar when she first woke up. *Strange.* She could have sworn she'd locked it before going to bed.

Feeling a need to hurry, she didn't allow herself to wonder about it. She wanted to get dressed as quickly as possible and return to the stable. She might be a total loss when it came to helping with the horses, but there were surely other things she could do.

She flipped on the overhead light as she stepped into the bedroom. Halfway across the room, she lurched to a stop, her gaze riveted to her rumpled bed. The white sheets were smeared with dirt and peppered with pine needles. Bewildered, Molly stepped closer for a better look. Her heart flipped and fluttered. She picked up a pine needle and stared stupidly at it. How on earth had debris gotten on her sheets? They'd been clean when she went to bed.

Feeling numb, she sank onto the edge of the mattress. A cold feeling washed over her. The pine needle slipped from her fingers and drifted to the floor. Once again, she recalled finding the front door ajar when she first woke up, a door she felt sure she had locked before going to bed.

Oh, God. Had she been sleepwalking?

The mere thought made Molly's stomach drop. Though she tried never to think of those days, she *did* have a history of somnambulism.

She turned to stare at the sheets. Then she looked down at her feet. They were filthy from running outdoors barefoot. If she climbed back into bed right now, she would rub dirt off on the linen, leaving smears much like the ones already there.

Oh, no . . . please, no.

Molly clamped a hand over her mouth, remembering her bouts of somnambulism in college. Had she sleepwalked and left the cabin when she wasn't aware of it? She'd been so certain that her more recent sleepwalking episodes had been staged by Rodney to make her look crazy. But maybe she'd been wrong.

Someone had left the front door standing open.

Someone had gotten dirt all over her sheets.

This couldn't be Rodney's handiwork. He was nowhere around.

She glanced at the window where light from the fire still played over the glass. An awful, sick feeling moved through her. She thought of White Star's sweet little foal. He might have died in that fire, and all the other horses could have as well.

Dear God. What had she done?

Pressing her hands over her face, Molly struggled to calm down. *Don't jump to conclusions.* Back in her college days, she'd had difficulty coming to grips with her best friend Sarah's suicide, and after her death, she had sleepwalked for a time. Once, she had wandered into the dormitory kitchen during the breakfast rush and awakened to find herself on display in nothing but a nightgown. Another time, she'd gone outside and awakened standing in a busy intersection. Those incidents had been alarming and undeniably bizarre, but she'd never done anything destructive or violent during the sleepwalking episodes until a year ago, shortly after her dad's death. And she had reason to believe Rodney had staged those episodes for his own nefarious reasons.

Why, then, should she automatically assume that she was responsible for setting that fire?

Molly dropped her hands and hauled in a deep, bracing breath. There was really no reason for her to believe she'd been sleepwalking. There was another explanation for the open front door and the dirt on her sheets.

There had to be.

By midafternoon the next day, Molly was so tired she could barely move. Since breakfast she'd been helping the men build emergency pens and lean-tos for the horses. Despite the chill air, the sun felt hot on her shoulders, and sweat trickled down her spine. Each time she raised the ax, her muscles quivered and jerked. For what felt like the millionth time, she swung at the base of a branch, her aim to denude a young lodgepole pine so it could be used as a fence rail.

At the edge of the forest, Bill manned a chainsaw to fell more trees. A woody smell drifted on the breeze along with particles of sawdust that coated her nostrils. Occasional puffs of smoke from the smoldering fire stung her eyes.

"Here's another one, Molly." Danno heaved a tree onto

the growing pile that awaited her attention. "If you need a rest, holler. I'll take over for you."

As much as Molly appreciated the offer, she couldn't accept. Danno was needed to drag the fallen trees over to the pile, a job she lacked the strength to do. At least she was helping here. Sort of, anyway. No matter how fast she worked, she was unable to keep up with the men who labored behind her.

Each time they ran out of poles, one of the older hands helped Molly catch up, his skill and speed at wielding an ax putting hers to shame. They all seemed to appreciate her willingness to help, though, and that was what mattered.

"Got it!" Nate yelled to Ben. "Hold her steady." That directive was punctuated with loud hammering. "Okay, she's sturdy!"

Molly tried to swing the ax again, but her arms refused to cooperate. Accepting the fact that she had to rest for a few seconds, she propped the ax handle against the log, pressed a fist to the small of her back, and stood up straight. Pain. She could have sworn she heard every joint in her body pop.

She stared at the remains of the stable to her left. Warped and blackened by the extreme heat, the sheets of corrugated steel had collapsed helter-skelter, reminding her of a flattened house of cards. She remembered how the structure had once looked, a mammoth green pole building with tidy paddocks. Now the interior had been reduced to chunks of charred timber and ash.

"Pretty sad, isn't it?" Hank commented as he came to get another pole. "Why anyone would do such a thing is beyond me."

According to the Crystal County fire chief, who had concluded his investigation and left only a couple of hours ago, the stable blaze had been deliberately set. After dousing the back of the building with diesel taken from Jake's machine shop, someone had ignited the fuel with a match.

"I can't imagine it, either." Parched with thirst, the

walls of Molly's throat rasped together. "At least you got all the horses out."

"That's true." Hefting a pole onto his shoulder, Hank walked away.

After he left, Molly wanted to just stand there for a few minutes. She checked the position of the sun. There wasn't much daylight left. Of the horses now grazing in the front pastures, two of the mares were due to foal soon, one of the geldings had a respiratory infection, another had been suffering with diaphragm spasms, and White Star's new baby still needed shelter at night when the temperature dropped. They *had* to get the lean-tos up before dark.

She clenched her teeth and bent to grab the ax. Just then she heard the front door of the house slam shut, the sound cutting through the air like a rifle shot. She glanced over her shoulder to see Jake coming down the porch steps. The erect set of his shoulders and the brisk way he moved told her he was angry.

In the middle of notching a pole, Hank stopped and swept off his hat to wipe sweat from his brow. "Well?" he called. "What'd the insurance guy say?"

Jake kicked a charred board from his path. "Son of a bitch is trying to renege. Says the machine shop should've been locked, that they aren't liable."

Hank slapped his Stetson back on his head. "That is such bullshit. Name me one working ranch where they keep all the outbuildings locked."

As Jake drew closer, he cut Molly a glance. Then he settled his hands at his hips. "If I have to, I'll hire a lawyer. There isn't a single clause in my policy that says the outbuildings have to be locked." Looking bone weary, he rubbed the back of his neck. "I spoke to the sheriff as well. He thinks kids set the fire."

"Kids?" Tex leaned over to spit. "This wasn't the work of youngsters."

Jake sighed as he surveyed the devastation. "Maybe the

sheriff has a point. A sane adult would draw the line at setting fire to a stable full of horses."

Molly's stomach clenched. A *sane* adult? Sweat beaded her face. She resumed her task of hacking off branches. With every swing, the ax grew heavier. Half the time, she missed her mark and left big gouges in the log.

"The fuel cans were full and handy," Jake went on. "You take a bunch of drugged-up kids out on the prowl, and they might think setting a fire was fun."

"Oh, horse puckey," Levi said as he hammered a nail. "Even dopey kids have more sense than that. He gonna check for fingerprints on those cans?"

"Sure. Problem is, they may not match up with anything on file. If it was kids, they may never have been fingerprinted."

Molly was about to take another swing with the ax when a brown hand locked over her forearm. Startled, she glanced up into Jake's brilliant blue eyes. "You're finished," he said softly.

Molly gestured at the poles she still needed to strip. "I've got at least—"

"You're finished," he said again. "Go on up to the house and have a cup of coffee. You're so tuckered you can't spit. That ax could jump back at you."

Molly had narrowly missed hitting her shin a few minutes ago, so she didn't argue the point. She really *was* exhausted.

As she started away, Jake called, "Why are you limping?"

She paused to stare stupidly at her filthy sneakers. Recalling her race to the stable last night, she shrugged and said, "Stickers, I guess."

No sooner had she reached the kitchen than she heard the front door open and close. The thud of heavy boots followed her path through the house. She was about to pour a cup of coffee when Jake appeared in the archway. Without a word, he settled his hands on her shoulders and steered her to a chair.

Molly sank down, too weary to protest when he hunkered before her and lifted her foot onto his knee. Off went her shoe, then her sock. Turning her ankle, he bent to examine her sole. "Holy hell. Why didn't you get these out right away? Now they're all inflamed."

Molly craned her neck to see. The bottom of her foot was dotted with red spots. "I was so upset I didn't really notice the tenderness."

He lowered her foot back to the floor and went to a drawer for the kitchen matches. When he returned a moment later, he fished his pocketknife from his jeans, struck a match, and sterilized the blade. Molly watched him dubiously.

"If you plan to dig stickers from my feet with that, think again."

He chuckled and hunkered back down in front of her. Curling a warm hand over her ankle, he lifted her foot back onto his knee. "Trust me. This is the best sliver picker you've ever seen. Hold still, okay?"

"I don't dare move. I could lose a leg."

He smiled, his ministrations so gentle that Molly barely felt them. She sighed and relaxed. Well, almost. It was difficult to completely relax with his long fingers curled over her foot.

When he finished extracting all the stickers, he kept her left foot on his knee, his big, calloused hand wrapped over her ankle. His pinky found its way under her pant leg and lightly caressed her calf, setting her skin afire. He gazed solemnly up at her, the expression on his face unreadable.

"I guess you'll live," he said softly.

This was the first opportunity they'd really had to talk since the fire. "I'm so sorry about your stable, Jake."

"No need for you to be sorry. It wasn't your doing."

Molly prayed not. "I'm pleased that all the horses are okay."

He nodded. "They're all that really matters."

Molly gripped the edges of the chair. "I know it's none of my business, but you've said things that lead me to believe you may be in difficult financial straits."

"Now there's a nice, fancy way of putting it."

"So I haven't misread it?"

He lowered her foot to the floor, then reached for her shoes. "I'm in hock up to my gonads and feeling the squeeze."

Molly thought of the huge amounts of money that would be hers when she regained control of her inheritance. It didn't seem fair, somehow, that she should have so much when someone like Jake had so little. "I'm so sorry."

His mouth twitched. "You have a bad habit of saying you're sorry for things that aren't your fault. No one twisted my arm to make me buy this ranch back."

"Why did you then?" Again Molly realized she was asking a question about something that was none of her business. "You've been to college. You could probably make a far better living working for someone else."

He nodded. "Without a doubt, but money isn't everything. I grew up here." He shrugged. "It's hard to explain what that means to me. I thought us boys would take it over one day, that we'd live on this land, raise our families here like generations of Coulters had before." His mouth curved in another slight smile. "From the time I was a little guy, I was good with horses. When I grew older, I dreamed of raising my own line, of training them from birth. I always thought I'd be able to do it here, that one day I'd make the Lazy J famous, in its way. When I got the chance to buy it back, it wasn't a decision I made with my head, but with my heart."

Molly knew how that went. Helping Sunset had been a decision of the heart. "How did your dad lose the place?" She imagined him drinking or gambling himself into deep debt. "Or is that too personal a question?"

"He went bankrupt and lost everything," Jake said solemnly. "Everything but the dream, anyway."

By his husky tone of voice, Molly knew that had been a painful time for him.

"As soon as I got out of college, I started working and saving to buy another place," he went on. "It took me a few years to scrape up a down payment and the working capital, but I finally managed. I was watching the market, never dreaming the Lazy J might be available. One day, after looking at a spread out this way, Hank and I stopped by here on impulse to take a stroll down memory lane. The man who owned the place was ready to sell. I leaped at the chance."

Molly dug her nails into the underside of the chair seat. "What caused your dad to go bankrupt?"

He ran a hand over his rumpled hair. He'd scrubbed the soot from his face, but he still looked tired. "My sister Bethany was paralyzed in a riding accident. She underwent three surgeries, and our health insurance wasn't that good. My dad went into hock, hoping she might walk again. She never did."

Some men might resent that, but not Jake. She'd seen his disregard for the burning stable last night, his sole concern for the welfare of his horses. He undoubtedly would have sacrificed anything for his sister. "If the insurance company won't cover the fire damage, what will you do?"

"There's no way I can scrape up the money to rebuild the stable by myself." He pushed wearily to his feet. "They'll cover it. I won't take no for an answer."

Molly couldn't let it go at that. "But if it happens that they don't?"

His brows pleated in a frown. He stared out the kitchen window. Voice husky, he said, "Then I'll be back to square one, with only a dream in my pocket."

Molly fixed supper alone that night. Jake was far too busy working outside to help her cook. At his suggestion, she made a tuna-and-rice casserole, a simple concoction of rice, canned tuna, and cream of mushroom soup, which she sprinkled with cheddar cheese and baked. Two huge pans of cornbread and a giant mixing bowl filled with canned corn complemented the meal. High starch, high fat. Molly felt sure the men would love it.

She was about to call them in to eat when the kitchen wall phone rang. Grabbing a towel to wipe her hands, she hurried to answer it. "The Lazy J."

"Howdy. This is Sheriff Dexter. Is Jake handy?"

Molly had steered clear of the sheriff that morning. Knowing it was he on the phone made her nerves leap. "I, um—yes. Can you hold for just a moment?"

She raced through the house and out onto the front porch. "Jake?" she called. "The sheriff is on the line."

He abandoned the section of fence he was building and came loping up to the house. Molly preceded him as they made their way to the kitchen. While Jake conversed on the phone, she put glasses on the table, along with two gallons of milk. She'd just finished when he broke the connection.

"Bad news?"

He nodded. "There were no prints on the fuel cans. Chances are the person or persons responsible will never be caught."

"No prints? That doesn't sound like the work of kids to me."

Jake scowled. "Not to me, either. Seems strange that a bunch of kids would have thought to wear gloves."

"Yes, it does." It also struck Molly as highly unlikely that a sleepwalker would have the presence of mind to be that clever.

The relief that coursed through her made her bones watery.

Directly after supper, the men went back outside to work on the lean-tos, using halogen floodlights to see in

the deepening darkness. By the time Molly had finished all
her kitchen chores, only half of the needed shelters were
done. Jake was busy moving horses in from the pastures to
put them in the few available lean-tos. The moment he saw
Molly, he turned over the task to one of his men and
walked to meet her.

"How can I help?" Molly asked.

He shook his head. "You've done enough for one day."

"Some of the horses need shelter, and the work still isn't
done."

"But you are." He took her arm. "I want you to get a
good night's rest."

"While you stay up half the night, finishing the lean-
tos?"

"I'm used to losing sleep. You aren't."

As they fell into a walk, Molly realized he was heading
for her cabin. "You don't need to see me home tonight,
Jake." Gesturing toward the lights, she smiled. "I'll be able
to see well enough. It's as bright as day out here."

"Not away from the lights, it isn't." He jerked off his
soiled leather gloves and tucked them over his belt. "Besides, I'm due for a short break."

Molly saw no point in arguing. She'd come to know
Jake well over the past three weeks. No matter what she
said, he was going to walk her home.

"No detours tonight. You've got work to do, and my
feet are sore."

Shortening his strides to match her pace, he chuckled
and cast her an inquiring look. Light from behind them illuminated one side of his face, casting the other in shadow,
which served to delineate the sharp bridge of his nose, the
muscular line of his jaw, and the nearly perfect bow shape
of his hard mouth.

"How's the rest of you doing?" he asked. "Any muscles
screaming yet?"

Her muscles had started screaming hours ago, but she

wasn't about to complain. Everyone else had worked hard, too. "I'm sturdier than most women."

The corner of his mouth twitched, telling her he was trying hard not to smile. "A veritable Amazon, that's you."

Molly shivered at the cold and drew her jacket closer around her. "Laugh if you like. I may not be well toned and athletic, but I *am* stout."

He said nothing to contradict her. As they walked along, Molly stared at their shadows, which danced like dark specters ahead of them, his tall and lean, hers short and squat. There was no denying that she was solidly built. Next to Jake's, the outline of her legs put her in mind of tree stumps.

Once at the house, he insisted on going in to check the rooms. Though touched by his concern for her safety, Molly couldn't resist teasing him when he entered the small, U-shaped kitchen to open the broom closet.

"That's barely big enough to hide a midge," she observed. When that didn't deter him, she laughed and added, "Don't forget to look under the sink."

"Go ahead, make fun. Anyone who'd set fire to a stable has a screw loose. Every last one of those horses could have burned to death. The person who did it has no conscience, and mercy is a word beyond his understanding."

Molly immediately sobered. "You're right. I'm sorry for giving you a hard time. I just—" She glanced at the broom closet. "I think a man would have a difficult time hiding in there, is all."

He nodded. "I'm not necessarily looking for a man." He closed the closet. "I'm not entirely convinced the sheriff's right, but on the off chance it was kids, caution is in order." He winked at her and looked under the sink, which made her laugh. "All secure," he said. "If you lock up tight, you should be safe enough." He arched a questioning eyebrow. "Will you feel comfortable staying over here alone? If not, you're more than welcome at the house. You do realize that."

Molly noticed a pair of brown cotton gloves lying on the counter behind him. She had no idea how they'd gotten there. Last night when she'd raced back here to dress, she hadn't come in the kitchen. The only other time she'd been in the cabin since the fire was this morning when she'd grabbed a shower.

"I-I'll be fine," she murmured. "I appreciate the offer, though."

His gaze sharpened on her face. "Is something wrong?"

Molly fiddled with a button on her new pink blouse. His eyes always unnerved her, making her feel as easy to read as an open book. "I'm just tired and need sleep."

His expression turned amused. "Sleep? What's that?"

"I'll think of you when I'm snuggled down in my warm, comfortable bed."

He grinned. "You do that."

Molly realized what she'd just said and blushed. Seeing her embarrassment, he chuckled and moved past her. Heart pounding, she followed him to the door.

Before stepping out, he cupped a hand to her cheek. "Get a good rest," he said.

For a fleeting instant, Molly thought he might kiss her. Instead he stepped out and closed the door firmly behind him. "Lock up tight, honey. If you need anything, just holler. I'll be here in two shakes of a lamb's tail."

"I'll do that," Molly called. "Good night, Jake."

As his steps faded away, she locked up and returned to the kitchen. When she found the courage to pick up the gloves, she saw dark splotches on the knit. The rank smell of diesel burned her nostrils.

Molly sucked in a sharp breath. With a shudder of revulsion, she opened the broom closet and flung the gloves inside. After slamming the door, she held it closed with the press of her palms, knowing on some level that it was silly. Out of sight, out of mind? She couldn't hide from this.

"There were no prints on the fuel cans," Jake had told her after speaking on the phone with the sheriff earlier. At

the time, Molly had been relieved to hear the news, convinced it vindicated her.

Those gloves were glaring proof of her guilt.

It hadn't been kids who'd started that fire. It had been *her*.

All this time, she'd been so convinced that her illness of a few months ago had been induced, that Rodney had drugged her and staged all her bizarre behavior to make her look crazy. Now she had to face the terrible truth, that she might be as nuts as everyone deemed her to be.

She had to tell Jake. If she had sleepwalked and set that fire, there was no telling what she might do next.

She had reached the front door and was about to unfasten the bolt when sanity returned. If she told him she had reason to believe she might have set the fire, there was no predicting how he would react, except that he would want her off his ranch. To that end, if he contacted Rodney, she could soon find herself in an asylum again.

Memories flashed through her mind—awful memories of ice baths, shock treatments, and mind-numbing sedatives. In the early days of her treatment, she'd been a screaming recalcitrant, pounding on the door, begging to be let out, and refusing to eat. Her attendants had thought she was crazy. Even Sam Banks had believed that at first.

She would rather die than go through a similar experience again.

There was also Sunset to consider. If Rodney learned where she was, what would become of the horse? Her ex-husband would take his stallion back to Portland. If Sunset acted up, which he surely would, Rodney's solution would be to whip him. She couldn't bear the thought of that happening. No matter what became of her, she had to save Sunset from enduring any more abuse.

Think, Molly. Laying the truth out before Jake was the obvious course of action, but that didn't mean it was her only option. There had to be a way to protect herself and Sunset while safeguarding the ranch as well.

Trembling with nerves, Molly turned from the door to survey the cabin. She couldn't prevent herself from sleepwalking, but she could take measures to make sure she did nothing destructive.

She went to work. After locking all the windows, she used a roll of masking tape she'd brought from Portland to seal them shut. Then she located the sack of wind chimes that she'd stowed in the closet. After dismantling them, she used yarn from her crochet satchel to string the noisemakers over the windows and front door. Hopefully, the loud tinkling sound would awaken her if she tried to leave the cabin. As an added precaution, she scooted the heavy old easy chair and the antique trunk in front of the door to form a barricade.

Only then could she bring herself to go to bed and try to sleep, *try* being the operative word—she was afraid to close her eyes. Despite all her precautions, what if she left the cabin?

Madness. Every conceivable exit was either taped shut or barricaded, and she'd booby-trapped every opening with noisemakers. She was bound to jerk awake the instant she touched those wind chimes.

Molly had nearly convinced herself that it was safe to close her eyes when a knock came at the door. "Molly, it's me, Jake."

She sprang from bed, thinking of the furniture and wind chimes in front of the door. Grabbing her white chenille robe, she thrust her arms down the sleeves and knotted the sash as she dashed to the living room. She grabbed the chair to move it, cringing when the wooden feet scraped loudly over the floor.

"Coming!" she cried when Jake rapped the door again. "Just a sec."

"Are you all right in there?"

Evidently she hadn't been all right for a very long time, and she'd been too blind to see it. The wind chimes tinkled loudly as she ripped the string away from the door. She dropped them on the chair before opening up. Jake's expression was bewildered as he took in the furniture behind her.

"Sweetheart, I said you were welcome at the house. You don't have to stay over here alone if you're afraid."

Molly's mind raced for an explanation. "I, um, just felt better, knowing I'd wake up if anyone tried the door. That's all."

He leaned a shoulder against the frame, his gaze dark with worry. "Come up to the house. There are plenty of spare beds."

Molly didn't dare do that. She needed the chimes and barricade to ensure that she didn't wander in her sleep. She pushed at her loose hair, which was already tangled from tossing and turning. "No, really. I was already dozing off."

He straightened to reach for something tucked under his belt. Eyes widening, Molly saw that it was a pearl-handled, nickel-plated revolver. He thrust the weapon at her handle first. "I want you to have this. Just in case."

Her father had died of a gunshot to the head. Even now, she couldn't forget the way the pistol had looked, loosely grasped in his blood-splattered hand. Molly recoiled. "Oh, no. I don't like guns."

Pointing the barrel at the floor, Jake spun the chamber. "This is an old .357 and very simple to use, the only drawback being that it's got a hell of a kick."

Molly shook her head. "No, thank you. I couldn't bring myself to shoot anyone, so what's the point?"

"You don't need to shoot anyone," he assured her. "If there's trouble, just aim at the ceiling. Call me a worrywart. I'm afraid I won't hear you calling for help. If you fire off a round, I know it'll get my attention."

He grasped her wrist and slipped the gun into her hand. Then, bending forward, he quickly showed her how to cock the hammer and take it off safety. "Just point and pull the trigger," he said. "It's as easy as that. If you won't come stay at the house, please keep it here with you. I'll feel better if you do."

Put like that, how could she refuse? She lowered the weapon, acutely aware of how cold and heavy it was. "Thank you. I'll keep it next to my bed."

"See that you do, and don't be afraid to use it. If you even *think* someone's trying to break in, fire off a round." He glanced up. "We're going to patch the roof this summer, anyway. You won't be hurting anything."

A moment later, Molly was bidding him farewell through the locked door again. After hanging the chimes and replacing the barricade, she took the gun to the bedroom. Fearful of what she might do in her sleep with a loaded weapon at her disposal, she took all the bullets from the cylinder and hid them at the bottom of her underwear drawer.

Only then did she feel it was safe for her to sleep.

Chapter Seventeen

Molly hadn't even reached the main house the next morning when she heard Jake cursing. Following the sound of his voice, she circled the machine shop and found him crouched beside an old yellow tractor. Peering over his shoulder, she saw that the tire was flat as a fritter.

"What on *earth* happened?"

"It's slashed!" he fairly snarled. "Every damned tire on the place, *slashed*."

Staring in horrified fascination at the tire, she recalled all the times she and Rodney had awakened to find their house in disarray, gouged sofa cushions vomiting stuffing, expensive paintings hanging in ribbons from their frames.

"Oh, no," she said hollowly.

"Oh, no, is right." Jake's face looked gray as he pushed to his feet. "First my stable, now all the tires." He jerked off his hat and thrust a taut hand into his sable hair. "*Damn!* Tractor tires cost a fortune. Someone's out to ruin me."

Molly gulped and directed another glance at the tire. Her fingers and toes felt suddenly numb. "I didn't do it," she said shakily.

He gave her a curious look. "Of course you didn't."

Embarrassment washed through Molly for having said something so stupid. It was just—*oh, God*—always before, everyone had blamed her.

Jake swept past her, the heels of his boots sending up puffs of dust.

"Where are you going?"

"To call the sheriff! I'll be damned if he'll blame this one on kids. It took a man's strength to do that."

A man's strength? She wanted to believe him, but her conscience wouldn't allow it. Seven months ago, she'd seen her handiwork. While sleepwalking, she had slashed Rodney's paintings with such force that the butcher knife had penetrated the backs of the frames and gouged the walls. She'd heard that people could exhibit extraordinary strength when their adrenaline was up. Maybe that held true for sleepwalkers.

She retraced her steps to the cabin. Once inside, she checked the windows for the second time that morning. None of the tape or chimes looked disturbed, and the front door had still been barricaded when she first woke up. If she had sleepwalked, she supposed she might have pushed the furniture back in front of the door when she returned to the cabin, but it didn't seem probable. How exacting was a sleepwalker likely to be?

Still concerned, Molly drew back the covers on the bed to check the sheets. She'd changed the linen last night before retiring, and it still looked clean, no smudges of dirt or debris. If she had gone outside last night, she'd either worn shoes or washed her feet before returning to bed.

Suddenly exhausted, she sank onto the mattress and rested her head in her hands. Oh, God . . . oh, God. Had she slashed all those tires? There was no evidence that she'd left the cabin during the night. But what if she had?

All the while she washed the breakfast dishes later that morning, Molly circled the possibility that she had slashed the tires, a part of her convinced she was the culprit, another part of her unable to believe it. But if not her, then who? Rodney couldn't be blamed for this, not unless he'd somehow managed to track her down and was perpetrating the vandalism to convince Jake she was crazy.

The thought made her freeze. About to put a large fry-

ing pan into the drying rack, she stood there, staring at
nothing, her fingers clenched over the wooden handle.
What if Rodney *had* found her? Until now, that possibility
hadn't occurred to her.

Her skin went icy. She glanced uneasily out the kitchen
window, searching the line of trees that grew at the edge of
the yard. For months now, she'd been convinced that her
ex-husband had deliberately made her look crazy so he
could gain control of the investment firm. Given her rapid
recovery after she'd entered the clinic, it had been the only
explanation that made sense. In less than seventy-two
hours after she'd escaped Rodney, her head had cleared
and she'd stopped feeling dizzy and nauseated. The sleepwalking incidents, about which her husband had complained so bitterly, never occurred in the clinic at all.

Sam had theorized that Molly's rapid improvement was
due to the abrupt cessation of stress in her life. She was far
removed from her overbearing husband's influence. She
had escaped the tension at work. Lastly, he argued that the
change of scenery had distanced her from all reminders of
her father's suicide. No stress, no symptoms, it was as simple as that, he'd assured her in the beginning.

Molly had never bought into that explanation. Granted,
stress had been known to make people dizzy and unable to
think clearly, but her symptoms had been extreme. Toward
the last, she'd been too weak and disoriented even to walk
from her bed to the adjoining bathroom. One night Rodney
had come home to find her lying half-conscious on the
floor. After carrying her back to bed and helping her into a
clean nightgown, he'd descended on her with yet more
pills. *"Take your medicine, darling."* She had tried to tell
him the drug was making her sick. He'd refused to listen,
and when she wouldn't open her mouth to take the pills, he
had poked them down her throat.

It had been a nightmare, a nightmare that had only
grown more horrible when she awoke at the clinic. Molly
shuddered at the memories. It had been glaringly obvious

to her, if not to her doctor, that her husband had been drugging her and that her illness had been chemically induced. It followed that the recent sleepwalking incidents had been staged as well. Until Sam had finally come around, she'd tried frantically to make someone listen to her, experiencing a gamut of emotions when she failed—rage, fear, frustration, and an awful sense of helplessness.

Now, suddenly, it was all happening again. She was apparently sleepwalking, and this time Rodney couldn't be blamed. She was frightened, starting to question her own sanity, and mere inches away from losing her grip.

Rodney would be so pleased.

Oh, God, it would be just like him to wage an insidious attack, chipping away at her self-confidence until she began doubting herself at every turn. Even worse, such tactics would eventually lead Jake and everyone else on the ranch to doubt her sanity as well, robbing her of the only friends and support she had.

Poor, crazy Molly. An awful weak feeling attacked her legs as she recalled the stable fire. Until that night, she'd always slept with her bedroom window open so she could hear Sunset in case he needed her. Wasn't it possible that after setting the fire, Rodney could have slipped into her cabin through that window? Was she out of her mind to think he might have hidden somewhere in the house until she left so he could put debris in her bed and plant the gloves in the kitchen?

Molly remembered the nightmare she'd had that night about Sarah and her dad. Rodney knew all about her past. In movies, she'd seen people whisper suggestively to a sleeping person to induce a terrible dream. It would be very like Rodney to enjoy the risk of that, not knowing for sure when she might wake up. *"Molly, help us."* A shudder coursed over her. She could almost hear his whispering voice in her mind.

She could easily imagine him showing up at the ranch. He could be so convincing when he chose. He'd pretend to be concerned about her welfare even as he regretfully informed Jake that she was emotionally ill and undoubtedly responsible for all the vandalism on the Lazy J. Poor, crazy Molly, who sleepwalked. Poor, crazy Molly, who was a danger to herself and everyone around her. He would tell Jake that she needed constant supervision.

Molly felt as if she might vomit. *Rodney.* There had been a time when she never would have believed him capable of such heinous behavior, but no more. After her father's death, her rose-colored glasses had been ripped away, and she'd begun to see her husband not as she wished him to be, but as he truly was, a man who would stop at nothing.

Terror sluiced through her. If Rodney had found her, she didn't have a prayer of escaping him. The tires on her Toyota were flat. Until they were replaced, she didn't even have transportation.

Oh, God. With Claudia and Jared's help, he might be able to get her committed again, and once that happened, no telling how long it might be before she was released.

Molly sank down at the table and covered her face with her hands. She'd been on the Lazy J for about three weeks. She hadn't heard a word on the television or radio about a stolen horse. It was possible Rodney hadn't even reported the theft, choosing instead to track her down and deal with her himself.

Only how had he found her? She'd told no one where she was going, not even her mom. Without the help of law enforcement, how on earth could he have pinpointed her exact location?

The trainer.

Lowering her hands, Molly clutched the edge of the table with such force her knuckles began to ache. The *trainer.* Of course, that was it. Somehow, Rodney had coerced the man into revealing her whereabouts.

Molly leaped up from the chair and advanced to the wall phone. A few minutes later, she'd spoken to an information operator and was ringing Shamrock Greens, the Portland stable where Sonora Sunset had been boarded. A woman answered the call.

"Yes, I'd like to speak with Keith Sandusky, please," Molly said shakily. "Would you mind having him paged for me?"

"Oh, I'm sorry," the woman said. "Keith no longer works here."

"He doesn't?" Molly flattened a hand against the wall. "Are you certain of that?"

"Quite certain. I make out the payroll here."

Sandusky had told Molly that he'd worked at Shamrock Greens for thirty years and hoped to retire from there, which was why he hadn't wanted any kind of trouble with Rodney. He'd been afraid her ex-husband would have him blackballed from the racing circuit if he dared to cross swords with him. An odd-turned, funny-looking little man, Sandusky had worn riding silks even when he wasn't on the track. *"These horses are my life,"* he'd informed Molly. *"No wife, no children. This job is all I've got. That's why I didn't call you after the first whipping, why I waited until it got so bad. I was afraid of losing my job. That's no excuse, I know. The horse has suffered for my cowardice."*

Remembering the passion in Sandusky's voice, Molly couldn't believe he had suddenly left the stable. "When exactly did Mr. Sandusky quit?" she asked.

There was a long silence. Then the woman said, "Are you a friend?"

"Yes." The man had lent her his horse trailer, after all, so Molly didn't feel that was really a lie. They were friends, of sorts.

"Well, I suppose I won't be speaking out of school, then. Keith didn't exactly quit, he just up and left about three weeks ago. Not a word to the owners, no forwarding address. He didn't even collect his pay."

Molly frowned. "Isn't it strange that he didn't come by to get his check?"

The woman sighed. "There's just no figuring people sometimes. I keep expecting him to call or to find a note from him in the mail. So far, nothing. If he should get in touch, would you like me to give him a message?"

"No, thank you."

Molly hung up the phone. She doubted anyone at Shamrock Greens would hear from Keith Sandusky again. Something had happened. Maybe Rodney had grown so furious when he'd found Sunset missing that he'd threatened Sandusky, and the trainer had become so frightened that he'd pulled up stakes rather than stay and face the music. Molly just hoped Rodney hadn't actually harmed the man. Maybe Keith was down in Kentucky somewhere, happily working with expensive purebreds at a highfalutin stable where Rodney would never think to look for him.

The thought comforted Molly even though the news of the trainer's sudden departure from Portland left her with more questions than answers. Had Sandusky revealed her whereabouts to Rodney before he left, or had he run before Rodney could force the information out of him?

Molly had no way of knowing. There was still a possibility that Rodney had learned of her whereabouts and was responsible for all the vandalism on the Lazy J. There was also a strong possibility that Sandusky had told Rodney nothing, which took her back to square one. Rodney couldn't be responsible for the vandalism if Sandusky hadn't told him where she was.

The blame for the fire and those slashed tires might be hers, after all.

"Where's Jake?" Molly asked Hank a few minutes later.

Jake's brother turned from the pile of poles they'd stripped for fencing. Beneath the brim of his hat, his burnished face glistened with sweat. "He went to town to buy tires and have it out with the insurance company."

Molly had hoped to talk to Jake before she lost her courage. "I thought all the trucks had flats." She glanced to the right of the house where the vehicles were parked. Jake's battered green Ford was there. "How did he get to town?"

"He went up the road and borrowed the neighbor's truck." Hank's gaze sharpened on her face. "Are you okay? You're pale as milk."

Molly wasn't okay. She wasn't sure if she'd ever be okay again. *"Someone's out to ruin me,"* Jake had cried this morning. She gazed out across his ranch. This was no longer about just her and Sunset. Jake Coulter's heritage was at stake. If she didn't take immediate steps to stop herself from doing any more damage, he could lose everything he owned.

Jake was gone until late afternoon, and immediately upon his return, he went to work building corrals with feverish determination. Since it was time for her to start cooking the evening meal, Molly decided to postpone talking to him until after dinner. He always saw her home once the kitchen was put to rights. That would be a perfect time to confess her sins to him.

Molly had no idea what she meant to say, only that somehow she had to get it said. She would leave nothing out. She'd tell him that she'd been lying to him from the start, that she'd brought this trouble to his door, and that she was sorry, so very sorry, for unintentionally hurting him.

Knowing what lay ahead, Molly could barely eat supper. Occasionally, she caught Jake watching her, his eyes dark with concern. She avoided his gaze, so upset and ashamed that it was all she could do to remain sitting at the table.

When dinner was over, Jake didn't stay to help her clean up as he usually did, and when the dishes were done, it was Hank who grabbed his hat and jacket to walk her home.

"Where's Jake?" Molly asked, scarcely able to believe

he'd altered their usual routine. Not tonight when she most needed to see him.

"He crashed," Hank told her softly. "I don't think he's slept more than two hours, all totaled, since the fire. He's been running on nerves and caffeine."

As Molly passed through the living room, she saw Jake sprawled on the log-frame sofa. One arm angled over his eyes, he was snoring softly. He looked absolutely exhausted, and she was glad he was getting some rest. At the same time, she wanted to run over and shake him awake. She was desperately afraid she might lose her courage if she postponed talking to him.

Hank gently ushered her from the house. Once on the porch, he flashed her a grin. "I'm glad he didn't wake up. He'd insist on walking you himself."

Disheartened, Molly allowed Hank to guide her down the steps. Unlike Jake, he didn't detour to take her for a stroll, but headed directly for the cabin. Not that she wanted to go walking. She was too worried to appreciate the beauty of the stars tonight.

Once on her porch, Hank said, "If you don't mind, I'll do a quick walk-through." He stepped inside ahead of her. "When Jake wakes up, he's bound to ask if I made sure you were safe before I left."

Molly waited just inside the front door while Jake's brother made a fast tour of the cabin. When he returned to the living room, he said, "All clear."

"Thank you. I really don't think anyone would hide in here, but it's nice to have you check."

He stopped beside her and flipped the wall switch to turn on the floor lamp. "Three days ago, I wouldn't have believed anyone would hide in here, either. Now nothing would surprise me. Better to be safe than sorry."

"Right." Molly turned to watch him step out. As she pushed the door closed, she called, "Good night, Hank. Thanks for walking me over."

"Not a problem. G'night."

Molly shoved the deadbolt home. Then she pressed her forehead against the sturdy planks, weariness weighing heavily on her shoulders. What an awful day it had been.

The chill of the room seeped through her jacket, making her shiver. Grabbing the afghan that lay over the back of the sofa, she hurried over to lay a fire. A moment later, when the flames sprang to life, she stared vacantly at the licking tongues of orange, remembering the stable fire two nights before.

Tomorrow, she promised herself. She would take Jake aside first thing in the morning, and she would tell him everything.

Morning dawned bright and cold, a layer of frost dusting everything with silvery white in the first faint light of day. Molly bundled up in a jacket before she left the cabin, but even so, she shivered in the chill air. As she drew abreast of Sunset's pen, the stallion whickered and trotted over to the fence, clearly pleased to see her. Unable to walk by without stopping to say hello, Molly stepped up onto a rail and reached over to scratch between the horse's ears.

"I'm sorry," she whispered. "We no sooner make friends, and now I'm neglecting you. I just haven't had any time."

The stallion sniffed her jacket. Molly pressed her cheek to his velvety muzzle, wishing she could spend time with him that afternoon. Unfortunately, it might be impossible. Once she spoke to Jake, he could send her packing. He wasn't going to be happy when she told him her story.

Lifting her gaze, she looked out over the pastureland that bordered both sides of the creek for as far as she could see. This was Jake's heritage, a dream of his great-grandfather's that had been passed down through generations. He'd played here as a little boy, as his father had before him. Molly knew all about heritage and tradition, how the sentiment of it became even more important than the business itself. Wasn't that a large part of the reason she'd remained here, to give herself time to heal so she might return to Portland and reclaim her share of the firm her dad had built?

Now, because of her, Jake could lose the Lazy J. All his dreams and aspirations would be little more than dust in the wind, and it would be her fault. The thought brought tears to her eyes.

It was tempting to linger at Sunset's pen rather than go face him. She had dreaded doing a few things in her life, but this took the prize.

Swinging off the fence, she hurried across the stretch of gravel to the house. She kept her gaze carefully averted from the charred remains of the stable. About halfway up the front steps, Molly saw a brownish-red lump lying on the porch. Her knees almost buckled. It was a dead chicken. The poor thing's head had been chopped off. Crimson neck tendons straggled from the gaping wound.

She rushed to the edge of the porch, grabbed the rail, and promptly lost what little was in her stomach. When the spasms passed, she slowly straightened. A quick glance over her shoulder verified that it was a beheaded chicken, all right, or what was left of it, anyway. The poor creature's feathers were half gone, as if it had been mauled.

She gulped, fighting back another wave of nausea. Then she raced for the front door. Once inside the entry hall, she leaned against the log wall, hoping to calm down before she proceeded to the kitchen.

"How the *hell* should I know?" she heard Hank say. "Damn, Jake, I can't believe you're trying to pin all this on me."

Curious, Molly followed the voice toward the downstairs bathroom, situated to the left just off the hall. Halfway there, she heard Jake say, "Well, I sure as hell don't know her." A loud thump and what sounded like water splashing punctuated the statement. "If I find out that this is all the result of some fatal attraction, Hank, I swear, I'll kick your ass clear into next week."

"I haven't gone out with a woman in months, let alone some fruitcake who'd do something like this. Why automatically blame me, anyway? Like you never dated any women? I'll bet there's a Sarah somewhere in your black book."

"*What* black book? If I had one, I've long since lost track of it, and I've *never* dated a woman named Sarah." Silence. "Well, maybe one. But that was almost two years ago. If she was pissed because I stopped seeing her, why the hell did she wait until now to do something about it?"

Molly reached the bathroom just then. She stared bewilderedly through the open doorway. For an instant, her brain couldn't assimilate what her eyes were seeing. *Blood.* It was everywhere, all over the floor, all over the sink and commode. Her gaze jerked to the bathtub where Jake knelt on one knee, wringing out a crimson-stained cleaning rag. Above his shoulder, she saw writing of some kind on the white ceramic tile. She stared incredulously as the letters came into focus. *Sarah.* Someone had written the name in blood.

Molly heard the ocean in her ears. Black spots danced before her eyes. *Sarah.* Memories hit her, hard and fast. She gasped and whirled away, covering her face with her hands. *Sarah.* Oh, dear God.

She broke into a run, not sure where she was going, only knowing she had to get out.

"Molly!" Jake called.

She kept going. When she reached the front door, she remembered the dead chicken on the porch. Wheeling, she raced back through the house into the great room. From there, she spilled into the kitchen. She aimed her lurching steps for the back door. *Out.* She had to get out. Fresh air. She needed to *breathe.*

Once outside, she nearly fell down the back steps in her haste to escape.

* * *

After searching high and low, Jake finally found Molly sitting by the creek several minutes later. Arms wrapped around her upraised knees, she sat on the grassy bank, staring off at nothing, her face so pale it frightened him. He started to speak. Then he thought better of it and simply joined her instead.

When she made no offer to say anything, he ventured a soft, "Hi."

"Hi," she said thinly.

She sounded perilously close to tears. Believing she was upset about the chicken, Jake tucked one leg under his rump and bent the other, using his raised knee as a rest for his arm. He joined her in staring across the creek.

"If it's any consolation, honey, the chicken didn't suffer. Beheading is a quick and merciful way to kill them. I know it looked bad, but I think that was a result of someone swinging it around the bathroom after it was dead to spread its blood every damned place."

It took her a moment to respond. Her voice was faint and quavering. "I need to tell you something, Jake, and I don't know how to start."

Jake angled her a searching look. "Start with the first thing that comes to mind, honey. I won't critique your delivery."

She tried to smile, but the attempt was ruined by a tremulous wobble of her chin. Her big, butterscotch-brown eyes went luminous with tears. "I've been lying to you. From the very first, I've done nothing but lie."

Jake rubbed a hand over his face and blinked. That came as no surprise. He'd always known she was lying to him about certain things.

"My last name, for instance. It isn't Houston like I said. It's really Sterling Wells. It'll be just Sterling when I legally drop my married name."

Jake arched an eyebrow. "Is that what this is about, honey? The fact that you've lied about a few things?"

"Not just a few things," she protested shakily. "About

practically *everything*. And all of this"—she swung her hand to indicate the ranch—"has been my fault, if not directly, then indirectly, and the end result is the same, either way. You've been pushed to the edge of bankruptcy."

He wanted so badly to hug her. Seeing her cry nearly broke his heart. "I thought you were upset over the silly chicken."

Another rush of tears filled her eyes. "It upsets me, all right. I didn't think I had it in me to kill anything. Now just look at what I may have done."

"What?" Jake said carefully, convinced his ears had deceived him.

"You heard me." With trembling hands, she wiped her cheeks and sniffed. Then she bent her head. "I may have done this. I could have done all of it." She cupped a hand over her eyes. "I'm so *sorry*. Please, forgive me, Jake. I'm so very, very sorry. I'll make it up to you one day, I swear. I'll pay you for all the damages."

"Whoa. Back up. I'm getting confused. Why do you think you might have done all this? The deputy who came out when we called seemed pretty sure some gal named Sarah did it." Heat crawled up Jake's neck. "A scorned lover of mine or Hank's who's come back to haunt us."

She looked at him as if he'd lost his mind. "First kids set fire to your stable and slash all the tires, and now a scorned lover paints her name all over your bathroom in blood?"

Jake knew it sounded far-fetched. The local law enforcement officials seemed more interested in offering explanations for all the bizarre incidents than in actually catching the perpetrator. "If someone named Sarah didn't do it, who did?"

Molly steepled her fingers. "Trust me, Sarah didn't write her name on your tile. She couldn't have." Her chin wobbled again. "She's been dead for almost eleven years."

Jake was growing more confused by the moment. He was about to make her back up and start all over when he heard Hank shout his name. He glanced up to see his brother waving at him from across the creek.

"You need to come up to the house!" he yelled. "We've got trouble."

Jake could believe it. Lately trouble had been raining buckets. He groaned and pushed to his feet. "I'm sorry, honey. I'd better go see what the hell has happened now." He leaned down to offer her a hand. "Come back with me. As soon as I get a minute, we'll find a quiet place to talk."

As he drew her to her feet, she threw a worried look toward the house. "Oh, God, I wonder what it is this time."

He flashed what he hoped was a reassuring grin. "Unless the house is burning down, it can't be too bad. Right?"

She didn't return his smile. "I'm so sorry, Jake." She lifted a tear-filled gaze to his, her expression filled with hopeless resignation. "Please believe that. I never meant to hurt you."

Jake cupped a hand to her cheek. Thumbing away a tear, he said, "Sweetheart, you don't even need to say it. I know you didn't."

After all the recent vandalism on the Lazy J, Molly wasn't surprised to see the sheriff's Bronco parked out front when they drew near the house. What did stop her cold was the cream-colored Lexus nosed in behind the county vehicle. She'd been half expecting Rodney to show up, but seeing his car was still a shock.

Her stomach dropped when the driver door opened and her ex-husband climbed out, looking just as she remembered him. Impeccably dressed, as always, he seemed taller to her as he unfolded to his full height. Walking toward them, he brushed the wrinkles from the sleeves of his expensive gray suit jacket, then straightened his tie and ran a hand over his perfectly groomed blond hair. Even at a distance, Molly could see the gleam of cunning and intelligence in his hazel eyes.

In that instant she knew, almost beyond a shadow of a

doubt, that he'd been behind every awful incident at the ranch. There was no mistaking that little smirk. She'd seen it a hundred times—when he lied to her about his women, when he was trying to cover up his gambling. It was a smirk that said, *"I'm so phenomenal, and you are so incredibly stupid."*

Her first thought was to run. "Oh, God," she whispered to Jake, her footsteps faltering again.

He gave her a sharp look then snaked out a hand to grab her arm. Even through the sleeve of her jacket, she could feel the steely strength of his fingers. "Rodney?" he asked.

Molly nodded stupidly, shudders racking her body as she reached to dislodge his grip. He tightened his hold. She cast a frantic glance around her.

"Please, Jake? You have no idea what he'll do!"

"Don't," he whispered when she tried to jerk away. "He can't hurt you, honey. Not here. There's no reason to be afraid."

There was every reason, Molly thought wildly. She knotted her hands into fists. Had Rodney enlisted the help of law enforcement agencies to find her? Or had he coerced Keith Sandusky into telling him her whereabouts? Mingled with the jumble of questions in Molly's mind was one clear thought, that she hated Rodney Wells with a virulence to last a lifetime.

Recalling the blood in Jake's bathroom, she quaked with trepidation. Always before, there had been a dual purpose behind Rodney's pranks, the primary one being to frighten her and make her doubt her own sanity, while at the same time convincing others she was crazy. Now he'd shifted his focus, his chief purpose to cast her in as bad a light as possible. The *bastard.* He'd staged that bathroom mess entirely for Jake's benefit, trying to make her look crazier than a loon.

Pain lanced behind her eyes. The truth would come out now. She had hoped to tell Jake herself. Now he would hear Rodney's version of the story instead.

An awful feeling of resignation settled in her chest. The taste of defeat was as bitter as gall at the back of her throat. Rodney was a silver-tongued liar, and nothing she said or did was going to stop him from talking. He would tell Jake everything, putting his own wicked spin on the story. Jake would hand her over into his care, and she would soon be staring at bare white walls again. It was as simple as that.

Rodney flashed an oily smile as he neared them. His spit-shined Italian loafers glinted in the morning sunlight. "Molly," he said softly. "I've been worried about you, darling. What a relief it is to see that you're all right."

It was all Molly could do not to fly at him with her claws bared. Oh, how she detested him. Her eyes dry and burning, she stared at him. She was effectively trapped, and there was nothing she could do. *Nothing.* Even worse, he knew it. She didn't miss the mocking gleam in his eyes as he turned his smile on Jake.

Sheriff Dexter avoided looking at Molly as he stepped forward. "Good morning, Jake," he said softly, as if he hoped Molly wouldn't overhear if he kept his voice pitched low. "I've got bad news, I'm afraid."

"What's that?" Jake asked. He shot a glittering glance at Rodney before shifting his gaze back to the lawman.

The sheriff darted a glance at Molly. "You're not going to like it."

Molly felt Jake's hand stiffen on her arm.

The sheriff cleared his throat. "This young woman hasn't been up front with you, I'm afraid. Are you aware that she was only recently released from a mental hospital?"

Jake glanced at Molly, then back at the sheriff. "There's very little about Molly that I don't know."

"I see. Can I take that to mean you're also aware that she left Portland in defiance of a court order mandating that she see her therapist twice a week?" The lawman narrowed his eyes. "Be careful how you answer that." He hooked a thumb toward Sunset's pen. "Not only have you been harboring an emotionally disturbed young woman who needs treatment, but you've aided and abetted her in grand theft."

A muscle in Jake's cheek started to tic. "Grand theft?" he said softly. "Call it what you like, Dexter, but in my opinion, it was a grand rescue. I've every confidence the Humane Society will agree with me."

"Don't draw a line in the dirt, son," the sheriff advised. "I've got no real quarrel with you, and I'd like to keep it that way." He inclined his head at Molly, no longer bothering to keep his voice down. "This woman is an emotional powder keg with a documented history of committing violent acts while sleepwalking. I'm convinced now that she has been responsible for all the vandalism out here—not juveniles, like we thought." The sheriff gestured toward Rodney. "The lady's husband has come to collect her and take her back home so she can get the treatment she needs."

Silence. Molly died a little with each passing second. There was nothing she could do but stand there while her fate was decided. Jake would undoubtedly hand her over to Rodney now. Why wouldn't he? He was probably absolutely furious with her. And who could blame him?

Jake bent his head, his expression thoughtful. When he finally lifted his gaze back to the sheriff, he was frowning. "I'm sorry. You say this man's her husband? You've got it all wrong." Jake glanced at Rodney. "Molly is divorced from Mr. Wells. He no longer has any control over her."

Rodney stepped forward. Just as Molly had imagined he might, he gave Jake a charming smile. "You're right. We are divorced, but that doesn't mean I no longer care about what happens to her—or that I'm completely cut out of the picture. Things aren't quite that cut and dry with a woman in Molly's condition. She never should have been granted a divorce in the first place. She wasn't thinking clearly when she made that decision. By court order, I'm also, to all intents and purposes, her legal guardian. And we still have strong family ties as well." He glanced over his shoulder and crooked a finger, beckoning to someone in his car. "Her adoptive mother, Claudia, is now my dad's wife."

Molly glanced over just as the rear doors of the Lexus opened. Out stepped Jared Wells on one side, Claudia on the other. Jared looked just as he always had, an older version of his handsome son with a touch of steel gray in his blond hair. But the same couldn't be said for Claudia. Always impeccably dressed, she looked uncharacteristically rumpled in her expensive beige suit. As she picked her way closer on wobbly high heels, Molly saw that she had tears in her blue eyes, which were underscored with dark circles.

Being a Judas was obviously interfering with her sleep.

Molly knew then that she was lost. Only a miracle could help her now. Her ex-husband, her mom, and her new stepfather were all in cahoots against her. *Poor little Molly. It's time to lock her away.* It was the only kind and responsible thing to do.

When Claudia drew abreast of Rodney, she fixed an aching gaze on Molly. Her mouth trembled into a tearful smile. "You changed your hair," she said in a squeaky voice. Her face twisted, and she pressed her fingers to her mouth, looking at Molly through swimming tears. "My little girl. You're so beautiful. I love it done that way."

Rodney curled a comforting arm around Claudia's shoulders and drew her close to his body. He sent a commiserating look at his dad. To Jake, he said, "Have a heart, Mr. Coulter. By resisting the inevitable, you're only putting innocent people through a lot of unnecessary pain. As you can see, Molly is deeply loved. We're only trying to get her home to Portland so we can get her some help. She hasn't been herself for a very long while, I'm afraid." He turned his smile on Molly and reached to take her arm. "Come along, darling. Let us get you in the car."

Before Rodney could touch her, Jake shot out a hand

and grabbed his wrist. "Keep your hands to yourself, buddy."

Molly threw an incredulous look at Jake. She'd never seen him truly angry until now, and the sight was frightening. His blue eyes glittered like chipped ice, and a ruddy flush had darkened his burnished features. "The lady isn't going anywhere she doesn't choose to go. Got it?"

Hank, who'd moved up onto the porch, descended the steps to stand behind his brother. From the corner of her eye, Molly saw the hired hands gathering around as well. Their message was clear. She had more than one man to defend her. Even Tex, with his bad shoulder, had joined the ranks.

She stared up at Jake's dark face through a blur of tears. *Trust.* She had vowed never to give hers easily again, but she hadn't known Jake Coulter then. Was he real, this man? She didn't deserve this kind of loyalty, not from him or his men. From the very start, she'd lied to him and kept things from him. Now, instead of abandoning her, he was protecting her. She could scarcely believe it.

Rodney looked imploringly at Molly. "Don't involve these nice people in this, Molly. Haven't you caused them enough grief?"

Molly couldn't have spoken if she tried.

"You need treatment," Rodney went on gently. "Let us take you home to see the doctor." He gave her a cajoling smile. "I know you blame me for everything. But, Molly, *think.* Is that really reasonable? Surely you can't believe that I set you up this time." He shook his head slightly. "You've been cut off from Sam Banks for only three weeks, and just look what you've done. You don't want to stay here and do anything more. What will it be next time, the house?"

Molly knew that she had caused Jake more than enough trouble. Even though she no longer believed she'd been directly responsible, she'd set him up as Rodney's target by staying here.

"One way or another, we have to take you back," Rodney went on. "Like it or not, you've been deemed legally incompetent, and we're responsible for you."

Claudia sent Molly an imploring look. "It's true, sweetie." She swung her hand toward the burned stable. "Until a judge reverses that decision, we're both responsible for you, which makes us liable. If you won't think of us, think of the firm and all that your father worked for. Do you really want to jeopardize that?" A single tear slid down Claudia's cheek. "If I were sick, wouldn't you do everything you could to make sure I got help? That's all we want to do, darling, just get you some help. Soon, you'll be well, and then you can come home. Won't that be nice?"

"You know we love you, Molly," Jared inserted. "Trust us to do what's best for you."

They spoke as if they were addressing a very small child. Molly's head hurt. Their voices bounced around inside her mind. She wanted to scream at them to go away, to just leave her alone. With relatives like these, who needed enemies?

"We can do it the easy way, or we can do it the hard way," Rodney injected. "It's your choice, Molly. Just bear in mind that your friends may get in a lot of Dutch if they run afoul of the law, trying to help you."

"Don't listen to him, Molly," Jake interrupted.

Molly threw him an agonized look. "I've caused you enough grief, Jake."

"And you'll cause me even more if you listen to this bullshit and go with them," Jake retorted. "You're no crazier than I am."

Molly cupped a hand over her eyes. "Oh, *God.* I don't know anymore. I just don't know."

Jake's grip firmed over her arm. "You're just upset right now. Fortunately, I'm thinking quite clearly."

"Stay out of this, Mr. Coulter," Rodney warned.

Claudia drew away from Rodney and stepped closer. She fixed Jake with an imploring look. "I'm her mother. I sat up with her when she was sick. I was the one who put money under her pillow for the tooth fairy. Do you really believe I have anything but her best interests at heart?"

"No, I don't think that," Jake replied softly. "I'm sure you believe you're doing the right thing. Nevertheless, you're not taking her anywhere, not without a court order, which you obviously don't have. If you did, you'd be waving it under my nose."

Bright spots of angry red flagged Rodney's cheeks. "You're making a grave mistake, buster."

Sheriff Dexter scratched his jaw. "There's no point in this, Jake. Why is a court order necessary? We all have the same aim in mind, to do what's best for the lady. She's ill, and she needs help. You aren't doing her any favors by preventing her family from taking her back where she belongs."

"You're right about one thing," Jake agreed. "I have only Molly's best interests at heart, and the way I see it, she's best off remaining here on the Lazy J with people who truly care about her."

"Just one moment," Rodney interrupted coolly. "Are you suggesting that her own mother doesn't care about her? Or that I don't? She's my wife, damn it."

"Ex-wife," Jake reminded him. "And your feelings for her don't count for squat. She doesn't care about you. That's the bottom line."

Rodney's eyes sparked with fury. "Only because she's hopelessly confused right now. Stop and think. She needs hospital care, which can be very expensive. We can afford to give her that care. Can you?" Rodney shook his head. "We know Molly's history. We understand her as no one else does, and we'll take excellent care of her. You needn't worry on that score. She'll be in good hands."

"I know she'll be in good hands," Jake replied, "because she'll be staying here with me, end of discussion." He shot a look at the sheriff. "I don't believe she's sick. What's more, I know for a fact she wasn't responsible for the vandalism here." He glanced apologetically at Molly. "I've never been one to kiss and tell, but in this instance, I'll make an exception. Molly has been sharing my bed since shortly after she came here. I sleep with one eye open, and I know for a fact that she never left my side on the nights the vandalism occurred."

Molly's heart caught. She gaped at Jake, scarcely able to believe he would tell such a bald-faced lie to protect her.

The sheriff shifted his weight, angled Molly an appalled glance, and said, "Begging your pardon, ma'am. I never meant to falsely accuse you. I was told that—" He broke off and shot an accusing look at Rodney. "Well, never mind that. If you weren't responsible for the trouble, I apologize."

Molly swallowed to steady her voice. "That's all right, Sheriff. I know you're only trying to do your job."

"That's right." The lawman rubbed beside his nose and coughed. "Well, Mr. Wells? It would appear that you'll need a court order to remove the lady from the premises. Until you've obtained one, our business here is finished."

Rodney jabbed a finger at Jake. "I'll be back. Count on it. Not just for my wife, but my horse as well."

If Jake was intimidated by Rodney's threatening manner, he didn't reveal it by so much as a flicker of an eyelid. Instead he smiled. "You don't even want to open that can of worms, Wells. The horse stays right where he is."

"We'll see about that."

Jake's grin broadened. "My brother and I had the foresight to take dated photographs of that stallion when it first arrived to document his deplorable condition. He was one big, bloody lash mark, as you very well know, and the snapshots developed out in sharp detail. We also had the good sense to call out a vet who's willing to testify that it took a man's strength to cut the animal that deeply with a whip. You want to take it to court, Mr. Wells? Fine by me. In fact, it would do my heart good. I'm of the opinion that no man should be able to abuse an animal like that without paying the price. There are laws against that sort of thing, you know, and you'll find yourself in more trouble than you can handle if you make any for me."

"You have no proof whatsoever that I've ever lifted a hand to that stallion."

"There's where you're wrong." Jake glanced toward Sunset's pen. "In this instance, the proof will come straight from the horse's mouth. Walk over and climb in that corral."

Rodney followed Jake's gaze and paled visibly. "What kind of game is this?"

"Go on," Jake said sharply. "Say hello to your horse, Mr. Wells. If you never lifted a hand to him, he should be glad to see you."

Rodney bit out a curse. He leveled a long, hot glare at Molly before he spun on his heel and stalked back to his car, brushing past Claudia and Jared as if they weren't there. "You haven't seen the last of me!" he vowed. "Get your bags packed, Molly. I'll have that court order when you see me next. Don't think I won't. Your big, tough cowboy will find himself on the wrong side of the law if he interferes then!"

Claudia wrung her hands, her tearful gaze clinging to Molly's accusing one. "I know you question my love for your father now, Molly. That's a discussion for another day. But surely you have no doubt that I love you."

Molly ached to throw herself in her mom's arms. But this woman had remarried only a few months after her father's suspicious death and then abandoned her when she needed her the most. How could she be sure Claudia wasn't part of the plot to rob her of her inheritance? Any right-thinking person would seriously question her sincerity.

Rodney climbed inside the Lexus and slammed the door with such force that the side mirror vibrated. "Come on, Dad! We're wasting our time. We'll have to get the damned court order before we can do anything more."

Jared stepped over to take Claudia's arm. "Sweetheart?" he said gently.

Claudia nodded and curled a hand over Jared's, but her pleading gaze remained fixed on Molly. After a long moment, she shifted her attention to Jake. "If anything happens to her, Mr. Coulter, I will hold you personally responsible," she said shakily. "Do you understand me? If a single hair on her head has been hurt when we return, you'll rue the day you met me."

"I'll guard her with my life," Jake assured her.

"Come on, honey," Jared murmured.

Claudia allowed herself to be drawn away. Looking back over her shoulder as they drew near the Lexus, she called, "I love you, sweetie. Never doubt it."

Molly watched stonily as her adoptive mother and new stepfather disappeared into the back of the vehicle. The doors slammed simultaneously with a punctuation of finality. An instant later, the car engine roared to life. Tromping on the gas pedal, Rodney threw gravel with the tires as he backed up to turn around.

The sheriff sighed and shook his head as the Lexus disappeared over the rise. "Wells is right, you know," he told Jake. "You'll be on the wrong side of the law if you interfere when they show up with a court order."

"I'll cross that bridge when I come to it," Jake said softly.

Dexter nodded. "I have to do my job, Jake. Just so long as you understand that. If Wells gets a judge in his corner, this could get nasty."

"I know that, Dex." Jake extended a hand to him. "Just do what the taxpayer pays you to do. I'll worry about things at my end."

The sheriff nodded, his eyes reflecting displeasure with the entire situation. "Ma'am," he said, touching the brim of his hat and inclining his head. "Sorry to make your acquaintance under such unhappy circumstances. I hope our next meeting is more pleasant."

Molly hoped so, too. But somehow, knowing Rodney, she doubted it would be.

The sheriff left, and in less time than it took to draw a deep breath, Molly found herself being propelled up the steps to the house by her "big, tough cowboy." Jake's grip on her elbow didn't exactly hurt, but she could tell by the taut dig of his fingertips that he was furious.

Feeling like flotsam carried forth on a wave, she was pushed through the house and into the kitchen, where he jerked out a chair, pressed her onto the seat, and proceeded to lean down to glare at her, nose to nose. Molly inched her head back, intimidated in spite of herself. Under the best of circumstances, Jake Coulter was a lot of man to contend with. In a temper, he seemed to loom over her like a tree.

"Emotionally unstable, Molly? Sweet Christ. What else haven't you told me?"

There was so much she hadn't told him—so very much.

"What in God's name were you thinking?" he cried. "The bastard means to lock you up. Do you realize that? Why in the hell didn't you tell me?" He grasped her by the shoulders and gave her a little shake. "*Why?* If your mom backs him on this, you don't stand the chance of a snowball in hell. She's your closest living relative. You've already been in a clinic. There's a documented history of sleepwalking. They've already had you claimed legally incompetent. Who's going to believe they're lying if they say you need more treatment?"

"Nobody!" Molly cried. His anger had transmitted itself to her, and before she thought it through, she shot up from the chair, forcing him to rear back so their faces wouldn't collide. "Which is exactly why I was afraid to tell you. I was terrified you'd think I was nuts!"

"I never would have thought that."

"When should I have talked to you, Jake? The first night, maybe? 'Oh, by the way, please don't be alarmed, but I should probably mention that I was just released from

a mental ward.' Or maybe later? Let me see. When would
have been a good time? It's such an easy thing to tell someone, after all. I was afraid you'd think the worst and call
Rodney."

His grip on her shoulders relaxed, and his eyes went
dark with what looked like sadness. "You should have
trusted me," he whispered. "They could have shown up a
week ago, Molly. I could have come in from the fields and
found you gone."

"They're going to take me back, anyway. What difference does it make?"

"They'll take you off this ranch over my dead body."

Molly stared up at him through a blur of tears. A thousand times over the last year, she'd wished for just one person besides her doctor whom she could trust, completely
and without reservation. Now, here was Jake, willing to
take on the world for her without even knowing for sure
what he was up against.

"Oh, Jake," she said tremulously. "Who's the crazy one,
you or me?"

He ran his big hands up and down her arms. "I'm crazy
about you. Does that work? I don't need to know what I'm
biting off. He's not taking you anywhere."

Tears blurred her vision. "You won't be able to stop
him," she said shakily. "You heard the sheriff. You'll only
get in a lot of trouble if you try. Rodney will get his court
order"—she snapped her fingers—"just like that, and he'll
be back, probably with a police escort or the sheriff, to return me to Portland. I'm just his fruitcake ex-wife who,
he'll be fast to inform a judge, obtained a divorce while
she was institutionalized and not of sound mind. He has
control of my father's half of the investment firm, control
over my inheritance, and, by extension, control over *me*.
My own mom has joined ranks against me. As much as I
appreciate your wanting to, there's nothing you can do.
They want my money, and to that end, they'll do anything
to cut me out of the picture."

"No one can come onto my land and drag my wife away."

Molly blinked, convinced she hadn't heard him correctly. "I'm not your wife."

"Yet." He slipped his hands back up to her shoulders and firmed his grip. "Molly, how much do you trust me?"

Her heart lurched. "A lot, but not that much."

"Let me put it to you another way. Who do you trust more, me or Rodney?"

"That's not a fair question."

"Life isn't always fair, and right now, honey, it's throwing you a mean curve ball. I'm your only ace in the hole. We can be in Reno in five hours. As your husband, my legal rights will circumvent theirs. Even if they fight the legitimacy of the marriage in court, it'll take them months to do anything. Meanwhile, we can come up with another plan."

"Oh, *God.*" The air suddenly seemed too thin. No matter how deeply Molly grabbed for breath, she couldn't get enough oxygen. "Reno?"

"When we get back, we'll be man and wife. Rodney's power over you will be history. Claudia's will be as well. From that point on, your only worry will be me."

Molly refocused on his dark face. "And you're a triviality?"

"Compared to them, I am."

Chapter Eighteen

When Jake made up his mind to act, he didn't waste time second-guessing himself. Within thirty minutes, he had Molly bundled into his ranch truck and was breaking the speed limit to reach Reno. She sat in a huddle against the passenger door. There was a vacant look in her eyes that worried him.

"Sweetheart, you look scared to death." He gave her what he hoped was an understanding smile. "Am I such a bad proposition?" He glanced in the rearview mirror and swiped at his tousled hair. "I clean up fairly nice."

"It's nothing to do with you. I just don't want to be married again."

"Because I'll have control over your life?"

"That's one reason, plus a dozen others."

"Let's deal with one at a time. First the control issue. I have no intention of trying to control you. If that's how it was with Rodney, don't look for a repeat performance. Control isn't my thing." Taking in her sassy new hairstyle and the pretty pink blouse she was wearing, he could add with all honesty, "You've got good instincts. Within reason, you can do whatever the hell you want. I won't try to stop you."

"Within reason?"

Jake tamped down his annoyance at the question. "Yes, within reason. If you decide to walk a tightrope across the Grand Canyon without a safety net, I may have something to say about it."

She bent her head. When he glanced over, he thought he glimpsed a smile flirting at the corners of her mouth. When she finally looked up, she said, "I don't mean to be difficult. I should be thanking my lucky stars you've offered to do this. I'm sorry."

"I'm offering because I care about you, and for no other reason."

A distant look came into her eyes again.

Jake parted his lips to speak, then clamped his teeth closed, thinking long and hard before he said anything more, which was a virtue that didn't come easily for him. He'd spent most of his life speaking his mind.

He didn't blame Molly for being upset. She'd had a horrific morning, and though he still hadn't heard all the details, he had reason to believe the incident today was only the icing on the cake. He didn't want to say anything that might make matters worse.

Unfortunately, the way he saw it, there were matters they absolutely had to discuss. "Is it the sex that's worrying you?"

Her face drained of color. "Actually, I was hoping we might bypass that part. I have a really bad track record."

Jake shot her another look. "In your dreams. I want this to be a real marriage, Molly, not just a stopgap measure to hold Rodney at bay."

"I was afraid you were thinking that."

"Afraid? Your reasoning eludes me."

"I just don't want to go through all that again. I loved Rodney when I married him, and I believed he loved me. Then, in a twinkling, my fairy tale turned into a nightmare."

Jake mulled that over. The statement smacked of heartbreak. "Did your marriage to Rodney really go sour that fast?" he asked cautiously.

She laughed bitterly. "Our marriage went sour the first night. Rodney got drunk, deflowered his bride, and then passed out. And *that* was the highlight. After that, he mostly didn't bother. When he did, he had to charge his batteries by looking at porn magazines."

Jake felt sick. An awful, rolling nausea. He tightened his hands over the steering wheel, wishing it were Rodney Wells's neck.

"Remember that morning in the woods, Molly? How can you think it'll be anything less than wonderful between us?"

"Experience."

That was all she said, just that one word, but it conveyed a world of heartache. Jake wished he knew what to say to her—anything to take the wariness and apprehension from her eyes. But try as he might, he could think of nothing but platitudes. How could he assure her it would be different between them? How could he promise that he'd find her body attractive when he'd never actually seen it? More important, how could he guarantee that she'd enjoy intimacy with him? He could have all the best intentions and desire her with every fiber of his being, but unless she met him halfway with desire in equal measure, their lovemaking would fall far short of perfection.

Jake had never been a man to make promises he wasn't sure he could keep. He wasn't about to start now. Better to simply get a ring on her finger and deal with each issue as it presented itself, doing his best to make the marriage work.

That decided, he focused his attention on the road, hating the wall of silence between them, but feeling uncertain how to breach it.

Once in Reno, Jake made fast work of finding a parking place in a pay lot across from a supermarket. Just one block over was the main drag where casinos, hockshops, jewelry stores, and twenty-four-hour chapels lined the crowded sidewalks. He helped Molly from the truck, locked her door, and led her toward the street. She moved beside him like a well-programmed android, replying in a flat monotone when he asked a direct question, her movements rigid, her face pinched and pale. He felt like an executioner leading a condemned person to the guillotine.

Glancing at his watch, Jake decided he could afford to blow a little time before he herded her to a chapel. It was only shortly after noon. Maybe if he took her to lunch, she'd calm down a little and get some color back in her cheeks.

He found a nice café in the Eldorado casino, which had been remodeled since his last visit several years ago. He guided Molly to a booth, helped her out of her parka, and then took a seat across from her. Avoiding his gaze, she toyed nervously with the Keno cards and then pretended intense interest in the game rules.

"Would you like to try your luck?" he asked.

She shook her head and put the instructions back into the plastic holder. "No, thanks. I'm not very lucky. I've never won anything in my life."

Wrong. She'd won his heart. Jake studied her pale face, aching to see her smile. He was starting to feel like the world's biggest jerk for pushing her into this. Only, when he considered the alternatives, he honestly couldn't think of any other way to help her. With both Rodney and Claudia joined against her, she was in an extremely precarious legal position, vulnerable in a way that frightened him. By marrying her, he could protect her, at least temporarily. She'd be his wife. He would be able to block any attempts to have her institutionalized.

Jake realized he was mindlessly stirring his coffee, the spoon clacking loudly against the cup. He froze, staring stupidly into the black liquid. Normally, he used no sweetener, and he couldn't think why he'd chosen to now. Nerves, he guessed.

The waitress came for their order. Molly requested only a green salad with blue cheese dressing on the side. Since she'd eaten no breakfast, Jake didn't feel a salad was enough to sustain her until dinner that night.

After placing his own order, he asked, "Do you have a good garden burger?" When the waitress assured him that they did, he said, "In addition to the salad, the lady will have a garden burger and a bowl of fresh fruit as well, please."

As the waitress walked away, Molly fixed Jake with a sparking gaze made all the more vivid by her pallor. The tendons along her throat swelled to form pulsating cords at each side of her larynx. "Why did you do that?" she asked tautly.

"You need to eat, sweetheart."

Before Jake could guess her intent, she swept her arm across the table, sending the silverware flying and catching her coffee cup with the back of her hand. Hot liquid sprayed up and outward, a good measure of it spilling onto his lap. He shot up from his seat.

"Holy *hell*!" He swiped at his fly with his napkin, barely managing to bite back a string of colorful expletives. "What on earth possessed you to do that?"

She leaped to her feet as well. Hands knotted into fists at her sides, she jutted her chin and gave him a wild-eyed look. "How dare you? We aren't even married yet, and already you're taking over. If I wanted a garden burger, I would have ordered one."

Jake could scarcely believe his ears. "You just doused me with scalding hot coffee over a stupid *sandwich*?" He resisted the urge to dance and grab his crotch. *Pain.* No more worries about sex tonight. He wouldn't be functional for a week. "Don't you think you're overreacting just a little?"

"Go ahead. Make light of it." She jabbed his chest with her finger. "It's only a sandwich, after all. Why should it upset me that you consider it your right to decide what I'm going to eat?"

Jake realized they were causing a scene. He glanced uneasily around. People were gaping. An old lady to his left held a forkful of food poised before her parted lips, her eyes wide with stunned amazement.

"Keep your voice down," he whispered to Molly. "People are staring."

"Let them!" she cried. "Who cares?" To Jake's horror, she whirled around. "If any of you women are here to get married," she cried in a shrill, hysterical voice, "think twice! It may be the biggest mistake of your life!"

After screaming that pronouncement, she swept past Jake as if all the demons of hell were nipping at her heels. He barely managed to catch hold of her arm. "Where the Sam Hill do you think you're going?"

"To the ladies' room!" She tried to free her arm. When Jake tightened his hold, she turned up her volume. "Or are you going to start telling me when I can use the bathroom, too?"

That cut it. Jake turned her loose. Keeping an eye on her as she stormed from the café so he'd know in which direction she went, he tossed some money on the table, took a final swipe at his jeans with the soaked napkin, and made a fast exit himself.

The silence in the ladies' lounge soothed Molly's frazzled nerves. She sat forward on the sofa, elbows on her knees, head in her hands. The multicolored pattern of the carpet blurred in her vision, and tears tickled her nostrils as they dripped from the end of her nose. She was shaking, and no matter how hard she tried, she couldn't seem to stop.

Marriage. She couldn't go through with it. She just couldn't. No matter what Jake said, she'd feel like a prison inmate, and for her, it would be a lifelong sentence. Be it in a Reno chapel or a church, she couldn't make vows before God when she had no intention of keeping them.

Until death do us part.

Love, honor, and obey.

How many times had Rodney reminded her of the

promises she had made when she married him? It hadn't mattered that he was breaking all the rules himself. It hadn't mattered if his disregard of those marital tenets was making her miserably unhappy. Rodney had never given a flip about anyone but himself. She'd been left to preserve the union as best she could, which had boiled down to swallowing her pride countless times each day, looking the other way, and smiling when she wanted to scream, all to save a marriage that shouldn't have happened in the first place.

Never again. Molly clenched her fingers into tight fists over her hair. If she wanted salad for lunch, she would damned well eat salad. She was finished with being pushed around.

Reaching that decision made her feel somewhat better. She wiped her cheeks and gazed blankly at the flocked paper on the opposite wall. One question circled endlessly in her head. If marriage was out of the question, what exactly was she going to do? No ideas came to her mind. Her adoptive mother was apparently in cahoots with her ex-husband, and there was every possibility that the two of them could manipulate the court system to have her put back in a sanitarium. To avoid that, Molly needed a champion in her corner, someone who could legally circumvent the court process already in play. As her husband, Jake would have the clout to do that.

A swimmy, disoriented feeling came over Molly. Back to square one. Always back to square one. Did other people find themselves in situations where there seemed to be no way out? Or was it just her? *Jake.* He was her only ace in the hole, as he'd so aptly put it.

For a moment, she considered running. She had no doubt that Jake would care for Sunset. He was nothing if not an animal lover. A surge of hope filled her. The casino was crammed with people. She could easily slip out of the lounge, get lost in the crowd, and exit the building by a back door. There was probably a bus depot nearby. She could buy a one-way ticket to anywhere, change her identity, and leave the past forever behind.

The thought was wonderfully appealing, but then Molly thought of all she would be abandoning, not only the firm, half of which was her birthright, but her dad's estate as well, which he'd worked all his life to acquire. She'd also be abandoning the few precious dreams she still had—to one day sit behind her father's desk, to gain recognition in the field of finance and carry on the Sterling tradition. And what of her determination to see Rodney punished? If she bailed out now, her father's death would be swept under the rug as a suicide. Even worse, his killer would gain control of his assets. That would be the final and ultimate insult to Marshal Sterling's memory, forever tarnishing everything he'd stood for all his life.

Molly couldn't allow that to happen. Besides, even if she did want to run, what could she buy a bus ticket with, her good looks? She glanced down at her pretty new blouse, thinking of all the money she'd so foolishly spent on clothes. She was all but broke now. The little money she had left was in her purse. At last count, there'd been just over a hundred dollars.

Her heart caught as she glanced stupidly around her. Where *was* her purse, anyway?

Oh, dear God. She'd left it in the café.

A hysterical urge to laugh came over her. She wasn't just broke; she was *penniless*. She didn't have the money to buy a cup of coffee, let alone a bus ticket.

The realization brought her staggering to her feet. Jake was undoubtedly furious over her behavior in the eatery. What if he had left? That was exactly what Rodney would do, she knew. Bad behavior was always punished. What better way to punish someone than to leave her stranded for a few days? No money equated to no lodging and no food.

Oh, God—oh, God. Molly imagined herself wandering the streets, digging in dumpsters for morsels of nourishment. If she sought shelter in the casinos at night, she'd be tossed out on her ear by security guards the instant she fell asleep. Inside of two days, she'd be half-starved, dead on her feet, and ready to kiss Jake Coulter's boots while she begged for forgiveness. If he took a page out of Rodney's book, he would grant her absolution only under certain terms.

Molly's heart was pounding so loudly that her eardrums felt as if they might burst. She had to find Jake and apologize before he took off and left her. Even now, he could be back at the truck, preparing to leave. *No, no, no.* She was better off getting married. Facing penury in Reno was not a pretty picture. She doubted it was a city that was kind to the homeless. People were far too involved with gambling and counting their losses to be in a charitable mood.

Molly hit the swinging door with such force, her shoulder thudded against the wood. Her legs felt curiously disconnected from her brain as she spilled from the lounge into the casino area. The noise of the slots immediately pummeled her, jackpot bells ringing loudly, the whirring sounds of the machines and soft blips of music compounding to create a computerized cacophony.

She tried to blank it out. *Jake.* Where would he have gone? She had to find him. If she apologized, maybe he would forgive her and go ahead with the marriage.

"Molly?"

About to plunge through the milling crowd to go in search of him, Molly was jerked up short by his deep voice. She whirled around, scarcely able to believe her eyes when she saw him sitting on a padded bench just outside the ladies' lounge. One long leg extended, the opposite knee raised, he was slumped on the seat, his Stetson settled low over his eyes.

In that lazy, slow-as-molasses way of his, he pushed to his feet. As he sauntered toward her, she saw that he held her purse clutched in one big fist. She pressed a hand to the base of her throat to slow her galloping heart.

"I was afraid you had left."

He arched a dark eyebrow. "Why the hell would I do that?"

He thrust the purse at her. When she took it, he clamped a hand over her arm. Molly braced for the cruel bite of his fingers, expecting him to exert unneeded pressure in his anger. Instead, his grip was only firm, not bruising.

"Call me bossy and overbearing if you want, but don't you *ever* run off like that again. Not without telling me *exactly* where you're going first. Do you have any idea the kind of creeps who hang around these joints?"

After imagining him leaving her, Molly was so relieved to be scolded instead that tears nearly came to her eyes. "No, what kind of creeps?"

His hold on her arm tightened. "The kind who wouldn't hesitate to back you against a wall and put a knife to your throat. That's what kind. I was worried sick."

Not three minutes ago, she had envisioned herself digging through dumpsters to stave off hunger. The throbbing anger in his voice told her how wrongly she'd judged him. For all his faults, which were admittedly few, Jake was nothing like Rodney, and she never should have painted him with the same brush.

What was wrong with her? All he'd done was order her a sandwich, and she'd gone clear over the edge. It was as if venomous spiders were caged in some dark, secluded part of her mind, and every once in a while, a few escaped to inject poison into her thoughts.

"Didn't you know I was inside the lounge?" she asked.

He drew her around a woman who'd just won a jackpot and was hopping about in celebratory glee. "Not for certain." He ground the words out, his jaw muscle ticking. "I had to go back for your purse and lost sight of you in the crowd. I hoped you had ducked in there. It was the only rest room I could find on this side of the casino, so waiting for you there seemed like my best bet."

He was leading her toward the front exit. Beyond the

glass doors, she could see people milling about on the side-walk in a wash of brilliant sunlight. "Where are we going?"

"Somewhere to talk."

"About what?"

He shot her a hard look. "What the hell we're going to do. What do you think?"

Molly supposed it had been a stupid question. Following the pull of his hand, she walked obediently beside him, feeling like a recalcitrant child being taken to the woodshed. Oddly, though, she wasn't apprehensive. Jake was nothing like Rodney. The fact that he'd waited outside the lounge for her was irrefutable proof of that. No games, no coercion tactics. Jake was just Jake, always up front with his thoughts and feelings. He'd told her that the very first night. *"I'm not much good at beating around the bush."*

Molly felt so small. His only sin had been to try his best to help her. Shame washed through her in waves. In that moment, every word Sam Banks had ever said to her came rushing back. He'd cautioned her dozens of times not to let the past influence her decisions now. *"Turn loose of it, Molly. Your life with Rodney is over. It's a whole new game from this point forward, with totally new players and completely new rules. Embrace that. Move ahead and don't look back."*

Sadly, it wasn't that easy, Molly thought as they exited the casino onto the crowded sidewalk. In so many ways, she was almost well. But in others, she wasn't, and she was starting to fear she might never be. Jake was nothing like Rodney, yet she constantly drew comparisons. As far as she knew, he'd never lied to her, yet she examined everything he said and did, analyzing his motives and reading between the lines. He'd never really tried to exert his will over her, either, but that hadn't stopped her from thinking he was.

It was fear that was trying to control her now, she realized, not the man who walked beside her. Jake had only been worried because she hadn't eaten breakfast, and he'd been thoughtful enough to make sure she got lunch. Even worse, he hadn't ordered her the kind of food he preferred himself, as Rodney would have done. No, he'd asked for vegetarian fare—a garden burger and fresh fruit. To someone else, that might be a small thing, but to Molly, it meant more than she could say.

"Oh, Jake, I'm so sorry. I behaved unconscionably. I'm so sorry."

Never breaking stride, he sighed and released his hold on her to slip his arm around her shoulders. After giving her a jostling hug, he said, "I'm the one who's sorry."

Just that. No explanation, no flowery words. As they drew up at the corner, Molly searched his dark face. "You're sorry? For what?"

He moved his hand lightly over her sleeve, the warmth of the caress seeping through the cotton. "For everything," he said huskily. The crosswalk light changed just then. He drew her out onto the street, his riding boots tapping out a sharp tattoo on the asphalt as he led her to the opposite curb. "For being a self-centered jerk. For railroading you into this. For treating you like a child at the café. You name it, I'm sorry for it. Hell, I even lost your coat."

Her coat? Molly realized her parka was missing. That he would even care about that at a time like this brought a wobbly smile to her lips.

"I was so upset when I went back to the café for your purse, I totally forgot it," he elaborated. "When I went back a second time, it was gone."

"You got my purse, at least. That's better than I can say for myself."

"Only because your identification is in it." He drew her toward the outer edge of the sidewalk to circle an approaching elderly couple. "Classic. I knew you couldn't marry me without ID. That's me, always focused on my own agenda."

As they crossed yet another street, she realized he was

taking her back to the truck. She knew then that he'd done an about face. The marriage was off.

Twenty minutes ago, she would have been relieved. Now her emotions were a crazy mix of relief and apprehension. If he backed out and refused to marry her, what on earth was she going to do?

After depositing her inside the vehicle, he circled to climb in on the driver's side. The report of the slamming door preceded a heavy silence broken only by the sound of their breathing. The window glass began to fog. Molly fixed her gaze on the windshield, stupidly watching the steam collect in an uneven line above the dusty dash.

Jake finally released a weary breath, folded his arms over the steering wheel, and rested his forehead on his wrists. The brim of his hat shadowed his features, making it difficult to read his expression, but the defeated slump of his broad shoulders spoke volumes.

"Ah, Molly." He sighed again. "I'm so sorry, honey. I should never have insisted on this. I don't know what I was thinking." He followed that with a self-deprecating laugh. "Strike that. I know what I was thinking. I just can't believe I was thinking it."

Molly traced a circle on her jeans, hating the dejected tone in his voice. This was her fault, not his. She was the one who'd gone berserk in the café.

"You only offered to help me, Jake. I don't think that's such a terrible thing."

"Yeah, I was a real prince. I offered you help, but only for a price. And for you, it's a dear one." He straightened away from the steering wheel. His dark face was drawn, his eyes lackluster. He searched her gaze. "Do you remember the night I told you an animal can't be owned, that it chooses its master?"

"Yes," she said faintly.

"The same holds true for people. Love can't be bought. You can't finagle your way into someone's heart. More importantly, though we may sign documents to make it legal, marriage isn't a contractual agreement. At least it shouldn't be." A suspicious shine came into his eyes. He swiped a hand over his mouth and directed his gaze out the windshield. "I want you as my wife, Molly. This morning, that wanting and my good intentions started riding double. You know what I'm saying?"

"I think so."

He smiled slightly. "I lost sight of the really important things for a while, namely that no one should ever be pushed into marriage, no matter how sound the reasons behind it." He drew his gaze back to her. "You aren't ready for marriage. When you are, I'll be first in line to pop the question and pray you'll say yes. But I don't want it to come about this way."

Molly hugged her waist. "So you're backing out, then?"

He huffed under his breath. "More like backing off. I guess I needed that douse of hot coffee in my lap to make me realize what I was doing. When ordering you a sandwich sends you into a tailspin, we've got some serious problems. They won't go away just because we get married."

Molly appreciated the fact that he'd said *they* had some problems. He wasn't pointing the finger or assigning blame. The fact that he wasn't prompted her to say, "I'm the one with the problems, Jake."

"Your problems are my problems," he said softly.

"I wish that—" She broke off, searching for words. "I can't explain what happened in there." Pressing a fist to her chest, she gave him an imploring look. "I'm all mixed up inside. It's like—I don't know—like an ignition of some kind. One minute, I'm fine, and the next, I'm losing it. I get so upset I can barely breathe, and reason flies out the window. The first thing I know, I'm doing and saying things I never would otherwise. Like the night you took my rotor. There was no excuse for the way I behaved. None at all. I felt trapped, and I couldn't get past that."

"Everyone loses it sometimes, Molly."

"Not in a restaurant."

"Yeah, even in restaurants. You just need time, honey. I'm sorry I lost sight of that and started pushing you." He drew in an unsteady breath. "We both need time, I think."

The way Molly saw it, there was no time. Rodney was closing in on her even as they spoke.

"You need to resolve a few issues in your mind," he went on. "And I need some time to show you I'm not the controlling bastard you think I am."

"I don't think that."

"Yeah. Yeah, you do." He held up a hand. "I don't blame you for that. Don't think it for a minute. You've been through a bad experience. Now I'm trying to herd you to the altar again." He puffed air into his cheeks and rubbed his forehead. "I can come off like a steamroller sometimes. I don't mean to, but there you have it. I don't stop to think before I speak, and even when I do, half the time I don't say what I mean."

Molly felt suddenly cold. She shivered and rubbed her arms. Jake swore under his breath and reached behind the seat.

"Here, honey. Put this on."

Molly accepted the denim jacket he handed her. Instead of slipping her arms down the sleeves, she pulled the wool lining over herself. "I'm scared, Jake."

He swore again, then dragged a hand over his face. "I know. Who wouldn't be? But, hey. We're going to lick this. Rodney isn't invincible, and there's always more than one way to skin a cat."

"Meaning?"

"Meaning that marriage isn't the only answer. Granted, it's the most surefire. But we've got options."

"Like what?" she asked thinly.

"I had some time to think while I was waiting outside the lounge for you. How about if I hire you a damned good lawyer? I'm sure my brother-in-law, Ryan Kendrick, can recommend a sharp one."

Given her legal incompetence, Molly doubted they could find a lawyer willing to take her case. "What would you hire a lawyer with? You're barely staying afloat financially as it is."

"I've still got some money in the bank."

"Isn't that your working capital?"

He shrugged. "I also have a few horses I can sell. I should be able to come up with enough for a hefty retainer fee. If not, I can always tap my sister Bethany for a loan." He flashed her a grin. "She married into money. Her old man's so rich, they'll never miss it."

Molly remembered that afternoon in the kitchen after the stable fire when he'd picked the slivers from her feet. He'd said nothing then about selling his stock or being able to borrow money to cover the cost of rebuilding. Instead, he'd stared out the window with a hollow-eyed hopelessness, saying he'd be left with only a dream in his pocket if the insurance company refused to cover the damages. By that, she knew that Jake Coulter was a man who believed in standing on his own two feet. Borrowing money wouldn't be easy for him.

"If you sell your horses, won't that seriously deplete your assets?"

The crease lines deepened at the corners of his intense blue eyes as he frowned past her out the window. "Nah."

Molly knew he was lying. Not because he didn't carry it off well, but because he couldn't look at her as he spoke. "Oh, Jake," she said shakily.

His gaze jerked back to hers. "What?"

She shook her head. "I can't let you do that. Besides, it's a long shot. Even if we can get a lawyer to take my case, there's no guarantee he can help me. I've got a documented history of emotional instability, I've already been institutionalized once, I've been judged legally incompetent, and my adoptive mother will testify in court that I'm a basket case. Realistically, what are my chances?"

"Will your doctor testify on your behalf?"

"I'm sure he would, but his professional opinion may be secondary if they put me in a different clinic. The attending doctor's testimony will carry the most weight with a judge."

"It's a chance we have to take. If we don't get married, hiring an attorney's your only hope."

"At what cost? The Lazy J means *everything* to you. If you deplete your funds and assets, you could end up losing the ranch."

This time, he was able to look her directly in the eye as he spoke. "The Lazy J doesn't mean everything to me, Molly. There are other things far more important."

Molly realized he was referring to her. An awful ache filled her chest. For a second, she was afraid she would burst into tears. That he would do this for her—that he would even *consider* doing it—nearly broke her heart.

"I won't let you throw away your dream," she finally managed to say. "Rodney's already destroyed most of mine. I won't let him take yours, too. I won't."

"Sweetheart, let's be reasonable."

"I am being reasonable. That ranch has been in your family for generations. It was a miracle you ever got it back in the first place. If you lose it a second time, chances are you'll never get your hands on it again."

"It's only a patch of dirt," he said. "I can always get another spread." His gaze trailed slowly over her face, as if he were committing every line to memory. "The same can't be said for a certain lady I know. She's one of a kind."

Molly felt her chin start to quiver. Then, as if an invisible hand nudged her from behind, she launched herself across the seat and into his arms. "Oh, Jake," she cried, nearly strangling on a suppressed sob as she hugged his neck. "I'm so sorry. So very sorry."

He was clearly startled by her embrace. She felt his body snap taut. Then the starch suddenly went out of him, and he tightened his arms around her. A hundred times,

Molly had tried to imagine how it might feel to seek sanctuary in his strong arms. He'd held her twice, once out in the woods and another time in the kitchen, but both those times, her thoughts had been fragmented by other emotions, not allowing her to really absorb the essence of him.

Such was not the case now. All her senses were focused on how he felt. The breadth of his chest—the steely strength of his arms—the gentle brush of his big hand over her back. Molly closed her eyes and pressed closer to him, heedless of the gearshift that jabbed her thigh, heedless of everything but him. *Jake.* This was how it was supposed to be, she thought nonsensically. Two people, holding each other, with nothing but feelings between them.

"I can't let you lose your ranch," she murmured against his neck.

"Did I ask your permission? Done deal, lady. It's the only way I can think of to help you."

"*No.* Just marry me. I've resolved all my conflicts. Really. Getting married is the simplest way."

She felt his lips curve in a smile. "That was a mighty fast turnaround."

"If I can't trust you, who can I trust?"

He ran his big hand slowly up her spine. "No one," he admitted huskily. "As much as I love you, Molly, if you can't trust me, you're sunk."

She laughed, the sound shrill and a little hysterical. "So marry me. I'd rather do that than gamble with the Lazy J."

She could feel his hesitance. "Such unbridled enthusiasm."

"I'm sorry. I didn't mean it like that."

He fell silent for a moment. "I just don't feel right about it now. I'm afraid you're getting pushed into something you'll regret later, and I don't want to be one of your regrets. You know?" He ran a hand into her hair. "You're not ready for a real marriage. Not yet."

Molly wished with all her heart that she could deny that charge. But the truth was, she wasn't ready. She'd come a very long way since that fateful morning when she'd awakened at the clinic. With Sam's help, she'd been going through a healing process ever since, taking giant strides toward emotional wellness. But she hadn't made it to the finish line yet. She felt that she was nearly there—that she was poised on an edge and about to take that last, freeing leap. But until she did, she wouldn't be whole.

She was functional. She could take care of herself and get by. But a healthy relationship demanded more than that from a person. She wasn't the only one with needs. Jake had them, too—needs she wasn't yet ready to fulfill. And, like it or not, she had fears he couldn't dispel. She wished that he could. Oh, how she wished that he could. But that wasn't the way of things in real life. Knights in shining armor existed only in fairy tales, and to slay her dragons, she needed to deal the killing blows herself.

"I guess we could go for a marriage in name only," he whispered. "Unless we go ahead and have sex, it won't be valid."

She stirred to look up at him. "I thought you wanted this to be a real marriage. No stopgap measure, you said."

He tucked in his chin to smile ruefully down at her. "Yeah, well, I don't always get my druthers." He smoothed a hand over her hair. "Maybe in time, huh? For now, the important thing is to stonewall Rodney. We can deal with the other stuff later. Preferably sooner than later." He bent to kiss her forehead. "Hope springs eternal, and all that. I'll keep a positive outlook and work on you every chance I get."

Molly searched his expression. "You'll be happy with that arrangement?"

"Hell, no. I want more, Molly. A lot more. I love you."

She knew he did. After his willingness to sacrifice his ranch for her, how could she doubt it? Sadly, though, love wasn't always enough. Molly had learned that bitter lesson the hard way.

He waited a beat, his gaze still holding hers. "So, what

do you say, Stir-Houston? You willing to take on a cowboy for a while?"

Molly stared hard at his chin. "I feel uncomfortable, making vows I'm not sure I can keep. To me, it's the worst kind of sin."

A twinkle slipped into his eyes. "We'll make up our own vows then. You can promise to stay with me as long as you can stand me. I'll promise to stay with you until your tread starts to wear and you need an oil change."

Molly gave a startled laugh. "Surely we can't be legally married, saying stuff like that."

He assumed a mock frown. "Why not? This is Reno, darlin'. Anything goes."

Chapter Nineteen

Two hours later, they were headed back to Crystal Falls. For the first half hour, Jake left Molly to her thoughts. Except for the engine noise and the occasional rattling sound, the inside of the truck was as silent as a sepulcher. Arms folded at her waist, eyes straight ahead, Molly huddled against her door. Every once in a while, he saw her thumb the wedding band that he'd placed on her finger.

As rings went, it wasn't much. Using his charge card, he had purchased it at a jewelry store near the chapel where they'd gotten married. Chances were good that the gold would flake off later. Someday soon, he would buy her a nicer band and a pretty diamond to boot, he promised himself. For now, though, chintzy was all he could afford.

Not that Molly seemed to notice the quality of the ring. He had a feeling it was the meaning behind it that had her worried. He'd done his best to modify the set of vows they'd chosen from the chapel's selection of canned ceremonies. Unfortunately, he and the JP had been working at cross-purposes. Toward the end of the ceremony, the man had thrown in, "Do you, Molly Sterling, take this man to be your lawful husband, to love, honor, and cherish him, keeping yourself only unto him, until death do you part?" Molly had flashed Jake a panicked look. Then, before he could intervene, she'd said, "I do," in a thin, tremulous voice. After that, Jake had followed her lead. What else could he do without embarrassing her half to death?

Now they were hitched, with a string of promises be-

hind them that Molly hadn't wanted to make. On the one
hand, Jake wished she wouldn't take it all so seriously, but
in another way, he was damned glad she did. Who wanted
to be married to a woman who took her vows lightly? He
sure as hell didn't.

His hands were slick with sweat on the steering wheel.
His guts felt tied in knots. He found himself wanting to
talk to her, about anything and everything. He loved the
sound of her voice. He loved the way she wrinkled her
nose in thought before she said something.

Damn. He just loved her, he guessed. Even when she
grew difficult and unreasonable as she had in the café, he
found himself stepping back to analyze the situation, rather
than getting mad. He grinned to himself, remembering the
scene she'd caused. That was a meal a number of people
would never forget, himself included. In twenty years, he
had a hunch it would be one of his fondest memories.
Someday, he and Molly would tell their kids the tale, and
they'd all laugh together about it.

That she might not be a part of his life in twenty years
was a possibility Jake refused to contemplate. Somehow,
some way, he would work past all her reservations, he assured himself. He had to. Otherwise he would lose her, and
that simply couldn't happen.

He glanced over at her. "You okay?"

She pushed at her hair and nodded. "Yes, fine. Just
tired."

Jake swallowed and tightened his grip on the wheel.
"Can you tell me about it, Molly? I'm not real keen on
walking into this blind."

She might have asked him to elaborate on his question.
He'd left her that room. But, instead, she proved herself to
be as courageous as he'd judged her to be from the start
and began telling him about her marriage—about what she
termed her foolish girlhood fantasies, which had died a
sudden death after the marriage—about the endless string
of other women in Rodney's life from the very beginning.

"I wasn't enough," she admitted hollowly. "No matter what I did, I wasn't enough."

That statement made Jake's heart twist. She was so damned pretty, so sweet and pure of heart. How could any man think she wasn't enough?

He took his gaze from the road for a moment to look at her. "Some people should never get married. That's the truth of it. Nothing is enough. No one is enough."

"I wanted to be," she said shakily. "I tried so hard to be."

Jake had already guessed that much. In fact, he believed her sense of commitment and loyalty had nearly destroyed her. "And nothing you did pleased him."

"Nothing," she admitted.

"It wasn't you, Molly. Never you."

"Yes. I think there's something lacking in me, Jake."

"Is there something lacking in Sunset?"

She closed her eyes. "That's different."

"Bullshit. That horse gave Rodney everything he had, and it wasn't enough. Your words, not mine. I heard you talking to him that afternoon. What applies to him applies to you. He's a beautiful animal, and I'll wager he's pure magic on the track. He's also got a heart as big as Texas, and then some. How is he lacking, Molly?"

She shook her head. "He isn't. He's perfect."

"Damned straight, and so are you." He reached up to adjust his visor to block out the setting sun. "That's a subject for later, though. Your marriage—or more specifically, what wasn't a marriage—is past history. Let's move on to the more pertinent details, namely what landed you in this mess."

"I'm almost afraid to tell you."

"Don't be silly."

"No, really. I'm terrified I'm doing the wrong thing by getting you mixed up in it."

Jake patted his shirt pocket, wishing to hell he still

smoked. At times like this, he always craved a cigarette. "I can handle Rodney. Don't worry about it."

"You could handle Rodney in a confrontation. Unfortunately, Rodney won't be confrontational. He'll get you when your back is turned."

"I'm not afraid of him, and I don't want you to be. He can't hurt you now. You're my wife. If he lays a hand on you, I'll kill him."

"Rodney is treacherous, Jake. He lets nothing stand in the way of what he wants. Nothing. Now that you've married me, you'll be in his way."

"Short of murder, what the hell can he do about it?"

"That's just it," she said tremulously. "He may not stop at murder."

Jake was so shocked that he almost had to pull off the road. Surely he hadn't heard her right. "Say what?"

"I think Rodney may have killed my father."

"Dear God. *Why?*"

"I'm not sure. Rodney was gambling heavily, and Sonora Sunset was losing more races than he won. Maybe he was embezzling funds to cover his losses. I don't know. But I think Dad found out about it, and Rodney killed him to shut him up."

"Jesus Christ," Jake whispered. He seldom took the Lord's name in vain, but right now, he wasn't sure if he was cursing or praying. Murder? He'd known the instant he looked into Rodney Wells's eyes that the guy was a snake, but murder was beyond his comprehension. "What makes you think he killed him?"

"My dad was very upset about something the last few days before his death, and uncharacteristically of him, he refused to discuss it with anyone, not even Claudia. They were always very close, so that was strange. It was doubly strange that he refused to talk to me." She lifted her hands. "My dad was an honorable man and didn't make accusations lightly. If he found something suspicious, he would have kept it to himself until he had absolute proof. I think he may have been checking into it, trying to get the goods on Rodney, and Rodney found out."

"And your father ended up dead? How did he die?"

"A gunshot wound to the head. I'd gone in early that morning to try to talk to him and see if I could find out what was wrong. I was the one who found him."

Jake's heart caught at the expression on her face, which told him how desperately she was hanging on to her self-control. "Oh, honey. That must have been a nightmare."

"A nightmare, yes." She fixed her gaze on the dash. "It was especially hard because that was the second time for me. In college, my best friend Sarah slashed her wrists. We roomed together, and I was the one who discovered her body. You can't imagine how I felt when I found my father. It was like a replay of my worst memories, only worse because I loved him so much. I'd failed Sarah, and then I failed my dad. You just can't fathom how I felt. Right before both of them died, I knew something was horribly wrong, and I didn't *do* anything. After finding Dad, I grew completely hysterical."

"Of course, you did."

She hauled in a shaky breath and tidied her hair with nervous fingers. Then she dropped her hands to her lap and went back to staring out the glass. "The police said it was suicide. My dad had been acting strangely for about a week. They found evidence that the gun had been purchased in his name only a few days before." She shot him a meaningful look. "It was purchased with ID, but Rodney is so clever with computers, he could whip up a picture ID in thirty minutes. The police didn't think of that, of course, and neither did I at the time. The investigating officers told me that older men often get depressed for no apparent reason. A chemical imbalance, possibly. Or maybe just feeling that life is essentially over, and their dreams haven't been realized. They said suicide wasn't uncommon in men his age."

"But you didn't believe that."

"My father was a noble man, not the type to take the coward's way out unless there were some horrific, extenuating circumstances. No, I couldn't accept it. At that point, of course, I was still in shock, so I wasn't thinking in terms of murder. I thought maybe he'd lost a bunch of money on the stock market, or that he'd made a string of bad investments for his clients. I needed—" She broke off and passed a hand over her eyes. "I don't know. I needed an explanation, I guess. A *reason*. Before I could lay him to rest, I had to know why he'd taken his life."

"If that happened to my father, I'd feel exactly the same way," Jake assured her.

"Anyway, Jared and Rodney—"

"Jared?"

"He was the man with Claudia this morning. He's Rodney's father."

"Ah, the plot thickens."

She nodded. "He was my dad's partner and best friend. They went through college together, worked at the same firm to get their licenses after they graduated, and then opened Sterling and Wells. Until recently, I always called him Uncle Jared. My dad had no siblings, and I always thought of Jared as my only other male relative." She grabbed for breath again, giving Jake the impression she was feeling oxygen deprived. "Anyway, right after the funeral, Jared and Rodney removed all my dad's personal effects from our family home. I was afraid they'd clear out his office next, and I wanted to go through his business records before anyone tampered with them."

"So you went to the firm to do that?"

"It seemed like a perfectly natural thing to me. My dad was dead, and I needed to know why. Rodney didn't see it that way. When he found me in my father's office, he got upset. He said he would go through Dad's files, but he didn't want me doing it myself because it was too stressful. He was afraid I'd have another nervous breakdown."

Jake shot her a questioning look. "You'd had a nervous breakdown before that?"

Her face had gone deathly pale. "No, that's the whole point. When my friend Sarah killed herself, I had a rough time handling her death. I knew she was depressed, and I encouraged her to seek counseling. But when she refused, I didn't insist upon it. I should have, and she paid for that with her life."

"Ah, honey. You can't blame yourself for that. You were only eighteen."

"Seventeen, actually. I entered grade school when I was five, so I was only seventeen my freshman year. I realize now that I was simply too young to recognize how deeply troubled Sarah was, but at the time, I blamed myself. My dad had me moved to a new dorm, but you can't escape something like that. The memories followed me. I started having nightmares. Worry over my grades added to the stress. Pretty soon, between dread of the dreams and concerns about school, I could scarcely sleep at all, and when exhaustion did win out, I began sleepwalking."

The puzzle pieces began to fall together for Jake.

"The episodes were bizarre and alarming, but never violent. When my parents got wind of them, they insisted I drop out of school and come home for grief counseling. At about that time, Rodney had just returned to Portland after working for several years in Silicon Valley. He and his dad, who were recently divorced, were frequent dinner guests at our house. Rodney was privy to the problems I had over Sarah's death."

"And he called that a nervous breakdown?"

Her mouth tightened, and she flashed him a dark look. Jake returned his attention to the road, waiting for her answer.

"Until that morning at the firm, he had never called it a nervous breakdown. I think he only did so then because other people were within earshot."

Jake flipped on the turn signal to pass a slow-moving vehicle. "My God, he was setting you up."

He heard her release a pent-up breath and realized he was parroting her thoughts. "At the time, I was just incredulous and horribly embarrassed that he'd say such a thing in front of other people. Suddenly I was, in his words, 'emotionally fragile.' I refuted the statement. He patted me on the head and mollified me, playing the concerned husband. In my opinion, it was a performance deserving of an Oscar."

Jake mulled that over. "He was running scared. There was something in those files he didn't want you to see, and on the off chance that you had, he needed a backup plan to cast doubt on your credibility."

Silence. Jake glanced over and saw that she had bent her head and closed her eyes. When seconds passed, he grew concerned. "Are you okay?"

She covered her face with trembling hands. "I'm sorry. It's just—except for talks with my doctor, I've been dealing with this alone for a good long while, and to be perfectly truthful, there have been times when I've doubted my sanity." She wiped her cheeks and sniffed. "You can't know what a relief it is to hear you mirror my thoughts."

"You aren't crazy, honey. Get that notion straight out of your head."

She nodded. "It's just that—well, these last few days, I haven't been so sure a couple of times." She haltingly told him about finding the debris in her bed and the deisel-soaked gloves in her kitchen. "Until Rodney showed up this morning, I was half convinced it was *me* doing it all."

"You booby-trapped the cabin so you wouldn't sleepwalk? That's why you had all that crap in front of the door that night?"

"Yes, and then the tires got slashed. I realized you were in danger of losing the ranch. At that point, I felt so awful that I knew I had to tell you."

"Why didn't you?"

She reminded him that he hadn't been accessible for a couple of days. "I meant to tell you, wanted to tell you, but the moment didn't present itself."

She went on to tell him of the weeks following her father's death, how bizarre incidents began occurring in her and Rodney's home. "It always appeared that I had done it. You know? We found the bloodstained jacket my dad was wearing when he died, hanging on a dining room chair. Rodney asked why I had kept such a gruesome memento." She shook her head. "I never saw the clothes Dad died in after they took him away in the ambulance. I tried to tell Rodney that, but he didn't believe me."

"He was trying to make you think you were losing it."

"I *did* think I was losing it. Shortly after that, I began sleepwalking again, and the incidents had violent undertones. I had no recollection of them, but I'd wake up to find the house in a shambles. Slashed cushions, slashed pictures, overturned garbage. Red lipstick or catsup smeared on the bathroom walls to look like blood, with Sarah's name written in the mess. I didn't own a lipstick, but Rodney insisted I must have bought one and simply didn't remember."

Jake's heart caught at the agonizing trace of doubt he heard in her voice. "That must have been scary, thinking you had done things you couldn't recall."

"It was. Rodney was so convincing. You saw him today, how calm and gentle he seems. I thought I was going mad."

"But, of course, you weren't. That's only what he wanted you to think."

She nodded. "Finally, after one particularly bizarre sleepwalking incident, he called my mom in a panic early one morning."

"In a well-staged panic," Jake corrected. "Let's keep this story on track."

She flashed him another grateful look. "Claudia is a general practitioner with a thriving practice. She rushed over. When she saw the house, she concluded that I was having a hard time with my dad's death and had started sleepwalking again. She wanted me to see a good psychologist for counseling. Rodney wanted to wait. He said a few sleepwalking incidents didn't make me crazy. He suggested that Claudia write me a prescription for sleeping pills, his hope being that if I slept deeply, the incidents would stop. She finally relented, though I think it went against her better judgment, and wrote a prescription. Rodney got it filled."

Jake sensed what was coming.

"The pills made me sick. Horribly dizzy and disoriented all the next day. Rodney asked Claudia for another prescription that might better agree with me. I just got sicker. Pretty soon he was giving me pills to cure the symptoms caused by pills I couldn't function. I couldn't think. It got so I couldn't even make it to the bathroom without collapsing."

"Oh, my God. He was slipping you something."

Her eyes brimmed with tears. "Yes," she said shakily, "I believe he was. I think my illness was chemically induced, that he drugged me to make it appear I was having a breakdown. During that time, he kept trying to get me to sign some papers. My dad had stressed never to sign anything I hadn't read. I hadn't observed that rule during Rodney's and my marriage because he often wanted me to sign personal papers, and sometimes I was too busy to read the fine print. But the documents he wanted me to sign during my illness could have been firm related. I felt responsible for my dad's half of the business, which represented his life's work, and I refused to sign anything without reading it first. That created a problem. My vision was too blurred for me to make out the words."

"I'll bet Rodney was thrilled about that."

"He was furious." She gazed off at nothing. "To understand the shock element of that, you have to know how Rodney was before then. I know you think he was a jerk, but he was never overt about it. If I displeased him, he never yelled or hit me. He'd simply not speak to me for days on end. Or he'd humiliate me, often in front of other people. I always paid for my transgressions, but not in the ways you'd think."

"He was a calculating, vicious bastard, in other words."

She laughed tremulously. "Yes, and very good at hiding it. He never meant to humiliate me in public. He never *intentionally* hurt me. He was simply stating a fact, and I was being too sensitive." She shrugged. "I can't count the times he'd say something in front of people that left me bleeding. Then he'd thump himself on the forehead and apologize to me for putting it that way. It made him appear thoughtless, but not deliberately cruel, and people found it endearing, the way he apologized so profusely after he tripped over his own tongue. In the beginning, even I fell for it. Unfortunately, that didn't lessen the hurt any, and later on, it hurt even more because I knew he intended it to wound."

"What kind of things did he say to you, honey?" Jake asked softly.

Silence. Finally, she said, "Just stupid stuff. It doesn't matter now."

Jake thought it mattered a great deal. "Can you give me just one example?"

Another silence. And then, waving a hand as if to indicate the insignificance, she said, "Things like, 'My God, where did you get that dress? It makes you look like a fat cow.' Then he'd do his forehead thumping routine, hand me money to go shopping, and be all over himself, trying to flatter me."

Jake ground his teeth. He needed to say something, but he couldn't think of a single thing. In the end, he remained silent. Words weren't what she needed. Not from him, at least. He did his best talking with his actions.

"Anyway," she went on. "That's water under the bridge. My point was that Rodney hides behind a mask most of the time and only shows his real self when it suits his purposes. Afterward, he's very talented at glossing it over and winning people back. My father was a great judge of character. He never liked Rodney very much, but I don't think he knew until the end what kind of man Rodney really is. I certainly never knew. Not in the beginning. In the early years, I never suspected that he was being unfaithful to me, for instance. He was gone a lot, but he always had an explanation, and I had no reason to think he might lie."

"You were going to make him rich someday. If he'd been a blatant adulterer, you might have divorced him, not to mention that your father would have been down his throat. Rodney may be a snake, but he's a smart snake."

"Anyway," she said with another wave of her hand, "one night, when I refused to sign the papers, his mask slipped completely, and I saw the real Rodney in all his ugly glory. It was the most *awful* feeling, Jake. Even doped up as I was, I reeled from the shock. I looked into his eyes and saw a stranger. I know that sounds overly dramatic, but that was exactly how I felt. It was Rodney's face, but the man wearing it was a *monster*. He looked as if he wanted to rip me apart with his bare hands, and in that moment, I thought sure he would. The worst part was, I was so sick and dizzy, I saw three of him. I didn't know which fist would plow into my face."

"Oh, honey." Jake was tempted to pull over again, this time because he wanted so badly to hug her. Rodney Wells was a fairly big man, and Molly, for all her ample curves, was a slip of a woman. She must have been terrified.

"He intimidated me that night. But after losing my dad the way I had, I couldn't betray everything he'd taught me."

Jake smiled slightly, not at all surprised to hear that. He was coming to know that Molly would stand firm on her convictions no matter what it cost her.

"I refused to sign the papers. The next morning, I woke up in a clinic. I was strapped to the bed. I had no idea where I was or how I'd gotten there. My first reaction was to scream for help."

"Of course it was."

"My attendants didn't see it that way. They thought I was a raving lunatic. It was so awful, Jake." Her voice went whispery. "It was the first time I'd been able to think clearly in weeks, and they pumped me full of sedatives again to calm me down."

"At least you had a few minutes of clarity. Rodney wasn't there to shove pills down you."

She smiled sadly and sighed. "It is so *good* to tell someone all this."

"And find out your take on everything wasn't so crazy, after all?"

"Yes," she admitted. "After waking up at the clinic, I didn't immediately put two and two together, but in moments of clarity after that, I began to. At first, I didn't play by the clinic rules. I was so enraged. You know? My father was dead. I was locked up, and I wasn't crazy. I wanted to tell anyone who'd listen and try to get help. That only made me look crazier. It was a pretty outlandish story."

"Did they treat you kindly at the clinic?"

"Eventually. I had a fabulous doctor. His name is Sam Banks. In the beginning, he thought I was a certifiable basket case, but before long, he started to believe my story. After that, he became my champion. He petitioned the court to get me a divorce. He allowed Rodney to see me only when he was present. Rodney hated his guts and still does."

"I think I'll like Sam Banks."

"I know I do," she said. "With his help, I was able to recall details I had blocked out or forgotten, and eventually, I was able to pinpoint the exact moment everything started, the day I went to search my father's office. Rodney began a campaign then to make me look nuts. I think he slipped the debilitating drug into my prescription bottles just in case I read the labels. I don't know if he got it on the black market, or if Claudia helped him get it, but I'm convinced he gave me something that made me deathly ill."

"You really think Claudia may be involved?"

"She helped Rodney put me away. She took Jared into her bed shortly after my father's death. I can't rule it out. I'm suspicious of all of them. Maybe they want my share of the firm. A great deal of money will eventually be at stake. People have done more heinous things out of greed."

Right after meeting Molly, Jake had sensed how very lonely and lost she felt. Now he knew why. Even the woman she'd called mother may have betrayed her in the most horrible way.

"What kind of woman is Claudia?"

"I always believed she was wonderful. My mom died of ovarian cancer when I was only five. She was ill for a long time, and shortly after her death, my father met and fell in love with Claudia. She couldn't have children, and, after adopting me, she always treated me like her own." Her voice quaked as she added, "I would have trusted her with my life, Jake, and I never questioned her love for Dad. I truly thought she adored him."

Jake couldn't bear to hear that hollow, tortured ring in her voice. "Maybe she did, Molly. If you and your dad were fooled by Rodney, maybe she was as well. Let's not condemn her until we know for sure."

She flashed him a warm look, even though her eyes shimmered with tears. "That's exactly what Sam would say. And my dad, too, for that matter. You remind me so much of him sometimes."

"Sam or your dad?"

A glow warmed her eyes. "My dad."

Jake took that as the highest of compliments. "Thank you," he said huskily. He checked his speed, noted how much he'd slowed down while listening to her story, and sped back up a bit. "Maybe Claudia turned to Jared in her grief. From things you've said, she must have regarded him as a very good friend. Sometimes when we're hurting, we just need someone to hold us, and maybe Jared was there for her in a way no one else was because he loved your dad, too."

"I want to believe that," she said in a thin voice. "You can't know how much. But she never came to see me, Jake. Except for that one time when Rodney called her over to the house, she stayed away the entire time I was sick. I never saw her in the clinic until right before my release when she came to tell me she was marrying Jared."

Jake felt her pain like a knife in his guts. "That doesn't mean she didn't love your dad or that she was in on anything. It could very well be that Rodney was doing everything solo, and he said or did something to make Claudia stay away."

Keeping one eye on the road, he leaned over to open the glove box where he kept a roll of toilet paper. "My version of tissues," he said.

She sniffed and tore off a length of squares to blow her nose. "Claudia said Rodney told her I was furious about the thing between her and Jared, and that I didn't want to see her. Knowing I was so ill, she didn't want to further upset me, so she honored my wishes. She came that one day to the clinic only because she felt I deserved to hear the news of her marriage directly from her."

"Sounds reasonable. Did you tell her of your suspicions about Rodney?"

Molly shook her head. "I'd worked so hard to get out of there. I was afraid to tell her anything for fear she and Rodney would have me moved to another clinic away from Sam. I didn't know if I could trust her."

"So the one time you could have talked with someone outside the clinic who might have believed your story, you were held back by fear."

"Yes."

"Did you ever see her again after that? Before today, I mean."

"Right after I was released from the clinic, but I was still on probation. Sam had warned me not to do or say anything to rock the boat, that they could go over his head and put me back in a ward." She shot him a worried look. "That could still happen. Stealing a horse will definitely strike a judge as being irrational."

Until that moment, Jake hadn't understood how greatly she had endangered herself to help that poor horse. She'd risked her freedom, her dreams, everything.

"Anyway," she went on, "I was afraid to tell Claudia anything. If she was in on it, and I started accusing Rodney of killing my dad, they could have claimed I was delusional."

"Why did you see her after you got out?" Jake asked, hoping she didn't feel as if he were grilling her.

"She'd heard about my divorce through Jared, and she knew I'd be out on the streets after my release until I found a place. She took it upon herself to get me an apartment, and working through Rodney's dad, she arranged to get my SUV returned to me so I'd have transportation. Except for the times Rodney showed up at the apartment after I was released to try to get me to sign those papers, I never had to see him."

Jake drew his brows together in a thoughtful scowl. The thing with the papers worried him. He had a bad feeling there might be far more to this than Molly realized. If Wells had her power of attorney, why did he need her signature on something? It just didn't figure.

Pulling himself back to the subject, Jake said, "It sounds to me as if Claudia did everything she could, outside of denying herself a relationship with Jared, to make sure her little girl was taken care of. As for her relationship with Jared, you can't condemn two grief-stricken people for clinging to each other."

"No," Molly whispered. "And if that's all it is, God forgive me for being so cold to her this morning."

Jake's throat went tight. "No self-recrimination allowed. You've been through a hell of a time. I don't think you've said or done anything that wasn't perfectly understandable, and if Claudia is half the woman I think she may be, she'll agree with me when she realizes what's been going on."

"You liked her, didn't you?"

Jake considered carefully before answering. He'd seen such pain in Claudia's eyes. "She was mighty upset. It's hard for me to believe it was all an act."

Molly sighed and began fiddling with the tissue. "I love her a lot. If she's innocent of any wrongdoing, I'd like very much to mend our relationship. I always loved Uncle Jared, too. He's a nice man." Her eyes darkened again. "At least I always thought so."

Jake fell quiet for a while, thinking about all that she'd told him. Then he said, "Okay, now I know all the facts. Right?"

Judging by the way she avoided his gaze, he guessed that she'd left out some of the grittier details about her marriage. He could understand that talking about something so personal wasn't easy. "You know all the really important things," she agreed.

"You come with some pretty serious trouble riding drag, lady."

She nodded. "Yes. If you want to annul the marriage and wash your hands of me, I won't blame you. You didn't create this mess, and it's not your job to fix it."

"I disagree. The moment I fell in love with you, Molly, everything about you became my problem."

"That's me, one big problem."

He winced. "I didn't mean it like that."

"I know you didn't. But it's the truth. I've been nothing but trouble, and if Rodney has his way, that won't end any time soon."

"I'll take you, trouble and all."

*　　*　　*

Molly thought she would have to start cooking dinner the moment they arrived at the ranch, but when she and Jake pulled up out front, four unfamiliar pickups were parked at the edge of the yard. Jake took one look at them and swore under his breath.

"Who is it?" Molly asked.

"Family," he muttered.

Molly's stomach dropped. "What are they doing here?"

"Hank must have called them." His eyes gleamed in the light from the porch. "I'm sorry. I know you're probably not keen on the idea of a big celebration."

Her hand flew to her hair. She glanced down at her clothes, which were wrinkled from traveling. "I'm a *mess.*"

He grinned. "You look better than I do."

Molly stared at the house. "Are your parents here?"

Jake reached across the cab to touch her shoulder. "Don't bolt on me. My mom and dad are the salt of the earth."

Molly took that to mean yes. She gulped. At the moment, she didn't care how nice his parents were. She wasn't ready to meet them yet. They couldn't be happy about their eldest son's sudden decision to marry, not to mention that he'd chosen to elope without notifying anyone. The only thing this awful day needed to make it complete was familial discord and censure.

Jake piled out of the truck and came around to open her door. As he helped her down from the lofty four-wheel drive, he whispered, "Sweetheart, you look like you just swallowed a half-gallon carton of live guppies. Don't be nervous."

"They aren't going to like me."

"You're absolutely right. They're going to love you." He wrapped a strong arm around her shoulders as they set off for the house. "Just relax and be yourself. You'll have my dad wrapped around your finger in two seconds flat."

Molly wished she were confident of that. "Are they going to be upset with us for running off to Reno?"

He sighed. "Maybe. Under the circumstances, though, I'm sure they'll make allowances."

"You're going to tell them? About Rodney and the clinic, I mean?"

He started up the steps, drawing her firmly along, his embrace comforting on the one hand, yet unbreakable as well, the firmness of his hold a silent message that there was no avoiding this ordeal, no matter how much she might like to. "Hank probably told them already," he said. "The Kendrick brothers are here. It's my guess he called in the big guns just in case I need help handling Rodney or the law."

Molly cringed, so embarrassed she wanted to die. "Talk about having your dirty laundry aired in public."

"It's not your fault," he reminded her. "You have absolutely nothing to be ashamed of, Molly." Once on the porch, he paused to hold her gaze. "Head high, shoulders straight. I'll be right beside you."

For some insane reason, hearing him say that bolstered her confidence. She remembered how he'd stood beside her that morning, his booted feet spread wide, his big body braced for a fight. Jake Coulter was a man who could be counted on, no matter what. She had a feeling he would even take a stand against his family in defense of her, which made her chest ache with emotions she couldn't and didn't wish to name.

When they entered the house, they were greeted by the smell of food preparation and the sound of voices. Molly expected to find the great room crammed full of people, but to her surprise, all the noise seemed to be coming from the room beyond. Jake led her directly to the kitchen archway, then fell back a step to let her enter just ahead of him. The awful thought went through Molly's head that his lagging behind meant she would have to take the first bullet.

The kitchen brimmed over with people. In a glance,

Molly picked out three dark-haired women—a slightly built brunette in a wheelchair who was holding a newborn baby; a short, plump older lady who was stirring something on the stove; and another woman standing by the refrigerator next to a tall, jet-haired cowboy in neatly creased Wranglers and a white western shirt.

As curious as Molly was about the women, her attention became riveted to the men. To her wary gaze, they all seemed to have been poured from the same mold. Tall, lean, and dark, they were, to a man, impressive male specimens, but the most interesting thing she noticed was the marked resemblance they all bore to each other. Two of them were Kendricks, if Jake was to be believed, so why did they all look so much alike? Was it something in the water around Crystal Falls?

At first sight of Molly, Hank and the seven strangers turned in unison to stare. Then, as if by silent command, they all converged on her, crying, "Congratulations!" Molly was so startled by all the joyous shouts that she reared back against Jake. He caught her around the waist with one strong arm.

"Unko Jake!"

Molly glanced down to see a pint-size cowboy barreling toward them. He was the most darling little guy she'd ever seen. Perched upon his dark head was a black Stetson bigger than he was. His brown eyes danced with delight.

Bypassing Molly, he grabbed Jake's leg. "Up high!" he cried.

Jake gave Molly a reassuring squeeze, then let go of her to scoop the child into his arms. "Who are you, partner? If this isn't a fine how-do-you-do. I leave for a while, and when I get back, my house is overtaken by strange cowboys."

The child grabbed Jake's ears, nearly knocking his hat off in the process. "I'm Jaimie. You know me."

Jake squinted as if to see the boy better. "Jaimie? Nah. It can't be. He's a little mite."

"I growed up!"

Jake grinned. "I'll be. It is Jaimie. What's your mama been feedin' you, boy? She needs to put a rock on your head. You're sprouting up too fast."

The older woman who'd been working at the stove stepped forward. Molly had a fleeting impression of friendly blue eyes, a radiant smile, and a sweet, very lovely countenance. "You must be Molly," she said, and then, with no further ado, gathered Molly into her plump arms for a hug. "She's lovely, Jake. I guess I'll have to forgive you for running off to Reno to get married. She's too pretty to toss back."

Jake hadn't relinquished his hold on the child, but he stepped closer, offering Molly his silent support. "There'll definitely be no tossing her back, Mom. I finally found a keeper. As for eloping, I'm sure Hank explained that it couldn't be helped." He leaned around to smile at Molly. "This is my mom, Mary, sweetheart. She's an incurable hugger, and she's never in her life met a stranger. All I can say is, you'll get used to her."

Mary flapped a hand. "Get away with you. If I can't hug my new daughter, who can I hug?"

Molly thought Jake's mother was delightful, and she found the unexpected hug reassuring, the thought going through her mind that she would have at least one friend in the Coulter camp. "I'm pleased to meet you, Mary."

"Just call me Mom," Mary chided. "Out of six kids, all I got was one daughter, and I had about given up on any of my sons bringing me home another one. This is one of the happiest days of my life."

A tall, dark-haired older man stepped forward just then. The family resemblance was so strong that Molly knew at a glance he had to be Jake's father. Aside from the silver at his temples and the lines that had been etched into his bronzed face by years of living, he looked so much like her husband and Hank that it was uncanny.

Nudging his wife aside, he grasped Molly by the hands

to draw her away from Jake, whereupon he released her to give her a slow once-over with unsettling blue eyes. Molly felt a little like a mare on the auction block as he circled her. When he came to stand in front of her again, he caught her chin in his hand to turn her face this way and that. Molly half expected him to pry her mouth open and check her teeth.

His gaze warmed on hers. Then he flashed a grin at Jake. "She's a little on the short side, son."

Mary straightened her shoulders. "She's as tall as I am," she informed her big, burly husband.

Jake's father's eyes danced with laughter. "Like I said, she's a little on the short side, son."

Mary elbowed her husband in the stomach, making him grab for his midriff. He huffed and laughed even as his wife scolded him. "Leave off, Harv. The poor girl will think you don't approve of her."

Harv assumed an expression of mock dismay. "Well, we can't have that." He smiled at Molly. "I definitely approve."

Jake lowered Jaimie to the floor. The next instant, Molly felt his big hands settle warmly on her shoulders. "I thought you'd like her, Dad." To Molly, he said, "This is my father, by the way. He's a little on the short side himself when it comes to manners, but he's long on loyalty."

"Now we know where you got it, Jake!" Hank called out with a laugh. "You took after the old man."

Jake's father smiled at Molly. "Welcome to our family, honey." And with that, he followed his wife's example and caught her up in his arms for a hug, the crush of strength around her ribs threatening to rob her of breath.

As Molly slipped free from Harv Coulter's embrace, a tall, jet-haired man standing beside the brunette in the wheelchair said, "Run while you still can, Molly. The whole family's crazy. Worst of all, it's catching, and pretty soon, you start to think they're normal."

The woman in the wheelchair socked the man's thigh.

Molly knew instantly she was Jake's sister. She had delicate features, but they bore the Coulter stamp, her eyes a blaze of blue, her small chin sporting just a hint of a cleft, her dainty jawline squared. "We are not crazy, just sort of—eccentric." She rolled her chair forward. Cuddling her baby in the crook of one arm, she extended only one hand, which Molly grasped to be polite. "Forgive us, Molly. They've already started on the champagne and forgotten their manners. I'm Bethany, Jake's sister." She wiggled a hand free to pat her newborn. "This is your new nephew, Sly. Sylvester, meet your aunt Molly."

Still trying to assimilate the fact that she was married, Molly was startled to hear Bethany refer to her as the baby's aunt. "He's darling," she found the presence of mind to say and leaned down to properly admire the infant. "What a handsome fellow."

"He's a preemie and still a little small, but the doctor says he'll catch up quickly. Judging by his appetite, I believe it." She shot the jet-haired man beside her a teasing look. "This big-mouthed fellow is his dad. May I introduce my husband, Ryan Kendrick? I'll warn you right up front not to believe a word he says. He delights in maligning my family."

Ryan laughed and extended a work-roughened palm. Pasting on a smile, Molly shook hands with him, whereupon she was somehow handed off to another tall, dark-haired man who caught her up for a second breath-robbing hug. "I'm Zeke, Jake's brother, the second oldest."

"Hi." Molly took in his cobalt blue eyes and chiseled features, which also bore the Coulter stamp. "I'm pleased to meet you."

Instead of releasing her after the hug, Zeke slipped an arm around her waist and led her across the room to where the third woman stood beside the jet-haired cowboy in the white western shirt. Molly knew even before the introductions began that the man was Ryan Kendrick's brother. Upon closer inspection, she saw that the two looked enough alike to be twins. "Meet Rafe and Maggie Kendrick," Zeke said. "Rafe is Ryan's older brother. He and Maggie decided to crash our party."

Maggie laughed and rolled her sparkling brown eyes. "Don't believe him, Molly. We're family and don't need an invitation."

Drawing his arm from around Molly's waist, Zeke glanced over the top of her head at Jake, who stood just behind them. "I'm playing waiter. Would you and your bride like some champagne?"

Jake gave Molly a questioning look. Then he shook his head. "Thanks anyway, Zeke. We'll have some in a bit."

Maggie gave Molly a quick hug, then stepped past her to kiss Jake's cheek. "Congratulations, cowboy. It's about time someone got you snubbed down with a short rope."

"Shhh," Jake joked. "She thinks it's the other way around."

Maggie's cheek dimpled in a mischievous grin. She linked arms with Molly. "That won't last. Bethany and I will have her set straight in no time at all." Meeting Molly's gaze, she added, "I'm Jaimie's mom." She held out a hand to measure off the child's height. "The little guy with the big hat? He insisted on coming to Unko Jake's house. My sister Heidi is watching my daughter, Amanda."

"*Your* daughter, *your son?*" Rafe interrupted, his tone laced with teasing rebuttal. He winked lazily at Molly. "They're my kids, too. To hear Maggie talk, I'm nothing but a hat rack."

"Easy mistake. There's always a Stetson on your head," Maggie pointed out.

Touching the black brim of said Stetson, Rafe flashed his wife a wickedly sexy grin. "Not always. I take my hat off for one special lady on occasion."

Maggie's cheeks flamed. For a moment, Molly didn't get Rafe's meaning. Then her face grew as warm as Maggie's looked.

Jake stepped in to rescue her. "Don't mind Rafe," he

said with a laugh. "His mama taught him manners, but they
didn't stick."

Rafe slipped an arm around Maggie's shoulders and
drew her back to his side. "Come back here, girl. I need a
leanin' post."

His leaning post nailed him in the ribs with a sharp
elbow. He pretended to struggle for breath. While he was
hunched over, he took advantage of the opportunity to nibble on Maggie's neck. She leaped and squeaked. "Rafe
Kendrick, be good."

"I'm always good. Sometimes excellent."

"Am I going to be the designated driver tonight?" Maggie demanded.

"Prob'ly." Rafe reached for the champagne he'd set
atop the fridge. "This stuff has a kick like a sawed off shot-
gun."

"That's only his second glass." Maggie sent Molly an
apologetic look. "He seldom drinks. He had a problem
with it a few years back, and—"

"I didn't have a problem," Rafe objected. "It's only a
problem when you wanna quit and can't." He chuckled. "I
never wanted to quit." He nearly spilled his champagne as
he bent to nuzzle Maggie's ear. "Not until I met you, any-
how. Then I swore off."

"Maybe I'd better take him home." Maggie arched her
eyebrows and looked inquisitively at Jake. "Do you think?
I'm afraid he's a little drunk."

"Daddy, what's drunk?"

Everyone looked down to see Jaimie tugging on his father's jeans. Rafe immediately sobered. With exaggerated
care, he returned the champagne to the top of the side-by-
side, clinking the base of the glass against the porcelain
with an air of finality. Then he crouched to loop an arm
around his son. "Well, now," he said, frowning thoughtfully. "Drunk is one of the past tenses of drink." He ruffled
the child's hair and hugged him close. "Your mama was
just telling me I've reached the past-tense stage."

Jaimie climbed onto Rafe's knee. He smiled happily up at Jake. "I'm not all the way growed up yet, so my dad can still give me hugs."

"What d'ya mean, I can *still* give you hugs?" Rafe put both arms around Jaimie and gave him a fierce squeeze. "I'll always give you hugs, big guy."

"Even when I'm *great* big?"

"Even when."

Hank called out that it was time to toast the bride and groom. With a flourish, he uncorked another champagne bottle and began filling Jake's delicate crystal flutes, the ones that had been a housewarming gift. "Since I'm the best man who wasn't, I get to do the honors first."

A series of heartfelt good wishes followed, some humorous, some poignant. Molly noticed that Rafe Kendrick took only small sips from his glass after each toast. When he caught her watching him, he winked at her. The message was clear. For the remainder of the evening, he planned to be a past-tense imbiber.

Watching Rafe with Maggie, Molly felt a twinge of envy. They were clearly blissfully happy in their marriage. Jaimie and Amanda were very lucky children.

After the toasts, everyone began milling around to visit. Molly was a little overwhelmed, to say the least, not entirely sure how to interact with such a large, boisterous group. As if Jake sensed her discomfiture, he kept an arm around her, moving from person to person to chat while everyone except Rafe and Bethany, the nursing mother, sipped champagne.

When dinner was finally ready, Molly was touched to discover that the meal was vegetarian, compliments of Hank and the hired hands, who'd informed Mary Coulter that Jake's new wife seldom ate meat.

The teasing banter, which was nonstop, helped Molly to relax. Evidently sensing that she felt better, Jake quietly excused himself and went to collect his newborn nephew. Molly couldn't help but notice the tender expression on his dark face as he took the baby from his sister's arms. Unlike many men, he seemed completely at ease holding an infant. When the baby tried to suckle the button on his breast pocket, he smiled and offered his knuckle as a substitute.

The conversation around Molly seemed to grow distant as she watched her new husband with the baby. Jake had removed his Stetson, and his dark hair fell over his forehead in lazy waves as he bent to kiss his nephew's temple. There was such love in the gesture, and unmistakable yearning. Molly recalled the morning when he'd confessed to wanting a family. At the time, she had scoffed, but after watching him with Jaimie and seeing him now, she knew it was true.

Jake Coulter ached to have a child of his own.

A lump came to Molly's throat. *Shattered dreams.* She, too, had always longed for a baby. After ten years with Rodney, she'd given up on it ever happening. Now, observing Jake, she felt a faint surge of hope.

What if? He claimed to love her. Incredible as it seemed, after his offer to sell his horses to hire her an attorney, Molly was half-convinced it might be true. Did she dare to hope that this marriage might actually last? If it did, wasn't there every possibility that she and Jake might have a family?

The thought made Molly feel almost giddy, and because it did, she firmly shoved it from her mind. She'd walked that path once, and it had led to nothing but heartbreak. She was afraid to open herself up to that kind of hurt again. Jake Coulter was an extremely attractive, charming man. He could have almost any woman he wanted. Right now, he thought that woman was Molly, but she had no faith his feelings would last. She was too plain and dumpy to hold his interest for long, and if she let herself believe otherwise, it would nearly kill her when he developed a roving eye.

Despite the thought, she found herself smiling or laughing more times than not during the meal, which was served buffet style, allowing the diners to recline wherever they wished to enjoy their food. Molly sat in the great room with the women. By meal's end, she'd noted one marked similarity in all three of them. Whenever they mentioned their husbands, their eyes glowed. Molly couldn't help but feel envious. What must it be like to love so deeply and be loved in equal measure? She couldn't imagine it.

Feeling like the odd one out, she searched for Jake, who was chatting with Rafe Kendrick at the foot of the staircase. Still holding the baby, he stood with his dark head bent, his body relaxed against a banister. As if he sensed Molly's gaze on him, he glanced up, his blue eyes locking on hers. A faint smile played over his mouth. He murmured something to Rafe, then fell into a lazy saunter that carried him quickly across the room. After returning the infant to its mother, he took the empty plate Molly held on her lap and set it on the coffee table.

"We need to walk over to the cabin and grab a few of your things," he said softly.

Molly hadn't thought that far ahead. But, of course, he was right. If she meant to spend the night at the main house, she would need her toiletries, a fresh change of clothes, and something to sleep in. Her mind froze at the thought, for all she usually wore to bed was an oversize T-shirt and panties.

"I should stay until the kitchen is clean," she protested.

"A bride doesn't do dishes on her wedding night," Mary inserted. "Go with your husband. We'll handle the cleanup." Catching Harv's gaze, she smiled and added, "We should probably get to it. We've overstayed our welcome as it is. I'm sure the kids would like to be alone."

"Oh, no!" Molly assured her. "We're in no hurry for you to leave."

Ryan, who was hunkered by Bethany's chair, chuckled and glanced at Jake. "You hear that, Jake? You're in no hurry to get rid of us."

Jake only smiled, his warm gaze remaining fixed on
Molly, his broad palm still outstretched. "Come on,
honey."

It didn't seem to Molly that he was leaving her any option. Everyone in the room had turned to look at them. She
took Jake's hand and let him pull her to her feet. After
grabbing two denim jackets, they left the house, escaping
all the staring eyes. Jake slipped an arm around her waist
as they started down the steps, touching her with the same
casual possessiveness he had all evening, as was his right
now that they were married.

"You in there, girl?" He squeezed her hip through the
lined denim. "Hank's coat damned near swallows you."

In Molly's opinion, it would be a mighty big gulp. As
they walked along, she touched the wedding band on her
finger. Wearing it felt odd after going without a ring for so
many months, a silent reminder that she was no longer her
own person. *Married.* The word rang in her mind like a
key turning in a lock. She tried to remind herself that a life
sentence with Jake might not be such a bad thing, but
somehow that offered scant comfort.

Determined not to let panic get the best of her again as
she had in Reno, she tried to push her concerns from her
mind. Only she kept remembering her last wedding night,
how Rodney had drunkenly groped her body, thrust into
her with no thought for her pain, and then fallen into a stupor, crushing her with his limp weight. She'd been a possession to him, and nothing more. He'd had no regard for
her feelings whatsoever, not that night or at any time there-
after. The thought of being treated that way again made her
feel ill.

Jake wasn't like that, though, she assured herself. He
wasn't. It was stupid to compare him to Rodney. Each time
she made that mistake, he proved her dead wrong.

Though she'd walked this path with him many times, it
seemed different tonight, more intimate somehow. He'd
slipped his hand under the jacket, and his palm had found

a resting place just above her left hip. The contact set her heart to skittering.

"You're tense," he observed dryly, his shimmering gaze finding hers in the moonlight.

Molly nodded. "It's been an eventful day. I feel as if I've climbed onto a roller coaster and can't get off."

He made a low sound at the base of his throat. "Things will calm down now. You'll feel better after a good night's sleep." He waited a beat. "I hope you don't mind my insisting that we come over to get your things. Under other circumstances, we could forgo appearances, and you could just stay at the cabin as you always have. But with Rodney lurking in the wings, that wouldn't be wise. I wouldn't put it past the bastard to sneak in on you during the night. I'd play hell getting you back once he got you to Portland."

Molly hadn't thought of Rodney's sneaking in on her. "You're right. We shouldn't put it past him."

"Trust me, I won't. I'm not letting you out of my sight. You can bunk with me."

Bunk with him? In the same bed? Molly threw him a startled look, which he didn't seem to notice. Her hip nudged his leg as they circled a fallen log. At the contact, it seemed to her that he drew her even closer. She fleetingly wondered if he hoped to consummate the marriage tonight. Then she discarded the concern. Jake would never take a woman without regard for how she felt about it. Besides that, he'd all but promised not to.

"It's a beautiful night." Molly heard the nervous edge in her voice and wanted to kick herself. "Just look at the stars."

"They are something," he agreed, his voice pitched low and husky.

When they reached the cabin, Molly hurriedly collected her things so they could return to the main house and their guests. While she was digging in her drawer for something suitable to serve as a nightshirt, he stepped up behind her, nearly startling her out of her skin. Grasping her upper arms, he drew her back against him and bent to feather his lips over her hair.

"Molly, would you relax? Just because we're married, it doesn't mean I'm going to jump you. Why are you so nervous?"

That was a question Molly couldn't readily answer. She certainly wasn't afraid of Jake. The very idea was preposterous. He was the kindest, most gentle man she'd ever known.

Unfortunately, he was also the most physically attractive man she'd ever known. The mere brush of his hands on her arms made her skin tingle. She had little faith in her ability to resist if he set his mind to seducing her. He made her want to forget everything. Just the thought of his touching her bare skin made her stomach do cartwheels.

"I don't know what's wrong with me," she said weakly. "I guess the reality of what we've done is starting to sink in. I just—getting married wasn't exactly on my agenda when I woke up this morning." His big hands massaged her arms, forcing the knots of tension from her muscles. She leaned more of her weight against his chest, comforted by his sturdy hardness, yet unnerved by it as well. "I don't really know what to expect. I mean—well, we are married. I couldn't blame you for wanting to exercise your conjugal rights."

"Conjugal rights? Never in almost thirty-three years have I heard anyone use that term. It's hopelessly old-fashioned."

"Is it?" It didn't seem out of date to Molly, especially not now with Jake's big hands locked over her arms. "Men have always expected certain privileges in marriage. I don't think that has changed." She could feel that it hadn't in the way he touched her.

"I'm sorry the JP tossed in all the forever stuff during the ceremony," he murmured.

"It wasn't your fault."

"No," he agreed, "but it's worrying you."

"We ended up making all the traditional vows."

He feathered his lips over her temple. "True."

"Vows should be kept."

"I'll keep mine if you'll keep yours," he murmured with a teasing smile in his voice.

Molly squeezed her eyes closed. "I don't know that I have a choice. Maybe it was only a cheesy little chapel in Reno, but I feel that I made them before God, nevertheless."

"Me, too," he whispered. "That being the case, can I promise you one more thing?" At her nod of assent, he said, "You'll never regret marrying me. I'll spend the rest of my life making damned sure you've never got a reason."

Oh, how Molly wanted to believe that. She thought of how he'd looked holding his sister's baby, and she wanted to grab hold of the dream again with all her heart. "Does this mean you want to go ahead and have sex tonight?" she asked tautly.

"Molly, not everything in a relationship revolves around sex."

"You're thinking about it. Tell me you're not."

He went perfectly still. "Yes, I'm thinking about it. I want you so much that I ache. I won't lie to you about that." He ran his hands lightly downward until his fingertips found hers. He interlaced their hands. "I said I'd wait until you're ready, though. Do you think I was lying?"

Molly closed her eyes. "I think you know very well that in many ways I am ready."

He sighed, disentangled his hands from hers, and wrapped both arms around her, one large hand splayed and laying claim to the slope of her ribs just under her right breast. "In many ways, yes. I think I could kiss you and make you want me."

Molly almost denied it, but she'd told this man far too many lies already. "Yes," she admitted faintly. "You could."

He bent sideways to kiss the hollow just under her ear. "There's just one minor problem," he whispered. "You're afraid I won't want you. Until you're past that and start to feel better about a few other issues, it'll never be perfect between us. I think perfect is worth waiting for."

Chapter Twenty

An hour later, Molly was alone with her new husband at the main house. Even Hank had left, abandoning his room at the opposite end of the landing from Jake's in favor of a cot in the bunkhouse. Knowing that he had left to give her and Jake privacy on their wedding night set Molly's nerves on edge even more. It seemed the whole world expected them to have sex at the first opportunity.

She was trembling as she mounted the stairs in front of Jake. He'd flipped off the lights on the main floor, leaving them with only the ceiling fixture above the landing to illuminate the way. Over the course of her employment at the Lazy J, Molly had ascended these stairs dozens of times to put away freshly laundered clothes or to clean the bedrooms. She didn't know why the climb unsettled her so badly now.

The thump of his boots resounded on the steps behind her, the plastic bag of her clothing that he carried rustling against his jeans. Once on the landing, he placed a hand at the small of her back and propelled her toward the master suite, which Molly already knew was a warm, rustically charming trio of rooms, a large sleeping area, a cozy reading nook, and a spacious four-section bath with an adjoining powder room, dressing room, and huge walk-in closet.

At the doorway, he grasped her shoulder to stop her from entering. Tossing the plastic bag in ahead of them, he said, "We can forego some of the traditions of a wedding night, but there's one custom I refuse to let slide."

He bent and caught her up in his arms. Afraid that he might drop her, she squeaked in surprise and grabbed hold of his neck. "Don't try to carry me!" she cried. "I'm way too heavy. You'll hurt your back."

He gave her a bounce. "Ah, bull. You're not so heavy."

"Almost a hundred and forty," she corrected.

"*That* much?"

She drew an arm from around his neck to slug his shoulder. He laughed and turned slightly sideways to move through the doorway so her feet wouldn't catch.

"At least this is an improvement," she observed.

"What is?"

"When Rodney carried me over the threshold, he bonked my head."

Jake winced and smiled. "Yeah, well, stick around. This isn't the only thing I'll improve upon, and greatly, I might add." He carried her to the bed, gently laid her on the mattress, and then, after bracing a hand on either side of her, moved back to gaze down at her. "Just as I thought," he said softly. "You look absolutely right, lying there." A twinkle of mischief entered his eyes. "How can a man get so lucky? I've never seen such a gorgeous compass."

Molly frowned bewilderedly. "Compass?"

He grinned and trailed a fingertip over her mouth. "That's north. I'll leave you to figure out the other pointers by yourself."

Molly groaned, which prompted him to laugh softly. Her cheeks went warm. Strike that, her whole body went warm. She stared up at him, dry mouthed. Keeping his gaze locked on hers, he bent his arms and lowered his head to gently kiss her. After tying her belly into tight knots and making practically every muscle in her body start to quiver, he drew back to gaze at the pointed tips of her breasts that peaked the cotton of her blouse.

"Those little beauties are definitely thrusting like sword points and stabbing my loins with desire," he whispered.

Recognizing that line from the romance he'd left on her porch, Molly gave a startled laugh.

"So you *did* read it," he teased.

"I leafed through it."

He nodded, his eyes gleaming. "To the best parts?"

She laughed again.

"That's better," he said approvingly. "Much better. You need to relax and take life just a little less seriously. Has anyone ever told you that?"

"Not that I recall, but I'll make note of it. Any other suggestions?"

He shoved with his hands to bounce up off the mattress. "Yeah, but they'll keep." He grabbed up the bag that he'd tossed on the floor and set it on the bed. "For now, just seeing you smile is a step in the right direction."

He began unbuttoning his shirt as he strode to the bathroom. Over his shoulder, he said, "You may as well get comfortable. I think it's going to be a very long night."

Molly sat up and opened the plastic bag. The T-shirt she'd elected to wear lay at the top, a wash-worn white thing that hung lower over her thighs than all her others. She sighed, wishing, not for the first time, that she had some flannel pajamas.

She was still sitting there staring at the shirt when Jake emerged from the bathroom a couple of minutes later. Bare from the waist up, he reminded her of the first time she'd ever seen him. Her initial thought was that she'd never seen any man more beautiful. Her mouth and throat suddenly felt as if she'd just gargled with Elmer's glue.

His upper body was burnished, every muscle and tendon that roped his torso standing out in sharp definition. His tousled dark hair gleamed in the lamplight, the tips ignited to gold. "Is something wrong?"

"I don't have any real pajamas, only a T-shirt."

He arched his dark eyebrows and stepped over to the bureau. "I'm going to dig out some sweats for me." After opening a drawer, he shot her a measuring glance. "I have some thermal underwear that would serve as pajamas. You want a top and bottoms?" At her surprised look, he grinned. "If I'm going to behave myself, I figure the less skin I see, the better. I really, really hate to break my word to a lady." He tossed the underwear onto the bed. "You in nothing but a T-shirt would be a little too tempting."

Molly gratefully grabbed the underwear. "Thank you."

"Not a problem." He winked at her. "If you need help getting it on, just holler. I promise to make a difficult situation impossible."

She laughed nervously and pushed to her feet. "I think I can manage."

"I was afraid you'd say that."

For the first five minutes, Jake waited patiently for Molly to come out of the bathroom. For the second five minutes, he waited, but not quite so patiently. When ten full minutes had elapsed, he started to worry. He heard none of the sounds people usually made while preparing for bed, no rush of water, no swish of a toothbrush, no flush of the toilet. What the hell was she doing in there, counting grout lines?

He swung off the bed, stood, and advanced on the closed bathroom door, which he felt pretty sure was locked. Even worse, he'd built it so sturdy he feared it would take two men and a small boy to break it down. If something was wrong, he might have to call on Hank to help him reach his wife.

Rapping lightly on the planks, he said, "You okay, sweetheart?"

"Not really," she called back. "Would you mind handing me in my T-shirt?"

"Why? What's wrong with my long johns?"

"Nothing's wrong with them. They just don't fit."

Jake frowned and flattened a hand against the door. The underwear fit him. Molly was much shorter and weighed over eighty pounds less. "Are they way too big?"

"In my dreams."

"Then how don't they fit?"

"It's more *where* they don't fit."

Jake grinned in spite of himself. Now that he came to think of it, she was more amply endowed in a couple of places than he was. "I'm sure they'll be fine. We're just going to sleep, not have a fashion show."

"If you think certain parts of me thrust like sword points under two layers of cotton, you ought see them under tight knit."

His smile broadening, Jake leaned a shoulder against the door. Delightful images sprang to his mind. "Honey, the shirt can't be that snug."

"It isn't—in most places. And excuse me, but it isn't just the shirt."

"Come on out. I won't look," he tried

"Not a *chance*."

"I'll turn out the lights first. How's that?"

"No way. You can see in the dark."

Jake chuckled. She evidently heard him. "Hand me the blasted T-shirt."

He imagined cuddling up to her scantily clad butt and bare legs all night and knew he'd break his promise to her. "Molly, nothing but a T-shirt isn't a good plan."

"Trust me, my body vacuum packed in bubble wrap isn't a good plan, either."

Bubble wrap? Jake's eyebrows inched toward his hairline. The thermal knit was a little like bubble wrap. "Try stretching the stuff."

"How strong do you think I am?" Another silence. "The crotch hangs almost to my knees."

Jake pressed his forehead against the rough-hewn planks of wood. The images dancing through his head did not bode well for a celibate wedding night. "Molly?"

"What?"

"I love you."

"That's irrelevant."

It felt pretty damned relevant to him.

"I may as well parade out naked," she said crossly. "Do you have another pair of sweats?"

"No." And he wasn't about to part with the ones he was wearing. She'd run screaming from the room.

The bathroom door suddenly flew open, and Jake, caught off guard leaning against the planks, almost toppled onto his wife, who stood before him like a vertically challenged boxer, fists knotted at her sides, feet slightly apart, small chin jutting. His first thought was that his underwear had never had it so good. *Holy hell.* As much as he hated to admit it, he could see why she had been reluctant to come out. Every swell and dip of her body was revealed by the tight knit, some swells far more compelling to the male eye than others.

"Sweet mother of God."

She bent forward to tug at the apex of the underwear legs, which hung, just as she'd said, midway to her knees. Folds of extra knit were bunched around her slender ankles. The lady didn't measure up in height, but she sure had dimension.

Planting a hand in the center of his chest, she pushed him back a step and swept past him. "I told you to hand me my T-shirt."

Jake turned to watch her walk away. The fanny action was mind-boggling. She had the cutest butt he'd ever clapped eyes on, both cheeks jiggling with every step she took. He couldn't tell bubble knit from dimples. The part of him that was purely male and totally lacking in social graces sprang infuriatingly erect, poking eagerly against his sweats. He shoved himself down. The instant he turned loose, back up he went. Finally, he resorted to tucking himself between his legs, locking his knees together, and walking in awkward baby steps into the bedroom.

Molly, sitting with her back to him on the opposite side of the bed, had plopped all her glorious dimples down on the mattress, which had the spellbinding effect of magni-

fying her fullness. Above the temptingly plump swells of
bottom and hip, her waist dipped in, making his hands ache
to grab hold and never turn loose.

"I feel like a hippo stuffed into a knee-high stocking for
a giraffe," she said crossly. Tugging the covers out of her
way, she plopped onto her back. "Turn out the lights and
stop staring at me. You're giving me a complex."

In Jake's opinion, she already had a complex, and he
continued to stand there staring because he couldn't help
himself. Never had east and west looked quite so good.

Molly was his exact opposite in every way, soft where
he was hard, convex where he was concave, and temptingly full where he was streamlined. He couldn't look at
her without aching to touch her, and his blood heated when
he tried to imagine all that delicious softness pressed
against him.

Her breasts were shaped like plump, delectably ripe
melons. She'd once told him that they flopped. Not a problem. If her nipples tried to wander off during lovemaking,
he would damned sure enjoy the chase and delight in the
capture. Just looking at those sensitive peaks of flesh
thrusting against tight knit got his juices flowing.

Oh, man. He was in trouble. A promise was a promise.
He wouldn't touch her. But that didn't mean the temptation
would be easy to resist. Her breasts did give way to grav-
ity just a bit. The nipple pointed in his direction was nail-
ing him right between the eyes.

He flipped off the lights. She was right; he could see in
the dark. Relief flooded through him when she tugged the
blankets up over herself. He picked his way to the bed, sat
on the edge of the mattress, and stared at the eerily white
outline of his feet. Funny. He'd never noticed how ugly his
toes were before.

"What are you doing?" she asked in a faint voice.

Jake sighed. "Praying for fortitude."

She giggled. "Aw, come on. I've never overwhelmed
anyone in my life."

Jake figured that was because she'd never paraded around in front of a man wearing skintight thermal underwear. He wished he could see her nude. He didn't even know what color her nipples were yet. Pink, maybe? He clenched his teeth. The same color as her lips, probably.

"Lie down," she urged. "We'll talk until we feel sleepy."

Sleep would be a long time in coming. But he followed her advice and lifted the blankets to slip in beside her—flat on his back, arms crossed tightly over his chest so he wouldn't be tempted to touch her. He just hoped to hell she didn't suddenly develop decent night vision. Just below his waist, the sheet and blankets were having an uplifting experience.

She yawned. "It seems like forever since this morning."

"Yeah, it does."

Silence. Then she whispered, "What if he comes back with a court order, Jake? What if they discount our marriage as invalid because I'm legally incompetent?"

Hearing the fear in her voice tamped Jake's libido. He groped to find her hand. After enclosing her slender fingers in his, he whispered, "Don't worry about it, Molly. I won't let him take you away."

"What if you can't prevent it? He's got lots of money at his disposal, and he can hire the best lawyers."

"So can I," Jake assured her.

"No way are you selling any horses."

He squeezed her hand. "Rafe and Ryan offered to back me financially. Normally, I don't like to borrow money, but in this situation, I'll do it without batting an eye. The Kendricks are a powerful, very wealthy family with connections all over Oregon. Rafe told me this evening that if Rodney tries to cause any trouble, he'll hook me up with his attorney. The guy kicks ass and takes names."

He felt her body tense. "I hate for you to borrow money on my behalf."

Jake would have happily gone into debt for the rest of

his life to keep her out of Rodney's clutches. He'd seen the coldness in the man's eyes. He never wanted her near the bastard again.

"Rafe and Ryan are relatives by marriage. I don't mind asking them for help. It's different when you tap family."

She sighed wearily. "Well," she said softly, "if it's any consolation, I'll be able to settle the debt one day. If the courts ever grant me control over my inheritance again, that is."

It was Jake's turn to grow tense. "Just how much was your dad worth exactly? You never really said."

"A lot. Not all of it is liquid, of course. Several million are tied up in the corporation. He left me his share of the firm. The rest of the estate was divided up equally between Claudia and me. I can't remember exact figures, but in stocks, bonds, and cash in the bank, I think I got around four, plus what my share of the firm is worth."

"Four what?"

"Million. Daddy started investing as soon as he got out of college. He was good at what he did."

"Dear God, I've married into money."

She giggled again. "Yes, well—it's nice that you didn't realize in advance. Being married for my future net worth was the pits." She fell quiet for a moment. Then, in a tremulous voice, she said, "It doesn't mean anything, you know. Money doesn't make you happy. If anything, it's only made my life difficult."

"Maybe it can't make you happy, but it sure as hell helps."

She laughed again. Then her fingers clutched his. "Does it bother you? My having money, I mean."

Jake tightened his hand over hers. "Money or the lack of it doesn't define us as individuals. I love you for who you are, not what you have."

She sighed. "And who do you think I am, Jake?"

A lump came into his throat. "A very special lady."

"I'm afraid you don't really know me. I barely know

myself, so how can you?" He heard a hollow plunk and knew she'd swallowed to steady her voice. "Now I feel like I never will."

"Know yourself, you mean?" Her silence was all the answer he needed. "Molly, being married to me won't prevent you from achieving your own goals and chasing your own dreams."

"Yes. Yes, it will. Today, I became a rancher's wife. What did you become?"

He drew a blank at the question. "I'm not following."

"Exactly. I'll bet it never once occurred to you that you became a stockbroker's husband today." He felt her tension. It radiated from her like electronic waves. "That's who I am, Jake. Who I was raised to be, anyway. Being married to Rodney derailed my career. We were partners, he said, but in truth, I was little more than his girl Friday. He was the one with the impressive computer science degree. I dropped out of college and just took the state tests to get my license, which made me somehow less in his eyes, even though I'd teethed on finance and knew more about it than he did. I did all the legwork, he got all the recognition.

"After the divorce, I hoped to eventually return to the firm. I wanted to sit behind my dad's desk. You know? I wanted to take over my half of the business and carry on the Sterling tradition." A tremor ran through her. He felt the quiver in her hand. "I also wanted to investigate my father's death. Rodney did it. I'm almost *sure* of that. I wanted to prove it and make sure he paid."

"And you feel you can't do any of that now?"

"I'm married to a Central Oregon *rancher*. Been there, done that. I'll end up being an extension of you, just like it was with Rodney."

"Is that why you feel so lost sometimes?" he asked huskily.

"Yes." He could still feel her trembling. "It's not as bad now as it was, but yes."

"Ah, Molly. You just need time to rediscover yourself, that's all."

She went rigid. "How can I do that now? The cycle will just start all over again."

He tucked in his chin, trying to see her face. She pressed her thumb hard against his palm, and by that, he took measure of her agitation. "That's why I never wanted to be married again. They say we live in an enlightened age, but women still get absorbed into their husbands' lives, not the other way around. I'm not blaming you. I understand it's a societal condition, one that you didn't invent or perpetrate. You're the man. You don't have to change. I'm the woman, therefore I do."

"Do you dislike the idea of being a rancher's wife?"

She lay quietly beside him for a long while, saying nothing. When she finally spoke, her voice rang hollow. "I've become a rancher's wife. There's not much I can do to change it."

Jake smiled into the shadows. "I've become your husband as much as you've become my wife."

"No, you haven't. I'll bet it never once occurred to you all day that by marrying me, you'd changed from being a rancher into something else."

That was true. "It was a fast-paced day. I didn't have a lot of time to contemplate all the changes that are bound to occur in my life now."

"What changes?" she asked bitterly.

He chuckled.

"It isn't funny," she said tightly. "I told you why I didn't want to get married again, and you couldn't understand. I wanted to be me for a while. I needed to find out who I am again and just be me for a while."

The note of longing in her voice made Jake hurt for her.

"I gave up my freedom twelve hours ago, end of subject. I didn't have a choice, and I knew what I was doing when I did it. Now I just have to—" He heard her swallow again. "I just have to live with it, is all."

"No, you don't, Molly. That isn't what marriage is all about. I told you it won't be a prison, and I meant it. You want to be a stockbroker? Fine. Be the best damned stockbroker there is. Invest for me. Make me a rich man. I won't bitch."

"The firm is in Portland. If the court eventually rules in my favor, how can I work there and live here?" Her voice went thin. "Ever since I got out of the clinic, I've lived for the day when I could walk back into Sterling and Wells. Now I never will. I'll be the chief cook and bottle washer on the Lazy J, separating milk and making butter that will make me big as a barn if I eat it."

Jake disentangled his hand from hers, hooked an arm over her waist, and hauled her across the mattress into his arms. She gave a startled squeak, her body snapping taut. He pressed his face against her hair, hugging her fiercely.

"You listen up," he said huskily. When she started to speak, he gave her a squeeze to silence her. "You *will* walk back into Sterling and Wells again, and the first time you sit down behind your dad's desk, I'm going to be there to celebrate the moment with you. It's true that you've married a rancher, but that doesn't mean you have to wash my pots and pans. If you're working and I'm working, we can hire someone to do the domestic crap."

"You'd consider doing that?"

"I'll do better than just consider. As for living here, yeah, we'll have to at least part of the time. But what's to say we can't live in Portland part of the time as well? We're in a telecommunication age, Molly. When you're here, you can work out of a home office on a computer hooked up with the firm network. There are fax machines and telephones. And in case of an emergency, Portland isn't that far to drive. We can hop in a car and be there in three-and-a-half hours."

She sniffed. "You make it sound so simple, but it won't be. What'll you do with yourself if we stay for any period of time in Portland?"

He caught a silky curl between his teeth and gave it a gentle tug. "I'll be a stockbroker's husband. What else? If you can run a milk separator, I can run a calculator and become proficient on a computer."

He felt her mouth curve in a smile against his shoulder. "You'd really do that?"

"Damn straight." He ran a hand up her back, loving the way she felt in his arms. Now that he'd finally found her, he would move heaven and earth to make her happy. "During the winter, the snow gets so deep that the work here slacks off. Most cattlemen ship their cows down to California for winter grazing. I'll be able to break away and leave Hank in charge during that time, no sweat. Who knows? I may get a kick out of changing my occupation six months a year. It'll give us variety in our lives."

He felt her smile again. She sighed and slipped her arms around his neck. It felt wonderful to have her hug him back. "Jake Coulter in a suit. That I have to see."

"I look damned good in a suit, I'll have you know."

"When have you worn one?"

He grinned into the darkness. "I wore one—let me see. I went to a funeral last year. I wore one then. I smelled like mothballs, but I stayed downwind of everybody."

She rewarded him with a giggle. "You can't go to Sterling and Wells smelling like mothballs. We'll have to send the suit out for cleaning."

Jake gathered her closer, glad to hear that wondering, almost hopeful note in her voice. She still had a lot of reservations, but she was starting to believe it might be possible for them to make this work.

Jake had news for her. He'd make it work or die trying.

Chapter Twenty-one

The following day, Jake refused to let Molly out of his sight for fear Rodney might show up. She went with him while he fed the horses. She trudged beside him in oversized rubber boots while he changed sprinkler lines. That evening he insisted she accompany him in the pickup while he hayed the livestock.

"I never realized how hard you work all day," she commented when the last of the cattle had been fed.

He parked his truck near the house. After pocketing the keys, he looked over at her, his eyes as blue as sapphires as he traced her features. "Come for a walk with me."

"What about dinner?" She glanced at her watch. "It's after five, and I haven't started it yet."

"We're newlyweds. Screw dinner. We'll heat up leftovers. I'd like to spend a few quiet minutes with my bride. In lieu of a honeymoon, it's not much, but it's all I can offer for now, a walk by the creek."

It was a beautiful evening. Molly relented with a grin. "All right, but only if you'll help me fix something to eat. I'm tired from chasing after you all day."

"Done."

He held her hand as they walked along the stream. Their footsteps were slow, their bodies moving in lazy unison as they listened to the sounds that drifted on the air. Now early May, the days were growing longer, but even so, dusk was beginning to descend, forming pools of grayish gloom beneath the trees that fronted the woodlands. They startled a lone buck with beautiful antlers still in velvet.

Jake led her to sit on a grassy knoll by the stream. The valley narrowed there to only about a hundred yards wide, the north fence line across the creek running parallel with the encroaching forest. To the east, red Herefords dotted the landscape. Directly across the creek, Molly saw a rabbit foraging for its supper, and at the edge of the woods, she glimpsed a doe and fawn.

"Uh-oh," she whispered. "I think we're preventing that mama and her baby from having their evening snack."

Jake followed her gaze. "They'll mosey along to find a more private spot."

Molly watched the deer bound away. "They're so lovely and graceful."

"They're quite something, all right." After a moment, he whispered, "Listen."

Molly went still. All around them, she heard a beautiful woodland symphony—the wind whispering in the trees, the call of a hawk in the distance, the chattering of the squirrels preparing for night.

"Isn't that fantastic?" he asked.

Molly agreed wholeheartedly. It was especially beautiful to be sharing it with him. Gazing at his dark profile, she felt her heart swell with emotions she didn't want to name or acknowledge, but there was no avoiding it. She'd done the unthinkable and let herself fall in love with him. *Oh, God.* The realization frightened her. He was such a strong-willed man—and so very handsome. Loving him could be dangerous.

He caught her studying him. His brilliant blue eyes went cloudy with tenderness, and he reached over to touch a fingertip to her nose. "Don't be afraid, Molly mine. I'm the best long-term investment you'll ever make."

She hugged her knees. "How can you know what I'm feeling?"

"I'm good at reading feelings. That's why I'm so good

with horses." He gave her a slow smile. "When people love each other, they share all their feelings anyway. What's so wrong with my knowing how you feel without you telling me? On the bright side, it'll make me a better husband. I'll understand you and know straight off when I've stepped on your toes."

Silence. She sensed that he was searching for words. "You're only feeling the same thing I've been feeling for weeks," he pointed out gently. "It's scary when it first hits you, isn't it?" He trailed the back of a knuckle over her cheek. "Caring deeply leaves you so open to being hurt."

Molly glanced quickly away. "I don't think I could live through it again. I know it sounds pathetic, but I've been hurt enough to last me a lifetime."

"You won't ever be hurt again," he assured her. "Not by me."

She gnawed the inside of her lip. "I just—" A pent-up breath rushed from her. She turned her gaze back to him. "I know I'm not being fair to you, Jake. You're not Rodney. I'm very aware of that. But inside me—way down deep—there's this terrified *child*. She believed in fairy tales and heroes once. Now, just thinking about buying into all of that again terrifies her. I try to tell her to grow up, that she's being stupid. But I think she's got the covers pulled over her head."

He grinned and nodded. "There's a child in all of us, Molly. You're not unique in that."

"Is there a child in you?"

"More a teenager, actually. High testosterone levels, horny as hell. And I'm pretty sure the little shit's wearing earplugs because he doesn't hear very good, either."

Molly laughed. She couldn't help herself. "What do you try to tell him?"

"To keep his damned hands off you, to keep his eyes where they belong, and to keep his thoughts out of the gutter."

Molly smoothed her hands down the legs of her jeans. "I'm sorry I've done this to you."

"Do you realize how often you apologize for things that aren't your fault?"

"I'm nearly thirty years old. I should just sleep with you and get it over with. It's no big deal to other women."

"I didn't marry other women. I chose you."

"Hopefully, that wasn't a mistake. I know I'm being ridiculous, Jake, but deep down, I'm afraid, and I just can't shake it off."

"Of what?" he asked softly. "Not of me, I hope."

"Of course not. I'm coming to trust you more than I've ever trusted anyone. It's not that kind of fear."

"What kind is it, then?"

"I'm afraid you won't find my body attractive." The words came hard, and Molly dug her nails into the denim of her jeans as she forced each one out. "I'm afraid you'll pretend otherwise, but that I'll see the truth in your eyes. Just *thinking* about how humiliating that would be makes me cringe. I'd rather die."

He gazed off across the creek, his expression solemn. Molly expected him to comment on what she'd just told him. Instead, he surprised her by saying, "I played out here as a boy. I loved it here, and I still do." His voice had become hushed with something very like reverence. "When I want to remember the most important moments of my life, both good and bad, this is where I come. Aren't the trees beautiful?"

Baffled by the change of subject, she followed his gaze. The trees were indeed lovely, a grand mix of ponderosa and lodgepole pine that rose majestically against the darkening sky. "Yes, they are lovely."

"Which do you think is the prettiest one?"

Molly searched the tree line. "That's a hard one. They're all so beautiful in their own way. I can't really decide."

"That one's a beauty." He pointed to a ponderosa that

stood straight and tall. "And just look at that one. Isn't it grand?"

Molly looked where he pointed next and smiled. "I've always loved trees of all kinds."

"Me, too." He inclined his head toward a half-dead, gnarled oak growing across the field at the forefront of the forest. "But that's the most special one of all to me. The most beautiful one, by far."

Bewildered, Molly stared at the tree he indicated. There was a split down the center of its once magnificent trunk, and half of its branches were dead. "What happened to it?"

"Lightning," he whispered. "And age, too, I guess. Time takes its toll."

"It looks as if it's dying, Jake."

"I don't notice that." He rested his folded arms on his upraised knees, staring at the dying oak with a dreamy expression on his face. "We're old friends, me and that tree. When I was little, I couldn't climb any of the ponderosas, and the junipers hardly seemed worth the effort because they were small. But I could climb that old oak."

Molly tried to picture him as a child. A likeness of little Jaimie slipped into her mind. "Did you ever fall?"

"Nah. Never once. That old tree has branches as big around as my waist. I built myself a fort up there. I think I was about six then. That poor old tree took a beating. I couldn't swing an ax or hammer very straight, and she's got scars all over her, way up high. Every single one of them is a memory for me. To this day, I can climb up there and go back in time, recalling a thousand afternoons and all-night sleep outs. It's like those times happened only yesterday. I spent a lot of happy hours up there, feeling like I was on top of the world and safe from everything. A lot of sad hours, too. Whenever anything bad happened, that was where I went. It was my secret place, apart from the world."

Molly sighed.

"One time, my dad nearly cut her down." He inclined

his head. "If you look, you can see how close she grows to the fence. Her big old roots were pushing up a post."

"What stopped him from cutting it?"

"Me. I wrapped both arms around his leg and begged him not to. He tried to tell me there were other oaks growing on the place, that I'd never miss that silly old tree. But I finally convinced him that particular tree was special, that no other oak could take her place." He chuckled softly. "Dad put a jog in the fence and left her to stand."

Molly could see the jog in the fence now that he'd pointed it out. "How sweet of him."

"My dad's a good man. He has a heart of gold, for all his gruff ways." He grew solemn again, his gaze still fixed on the tree. "The night my sister was hurt in the barrel-racing accident, I came out here when I got home from the hospital. It was about four o'clock in the morning, still dark as pitch. All that evening, I had to be strong for my mom and dad, and my younger brothers. And for Bethany, too, when she woke up." His jaw muscle tightened. "She screamed when she realized. Just screamed and screamed. I had to hold her to the bed. I kept telling her it was going to be all right. The entire while, I knew I was lying, that nothing would ever be all right again. I loved her so much, and she was so damned beautiful. In a split second, her life had been destroyed, and there was nothing I could do to fix it. Being her big brother, I'd always fixed things for her, you know? And that night I couldn't."

His voice had gone gravelly with remembered pain. Molly closed her eyes. "Oh, Jake," she whispered.

"Seeing her like that really shook my faith in God. I kept asking myself *why*. How *could* He let that happen? To me, maybe, but not to someone like her. She'd never done a wrong thing to anybody, and she didn't deserve that." He sighed and ran a hand over his face. "I was so *angry*. I'd believed in God all my life, and suddenly it was all a lie, one great big *joke*. I needed to be alone."

"So you came out here."

He nodded. "My folks were a mess. My brothers, too. I felt like the world had ended. When I got out here, I climbed up to my old fort. The floor was rotting out, but I lay down on it anyway. It felt like home to me, a familiar, peaceful place when everything else had become a nightmare. After I cried myself dry, I cursed God and shook my fist at the sky, swearing I'd never believe in anything again. At that moment, I meant it with every fiber of my being."

"What changed your mind?" She had no doubt that something had. She'd never met anyone with more soul than Jake Coulter.

He turned his gaze eastward. "Dawn broke across the sky," he said softly. "You've never seen beautiful until you watch the sunrise from the top of my old tree. I sat up there, and I swear, it felt as if the light was moving clear through me. I knew then. I just *knew*. Me and my old tree were seeing the face of God, and He was saying 'good morning.' " He smiled at the memory. "The world hadn't ended, after all. I knew Bethany would somehow be all right eventually, and that no matter what happened, the sun would always rise again. Life goes on. We just have to find the strength to face it sometimes, and the only way we can do that is to reach deep for faith and believe with all our hearts."

The conviction in his voice brought a lump to Molly's throat. A peaceful silence fell over them. For a long while, they simply sat there, staring at the old oak. Hearing his story gave her a sense of place and history. It also revealed yet another side of this man she had grown to love. Just when she thought she'd learned all there was to know about him, he revealed another layer.

"When you look at my tree, you probably see the dead branches and that big split down her trunk."

"I see more than that now," she assured him. "I can understand why it'll always be the most beautiful tree in the woods to you."

He turned his gaze back to her. "Then why can't you understand that you'll always be the most beautiful woman in the world to me?"

Molly tried to look away, but she couldn't, and her eyes began filling with tears.

"I *love* you," he whispered. "I think I fell in love with you the first time I saw you, Molly mine. And when I look at you, that's all I'm ever going to see, the woman I love. It doesn't matter if you're perfect. To me, you will be, and that's all that counts. It'll be that way always. Even years from now, when you're old and withered, I'll see you with my heart, not my eyes. That's just the way it is when you love someone. The imperfections don't exist. If you see them at all, you think they're beautiful."

"Oh, Jake."

He cupped her chin in his hand. She squeezed her eyes closed as he gently kissed her cheek. Then he released her. A moment later, she heard his clothing rustle and knew he'd pushed to his feet. The wind whistled through the trees, its song lulling her and wrapping around her like an embrace.

"You gave the bastard ten years," he said huskily. "Don't let him ruin the rest of your life. Reach deep, Molly mine. Have some faith in me."

He left her then, his words replaying in her mind long after the sound of his footsteps faded away. *"Have some faith in me."* More tears welled in Molly's eyes. She stared across the clearing at the old oak, wanting so badly to go after him, but lacking the courage to do it.

When several minutes had passed, she pushed to her feet, scaled the fence, and walked across the pasture. When she reached the other stretch of wire, she gazed up into the oak, taking in the tangle of dead and living branches. The tree was huge, at least four feet in diameter at its base, with a towering height bearing testimony to its impressive age. Way up high, she could see the rotted remains of Jake's childhood tree fort. On the tree's massive trunk, she saw carvings in the rough bark, some of them weathered with age and others that looked fairly new. Slipping through the barbed wire, she moved closer to read the inscriptions.

A smile touched her mouth. Jake had chiseled a chronicle of his life on this old tree. One carving commemorated his graduation from college, reading, PIGSKIN, 1993, in painstakingly shaped, small block letters. Another inscription said, MY BEST FRIEND, PEDRO, 1976–1983. The letters weren't as even, indicating a boy's less accomplished skill with a knife. Counting back, Molly figured that Jake had been about thirteen at the time. Touching the dates, she wondered who Pedro had been. She guessed that he had died and that Jake had loved him so much he had tried to immortalize him in this special place.

It was the strangest feeling, reading those old inscriptions. Molly felt as if she were snooping through a personal journal that held all the secrets of Jake Coulter's heart. The freshest-looking inscription on that side of the tree recorded the birth of his nephew, SLY, APRIL, 2001. Molly touched that date as well, recalling the tenderness she'd seen on his dark face when he held the baby in his arms. A tight sensation filled her chest as she moved further around the tree, taking in other inscriptions, some old, some new. Every major event of his life, both joyous and sad, had been recorded, including the dates of Bethany's accident and her marriage to Ryan Kendrick.

It was incredible, making her want to smile and cry, both at once. High in the network of huge branches, she could even see the crusted wounds that had been left in the bark by a little boy's ax blade. She pictured Jake as a child, struggling on a summer afternoon to drag boards up there and build a miniature mansion in the sky. From that point on, he'd spent much of his time in this place, and every mark on the tree was a memory.

As Molly turned to leave, she spied what looked like fresh cuts on the other side of the old oak's trunk. She stepped around to better examine them. What she saw nearly took her to her knees. It was a recently carved heart. Inside, he had chiseled out the words MOLLY, MY LOVE, 2001.

"Oh, Jake," she whispered shakily.

She lightly traced the engraving. Judging by the freshness of the cuts, he'd done this recently. She imagined him, laboring with his knife, recording yet another memory on his tree so he could come here years from now and remember the moment as if it were yesterday. *Molly, my love.* She could almost hear him whispering the words, his voice deep and raspy with emotion. If ever she had wished for irrefutable proof that he really loved her, this was it. She'd become part of the chronicle, her name inscribed in his secret place, never to be erased or forgotten.

Recalling the story he'd told her about the night of Bethany's accident, Molly wrapped her arms around herself and tipped her head back to gaze at the sky through the network of old branches. She couldn't say that she actually saw the face of God, but she did see and feel the incredible beauty of Creation all around her. And she came face to face with an undeniable truth.

Years from now, when Jake Coulter returned to this special place and looked at the carving that bore her name, she didn't want to be nothing more than a fond memory in his mind.

She wanted to be the woman who stood beside him.

True to his word, Jake helped Molly cook dinner that night, and after the meal was over, he rolled up his sleeves to wash the dishes. Standing beside him, Molly waited with a dishtowel in her hands and butterflies in her stomach while he rinsed a large pot and slipped it in the drainer. Watching him, she tried to think how to best broach this conversation, but every idea she came up with seemed dumb, and she discarded it.

Finally she simply blurted, "I've reached a decision."

Scrubbing a blue Pyrex baking dish, he paused in his

work to fix a questioning gaze on her. "You've reached a decision about what?"

Molly gulped. Her hands tightened on the dishtowel. "That I'll have sex with you."

He almost dropped the baking dish. To his credit, he quickly recovered. "When?" he asked, his eyes glinting.

Molly hadn't planned the time and place. "I, um— whenever you'd like. Tonight, I guess. If you want to, that is."

"If I *want* to?" He grinned slowly. "Do I have to finish the dishes first?"

Molly. Jake had been in so many relationships that he'd forgotten what it was like to be with a woman who was shy and hesitant. After they finished up the dishes, she thought of last-minute tasks to delay the inevitable. The rug by the back door needed to be shaken out. She called Bart in and spent ten minutes chasing him around the kitchen to brush his teeth. A stove burner needed a quick scrub. Her hands were trembling so that she could barely hold onto the steel wool pad.

He thought about fetching the leftover bottle of champagne from the fridge and cracking it open, anything to help her relax, but he was afraid it would take a bathtub of bubbly to cure what ailed her. He didn't want her numb with drink the first time he made love to her.

"Molly, we don't have to do this tonight if you'd rather wait," he finally offered, praying to God and all His angels that she wouldn't take him up on it.

"Oh, no," she said shakily. "I want to."

Jake had seen people more enthusiastic about having major surgery. He schooled his expression, biting back a smile. The last thing he wanted was for her to think, even for a moment, that he was amused by her nervousness. Just the opposite was true. It caught at his heart and made him want to hug her.

Once upstairs, she stood by the bed, fixed worried eyes

on him, and reached with violently trembling hands to unbutton her blouse.

"Sweetheart," he said cautiously, "this isn't how it's
supposed to happen."

"It isn't?" Her voice was little more than a squeak.

"No, it isn't," he assured her. Stepping close, he caught
her wrists and bent to kiss the corner of her mouth, which
was also tremulous. Was she quivering this way all over?
The thought ignited his imagination. "It's not an official
unveiling. We're supposed to kiss and—" He pressed his
face against her hair. "It's supposed to happen naturally."

"No," she said faintly. "Not this time, Jake. I, um—I
need for you to see me first. That way, if you don't like me,
we can just call it off."

Sweet Lord. She was so sweet and beautiful. How on
earth could she believe that he could fail to like her? As if
like were an appropriate word? He wanted her in a way
he'd never wanted anyone. He also preferred to unwrap
her himself. Nevertheless, he could tell by the determined
ring in her voice that she needed to do this. In some con-
voluted reasoning, she had concluded that this was the
only way she could slay her demons.

Sighing, Jake stepped back, lifting his hands in defeat.
"All right. Have it your way."

She nodded decisively and resumed her struggle with
the buttons. Never in Jake's memory had a blouse had so
many. *One . . . fumble, fumble . . . two.* She was killing
him. His hands itched to rip the damned thing off her.

Instead, he leaned against the door, crossing his arms
and ankles. *Waiting.* The cotton slowly parted. Once in college, he'd gone to a strip show. All the other guys had
whooped and hollered and made asses of themselves, tucking money under the performer's G-string and copping
feels. Not him. He'd found the entire display disgusting,
giving him cause to wonder if he was abnormal. *Not.* He
knew now, beyond a shadow of a doubt, that watching a

woman slowly, ever so *slowly,* remove her clothing could
turn him on. She just had to be the *right* woman.

Molly. God, how he loved her. He leaned more heavily
against the door, thankful for the constraints of denim,
which made his arousal less apparent. He could do this. It
might be the death of him, but he could do this.

Finally the damned blouse was unbuttoned. Her cheeks
turned a painful pink as she peeled the cotton down her
arms. *Plop.* The sound of the cloth hitting the floor went
off in his head like a bomb. He hoped, *prayed,* that the bra
would be next. But, oh, no, she reached for the waistband
of her slacks instead, driving him nuts as she endeavored
to unfasten the catch.

What the *hell* was the hold up? She jerked and fussed,
then bent her head. The girl had fifty thumbs. He could
have had that fastener undone in a blink. He settled his
gaze on the swell of her breasts above the lacy edge of her
bra and damned near swallowed his tongue.

After unfastening her slacks, she kicked off her shoes
and bent to tug off her socks. His gaze dropped. He knew
he was losing it when he got turned on looking at her toes.
They were itty-bitty, the nails an iridescent pink. He imagined nibbling on each one.

With a wiggle of her hips, the slacks slid down her legs,
pooling at her ankles. She stepped away, giving the gar-
ment a little kick. Jake wondered what would go next, bra
or panties. She looked like a vision standing there, her
most feminine parts still covered with bits of white nylon
and lace.

He was a saint. No question. His shoulder blades had
drilled holes through the door.

Next she pulled down her panties. As the nylon slid past
her hips, she sucked in her tummy. The moment the underwear puddled at her feet, she pressed a hand over the
abdominal roundness she obviously thought was a less
than attractive feature. Jake liked her belly just fine. He
honestly did. But it was that nest of butterscotch curls just

below that made his eyes feel as if they might part company with their sockets.

"I, um . . . " Her voice trailed away, the sound reminding him of a tremulous note on a reed whistle. "My stomach is fat."

Jake's stomach was somewhere around his knees. He stared at her well-rounded hips and thighs. Her skin was as flawless as cream, and her shape was what men's dreams were made of—every inch of her soft and enticing.

The *bra*. He wanted it *off*. But, oh, no, those gorgeous breasts were the last things she wanted to unveil. She lifted trembling hands to the front clasp of the undergarment. Jake's brain snagged on the thought that there were probably four fasteners there for her to undo. His larynx was stuck at the back of his throat.

Patience was a virtue, he reminded himself. The bra would come off—eventually. Never in his memory had a clasp proved to be so stubborn. She jerked, she twisted, her breasts jiggling with every tug. He was going to have a coronary. He stared hard at the crests of her breasts, wondering what color her nipples were.

When the bra finally came open, she grasped either side of the front clasp, her body tense. A study in humiliation, she just stood there, not moving, her nipples still shielded by lace. Her eyes had gone dark. Bright slashes of crimson rode high on her cheeks. She looked so miserable, nearly naked, but not quite, her arms frozen in a torture of embarrassment.

He felt ashamed of himself for ogling her. He never should have allowed her to do this. He stepped toward her. He was about to grasp her wrists and force the issue when warning bells went off in his mind. She'd come this far. He sensed that she needed to go the remainder of the way, that somehow it was important to her that he stand back and see her. Really see her.

"Let me look at you, Molly love."

She gulped and stared at him. Damn, she was so pretty.

How could she not realize that? In the faint light coming through the window, her skin shimmered like creamy satin. He wanted to kiss every sweet curve, every delicious hollow—to taste and nibble on her until she sobbed for more. In that moment, Jake could have killed Rodney Wells with his bare hands. The *bastard*. He'd hurt her so deeply, leaving wounds that still bled.

His voice grated like sandpaper over a knife blade. "Molly, let me look at you."

The tendons along her throat stood out. Her shoulders went taut. He felt her struggle. Bless her heart.

With a tug, she drew the cups of the bra from her breasts, and then she just stood there, trembling. Oddly, now that her lovely bosom was bare to his gaze, he hardly noticed the rose pink nipples he'd been fantasizing about for so long. How could he enjoy looking at them when she was cringing? Without the heat of passion to ease her shyness, this was awful for her.

Jake wanted so badly to take her into his arms, to reassure her with whispers and soothing strokes of his hands. Even he might feel embarrassed to stand there naked while someone stared at him.

But, no, comfort wasn't what she needed from him right now. For her, these next few seconds—and his reaction—were pivotal.

Instead of embracing her, he slid the bra straps down her arms and let the undergarment fall to the floor. Then, grasping her by the wrist, he drew her away from the bed so there was room for him to walk a full circle around her. When this was finished, he vowed, she would know that he had examined every inch of her and looked closely at every imagined flaw.

And imagined flaws they were. She was exquisite— sweetly ample, but perfectly formed. The curve of her back was smooth without a hint of ribcage to mar the effect, the layer of feminine flesh over bone just generous enough to give her a lush softness that made his hands itch to touch her.

For the life of him, he couldn't see why she was so self-conscious about her breasts. Granted, they were large and heavy. She'd never pass a pencil test, that was for damned sure, but few full-figured women could. For all of that, her breasts were beautifully shaped. If that downward dip was a sag, he'd take her, sag and all, and count himself the luckiest man on earth.

Molly was dying. Each time she tried to draw breath, her lungs hitched. An airless pounding had started in her temples, making her afraid she might faint, a fear compounded by the violent slugging of her heart against her ribs. Her skin felt both cold and hot at once, pebbling from the chill air but burning wherever Jake's gaze touched.

When she could bear the agony of it no longer, she crossed her arms over her chest and forced herself to meet his gaze. He was staring back, only not at her face. She wanted to disappear. Under the bed, through a crack in the floor, anywhere, just so long as he couldn't look at her like that. Much as his father had done the evening before, he walked a slow circle around her, making her feel like an object up for bid on an auction block.

Coming to stand behind her, he lightly grazed a hand over the right cheek of her butt. "Dear God, that's the cutest fanny I've ever seen in my life."

Molly squeezed her eyes closed. *Cute?* Oh, God. That fell short. She needed him to think she was pretty even if she wasn't. Anything less simply wouldn't do.

He curled big, work-roughened hands over the sides of her waist, making her jump. His shirt grazed her shoulder blades. She felt his warm breath feathering over her neck just below her ear. He moved his hands down to rest them on her hips, his long, thick fingers pressing gently into her softness.

He moved in closer, sliding a palm from her hip to her

tummy, where he explored the swell she so detested. His fingertips lightly traced the roundness, making her belly muscles quiver and jerk. "Oh, Molly," he murmured, "you feel so wonderful. Your skin is like silk. Are you this soft all over?"

She gulped and a low mewling sound she couldn't squelch came up her throat. He bent his head, kissing the line of her collarbone, his big hand pressing in hard against her abdomen to force her posterior against his hard thighs. The denim of his jeans felt warm and abrasive as he moved against her.

He suddenly released her to step around and face her again. His eyes a blaze of blue in his dark face, he ran his gaze the length of her, ending at her toes. On the return journey back up her body, his attention lingered at her knees, and a slight smile slanted across his mouth. Moving up from there, he spent a moment appraising her thighs, one of her worst features. Next, he settled a burning gaze at their apex.

When his eyes finally flicked back up to hers, he said, "Drop your arms, sweetheart."

They felt frozen across her chest, and Molly couldn't have moved them for anything. He stepped closer, curled his fingers over her wrists, and forced her hands down to her sides. Moving back, he stared at her breasts, his eyes an intense, piercing blue that seemed to touch and caress in an almost physical way. Seconds crawled by. Molly tried to cover herself again, but he braced against her.

"Don't," he whispered. *"Don't."*

She was shaking, shaking horribly. She wanted to stop, tried to stop, but her jerking muscles seemed to have a will of their own. With every shudder that ran through her body, her breasts jiggled.

He said nothing. And she needed him to say *something*. Instead he freed her hands to slide his palms up her sides and cup her fullness. She jerked and mewled again when he circled her nipples with his thumbs, torturing the pebbled areolas with feathery passes but avoiding the sensitive, hardened centers. A throbbing ache filled her breasts. Her breathing abated to soft, shallow pants that didn't reach her lungs. Her peripheral vision blurred until only his face was visible, dark and chiseled of feature.

"Dear God," he finally said in a throaty whisper, "you are so pretty, Molly. I knew you would be, but my imagination didn't come close to the reality."

Tears rushed to Molly's eyes. Her mouth suddenly felt as if it was all over her face, twisting every which way. Jake bent to kiss the quivering corners, every brush of his lips incredibly light.

"Don't cry, Molly love. Please don't cry. I'm sorry this has been so embarrassing for you. You are *so* beautiful, Molly. So very beautiful." He gathered her into his arms, his body taut, his hold vibrant with emotion and fiercely possessive. "There's not a spot on you that isn't perfect. From the top of your head to the tips of your toes, you're glorious. I love those little dimples on your butt."

"You do?"

"I do," he assured her.

"You don't think I'm fat?"

He grabbed one of her hands and shoved it between their bodies to press her palm over his fly. "Does that feel like I think you're fat?"

Molly felt throbbing hardness under the denim. Relief made her bones feel as soft as pudding. If not for the support of his arms, she felt sure she couldn't remain erect. Pressing her face against his shirt, she said in a muffled voice, "No."

"I told you, I think you're beautiful. I *like* the way you're made, Molly. If I wanted a woman built like a railroad tie, I could go find one. That's not what I want." He cupped a hand over her bottom, squeezing and releasing. "I love the way you feel, so soft everywhere. And I love the way you look. You have gorgeous breasts, I love all your dimples, and I've never seen prettier legs."

He slipped his hands to her hips then embarked on a slow, burning journey upward from there to cup his palms under her breasts again. This time, after tormenting the areolas with feathery caresses, he drew his thumbs over her nipples, teasing the tips until they budded and throbbed. "I want to kiss those little beauties. Will you let me?"

Molly was trembling—trembling so hard she feared her legs were going to buckle. All the way up the stairs and the entire while she'd been undressing, she'd imagined him turning way in disgust. Now, despite his reassurances, she couldn't quite believe he hadn't—or that he wouldn't yet.

"Are you sure you really want me?"

"Am I sure?" he asked with a husky laugh. "Molly, I want you so much I'm about to die." His voice was so low and throbbing it seemed to move clear through her.

He flicked her nipples again and tickled the inside of her ear with his tongue. With every drag of his thumbs, fiery shocks ribboned through her breasts, making her whole body jerk. Low in her belly, her muscles turned to a quivery mass of heat that made everything tingle and ache. Oh, God, he made her *want*. She'd never in her life wanted anything so much as she wanted Jake Coulter.

He trailed kisses down her neck. His breath wafted hot and steamy over the uplifted swells of her breasts. Molly moaned and clutched the sleeves of his shirt. With darting passes of his tongue, he traced the line of her cleavage, his dark hair whispery soft against her arched throat. Beneath her fingers, she could feel the bunched power in his arms, and his coiled hardness called together everything within her that was feminine to form a fiery, twisting ache at her center.

Lifting one breast, he touched the very tip of his tongue to her nipple. The wet heat sent a jolt of sensation clear to her toes, and her breath whistled in her throat. "I want you so much," he said in a gruff, imploring voice that hummed over her nerve endings.

Molly locked a fist over his hair so he couldn't get away. She wanted his mouth on her there. He licked her again, making her cry out. He moaned and blew softly on her moist flesh, the sudden shock of coolness making her crave his heat even more.

He abandoned her breasts to catch her face between his hands. His long fingers stretched to her hairline, the padded tips pressing possessively against her scalp, his roughened palms warm on her cheeks.

She struggled to focus on his burnished features. He rubbed the pads of his thumbs along her cheekbones. She felt him trembling slightly, and by that she knew he really did want her, and badly.

"Oh, Jake," she said shakily. In these moments of sensual respite, her head had started to clear a bit. She looked into his beautiful eyes and saw need burning in their depths, hot, raw, gut-clenching need. It was the first time in her life any man had ever looked at her that way. The most wonderful feelings coursed through her—a light, airy joy that made her want to laugh and dance about the room—a sense of relief that drained the awful tension from her muscles. "I want you, too. So much I can't bear it."

"Do you, now?" He gave a low chuckle and moved his hands to her shoulders. Pushing her back a step, he said, "Well, never let it be said that I kept a lady waiting."

Molly really, really liked having him look at her that way. The front of his shirt teased her nipples, making her ache to have his mouth on her again. Her legs butted up against the bed just then. With a little push, he sent her sprawling. Before she could gather her wits, he'd followed her down to the mattress, his hands braced at her shoulders to suspend his upper body over hers.

His face moved slightly closer. "When I'm done with you, lady, there won't be a place on you I haven't tasted."

Molly gulped. His shoulders were nearly twice the breadth of hers, the bunched muscles in his arms and chest stretching the cloth of his blue shirt taut to showcase his powerful build. His sable hair lay in tousled waves over his forehead. One dark eyebrow was arched in mischievous challenge. He grinned, the flash of his teeth against his coppery skin making her heart do a funny little jig at the base of her throat.

Before she could start to feel truly nervous, he settled his mouth over hers. *Moist heat, the brush of silk.* His lips were soft yet firm, and he used them with mastery, forcing hers apart to gain entry with his tongue. With long, searching thrusts, he tasted the deepest recesses of her mouth, tickling the roof, grazing the inside of her cheeks, teasing her lips. Molly's head swam. He shared his breath with her, slipping an arm under her waist to lock her against him. *Jake.* As had happened before, she forgot everything but how he made her feel. She arched against him, made fists in his hair, and trembled at the sensations that stormed through her.

This time when he broke off the kiss to trail his lips to her breasts, she didn't want him to stop. His mouth closed over a nipple. Her spine arched of its own accord, her breath snagged in her throat, and she cried out at the sheer pleasure of it. With every flick of his tongue, with every draw on her flesh, her muscles jerked and her toes curled.

He loved her there like a starving man until he was finally sated, and then he stayed to lazily tease her with his teeth, catching her sensitive flesh in a gentle vise and tormenting it with laps of his tongue. Molly moaned. She cried out. And still he teased her.

The need within her mounted, becoming an ache that bordered on pain. Only dimly aware, she wrapped her legs around his thigh and drove her hips against all that deliciously hard male muscle, mindlessly seeking release in a grind of passion as old as womankind.

"Oh, no, you don't," he whispered. "I'll get to that little sweetheart later."

He reared up onto his knees to strip off his shirt. She

stared at his chest and upper arms, her heart locked in a struggle to keep its rhythm, her lungs grabbing frantically for oxygen. He was so beautiful. In the dusky light coming in the window, his skin looked shades darker than usual, his eyes an intense sky blue as he looked into hers. She wanted to run her hands over the bulge of muscle in his shoulders, skim her fingertips down his powerfully roped arms, and discover the texture of his skin.

"Jake?" she said tremulously. "I want you."

He flashed her a slow grin. She remembered thinking the first time she met him that he had the dark countenance of a wicked angel. He looked more than a little wicked now—a man who knew what he was about and had no intention of straying off course.

He cast his shirt aside and bent his dark head to lap at her navel. The shock of sensation jerked Molly's hips off the mattress. "Is there anything special you'd like—or anything in particular that you don't like?"

Molly could scarcely think, let alone formulate a coherent response. "I, um—I don't—with Rodney, I never . . ." Her voice trailed away as he flicked his tongue in a widening circle around her belly button. "Jake?"

He raised his head to stare at her, his eyes suddenly sharp and relentlessly intent. "With Rodney, you never what?" he asked softly.

Molly searched her muddled brain, trying to recall what she'd been about to say. He moved up, bringing his face closer to hers, his gaze filled with question.

"I never liked any of it," she found the presence of mind to say.

"It won't be that way with me," he whispered.

Molly knew it wouldn't. The beauty of what had happened so far assured her of that.

He bent to settle his mouth over hers again. After kissing her until she felt dizzy, he lifted his head to trail his lips over her cheek, then down the bridge of her nose. Then he kissed his way down her throat, lingering at the V of her collarbone. "If I do anything you don't like, you just tell me, all right?"

Molly couldn't imagine not liking anything. "All right," she managed to say.

He grazed his lips down her sternum. When he reached her belly again, Molly made fists on the bedspread and stared blindly at the knotty pine ceiling. She'd read about this kind of thing in romances and guessed his intention, but she'd never experienced it herself.

Jake circled lower to the nest of butterscotch curls at the apex of her thighs. She quivered and gulped, her insides clenching. He traced a teasing trail over her pelvis with his lips and tongue. When her stomach convulsed, he chuckled, the hot waft of his breath and the vibration of his chest against her thigh making her moan.

He circled out to her hip and took a lazy journey south, the hot skin of his chest grazing hers as he moved down. He kissed her toes. He made her ankles tingle. He trailed the tip of his tongue up her shins, tantalizing her with the titillating strokes until she felt sure she would go mad. By the time he moved higher, Molly thought she would die when he delved his tongue between her knees and licked his way up her inner thigh.

"Are you okay with this?" he asked huskily.

Molly couldn't have answered if her life had depended on it. He reached his target and dipped past her curls with the tip of his tongue, sending electrical shocks coursing through her whole body. What little breath remained in her lungs came rushing out. The ceiling did a slow revolution. He tickled her there again.

"Sweetheart, answer me. Is this all right with you?"

Molly's throat strained. She arched up, trembling so badly she felt the mattress shiver. "Yes," she managed to say breathlessly.

He thrust his tongue in, laving her with shocking heat. "Are you sure?" he murmured against her. "If it's too much, too fast, I'll understand."

The movement of his lips made bright spots dance before her eyes. Her only fear was that he might stop. "I'm—sure."

He closed his mouth over her then. Molly bucked and sobbed. It was the most incredible sensation. Far better than anything she'd ever read about in books. It was—she arched up. He teased her so gently that she held her breath until her temples pounded. She sobbed again and made fists in his hair, trying to press him closer. Still he tormented her with light strokes, making her insides twist and knot, making the urgency build.

When she thought she would die with the wanting, he shocked her by drawing hard on her with his mouth. Molly felt as if every nerve in her body had converged to that one spot. He dragged the rough of his tongue across her in rhythmic passes, pressing harder, taking complete possession, and sending her body into helpless spasms. When release finally caught her in its throes, Molly shrieked—shrill bleats of sound emitted with every convulsive expulsion of breath. He stayed with her until her throbbing flesh could stand no more, and then he brought her down with gentle strokes, soothing the pulsating nerve endings that he had just teased so mercilessly.

Afterward Molly felt as if she'd melted into a puddle. She couldn't move, couldn't think or focus clearly. She heard boots thump on the floor, followed by the plop of denim and pocket change rolling across the hardwood floor. Jake moved over her in a dark blur. He gently kissed her. Then he curled his hands over her hips and lifted her to him. Molly didn't think she could bear to feel anything more, didn't think the finale could possibly compare to what he'd just given her.

But she was wrong.

When the hard, hot heat of him pushed into her, she felt as if starbursts were going off low in her belly. He pressed forward gently at first, testing his way as if she were made of fragile silk. When he was buried to the hilt, he eased back and then carefully moved forward again.

"You okay?" he asked in a strangely tight voice.

Molly curled her hands over his rippling shoulders. "Oh, *yes*."

He picked up the tempo then, increasing the force of his thrusts. Pleasure bursts exploded inside her. She cried out and started to move with him, locking her legs around him to better gauge his strokes. Up, up. She felt as if he were lifting her toward a fiery crest. Her heart slugged against her ribs. Her breath came in sharp gasps. Black spots danced before her eyes. He increased the power of his thrusts, sliding her over the mattress with each impact until all that kept them joined was the clutch of her legs.

Heaven. Just when she felt his body snap taut, Molly reached her second climax. Through a dizzying blur, she focused on his dark face, loving him as she'd never loved anyone. *Jake.* She felt a rush of electrical heat spill into her. His hardness went into spasms deep within her. And then there was only spiraling delirium as they went over the edge together.

Chapter Twenty-two

Jake held his world in his arms. Molly cuddled against him like a delectably shaped body pillow, so soft that he was sorely tempted to have her again, even though he knew she was still exhausted from last time. Completely without inhibition in slumber as she never was awake, she pressed so close that one full breast rested on his chest. Her relaxed tummy, which she'd tried to suck in earlier, pressed into the hollow above his hip, and one plump thigh angled across his as though to anchor him in place.

He smiled into the darkness that had descended over the bedroom. As if he was going anywhere? Not a chance. God, she was precious. If he ever saw her eating nothing but salad for lunch again, he'd turn her over his knee. He *liked* her round. There wasn't a place on her he could touch without going rock hard. He wanted to squeeze and kiss and fondle every soft inch of her, and doubted he would ever tire of the experience.

He toyed with her hair, loving the way the short tendrils curled over his fingers. He pressed close to inhale the scent of shampoo and feminine essence that were exclusively her own. *Damn.* Letting her hair slip from his hand, he ran his palm over her fanny. His fingertips searched out the dimples, and he grinned.

He couldn't help but marvel over how fantastic she felt. Everything in his life was hard. He got up of a morning and endured the harsh elements. He bucked hay. He wrestled bulls. He pitted his strength against recalcitrant horses.

It was so incredibly arousing to feel satiny softness for a change. He cupped a hand over her shoulder and felt for bones. They were in there, but he had to search to find them, and that suited him just fine.

Molly moaned in her sleep. *Uh-oh.* He kissed her forehead and whispered, "It's all right, Molly mine."

"Mmm," she murmured and snuggled closer. Her body went limp again.

Jake ran his hand down her arm, testing for muscle. He found only a cute little dimple above her elbow. He made a mental note to trace it with his tongue the next time he made love to her. He touched the small knob of her elbow. Next he explored her wrist and hand. Under all the softness, there wasn't a whole lot to her.

Journeying south, he ran his hand over her bent leg. On the inside of her thigh, he found squishy little lumps under her skin that he guessed were cellulite. *Warm,* squishy little lumps. His dick went hard and stood at attention.

He sighed. Determined not to wake her, he closed his eyes and moved his hand to his chest. Only instead of chest, he found breast. He was lost. He wanted her again, and if he meant to get any sleep at all, he had to have her. He cupped his hand over the silky fullness of her. The instant he grazed her nipple with his thumb, her flesh went hard. Pushing her upward, he dipped his chin to flick her with his tongue. Her body flinched. She sighed in her sleep. He pushed her a little higher to take her into his mouth.

That sensitive rivet of flesh swelled and thrust eagerly against his tongue. He grazed it with his teeth, then suckled, teasing the crest to a throbbing rigidity. Molly moaned. Her slender fingers tightened over his ribs. He saw her lashes flutter. He nipped her lightly and felt her muscles jerk.

"Jake?" She fluttered her lashes again. "What are you doing?"

"Nothing. Just go back to sleep, sweetheart." Like he

would let her? Ah, but she was so sweet like this, all relaxed and unguarded. He pushed her onto her back, following her over to keep her nipple caught between his
teeth. He dragged his tongue over the tip. Once, twice. Her
eyes came wide open. He lifted his head to grin at her.
"Hi."

She sighed and arched her back. Her slender hands
threaded into his hair. "Oh, my."

"I want you again. Do you mind?"

Her only answer was a dreamy sigh. Jake took that as a
positive response and made love to her, this time paying
special attention to all the dimples he'd missed during the
first round.

Happiness. Molly realized now that she'd never really
experienced it before. Being in love, being loved . . . it was
such an incredible joy, and it was made all the more special by Jake's penchant for laughter. With him, Molly
quickly learned that lovemaking would always be something to be enjoyed, not only during the act itself but before and after. He joked, he teased, he played with her.
Sometimes he had Molly laughing so hard that when he finally kissed her the passion she felt came as a shock.

There was only one cloud on their horizon. *Rodney.* It
worried Molly that her ex-husband had not returned with a
court order as he'd threatened. She knew him. When he
thought he had the upper hand, he moved in with merciless
intent.

Why hadn't he come back? Molly knew he could easily
have gotten his court order. He had no way of knowing she
and Jake were married. Something wasn't right. Jake was
worried about it, too, Molly knew. She often saw shadows
in his eyes and knew he was pondering the situation.

On the third evening after their marriage, Jake invited
her to take one of their frequent walks along the creek.
Hand in hand, they strolled in silence for a long while.
Then he finally said, "I feel like there's a bomb hanging

over us by a slender thread and any little thing may bring it crashing down."

Molly squeezed his hand, knowing exactly what he meant. Not even in her most blissful moments with Jake could she forget that there would be unpleasantness to face. The possible outcome terrified her. She could never return to a clinic now—and stay sane. Jake had shown her what magic was like, and now anything less would equate to unbearable misery. She didn't think she could live without him.

"He wants something," Jake said softly. "If he once killed over it, Molly, it stands to reason he won't give up. He'll be back."

"I know."

His hand tightened over hers. "I hate waiting like a sitting duck. It's not in my nature." He sighed wearily. "I keep circling back to those papers he wanted you to sign. I think that's why he drugged you—why he had you locked away. He hoped to break you down, to reduce you to such a helpless mess, you'd do whatever he said, even if it meant signing papers you couldn't review first."

Molly's stomach clenched when she recalled how very close she'd come to being beaten. There had been times during her illness when she'd been so terrified, she would have done anything, *anything*, to escape the nightmare her life had become.

"If he's got your power of attorney, that makes no sense," Jake pointed out. "He should be able to sign in your stead, so why does he need your signature on something?"

Molly had been thinking about that as well. "Maybe the documents aren't covered by my power of attorney. Something he can't sign for me."

"What, though? A good attorney would draw up an all-inclusive power of attorney that would cover your business affairs in all fifty states."

Molly's heart caught as a horrible thought occurred to her. "Maybe it involves something outside the states."

Jake's eyes narrowed. "Damn it, I hate playing these guessing games."

Molly did as well. "I need to go through the firm records," she whispered.

She felt his body go still. He cast her a worried look. "How?"

"I could return to Portland, breach building security, and get on one of the network computers."

"No way! That'd be dangerous."

"Waiting for him to make a move is dangerous, too," she argued. "I know him, Jake. He's scheming and planning. If we wait for him to make his move, we may find ourselves in more trouble than we can worm out of."

"Forget it. You're not going."

A week ago, his authoritarian manner would have struck terror into Molly's heart. Now she looked into his eyes and saw only the fear he felt for her. Control wasn't the issue with Jake. Keeping her safe was his only concern.

"You could come with me."

He gazed off at nothing, his jaw muscle rippling as he clenched his teeth. "I guess I could, at that. At least then I'd know if something happened. You wouldn't have to face the son of a bitch alone."

Molly took both his hands in hers. "I'd feel a lot better if you were there, that's for sure."

His gaze locked on hers. "Deal. We'll go together."

Molly's heart started to gallop as she considered all that they'd have to do, most of it illegal. "We need to make plans."

He startled her half to death by releasing her hand, bending his legs, and locking an arm around her knees. Just that quickly, Molly found herself upended over his shoulder, her head dangling. She grabbed his belt to lever herself up. "*What* on *earth*? Jake, have you lost your *mind*?"

"Hell, no. I had a reason for bringing you out here, and I'll be damned if I'll let Rodney Wells screw it up. This is your one evening of the week off, and I'm going to enjoy every second of it."

He set off through the woods with Molly draped over his shoulder. She shrieked and playfully pummeled his back. He retaliated by smacking her upturned rump.

"Ouch!" she cried, even though it didn't hurt.

He cupped a hand over her butt and gave it a squeeze. "Damn, that was fun. I'm kinky and didn't even know it."

She giggled. "Forget it."

He jostled her to get a better hold and veered right. "Ah, come on. Let a guy have some fun."

"Have fun with someone else's fanny."

"I can't. Only yours will do." He suddenly braked and crouched to settle her feet on the ground. When she'd gained her balance, he grinned and patted the ponderosa pine beside them. "Remember this tree?"

Molly threw a startled look at the tree in question. "Is this the one?"

He patted the bark again. "Trust me, this is it. I'd know this tree anywhere. I've seen it in my dreams a hundred times."

Molly giggled. "Forget it. I'd get slivers in my already abused posterior."

His eyes began to twinkle, and he reached into his pocket to flash his pocketknife. "I brought my sliver picker. Afterwards, I'll lay you over my knees and—" His eyes filled with an ominous glint. "Holy hell. That'd never work. I'd forget what I was about and make love to you again."

He slipped an arm around her waist. Dipping his head, he nibbled on her ear.

"No!" she cried halfheartedly. "Not against a *tree,* Jake."

"Please?" He nibbled some more. "I have to do this just once and get it out of my system. Otherwise it'll never leave me alone." He tightened his arm suddenly. The next instant, Molly found herself pinned against the tree trunk. "Wrap your legs around my hips."

She did as he told her. Her blood began to slog through her veins when she saw the heat in his eyes. Pressing in with his lower body to support her weight, he reached to touch her hair. The love she saw in his expression made her feel gloriously beautiful—so beautiful that she felt not a twinge of embarrassment when he started to unfasten her blouse. His gaze moved lightly over her face like lambent tongues of flame.

"Did you bring a rope?" she couldn't resist asking.

Surprise flickered across his dark countenance, and then he barked with laughter. "The love scene in the romance, right?" Before she could reply, he was kissing her—deeply, passionately, his tongue claiming hers in a rhythmic parry and thrust that made her think of the way he possessed her body. Molly gave herself up to the sensations. Oh, how she loved him. The feelings that coursed through her were indescribable—delicious, sweet, her yearning for him so sharp she thought she'd never feel sated.

She was wrong, of course. Jake never left her on the edge. He drew her over into the abyss with him, taking all she had to give, giving all she could take. When the moment came, he jerked off his shirt to wedge it between her bottom and the bark, protecting her even in the throes of passion.

He then proceeded to make one of her wildest fantasies come true. He flattened her against the tree, thrust himself into her eager body, and took her with a forceful urgency that made her heart soar.

One short month ago, Molly had never envisioned herself as a criminal sort. Then she'd stolen a sixty-five thousand dollar racehorse, and her moral character had deteriorated from there. Now she found herself breaking and entering. It was one of the most terrifying experiences of her life. All during the drive up from Crystal Falls, she'd dreaded this moment.

Her hands shook violently as she groped in her purse for her firm keys, one of the few things Rodney had forgotten to strip from her possession. Jake stood beside her in the shadows, one side of his face illuminated by the parking lot lights. In honor of their foray to the city, he'd doffed his Stetson and wore a white shirt and sport coat over his Wrangler jeans. He still looked every inch a cowboy. Molly figured he probably would even in an expensive three-piece suit, but she wouldn't have changed him for the world. He looked so big and sturdy and wonderfully dependable. Having him there made her feel less terrified.

"Oh, Jake," she whispered, staring down at the alarm key on her palm. "What if they've changed the system and I set off the alarm?"

"Then, Molly mine, we run like hell."

She giggled. "A big help you are. Criminals never outrun the cops. They always get caught."

"Most criminals don't have four-wheel-drive trucks with all-terrain tread," he said jokingly. "I'll leave them to eat our dust."

Gaining courage from the confidence in his voice, Molly took a deep breath and thrust the odd-shaped, tubular key into its niche. She held her breath as she gave it a turn. The little red light on the panel went out. Her shoulders sagged with relief. "Thank you, God."

"Amen." The moment Molly unlocked the door, he opened it. "Hurry, Molly girl. We're sore thumbs out here."

They stepped inside. Darkness enveloped them when he closed and relocked the door behind them. Molly knew her surroundings by memory. They stood in a carpeted hallway. On the right just a few feet away was the coffee lounge. To the left was the janitorial supply room where she'd once caught Rodney banging a girl Friday. The memory no longer hurt. It didn't even rankle. That rude shock had marked the beginning of her awakening, which had eventually led her into Jake Coulter's arms.

"Follow me," she whispered.

"Try to lose me," he said near her ear. "I'm joined to you at the hip."

Molly went directly to her dad's office, waiting until they were inside with the door closed before she flipped on the lights. *Memories.* They hit her hard and fast, so gruesome and clear they hurt like physical blows. Her dad's desk, where she'd found him with half his head blown off. The chair that she'd so often occupied as a girl while he worked.

Jake's arms came around her from behind. He drew her back against him. "Ah, Molly, honey. Talk to me. Don't remember alone."

Her voice quavered. "I can almost see him. All the blood." Her body started to shake. "I loved him so much, Jake. He was so *good.* So wonderful. No one ever had a better dad. I always knew he loved me, no matter what. During the worst times, knowing that was all that held me together. And then, just like that, he was dead, and in such a horrible way."

His embrace tightened. It was as if he knew how desperately she needed his strength right then. "I love you that way now, Molly mine. No matter what, and forever." He lifted his head to scan the room. "Remember past it, Molly. You must have had good times in here."

"Oh, yes," she said softly. Oddly, it wasn't the joyful memories that rushed to her mind, but those that were bittersweet, the things that had defined her relationship with her dad. Being eleven and heartbroken over not getting the lead part in a play. Developing breasts before all the other girls did and feeling acutely self-conscious. "My dad was always my rock," she whispered. "Somehow, no matter how upset I was, he could make me laugh, and he always made me feel special."

"That's what you should remember, all those special times. Death is our final scene, not the one that comprises our life. Remember your dad as he was, not the way he ended."

A feeling of peace settled over Molly. She hugged all the good memories close and leaned her weight against Jake's solid chest, closing her eyes for a moment. When she opened them again, she felt restored and knew she had the strength to face anything as long as this man was beside her.

When she said as much, Jake whispered, "You can face anything even without me. You've got steel in your spine, Molly. I've seen it a hundred times. You don't need me. You don't need anyone. If you did, you never would have made it this far."

Molly straightened away from him. Dropping her purse onto an upholstered Victorian chair along the wall, she stepped forward. One foot in front of the other. Not allowing herself to think of that morning when she'd found her father's body, she walked to his desk.

As she lowered herself onto his chair, tears stung her eyes. *This* was who she was. From infancy, she'd teethed on investment journals. *This* was her destiny, what she'd been groomed to do all her life.

"You look transformed sitting there," Jake whispered.

Her gaze clung to his. It pleased her to know that he understood exactly how she felt without her saying a word.

"Hello, Molly Sterling," he said softly. His eyes searched hers, delving deep. Then he held out a big, brown hand to her. "I've been waiting a hell of a long time to meet you."

Molly took his hand. An electrical surge seemed to run from his arm up hers. She slowly smiled. "How do you feel about being a stockbroker's husband?"

"Like the luckiest man alive. How do you feel about being a rancher's wife?"

Molly took a moment to reply. "Blessed," she said softly. "I feel so blessed."

He grinned and inclined his head at the computer. "Go to work, lady. Get the son of a bitch by the balls."

"Can I have them freeze-dried and hang them on our living room wall as a trophy?" she asked as she flipped on the computer.

"Hell, darlin', I'll make you a special display case."

She giggled and went to work. The computer was connected to the mainframe, giving her access to all the firm's files. Jake watched with keen interest over her shoulder as she invaded the firm's system. "Damn, you're good at what you do."

Molly's chin came up. A feeling of purpose surged through her. "Damn straight, Mr. Coulter. I was taught by one of the best."

For all of Molly's renewed confidence and sense of purpose, her search of the computer files revealed nothing. "Oh, Jake, there's nothing here. I can't find a single thing that looks out of the way." She logged into her dad's personal files. Still, nothing. "Now, what?"

"We take a break and calm down," he said sagely. "Get all worked up, and you won't be able to think straight." He leaned a hip on the edge of the desk and grinned down at her. "How do you feel about sex on a Victorian chair?"

She giggled. "Not in *here*. It's a shrine."

He sighed and raked a hand through his hair. Glancing around, he said, "When we move up here six months out of the year, where'll I grab my afternoon fix if we can't do it in here?"

Molly grinned. "Maybe we could partition off one corner and designate it a nonshrine area."

"Done."

She ran her hands lovingly over her father's mahogany desk. Just touching it brought back so many memories.

"When I was growing up, Daddy left me surprises in his secret compartment."

"What secret compartment?"

Molly leaned back in her chair and gave him a challenging look. "The one in his desk. Bet you can't find it."

He crouched beside her to study the desk's structure. He ran a hand over the left side panel.

"Nope, not even warm," she teased.

He flattened his hand against the opposite panel. "Cold, cold," she said. "Try north."

He reached up, feeling the panel beneath the center drawer. His gaze suddenly sharpened on hers. Then he grinned. The next instant, an invisible drawer beneath the center one popped open. "Voilà!" he said.

"Every time my dad went away, he'd buy me a little something and hide it in here for me," she said softly. "I'd come racing in here after school to—" Molly broke off and stared. Inside the drawer lay a computer disk. The hair on her nape prickled. Her skin developed goose bumps. "Oh, my God, Jake."

He twisted around. "What?" he said, and then he saw the disk. "Sweet Christ, Molly, I think he left you a final sweet nothing."

Molly liked that. *A sweet nothing.* It reminded her of all the little gifts Jake had left her on the cabin porch. With trembling fingers, she picked up the square of plastic. It gave her the oddest feeling to know her father had touched it last. Possibly right before he died. Her heart kicked in excitement.

"Let's not get ahead of ourselves," Jake whispered. "Have a look at what's on it first."

She nodded. "You're right. Daddy said secret panels were a joke because all desks have them. He never hid anything of importance in there."

"Maybe he broke that rule just once," Jake suggested huskily. "If you're right and Rodney shot him, it could be he didn't have time to hide it elsewhere. Or maybe he knew you'd be sure to look in there eventually, for old time's sake if nothing else, and he felt it was a sure way to get information to you."

"I thought we weren't going to get ahead of ourselves."

He smiled. "Just look at the damned disk," he urged, his tone edged with excitement.

Molly was shaking so hard, she had to take two stabs at inserting the disk into the drive. Telling herself not to get her hopes up, she began viewing the files.

"Oh, my God, Jake. Oh, my *God!*"

"What? It's all Greek. Talk to me."

"He used dummy corporations as a cover to invest heavily in stock, hedging his bets with insider information, which is against the law."

"Your father?"

"No," Molly whispered. "Daddy would never have done this. It was done under his name, though. Rodney's machination, I feel sure."

"That miserable son of a bitch," Jake said softly. "He couldn't even make his dirty money without setting up someone else to take the fall."

Molly opened another file. Again all she could think to say was, "Oh, my God." After the first shock wore off, she whispered, "He must have raked in millions, Jake. *Millions.*" She anxiously opened another file. "Email messages. Oh, dear God, Jake, just look at this. Information from other companies about new products, upcoming mergers, swings in the market." Molly's heart caught when she saw that every message had been addressed to Marshal Sterling. "Using insider information like this, Rodney was making a killing, all under dummy corporations and in Daddy's name so it wouldn't appear that the gains came to him."

As Molly continued to search through the files, her alarm mounted. "It's all under my father's name, Jake. If I go to the authorities with this, the blame for it will be pinned on him." She fell back in the chair and looked at her new husband with sick apprehension. "Rodney did this. I know it. But there's no way I can prove it." Her heart twisted in her chest. She glanced back at the computer screen. In a hollow voice, she said, "Maybe my dad killed himself after all. Maybe he was so devastated when he saw this that he decided to take the easy way out, rather than face the scandal."

Jake shook his head. "I never had the honor of meeting Marshal Sterling, but I know his daughter. No faint heart who would blow his brains out over a patch of trouble could have raised a woman of your caliber."

"Oh, Jake, thank you."

He stared hard at the computer display. "Why is it that all these files aren't on the main network?" he asked. "It's as if your dad copied them from a separate hard drive or something."

A chill zipped down Molly's spine. "Oh, Jake, I've been so upset I wasn't thinking straight. You're right. You're absolutely *right*." She jumped up from the chair. "These are records of company transactions, alleged activity in accounts of my father's. That being the case, they should be on the main system like all his other firm accounts, not hidden away on a disk."

Jake stood beside her.

"My father was worried sick about something for about a week before he died. Maybe he was suspicious of Rodney. The morning of his death, he came in early. He seldom did that, choosing instead to enjoy the mornings with Claudia before she left for the clinic. What if he came in early that day, expressly to get here before Rodney to have a look at his computer? Rodney came to the firm early that morning, too. At least he was supposed to. When I arrived, he still wasn't here, and I thought it strange. But what if he'd been here already and left?"

Jake nodded. "Go on. It's making sense to me so far."

Molly was trembling. "Maybe he caught Daddy in his office *after* he'd copied this information onto a disk and put it in his pocket. Rodney may have been angry and followed him back here. Dad would have sat at his desk while they talked. Maybe he sensed that things were turning lethal, and he slipped the disk into the secret compartment right before Rodney shot him."

Molly swung around the desk to go to Rodney's office, Jake fast on her heels. "Knowing my ex-husband, he's still investing heavily in stock illegally. Rodney, the gambler. Investing turns his crank. He says it's a sophisticated way of betting. Only he found a way to swing the odds in his favor."

"Let's just hope we can find some proof to nail the bastard."

"He *knew* Dad had gotten the goods on him," she cried shrilly as they raced along the corridor. "Don't you see, Jake? *That's* why he was so upset that day when he caught me searching Daddy's office. He didn't know where my father had stashed the evidence, and he was terrified I'd find it if I hadn't already. That's why he immediately started trying to make me look nuts. He *had* to cast doubt on my credibility so no matter what I found, I couldn't have him thrown in prison."

After sitting at Rodney's desk, Molly closed her eyes and reached deep within herself for calm. Justice would be served, she promised herself. Rodney would pay dearly for the lives he'd ruined. She lifted her lashes, focused on Rodney's computer screen, and determinedly went to work.

Jake folded his arms on the back of the chair to watch over her shoulder. "Your scenario all figures except for one thing," he mused aloud. "It doesn't explain why Rodney needs your signature on something so desperately."

"Maybe the answers are here," Molly said.

"If he's made millions, why the hell doesn't he just take his profits and scat?" Jake asked. "He could go to a foreign country, assume a new identity. If those account records

we just saw are any indication, he made some huge profits."

"True, but Rodney's never satisfied. Greed is his middle name. He'll stay and rake in cash as long as he can. It's
gambling to him. He's compulsive about it."

"If that's the case, why not just let you remain on the
ranch, well out of his way, while he hauls in dough for the
next few months? Until the power of attorney expires, he
can run this place without any input from you." Jake
growled low in his chest. "I smell a rat. I'm not sure what
it is, but this stinks to high heaven."

Molly had barely gotten into Rodney's system before
she hit a brick wall. "A bunch of these files are protected."

"Go for it. That's where he'll hide the good stuff."

"I need the password!" Molly cried in frustration. "Oh,
God, Jake. Rodney is a genius with computers. The Silicon
Valley guru, remember. I'm a babe in the woods by com-
parison. I'll never be able to crack a system he protected."

Jake laid a hand on her shoulder. Just his touch served
to calm her. "Molly Sterling Coulter, you can do anything
you set out to do. Didn't you steal a horse and put your
whole life on the line?"

"Yes," she said weakly. The memory of that horrific day
made her grin. "I did."

"Shhh." Jake's hand convulsed on her shoulder. "What
the frigging hell is that?"

Molly's heart leaped at a shrill sound, pealing in the
outside corridor. She almost jumped out of the chair, thinking they'd been caught and the alarm was going off. Then
she laughed and went limp with relief. "It's the grandfather
clock."

Jake listened and chuckled. "Damn. I thought our asses
were grass for a second."

Molly relaxed and went back to password guessing. She
tried everything she could think of—Rodney's name, his
initials, his birth date, his social security number. Nothing
gave her access to the protected files.

"What we need is a little blind luck," Jake whispered.

Luck. Rodney was a gambler. Molly typed in the word. It didn't work. "Well, that wasn't it." She thought for a moment. Then a thrill of excitement coursed through her. Going on a hunch, she typed in Sonora Sunset, the name of the horse Rodney had placed so many bets on.

"Bingo," Jake whispered. "That's it, Molly."

"I'm in," she said joyously. "I'm *in*, Jake."

"Holy Toledo," Jake said as she began opening files. "Rodney has been a very busy boy."

Molly found records of several illegal stock transactions. Then she stumbled upon entries of her ex-husband's betting at the track. "Now I understand why he whipped poor Sunset. Luck has not been Rodney's friend. Just look at this, Jake. He's suffered some very heavy losses, the largest when he last wagered on Sunset and the poor horse lost."

Jake whistled at the huge amounts of money Rodney had tossed away. "He's crazy. No wonder the bastard isn't lounging on an exotic beach somewhere. He's been betting at the track like a lord. Is that his present bottom line? How the hell can that be? It looks like he's damned near broke."

It made no sense to Molly, either. All those millions that Rodney had made illegally appeared to be gone. "I guess gambling finally got the upper hand," she whispered.

"Blowing money like that makes no sense at all to me." Jake said. "He has to know he can't continue with the insider trading forever without being caught. He should be using this window of time to make a killing, and then run when the heat turns up."

Molly sadly reviewed the accounting of all Sonora Sunset's losses at the track. The poor horse. He'd run his heart out for Rodney, but he just hadn't had what it took to win. He'd been too young, too green. His failures had earned him his owner's rage. "Oh, Jake, do you think Rodney whipped Sunset every time he lost?" she asked thinly. "It breaks my heart to think of it."

"I just thank God he managed to control his mean nature with you," Jake murmured.

"Sunset was just an animal. He had no recourse, and Rodney knew that I did. My dad would have been enraged if he'd laid a hand on me." Coldness filled her. "He killed my father, Jake. Looking at all this just drives home to me how very ruthless he actually is. I know he killed him. He probably did it without a twinge of conscience. He has no stops. No compassion for anyone or anything."

"Sonora Sunset, his password to a life of luxury," Jake said softly. "Who's the animal—the horse or him?"

"I'm just so glad I'm free of him," she whispered.

"Free, yes. It's time to heal and move on, Molly mine."

She smiled. "Yes, but to do that, I have to bring the bastard to justice."

"Is this enough to take to the Securities and Exchange Commission?" Jake asked.

Molly nodded and began copying all the protected files onto disks. "More than enough. The dates of the more recent transactions prove that my father had nothing to do with it. Dead men can't do insider trading, and thanks to Rodney, I've been effectively cut out of the picture for months, so he can't pin it on me, either."

When she'd finished making the copies and pushed up from the desk, Jake glanced around the plush office. "Do you have bad memories of this room?"

"A host of them," she admitted.

A twinkle slipped into his eyes. "Is it a shrine?"

"More like a horror chamber."

He caught her chin on the edge of his hand. "Do you think he ever screwed around on you with someone in here?"

"Undoubtedly."

He grinned. "Wanna get even?"

Molly giggled. "I think we'd better save it for later, Mr. Coulter. If we get caught, you could have difficulty running with your Wranglers around your ankles."

"Good point."

But he kissed her anyway. For Molly, the magic of that was enough to dispel all the bad memories and fill her mind with glorious new ones. Rodney Wells no longer had any power over her life.

On the way out of the city, Molly asked Jake to make just one stop—at the cemetery. She hadn't visited her father's grave since the day she buried him. It was time. High time. She felt ready now to face the pain.

Typical of Portland, it was raining by the time Jake parked near her dad's grave. Huddling inside her trench coat, which she hadn't had occasion to wear since that fateful morning when she'd left the city, Molly soon got soaked standing beside the headstone. Her short hair was plastered to her head and dripping wet. Still she just stood there, staring down at the stone. It seemed so sad, so terribly sad that a man's entire life could be synopsized with a dash between two dates. It was as if he'd never existed. It reminded her of the inscription on Jake's tree, PEDRO, 1976–1983. Life was so short, death so final.

"I'll be contacting the authorities on Monday, Daddy," she explained quietly. "Tomorrow being Sunday, I can't do anything sooner, but I promise you, I won't rest until it's done. I pray that I can present a convincing case against Rodney. Regardless, it's a risk I have to take to bring him to justice. If I fail, I could end up dragging your good name through the mud, and by extension, the reputation of Sterling and Wells may suffer. I know how much the firm meant to you."

Molly swallowed and closed her eyes. "If that happens, I'll be so sorry, Daddy. But this is something I have to do. I hope you can understand and that you'll forgive me if it all turns sour."

Jake, who'd been standing nearby without her realizing it, joined Molly just then and wrapped her in his strong arms. "You have to stop torturing yourself like this," he whispered. "Why do you think your father made a copy of Rodney's files? To turn the bastard in, of course. Under the same circumstances, I know I would have, and I'm beginning to think your dad was like me in many ways."

Molly smiled through the raindrops and tears, knowing Jake was right. Though she knew it was an inappropriate moment for the question, she shakily asked, "Who was Pedro, Jake?"

He stiffened. "What?" The tension slowly slipped from him. "You visited my tree."

"Yes." Inclining her head at the stone, she said, "Seeing the dates reminded me."

He rested his cheek against her hair. "Pedro was my dog. He got killed trying to protect me from a charging bull."

Molly's heart caught at the sadness in his voice. "He must have been a very special dog."

"My one and only. When I buried him, I swore I'd never get another one to take his place."

"And you never did?" Molly smiled through her tears and the raindrops, for it wasn't really a question. She was coming to realize that this man loved with his whole heart and soul. It comforted her to know that Pedro lived on in his memory. The dates on her father's headstone weren't just numbers chiseled in stone; they commemorated his life, and the dash was representative of the most important parts, all the events that had transpired between his opening scene and the final act. She would never forget him, and because she wouldn't, he would never really be gone. "May I ask a favor?"

"What's that?"

"Can I carve Daddy's name on your tree?"

He tightened his arms around her. "It's our tree now, Molly mine. I think your father's name belongs there."

Their tree. Oh, yes. She loved the sound of that. One day, she would carve the name of her father's first grandchild on that beautiful old oak. Marshal Sterling would live on in her, and in her and Jake's children.

For the first time in so long, Molly felt as if she were coming close to being the woman her father had raised her to be. "I can feel him here," she said. "I think he's looking down on us right now. And you know what?"

She felt his mouth tip in a smile. "No, what?"

"I think he's celebrating in heaven with the angels right now to see his daughter in the arms of such a fine man." She turned to frame his face between her hands. "You know what else, Jake? Nothing can stop us. Together, you and I are going to bring Rodney Wells to his knees and make him pay dearly for all that he's done. To Sunset, to me, to my father. He's going to pay. I'm going to see that he does."

Chapter Twenty-three

Morning sunlight streamed in the kitchen window, bathing the log walls and wooden floors in a wash of gold. Sitting catty-corner together at the table, Jake and Molly fed each other breakfast, vegetarian fare aside from the eggs in the garden omelet. Licking the juice of a fresh ripe peach from her lips, Molly guided a forkful of fruit to her husband's mouth, giggling when he dodged the food and nipped at her knuckles instead.

"I'd much rather have you," he said huskily. "Come back upstairs with me."

"It's morning," Molly protested, glancing toward the window. "My day off as well, I might add. I don't want to spend all of it in bed."

He waggled his dark eyebrows at her. "Come on up, and I'll have brunch, Jake Coulter style."

She curled her toes inside the oversized wool socks she'd borrowed from his drawer. "Brunch?" Her gaze moved to his mouth. She imagined his lips trailing over her skin, and a delicious shiver ran up her spine. In a voice gone oddly thick, she said, "I might be convinced. Tell me more."

He took the piece of peach between his teeth, barely skimming the ripe flesh, then flicking it with his tongue. "Come upstairs," he whispered. "I do my best convincing with my actions."

Molly laid down the fork and pushed up from her chair. Jake trailed his gaze over her T-shirt to the hem, where he spent a moment admiring her bare legs. "Did you know you have cute little dimples in your knees?"

She bent to look. When she glanced back at him, she wrinkled her nose impishly. "Some men are wild for dimples."

"I'm one of them."

Five minutes later, Jake was intent on showing her just how wild he was for dimples, and Molly felt like a smorgasbord, created expressly for his enjoyment. He nibbled the dimples on her bottom. Then he moved to kiss the dimples at the small of her back. Then he slowly licked his way up her spine. Her skin was tingling everywhere by the time he turned her over to kiss her front.

"Have I told you this morning how much I love you?" he asked.

"Not for at least twenty minutes or so."

He grinned. "I love you more than words can say. You know what that means, don't you? I guess I'll just have to show you."

He was much better at showing than telling, Molly decided some thirty minutes later. He also knew how to totally monopolize a lady's day off. When he was done with her, she only wanted to snuggle up against him and sleep.

"Take a nap with me," she coaxed.

He frowned. "I have things to do today."

"Like what?"

"Work, as much as I hate to say the word. It's the men's day off. Hank and I have to carry the load on Saturday and Sunday."

Molly huffed under her breath and nipped his chest. "Well, then, I demand a change in my schedule. I want days off that you can enjoy with me."

"Speak to the lady of the manor. I don't handle the domestic crap anymore. I got smart and found myself a wife."

She playfully punched his ribs. Then she decided to

change tactics and kissed them instead. "Take a nap with me, and I'll make it worth your while when we wake up."

He grinned and closed his eyes. "I might be convinced. Tell me more."

Molly rose to her knees. "I'd much rather give you a preview. I'm much more convincing with my actions than I am with words."

Jake chuckled. "It's a losing proposition. We just finished. I need some recharge time."

"Wanna bet?"

"How much are we talking?"

Molly giggled. "Who said anything about money?" She whispered in his ear what she wanted him to do to her if she won. "What do you say?"

He gave her a heavy-lidded look. "You're on, and I just lost the bet thinking about it."

Molly glanced down, saw the proof of his words, and burst out laughing. He didn't allow her to gloat for long. Before she knew it, he was making love to her again. Slow, languorous lovemaking that ended with snuggling and a snooze.

"Jake!"

Molly jerked awake to the sound of Hank shouting her husband's name. An instant later, she heard booted feet on the stairs. Jake sat up in bed, rubbing his eyes. Molly jerked the sheets up over herself just before the bedroom door flew open.

"Hurry up and get dressed," Hank cried. "Somehow the horses got loose. They're scattered from hell to Texas. The rancher down the road just called, and two are clear down at his place."

"That's two miles away!" Jake swore under his breath. "Damn it. How did they get out?"

"Beats me, but we've got to get them home before one of them gets run over."

The instant his brother exited the bedroom, Jake threw

back the covers and swung out of bed. "Well, that shoots the nap all to hell."

Molly pushed up on her elbow. "Can I help catch them?"

He leaned back to kiss her, then pushed to his feet and jerked on his pants. "It'll be more time consuming than anything else." He winked at her as he bent to pull on his socks and boots. "I'd much rather you wait here. I haven't gotten to pay up on that bet I lost yet."

Molly sighed and snuggled back down, feeling deliciously lazy and content. "I'll be here then, waiting."

He grabbed his Stetson off the bedpost and put it on his head. "Stop looking at me like that, or I'll let the damned horses go to the devil."

She giggled sleepily. "Go on and do your cowboy thing. I need some recharging time myself now."

A moment later when he left the bedroom, Molly snuggled back down, hugging his pillow close so she could drift back to sleep with the scent of him all around her. *Jake*. She drifted in lazy contentment, half asleep and caught in that shadowy world between wakefulness and dreams. Oh, how she loved him. She felt as if some magical fairy godmother had waved her magic wand and made all her wishes come true.

She had just fallen back to sleep when a sound awakened her. She blinked sleepily and tried to focus. Lifting her lashes, she was surprised to see that the bedroom door stood ajar. She knew her husband had shut it when he left. She propped herself up on one arm.

"Jake? Did you catch the horses already?"

From behind her, a hand clamped over her hair. Molly screamed as pain exploded over her scalp. The next thing she knew she was being dragged off the bed. She glimpsed gray slacks and shiny loafers.

"No, you fat bitch, he hasn't caught the horses already."

Rodney. Molly's brain went cold with terror. She grabbed frantically at his hand to ease the pull on her hair.

He hauled her out onto the floor and jerked her head back with such force she feared her neck might snap.

"God, you're disgusting." He pressed his face close to hers. "The poor bastard is so used to cows, he doesn't know udders when he sees them."

Molly stared up into her ex-husband's hazel eyes. Oddly, his words had no effect on her. He'd hurt her all he could. Nothing he could dish out now was going to bruise her feelings. Jake had given her a beautiful memory for every cruel thing Rodney had said. "What do you want, Rodney?"

Something cold pressed against her temple. She knew instantly that it was a gun. Her stomach clenched.

"One sound, and I'll pull the trigger," he whispered. "Get your fat ass dressed. We're going to have a little party."

Molly scrambled away from him the moment he released her. Keeping the weapon pointed at her, he followed her to the dresser where Jake had emptied some of his drawers to make room for her clothes. With fear-numbed fingers, she took out underwear and hurriedly put it on. Then she went into the walk-in closet for jeans and a blouse, Rodney following close behind her.

"Where are the computer disks?" he said as she put on the blouse.

Molly gave him what she hoped was a bewildered look. "What computer dis—"

He backhanded her across the mouth. The force of the blow sent her reeling into the wall, her head cracking against a log. Her legs suddenly rubbery, she slid down to the floor and then just sat there, staring stupidly up at him.

Pressing the barrel of the gun between her eyes, Rodney said, "Don't fuck with me, Molly. I blew your father's head off. I sure as hell won't hesitate to blow off yours."

That came as no surprise to Molly. She blinked, trying to regain her senses. Her jaw throbbed where he'd struck her, and her head was whirling.

"Did you really think I wouldn't know if someone messed with my computer?" he asked acidly. "You're as stupid as your father." He jabbed his chest. "My system is inviolate. No one can touch it that I don't immediately know when I log on. You left your fingerprints all over it, and I want the copies you made."

Molly was afraid to defy him. She staggered to her feet and withdrew the computer disks from the pocket of Jake's sport coat. Rodney snatched them from her hand. After looking at them, he shoved them in his suit pocket.

"Thank you," he said softly. "Now finish getting dressed."

While Molly drew on some jeans and leaned against the closet wall to tug on her sneakers, Rodney talked. "It's too damned bad your big, tough cowboy didn't listen to me and stay out of this," he bragged. "Instead he kept a crazy woman on his ranch, and now she's going to commit a final, crazy act, costing him dearly."

Molly had no idea what he meant until he forced her at gunpoint out onto the landing. A five-gallon can of diesel sat just outside the bedroom door.

"Start dousing the floors." Smiling one of those oily smiles she'd come to detest so much, he added, "I'd lend you my gloves, but it's extremely important that your fingerprints be all over the can later. I'm sure you understand."

Molly understood all right. *Oh, God, oh, God.* He meant to burn down Jake's house. As sick as the thought made her, she couldn't help but be even more afraid for herself. Rodney had just openly admitted to killing her father. He wouldn't have done that if he meant to let her live to tell about it.

With Rodney following behind her, Molly doused the floors with fuel. When she had emptied the five-gallon can, Rodney motioned her downstairs. "Take the can down with you. We'll be leaving it outside as evidence for the police."

As Molly started down the stairs, she prayed mind-lessly, imploring God to intervene somehow. Rodney meant to kill her. She saw it in his eyes. Terror sluiced through her veins like ice water.

Once on the ground floor, Rodney smiled again, inclin-ing his head to indicate yet another gas can. "You know the routine. Don't drag your feet. If your cowboy comes back, he'll end up being a very dead hero. You wouldn't want that, now would you?"

Molly imagined Jake's rage if he were to walk in on this scene. Her heart gave a painful twist, for she knew very well it wouldn't be the house that her husband would fight to protect. Helpless anger welled up within Molly. She'd spent all her adult life believing herself to be second rate. Now, for the first time in eleven years, she was happy. Meeting Jake Coulter had transformed her life. She loved him so, and he loved her. Somehow he'd done the impos-sible and made her feel beautiful. Not just so-so, not just pretty, but absolutely beautiful. Now Rodney meant to end it all, and in the most horrible of ways, making it appear that she had been responsible for the misdeed.

As she poured diesel over the great room floor, she re-membered all the evenings she'd walked through the room with Jake. Tears nearly blinded her when she recalled the night Hank had teased her about the cougar threat. She had a *family* now. Jake's parents, who'd both called her daugh-ter and taken her into their hearts. Jake's brothers and sis-ter. She didn't want to die and miss out on that feeling of belonging.

"Now the kitchen," Rodney said in a low, venomous voice.

Molly swallowed hard to steady her voice before say-ing, "You're going to murder me, aren't you?"

"All in good time. First, we have business to conclude."

Molly flung diesel onto the middle of the floor. The fuel pooled around the cross-buck legs of the table Jake had built. *Oh, God.* She thought of the horseshoe clock. Then her mind conjured pictures of the downstairs bathroom where an antique Jack Daniel's barrel served as a sink vanity and horseshoes had been welded together as towel hooks. In the great room, all the furniture had been crafted from trees felled on this ranch. Every nook and cranny of this beautiful house bore Jake Coulter's stamp. He'd fashioned it all with those big, capable hands, making each room unique.

Rodney, who'd spent his whole life greedily taking and destroying, couldn't conceive what he was about to incinerate—not just a house, but Jake Coulter's dream.

"If you're going to kill me, I'm going to make good use of the minutes I have left." Molly straightened and turned to glare at the man who'd nearly destroyed her. "I want to make sure you know how much I detest you."

Rodney only smiled. "You weren't even a blip on my radar screen, Molly dear. Like I care?"

"No," Molly said, her voice quivering with revulsion. "You never cared. You've never cared about anyone but yourself. I look at you, and do you know what I see, Rodney? There's nothing to you. Not even the despicable parts amount to anything."

His beautifully drawn mouth, which she'd once admired, twisted into a sneer. "Shut up and just pour the damned gas."

"Diesel," she corrected. Molly had no choice but to do as he said. A feeling of separateness came over her. She fleetingly wondered if it was some sort of God-given protective device inside of her kicking in. *Numbness.* She was about to die, and she felt so apart from it, not really afraid any longer, just numb.

When she finished dousing the house, Rodney instructed her to carry the fuel cans outside and throw them over the porch railing into the front yard. Then, keeping the gun trained on her, he withdrew a cigarette lighter from his suit pocket.

"Don't do this, Rodney," she tried. "Jake's never

harmed you. He's an innocent player. If you torch his house, you'll ruin him. Can't you accomplish whatever it is you need to without involving him?"

"Oh," he said in a falsely sympathetic tone, "be still, my heart. I think dumpy little Molly has fallen in love. *Again.* Don't cry for him, dear heart. How long do you think it would have been before he got tired of you? Not long, that's guaranteed. Trust me to know. You're the most unbearably boring woman I've ever met."

Molly glanced at the doorway, where diesel lay in pools just beyond the threshold. Rodney moved sideways in a half-crouch, extending the flame toward the fuel. "Be ready to move," he said.

"Please, *don't!*" Molly cried.

Rodney only laughed. The fuel ignited in a *whoosh* of fire. He leaped back, his hazel eyes glittering madly. "You're so crazy, Molly. Why in God's *name* would you burn down your lover's house? People will shake their heads. They're even Lazy J gas cans, which makes it perfect. They'll think you got them from the shed."

He grabbed her by the arm and flung her ahead of him down the steps. From out in his pen, Sunset shrieked. Molly knew by the sound that the stallion recognized Rodney. She stumbled as Rodney dragged her away toward the woods. He drew to a stop in approximately the same area where she'd first seen Jake, sawing up the fallen pine. *Jake.* It broke her heart that the house he'd built might burn to the ground. She could only thank God that he had cleared off most of the trees near the dwelling, just as he had around the stable, forming a fire break. He'd done it to protect the buildings in case of a forest fire, she felt sure. Hopefully, the safety precaution would work in reverse, preventing the flames from catching on the trees.

Grabbing her viciously by the hair, Rodney forced her to her knees. Rocks jabbed into her shins. Sharp pain lanced her thighs. The next instant, he shoved a pen and some papers in front of her face. "This time, you'll by God sign."

Molly blinked and tried to focus. "The papers again?" Her hands shook violently as she took them. "If you're going to kill me, at least tell me what they are."

"Just sign the damned thing!" He rammed the barrel of the gun against her temple, making her see stars. "So help me, if you don't, I'll blow your gray matter from here to hell. I have nothing left to lose. *Nothing*."

"Of course you don't. You've gambled it all away."

Turning his wrist, he struck her on the head with the weapon. The front sight cut into her scalp, the sting bringing tears to her eyes. She tried to focus on the papers. The roar of the house fire snarled in her ears like a ravenous beast. She didn't need to look back to know that Jake's home would soon be an inferno. The print blurred, making it impossible for her to tell where the signature line was located.

"Sign it!" Rodney cried.

"I'm trying, damn you. Stop hitting me. I can't see."

He shoved the barrel of the gun against her temple again. "Toward the bottom. Sign it." He gave her a hard nudge. "Your refusal to do it before fucked everything up for me. *Everything*. Why, all of a sudden, did you have to get stubborn. A hundred times, at least, I brought home papers, and you always signed them without a question. Why, the one time it really counted, did you have to get so goddamned righteous on me?"

"It didn't matter before!" she cried, still trying to focus on the page. "After Daddy died, it did. I was in charge of the firm. I had to be responsible."

"Responsible. Jesus Christ. You caused yourself no end of heartache, you stupid bitch. I would have split town and left you alone if only you had signed off. But, oh no, you had to be difficult for the first time in our marriage."

"What am I signing off?" Molly asked, struggling to hold the pen in her shaking fingers.

"An offshore account! *Millions* of dollars, Molly. All of it automatically deposited by the dummy corporations under your name. That way, the profits never came to me, and if anyone ever found out, you and your dad would take the fall. I thought having your power of attorney would enable me to make withdrawals, only that jerkwater foreign country doesn't recognize it as a legal document! All that money, and I couldn't touch a cent of it. I was almost broke, and you refused to sign. The only way I could survive was to bet on the races with what money I had here, hoping for a win."

"Only Sunset kept losing," she inserted hollowly.

"The goddamned horse has four left feet," Rodney retorted bitterly.

"I was locked up over this?" Molly wanted to fly at him, claw out his eyes, bite him, kick him. "You deprived me of my freedom for *money*?"

"It wasn't by choice. You forced my hand. What was I supposed to do, let you waltz away before you signed this, and let millions of dollars turn to dust in a bank account I couldn't touch? I had to make you sign. I figured you would eventually, that sooner or later, you'd break down and see reason."

"Why on *earth* did you bank your dirty money under *my* name?" Molly cried.

"Why not? If something went sour, I had it set up so your father and you would take the heat, and I'd walk away without being implicated."

"To amass another fortune?"

He smiled. "I profited by my own genius. So hang me. You and your father were both so stupid, lending yourself so easily to be used. Why not?"

Molly pressed the pen to the paper, remembering all the many times she'd refused to do this. "So it was all for money. You consigned me to hell for money."

"You could have ended it any time. I asked you, time and again, to sign this for me, and you refused." He crouched beside her, leveling the gun between her eyes. "Do you realize how brilliant I am, Molly? You have a brain the size of a pea, compared to mine. You saw all those emails I received under your father's name. Do you think those companies voluntarily sent me all that insider information? Hell, no. I developed a worm virus when I was working in the valley. No antivirus software on the market today can detect it. I can attach it to any email message I send out from my computer. When the recipients open the file, the worm infiltrates their system's email program, creating an automatic alias mailing address that's executed any time electronic mail is sent or received by that system."

Molly stared along the blue-black barrel of the gun at his face. His features were contorted with feverish intensity. In his irises, reflections of the flames behind her danced like tiny demons caught up in the throes of evil. "So all those companies unwittingly sent you copies of all their electronic correspondence," she whispered.

"Exactly. The perfect insider-trading setup. I sent them introductory email brochures about our firm, and after that, I got all the upcoming information about their products, their business dealings. My own little crystal ball to show me the future and enable me to make millions."

Her vision was beginning to clear from the rap on her head. Molly lowered her gaze to the document he wanted her to sign. She saw that it was a withdrawal form to an offshore bank account. She thought of all the movies she'd watched where the imperiled heroine got the villain to keep talking and thereby bought herself precious seconds of time. Fat chance. Rodney had said all there was to say. Time had run out.

She thought about defying him. Oh, how appealing that thought was. As if he guessed her thoughts, Rodney smiled coldly. "I can make it painful. Is that what you want? Before I'm done, you'll beg me to die. For once in your misbegotten life, do it the easy way."

Molly considered her options. Jake was out there some-where. Even if it was painful for her, any delay might save her life. Her husband and Hank would surely see the smoke. At this very moment, they might be racing back to the ranch. How long did it take to cover two miles on horseback? She had no idea, absolutely none, but any chance she might have to live was one she couldn't ignore.

Molly looked Rodney dead in the eye. "If I sign this, I'm signing my death warrant."

A diabolical glint slipped into Rodney's eyes. "And if you don't sign it, you're signing his death warrant."

He smiled and pushed to his feet, aiming the gun away from her. For a moment, Molly couldn't think what he meant to shoot. Then her gaze followed the direction of the gun barrel—to Sunset. Her heart caught. She bit down hard on the inside of her cheek to keep from crying out and stared with burning eyes at the beautiful black horse.

Rodney sighted in, smiling evilly. "A knee first, don't you think? That's sure death for a horse. Slow, excruciat-ing." The gun clicked ominously. "If you think I can't hit him from here, don't delude yourself. I've been practicing weekly at a shooting range for almost five years. I can pick my target. And I assure you, darling, I'll make it very painful for him."

Molly told herself that Sunset was only an animal, that her life was far more precious. But, somehow, when she looked at that magnificent black stallion, knowing how horribly he'd already suffered at Rodney's hands, it wasn't that simple. The bond that had developed between her and the horse ran deep, and she'd risked so much to save him. If she allowed Rodney to kill him now, all her efforts would be for nothing.

The thought washed her mouth with bitterness. Rodney Wells had taken so very much from her. He couldn't have Sunset, too.

Rodney would probably kill her anyway. It took only a split second to fire a bullet. How much time could she conceivably buy for herself? A minute, maybe? Looking at Sunset, she couldn't bring herself to sacrifice his life on the off chance that Jake might return in time to save her.

"No, *don't*!" she cried. "I'll sign, Rodney. Don't hurt him. Please, don't."

Rodney turned the gun back on her. "Then do it, damn you."

Her hands trembling so that she could barely move the pen, Molly scrawled her signature on the appropriate line, knowing as she did that she might be signing her life away. She thrust the paper at him. "There, you bastard. You've got your money. Now why don't you just go?"

"And have you blow the whistle on me? Not a chance, darling. When I walk away, there'll be no evidence to haunt me. That means I have to shut your trap, make it look like you went over the edge and did all this." He tucked the withdrawal form safely inside his suit jacket, then grabbed Molly's arm and jerked her to her feet. "Come on. Let's finish this before your cowboy rounds up his beasts and comes back to complicate matters."

Molly stumbled along beside him, wincing at the pain of his grip on her arm. "How will you kill me, Rodney? Not with the gun, surely. Or is it registered in my name like the one you killed my father with was registered in his?"

"I seldom repeat a stroke of genius," he said with a laugh. "It worked once. Repeat performances are risky."

He led her to Sunset's pen. When he suddenly released her at the gate, Molly stared stupidly at him, not registering what he meant to do until she glanced down to see a large rock and a whip lying near her feet. She threw him an appalled glance. He kept the gun trained on her as he bent to pick up the rock.

"Open the gate," he whispered.

Molly glanced back at the whip. "What are you—?"

"Just do it!"

She jerked away from the thrusting gun barrel and turned to open the gate. Against her back, she could feel the intensifying heat of the house fire. She wondered if Jake might see the smoke. Prayed he might.

"Step inside," Rodney ordered.

Molly did as he said.

"Stop!" he said. "And don't turn around. Things always hurt less if you don't look."

Molly braced, trying frantically to think of something she could do to save herself. The next instant, her head exploded with agony. In that split second between consciousness and oblivion, she knew he'd struck her with the rock. Then—*blessed blackness.*

Jake cut his horse in behind the gelding, clicking his tongue and softly talking to keep the animal from panicking. Fifty yards up the road, Hank was going through similar motions with a frightened mare.

"It's all right, boy," Jake crooned. "Let's head home and have some oats."

Hank was already dogging the mare in that direction. He waved his Stetson at Jake in silent communication. Jake lifted a hand to let his brother know he'd be right behind him. He was shifting in the saddle, thinking of his wife and wishing he were back in bed with her already, when he saw what looked like smoke in the distance. He stared at it stupidly for a moment. Then alarm bells clanged in his brain. It was coming from the Lazy J.

He tensed, standing rigid in the stirrups, his heart freezing in his chest. "Hank!" he yelled. "There's a fire back at the ranch!"

Hank wheeled his horse, following Jake's gaze. His whole body snapped to attention when he saw the smoke. "Holy hell! It's the house!"

Sweet Christ. Jake had thought the same thing, but it had frightened him so that he'd pushed it away. The house. Molly was in there. She was sleeping. Oh, sweet Christ.

Jake left the horse he'd been dogging to race his mount along the edge of the drainage ditch toward his brother.

"Molly!" he cried when he got close enough to Hank to make himself heard clearly. "She's upstairs asleep!"

Hank leaned sharply forward in the saddle and dug in with his heels, urging his horse into a flat-out run. Jake fell in beside him in a breakneck dash for home.

Molly blinked dazedly. *Dirt.* In her mouth, in her eyes. She coughed and spat. Her fingers dug into the earth, the grit pushing up under her nails. Her head hurt. The pain was so excruciating, it was almost blinding. She didn't know where she was. There was a roaring in her ears, a loud snapping sound, and shrill bursts of noise that sounded like someone shrieking.

She moaned and rolled onto her side. In her blurry vision, black legs danced. She focused, blinked. *Hooves.* They flashed near her face with dizzying unpredictability, dust flying every time they impacted with the ground. Molly stared stupidly at them for a moment. Then it all came rushing back. *Rodney.* He'd hit her on the head. She was inside Sunset's pen.

She tried to push up on her elbow. Her body felt leaden, as if her limbs had become detached from her brain. She fell back onto the dirt, too disoriented to move or think clearly. She saw Rodney on the fence. He sat astride the top rail, and he was swinging one arm. As her vision cleared a bit, she realized he was snapping a whip.

Her brain froze with horror. She glanced up at Sunset, the source of all the shrieking sounds. The stallion danced in terror, trying to avoid the leather that whined in the air all around him. But there was no escape in the small corral.

"Trample her, you son of a bitch!" Rodney yelled. "Do something right, just once in your miserable life!"

Sunset screamed and sidestepped, narrowly avoiding the lacerating bite of the whip. Rodney laughed as the horse danced perilously close to Molly's legs. She tried frantically to move her feet, to escape the stallion's hooves, but her body ignored the commands. *Oh, God.* Rodney meant to make Sunset kill her. It would look like an unfortunate accident, Sunset would pay the price, and Rodney would waltz away scot-free.

To Molly's disbelief, Sunset didn't step on her. Coincidence? She threw another frightened look at the horse. The whip sliced through the air again, almost connecting with the stallion's nose. He threw up his head. Molly saw the whites of his eyes. He danced sideways—away from her.

Sunset. He'd looked at her. She'd seen the flash of his eyes. Even with Rodney terrorizing him, he was trying to avoid stepping on her.

"He won't hurt you, honey. I feel it," Jake had told her once.

Tears of sheer outrage sprang to Molly's eyes. She riveted a glare on Rodney, hating him as she'd never hated anyone. Fury sent a rush of adrenalin coursing through her body. She struggled up onto her elbows and knees. *Damn him, damn him.* He was a bastard without a heart. How could he do this?

"Step on her, you stupid beast!" The whip sang in the air again. "Do it, or I'll cut you. Do it, you son of a bitch!"

Sunset screamed again. Swaying dizzily on her knees, Molly looked up, and all she could see was the rearing horse and flashing hooves. *Dear God.* She threw up an arm to shield her face, knowing she was about to die. Only somehow Sunset wheeled at the last second, bringing his front feet down beside her instead of on her. Molly sobbed, her body quivering with relief.

Sunset tried to move away from her. Rodney cut him off with a snap of the whip. The horse circled the other way, and again, Rodney blocked his path. Molly knew the horse could only avoid stepping on her for so long. Eventually terror would blind him, and he'd kill her.

A snarl crawled up Molly's throat. She focused sharply on Rodney, despising him with a virulence that made her whole body tremble. *Enough.* He'd contaminated her life with his evilness, twisting and transforming everything into an ugly travesty, robbing her of everything precious. She wouldn't let him destroy Sunset as well. She *wouldn't*.

A sudden calm settled over her brain, even as she tensed her body to spring. She waited until Rodney swung the whip again. Then, with a speed and strength she didn't know she possessed, she vaulted from a crouch, throwing up her arms to catch the snaking leather in her hands. Dimly, she felt the whip cut into her palms. She tightened her grip, snapped her wrists to wrap the leather around her arms, and with all the force of her weight, she jerked.

With a surprised yelp, Rodney toppled off the fence rail into the pen. He hit the dirt in a facedown sprawl and shook his head as if to clear it.

"You bastard!" Molly cried, throwing the whip with all her strength through the rails of the fence. "You leave my horse alone!"

Rodney shook his head again. Then he tried to push to his knees. He fixed Molly with a dazed, bewildered look, as if his senses hadn't quite righted themselves yet. When his gaze cleared, he thrust a hand inside his jacket.

"Plan B," he said, and pulled out the gun. "It's registered in your name, darling. I lied."

Molly tensed, knowing a bullet would plow into her body at any second. This was it. She was dead.

Only she'd forgotten the third player in this scene. *Sunset.* The horse came from behind her like an avenging angel, mane flying, tail raised like a cavalry flag behind his gigantic black body. He advanced on Rodney, never slowing. Rodney screamed and tried to throw himself out of the stallion's path, but Sunset ran his heart out to reach him.

"Oh, God!" Rodney yelled.

The next instant, Sunset ran right over the top of him. Molly almost whooped. *Yes!* Rodney wasn't such a big man when he didn't have a whip in his hand.

Molly raced forward. The gun had slipped from Rodney's grasp and lay in the dirt. She kicked the weapon outside the pen, beyond Rodney's reach. Sunset circled to the far end of the corral. Molly, intent on Rodney, didn't realize the horse was racing back until she saw hooves flash. She glanced up. Sunset stood on his hind legs. Eyes wild, mane flying, his powerful body a sculpture of magnificent jet in the sunlight, the horse seemed poised there for endless seconds, a vengeful beast bent on destroying his tormentor.

With a scream of rage, the stallion brought his front hooves down on the man who had scarred him for life. Stupefied, Molly watched, a part of her cheering Sunset on. The horse deserved his moment of revenge. Rodney deserved to die. For seconds that seemed to last a short eternity, Molly felt smug satisfaction and sincerely hoped the stallion delivered a lethal blow. What a fitting ending to a totally misbegotten life.

Sunset shrieked again and crouched on his rear legs to pummel Rodney with his front hooves. In that instant, Molly regained her sanity. *Sunset.* The stallion was intent on killing Rodney, and she didn't blame him. But what would happen to the horse if she allowed it? No matter what the provocation, a stallion that turned killer would be destroyed.

She darted forward, afraid the crazed horse might turn on her if she interfered. "Sunset, *no*! Sunset, stop!" Molly leaped in to grab the stallion's halter, knowing even as she did that she lacked the strength to pull him off. "Sunset, please. Please!"

The instant the horse felt her hands on him, he grunted and backed away to stand motionless over the man he hated so much, blowing, snorting, every muscle in his glorious body tensed. Molly sobbed and hugged the stallion's neck. "I *know,*" she whispered. "I know just how you feel, Sunset, but it's better this way. It's better this way."

Rodney moaned and rolled over. Molly could tell by the way he moved that he wasn't seriously hurt. For Sunset's sake, she was glad of that. The stallion had already suf-

fered enough because of this man. Keeping an arm around
her horse's neck, she gazed down at her ex-husband, feeling detached. His suit was ripped and in a few places she
thought she could see a little blood. Compared to the
wounds he'd inflicted on Sunset, his injuries were mere
scratches.

"Dare to move, and I'll turn him loose on you," Molly
warned.

Rodney angled her a hate-filled glare. "And I'll see him
shot!"

"No, you won't, because I'll let him kill you." Molly
looked him dead in the eye. "I'll tell the authorities I blud-
geoned you myself before I allow anyone to touch this animal."

Rodney came up on one knee. Sunset snorted and
started to prance. Rodney froze, cast a wary glance at the
stallion, and lay back down. "Hold him, for Christ's sake!"

Molly smiled. "I'm feeling very weak and dizzy from
the blow to my head. Lie still, Rodney. If he starts to act
up, I may not be able to keep him off you."

Rodney's hazel eyes went dark with fear. He flattened
himself to the ground. "You bitch!" he whispered.

"Yes, and don't forget it."

Over the roar of the house fire, Molly thought she heard
something. Before she could identify the sound, she heard
Jake's voice. "Molly. Oh, sweet Jesus!"

Glancing around, she saw Jake swinging off his horse,
dust billowing around him. He emerged from the rust-red
cloud at a dead run, a blur of blue and burnished skin that
sailed over the fence as if it wasn't there. Molly felt as if a
locomotive had plowed into her when her husband
snatched her up in his arms. Sunset whinnied and backed
up a few inches, but he didn't run.

"Dear God, dear God." Jake turned in a half circle with
her locked against his trembling body. Molly wanted to tell
him she was okay, but he was hugging her so fiercely, she
couldn't talk. "You're bleeding. You're hurt." He loosened

his embrace to catch her face between his hands. "Oh, sweet Lord, your head's cut."

"He hit me with a rock." Molly reached to feel, wincing when her fingertips grazed the deep gash.

She was about to say that she was okay when Rodney rose to his knees. Molly staggered dizzily when Jake suddenly released her and whirled around.

"You son of a *bitch*!" He plucked Rodney up from the dirt and shook him like a rag doll. "I'll kill you. I swear to God, you're a dead man."

Rodney took a wild swing, grazing Jake's jaw. Jake retaliated by drawing back his fist and hitting Rodney squarely in the face. The blow sent the other man reeling back against the fence. Molly could only gape. She'd always known Jake was strong, but she hadn't realized he had the strength to lift a large man clear off his feet with one punch.

"My *nose*," Rodney cried, cupping his hands over his eyes. "You bastard, you broke my nose!"

"That's not all I'm going to break!" Face contorted with rage, big body taut, Jake advanced.

"Jake, no!" Molly cried.

It was as if Jake didn't hear her. He leaped on Rodney again, hauled him erect by the front of his jacket, and proceeded to rap his head against the fence post. Molly grabbed her husband's arm, screaming for him to stop. He paid her no heed.

"You miserable, worthless piece of trash!" Jake shook Molly off as if she weighed nothing and plowed his fist into Rodney's stomach, once again lifting him clear off his feet with the blow and bending him double. "Keep your filthy hands *off* my wife! Touch her—even *look* at her again—and I swear on all that's holy, I'll snap your neck."

Molly was afraid Jake might kill Rodney. She'd never seen him like this. His face was drawn. His eyes glittered. With every word he spoke, he bared his teeth in a snarl.

Suddenly Hank was there. He leaped on his brother's

back, locked Jake's arms behind his waist in an unbreakable hold, and then rode it out, with Jake cursing a blue streak, staggering under his weight, and trying futilely to shake him off.

"Stop it, Jake!" Hank yelled. "He's not worth it. Let the law punish the bastard."

With a mighty roar of anger, Jake tried again to free his arms. "Get *off* me, damn you. He hurt my *wife*!"

Hank didn't unlock his hold on his brother's arms. "She's all right, Jake. She's going to be all right."

Jake stood with his legs braced apart to bear the extra two hundred pounds draped over his shoulders. He heaved for air, his fiery gaze riveted on Rodney, who had slumped to the ground with his back against the fence, one arm angled over his stomach.

"He's down," Hank said. "You got your message across. If you pound it home when he can't fight back, you'll hate yourself for it later!"

"Like *hell* I will!" Jake cried. "Why show him mercy? Did he show Sunset any? Damn him! He bashed my wife's head with a *rock*!"

"I'm all right, Jake," Molly said shakily. "See?" She waved a hand in front of her husband's face. "Would you look at me? I'm fine. It's only a little bump. I'm okay."

Jake cut her a glance. Some of the wildness went out of his eyes. "Nobody touches my wife," he bit out.

"He'll pay for it," Hank assured him. "He'll pay, Jake. But not this way. You could end up in prison. Is that what you want?"

Jake staggered sideways. Then he suddenly stopped fighting. Heaving for breath, he bent forward to better support Hank's weight. Molly saw sanity returning to his eyes. "No, of course, it's not what I want," he ground out. "Get off me, little brother, before I beat the sass out of you."

Hank grinned at Molly and released his brother's arms. Patting Jake on the shoulder, he said, "You need to watch that temper of yours, bro. It could get you in trouble."

Jake straightened, leveled a burning look at Rodney, and then, cursing vilely under his breath, he kicked dirt into the other man's face. Molly almost laughed when Rodney sputtered and coughed. Since she'd eaten her own share of dirt only a few minutes ago, she felt it was just punishment.

"This is your lucky day," Jake told Rodney through clenched teeth. "You're not worth going to prison over, so I'll spare your worthless hide."

He came to Molly then. With shaking hands, he checked her for injuries, his touch so careful and gentle, she might have been made of fragile glass.

"I'm all right," she whispered. "I'm all right, Jake."

She looked up and couldn't believe what she was seeing. Jake Coulter's vivid blue eyes were swimming with tears. A muscle in his cheek bunched as he cautiously examined the wound on the crown of her head, his fingertips barely grazing the edges of the gash. "He could have killed you," he said in a husky voice that shook slightly.

"But he didn't. Sunset wouldn't step on me, no matter what Rodney did, and together, we took him down."

Jake slipped an arm around her waist and drew her against him. She could hear his heart pounding and felt his body trembling. By that, she took measure of how very much he loved her. She closed her eyes and pressed her face against his shirt. Never had anyone's arms felt so wonderful. To love and be loved truly was such a fabulous feeling.

"Your house," she whispered shakily. "All I've done is bring you heartbreak, from start to finish, Jake. I'm so sorry."

His embrace tightened around her. He didn't even look toward the burning house. "Never that, Molly girl. Never that. A spot of trouble, here and there, but no heartbreak. Don't you know how much I love you?"

Molly did know. How could she not? She went up on

her tiptoes to hug his neck. "Oh, Jake, I love you, too. But what of the ranch? He's destroyed everything."

"Not everything," he whispered against her hair. "Not even close. We have each other, sweetheart. Nothing can keep us down for long."

Sunset nickered just then. Molly opened her eyes to see that the horse was sniffing her husband's sleeve. Jake chuckled and reached out to curl a hand over the horse's halter. "So you've finally decided I'm okay, have you?" He tugged on the leather. "Come ahead. Love on her all you want."

Sunset nickered again and moved in closer to sniff Molly's clothing, then her hair. When the stallion smelled her blood, he snorted and pawed the dirt.

"I know," Jake muttered, tightening his grip on the horse's halter. "I'd like to stomp him, too. But we better not."

Molly grinned in spite of herself. In that moment, she knew Jake was absolutely right. Everything wasn't lost. They still had each other, and they still had Sunset.

Where there was enough love, anything was possible. The three of them formed a winner's circle, and together, they would start over. Sunset hadn't yet run his last race, and what had been razed by fire could be rebuilt. She would get her inheritance now. Money wouldn't be a problem.

Molly turned in her husband's arms to press her back against his chest. She barely saw Hank, who was bent over Rodney, relieving him of the computer disks and the papers he'd forced her to sign. She gazed instead at the burning house. Beyond the flames, the pastureland and forests of the Lazy J stretched like a promise, offering grazing land for the horses, timber for reconstruction, and an endless playground for all the little Coulters who'd someday be born. Molly meant to make sure that they grew up right there, on Coulter land, with their father's dream a reality around them.

She straightened her shoulders and took a deep, cleansing breath. She remembered all the many times she'd heard a voice whisper in her mind. *Who are you, Molly? Where are you?* Now, she could answer both questions unequivocally.

She was Molly Sterling Coulter, and she was right where she belonged, in her husband's loving arms.

Epilogue

Seven months later:

Snowflakes drifted gently through the air, flocking the Douglas fir trees with white and lending the gray-blue gloaming of twilight a magical feeling of Christmas. Pulling his very pregnant wife on a sled behind him, Jake trudged more deeply into the forest, keeping an eye out for the "perfect" tree. So far, nothing he'd found suited Molly. He glanced at his watch. If he didn't find a Christmas tree soon, they wouldn't get back to the house in time to greet their guests. Unfortunately, he couldn't tell Molly that. He didn't want to ruin her surprise.

With a sigh of resignation, he forged onward. It was rough going in places, the snowdrifts so deep they came to his knees. The coarse towrope bit through his lined denim jacket, making his shoulder ache, and his legs were growing weary from the strain of pulling the extra weight.

"What about that one?" he asked hopefully, pointing to a small fir.

Molly gazed critically at the tree he indicated. After a moment, she shook her head. "It's too scrawny."

The last one had been too fat. Beginning to wonder if there was any such thing as a perfectly proportioned Christmas tree, Jake set off again. He walked only a short way before he had to stop for a breather.

"You're getting tired," Molly called in a worried voice. "I *knew* this was a bad idea. Just let me get off and walk. A little exercise will be good for me."

"No way," he managed to say between gulps of air. Though he'd already told her his reasons for pulling her behind him on the sled, he added, "Not in this deep snow. You could fall and hurt yourself."

"I'm not made of fragile glass, and neither is the baby." She pouted prettily and gave her head a shake to rid her curly hair of snowflakes. "It'd be like falling on a pillow." She dragged her gloved fingers through the fluffy whiteness beside the sled. "I couldn't possibly get hurt."

"You could fall on a stump hidden by a drift," Jake pointed out. "Or on a big rock we can't see. Besides, I'm not that tired."

"Yes, you are. Please let me walk? Just for a while, then I'll let you pull me again."

Jake narrowed an eye at her. "You promised, no arguments. When it comes to the safety of my wife and son, I don't want to take any chances." Hoping to distract her, Jake scanned the small stand of evergreen trees around them. His dad had planted them as seedlings years ago, and now they were finally large enough to harvest. "Do you see one that you like?"

She frowned slightly. "You know what I think my problem is? They're all too beautiful. I've never found it difficult to choose a Christmas tree from a tree lot. I'm in and out in ten minutes. Here, I can't seem to make up my mind."

"You know what they say. Give a woman too many choices, and all it does is confuse her."

Her laughing gaze met his, and she poked out her tongue. "Yes, well, most men wouldn't recognize symmetry if it ran up and bit them on the behind."

Jake laughed and stepped around the sled to steal a quick kiss. Her warm, moist mouth tasted of Christmas toffee, and he was sorely tempted to forgo tree hunting to join her under the wool blankets he'd tucked so carefully around her.

"Have I told you lately how much I love you?" he asked huskily.

"Not for at least twenty minutes. I'm feeling neglected."

Jake reclaimed her lips, deepening the kiss this time until she pressed close and put her arms around his neck. Unable to resist the invitation, he sank onto the sled beside her and drew her across his lap. When the kiss ended, they sat in silence, taking in the beauty of the forest around them. The falling snow seemed to absorb sound, creating an almost mystical silence that made Jake feel as if they were the only two people in the world. He rested his chin atop Molly's head and sighed.

"Happy?" he asked.

"I've never been so happy," she murmured. "And I can barely wait for Christmas." She rested a hand over the front of her new parka where her swollen tummy stretched the nylon taut. "I still can't believe you managed to get the house rebuilt in time. Our very first Christmas together, and we get to celebrate it in our home. I can almost see the great room, with lights twinkling on the tree and garland draped over the river rock."

When Jake tried to envision it, all he could picture was Molly's smile brightening the room. He was so glad that fate had led her to him.

"Thank you, Jake," she said softly.

He stirred to glance down at her. "For what?"

"For working so hard to get the house finished. It wasn't really necessary, you know. I would have been just as happy to celebrate Christmas at the cabin."

He bent to kiss the tip of her nose. "I didn't want to bring our baby boy home to that drafty old cabin. I knew that if I didn't get all the work done before Christmas, the holidays would set me back."

She sighed and snuggled closer. "Yes, well, thank you. Because of you, the last of my pregnancy is going to be what dreams are made of."

Even as she spoke, Jake heard the trace of sadness in her voice and knew there was still one very important element missing in her life. "I couldn't have done it without help. Hank and the men worked almost as hard as I did. And you contributed, too. What about all those cushions for the furniture that you helped Mom and Bethany make?"

"That was nothing. While we sat around sewing, you were working the ranch all day and making log furniture at night."

He cupped his hands protectively over her swollen middle. It would have been a lie to say that he hadn't burned his candle at both ends to get the house finished in time for the birth of their child in February. But all the long hours had been worth it.

"Right after New Year's, we'll start getting the nursery decorated and furnished," he promised. "I found a great pattern for a cradle. It looks like Noah's ark."

She giggled. "You're kidding."

"You do still want to go with the Noah's ark theme, right? Or have you changed your mind again?"

"Nope, Noah's ark it is. Growing up on a ranch, our little boy will be surrounded by animals. We may as well get him acclimated to the lifestyle early on." She brushed her cheek against his jacket. "Oh, Jake, I love you so. A cradle that's shaped like an ark? It'll be darling. You're making all my wishes come true."

Not all of them, he thought, and glanced at his watch again. It was almost five o'clock, and Molly's most meaningful Christmas present was due to arrive soon. Jake hoped to hell they didn't have an accident. There was a full-fledged snowstorm occurring in the mountains, making the highway conditions between there and Portland treacherous. He felt certain that traction devices were being required on the passes.

"It's all pretty perfect, isn't it?" he whispered, struggling to stay on track with his side of the conversation.

Molly rested quietly against him for a moment, saying nothing. When she finally spoke, she injected a note of blissful happiness into her voice. "Oh, yes, absolutely perfect."

Jake grinned against her curls. *Sweet Molly.* She would never dream of admitting that her happiness wasn't complete and would never be complete until her relationship with one very important person was mended. Jake understood, though, without her expressing her feelings. Every young woman wanted and needed her mother with her when she gave birth to her first child.

Rodney's had been a nasty, emotional trial, and Molly had given the most damaging testimony, which had ended with her ex-husband receiving two sentences, one for life, the other for forty years. The justice system being what it was, Jake figured the bastard would probably get paroled eventually to enjoy his golden years as a free man, but that was the way of things in this country. There seemed little point in letting the unpleasant inequities ruin his and Molly's happiness.

What bothered Jake—what he absolutely could not and would not accept—was the lack of communication between Molly and her adoptive mother. It had come out during the trial that Jared Wells, Rodney's father, had suspected that his son was involved in insider trading. Not realizing the extent of Rodney's depravity, Jared had done what many fathers might have done under the same circumstances. He had turned a blind eye, telling himself that Rodney would hurt only himself.

Wrong. Jared's error in good judgment had caused a great deal of harm to others, costing his best friend and partner his life and putting Molly through untold hardships in a sanitarium. Jared Wells would bear the guilt of that for the rest of his days, and a terrible guilt it was. He had hung his head at the trial and been unable to look Molly in the eye, thinking she despised him and would never forgive him for his failure to come forward. Claudia, being the loving, loyal woman she was, had stood by her new husband, her eyes revealing a world of heartbreak and regret every time she looked across the courtroom at her daughter.

What a mess. It was a situation Jake was determined to rectify for Molly's sake. He couldn't count the times he'd found her standing by the phone with a wistful expression clouding her features. When he'd asked her what was wrong, she'd only shaken her head and said nothing.

Jake had known what was bothering her. She wanted to call her mother, but fearful of rejection, she couldn't quite muster the courage. He understood how she felt. After all the ugliness of the trial, it wouldn't be easy for anyone to make the first overture.

Oddly—or perhaps not so oddly, considering that she'd been raised by a fine person like Claudia—Molly didn't blame Jared Wells for loving and protecting his son. From the first, she had understood why her surrogate uncle had chosen to keep silent. What father worth his salt could turn his child in to the authorities without it tearing his heart out? Jared hadn't known the extent of Rodney's illegal activities, and the man had no way of predicting how foul his son's deeds would become before it was all over. Murder, betrayal. Such things were beyond the comprehension of normal, decent people, and Jared Wells was nothing if not a decent, caring man. Jake had picked up on that the first time he spoke with him on the phone.

No, aside from Rodney, Molly blamed no one—not Jared, and certainly not Claudia. But as often happened in complicated situations such as this, Molly believed with all her heart that Claudia and Jared resented her because she had been instrumental in sending Rodney to prison. Not only that, but Molly had been understandably joyous when the jury had found Rodney guilty on all counts.

After seeing that justice was served, however, Molly had gone into a holding pattern, reluctant to make the first contact with her mother and stepfather. *"No matter how wrong Rodney was, you know how Jared must be grieving over this. If they want to see me, it's up to them to make the first phone call!"* she'd cried to Jake after the trial.

As a result, she hadn't even returned to Sterling and Wells to take her rightful place behind her father's desk. Out of respect and concern for her mother's feelings, she probably never would, and that would be a shame. Molly had been raised to follow in Marshal Sterling's footsteps. The investment firm was important to her, and until she took up the reins, she would never be the woman she was meant to be—or the woman she needed to be. That couldn't be allowed to happen, and it wouldn't if Jake had any say in the matter. Six months out of the year, he wanted to see his wife helping to run the firm her father had worked all his life to build. The way Jake saw things, it was not only Molly's heritage, but that of their future children as well, and he meant to make damned sure Marshal Sterling's legacy was passed down to them.

On the outside looking in, Jake saw three people who had once loved each other deeply, and still did. It was time for all of them to talk, shed their tears, and get on with life. Molly and Claudia especially needed to patch up their relationship. A child was on the way. Jake wasn't about to let his son grow up without knowing his maternal grandmother.

To that end, he had telephoned Claudia and insisted that she and Jared come for a pre-Christmas dinner at the Lazy J. Claudia, concerned about how Molly might feel, had been reluctant to accept the invitation, but Jake had finally prevailed after a man-to-man talk with Jared. It would only be for an evening, after all. If things went well, Molly could ask her parents to stay longer. If the visit went badly, the misery would be over quickly.

"You feel tense," Molly whispered, jerking Jake from his reverie. She rubbed a hand over his arm. "Are you worried about something? You're all tied in knots."

Jake was praying to hear the faint sound of a car out on the main road. If Molly's parents had had an accident en route to the ranch, all his plans for a happy reunion might be forever spoiled. He didn't even want to think how Molly would react if something happened to her mother. At the very least, she'd probably be thrown into early labor.

"No, honey, I'm not worried. What's there to worry about? The insurance paid off on all the fire damage. The stable and house are rebuilt. Since the fall auction, we're actually operating in the black." He gave her shoulder a gentle squeeze. "And best of all, we're about to have a beautiful, healthy little boy. I've never been so content."

"Me, neither." Her gaze suddenly caught on a tree off to the right, and a delighted smile swept over her face. "Oh, Jake, look at that one. It's *gorgeous!*"

Jake turned to peruse the tree. His heart sank when he noted how huge it was. "Honey, that thing must be ten feet tall."

"We need a really tall one to go in front of the vaulted windows. A short tree will be dwarfed."

Setting her carefully off his lap, he stifled a sigh and pushed to his feet. He wanted their first Christmas together to be memorable for her in every way, and if that meant dragging a ten-foot tree all the way home, he'd do it without complaint. He grabbed the saw from where he'd stashed it on the sled and went to work. Minutes later, he jumped out of the way as the huge Douglas fir plummeted to the ground.

She struggled up from the sled in that awkward, tummy-first way of all pregnant ladies. Once standing, she appeared delightfully round in the parka and thick fleece pants he'd insisted she wear. Her hair fluffed in a brilliant cloud of curls around her head. "It'll be so beautiful, all decorated with lights."

"Not half as beautiful as you are." Jake meant that with all his heart. All his life he'd been told how radiant some women were during pregnancy, and Molly was one of them. Her eyes sparkled, and her skin seemed to glow.

After dragging the huge tree over and securing it across the sled with ropes, he and Molly began the homeward trek through the woods. "If you're not too tired, maybe we can get this monster decorated tonight after dinner."

"I won't be too tired," she insisted, her voice ringing with enthusiasm. "I haven't done anything but sit on the sled. You did all the work."

Jake guessed that was true.

As they drew near the house, he saw a beige Buick sedan coming up the drive. Relief flooded through him. Jared and Claudia had arrived safely. He drew the sled over the boards he'd laid out to bridge the creek. Then he stopped and glanced back at Molly. "It looks like we've got company."

She squinted to see through the falling snow. When she spied the slender woman stepping from the Buick, her eyes widened with incredulity, and her face drained of color. For an awful moment, Jake wondered if he'd made a mistake by inviting Claudia there without asking Molly in advance. But then his wife let out a glad little cry.

"It's my *mom*! Oh, Jake, it's my mom."

"Looks that way."

Her questioning gaze jerked to his. Then, before he could guess what she meant to do, she threw herself into his arms, their bodies connecting belly first. "You called her for me! Oh, Jake, *thank* you!" She rained kisses along his jaw. "I love you. You're the most wonderful husband who ever lived. I love you, love you, *love* you!"

Before he could think of a response, she shoved from his arms and whirled toward the house. Not wanting her to take a spill in the snow, Jake almost grabbed her hand. But then he thought better of it and let her go. This close to the house, there were no fallen logs or rocks hidden beneath the drifts. If she slipped and fell, the deep snow would provide her with a soft landing.

For a lady heavy with child, she ran with amazing agility. Pulling the tree-laden sled behind him, Jake followed at a much slower pace. This was Molly and Claudia's moment. He preferred to hang back until they said their hellos.

As Jake neared the barn, Hank emerged from the doorway. He tipped back his hat, his eyes twinkling with amusement as he watched Molly launch herself into her mother's arms. He flicked a knowing look at Jake. "You're going to be her hero for at least a month."

Jake observed the emotional reunion. Then he grinned. "I just set things in motion, that's all."

"You want me to run in the house and get a stack of towels?" Hank asked.

"What for?"

"To mop up all the tears." Hank rested his gloved hands at his hips, his dark face creased in a grin. "It's going to be ugly. She's been really weepy the last few days. Once the spigot gets turned on, she can't seem to shut it off."

Jake glanced at the women, who were locked in each other's arms and sobbing with joy as they swayed back and forth. "Most women cry easily during pregnancy. It's something to do with their hormone levels."

"I told her how big her stomach was yesterday, and she burst into tears," Hank said. "I felt terrible, but nothing I said made it better. I never meant to hurt her feelings. She's such a sweetheart, and she's cute as a button with that big tummy poking out."

"She feels fat and unattractive right now. I think most women do at this stage."

"She doesn't look fat," Hank observed. "I think it's cute, the way she waddles."

Jake shot his brother a warning look. "Do *not* say the word *waddle* in front of her. She'll be upset until after the baby's born."

Hank huffed. "Do I look that stupid?"

"Yes."

Another shrill wailing sound drifted to them. Jake turned to peer at his wife through the thickening downfall of snowflakes. His heart caught when he saw that Jared had joined the women and was now participating in a three-way embrace. Molly buried her face against her mother's shoulder, and then she turned to press her cheek to Jared's chest. Even from a distance, Jake could see the happiness in her expression.

He was glad—so very glad. From the start, he'd sensed Molly's loneliness. To someone like Jake, who'd grown up with so much love to sustain him, it seemed tragic that other people weren't so fortunate.

Smiling, he watched Claudia cup Molly's face between her hands. The tenderness in the older woman's actions spoke volumes, making Jake recall the afternoon he'd told Molly that everyone, both humans and animals, saw themselves as others did. He also remembered with a twinge of sadness how Molly had once gazed at her reflection in the bathroom mirror and told him she couldn't find herself anymore, that the person she'd once been was gone.

Jake had assured her then that the real Molly still existed, that she only needed time to rediscover herself. This reunion was the final step in that process, a reclaiming of childhood memories and a reestablishment of family bonds that defined who she really was and how deeply and unconditionally she was loved.

A lump came to Jake's throat. Eventually Molly and Claudia would have ironed things out on their own. The love between them ran too deep for it to happen otherwise. Nevertheless, he stood a little taller, knowing he'd been instrumental in making it happen today—before Christmas and before their son was born. What better gift could he give his wife?

As if Molly felt his gaze on her, she turned to search him out. The radiant smile she flashed his way was all the invitation Jake needed. He dropped the sled rope and started toward her. Breaking away from her parents, Molly ran to him.

Jake met her halfway and caught her up in his arms. She

laughed tearfully and leaned back to search his eyes. Jake allowed her to look deeply, hoping to convey his message without words.

Judging by her radiant smile, he knew she understood—that, in his opinion, she was and would always be the most beautiful woman in the world.

Here's an excerpt from Catherine Anderson's
next exciting contemporary romance

Back in My Heart

Coming in August 2002

Ellie Grant tugged her son Kody's basketball jersey from between the cream-colored sofa cushions. The white knit was streaked with mud and covered with black dog hair, and the team name, "Trojans," in green lettering across the front was smeared with what appeared to be mustard. Scrunching the nylon in her fist, she almost lifted it to her nose and then caught herself. What on earth was she doing? Granted, she missed her boys, but they'd be gone only until tomorrow night. She could survive another weekend without them—no shirt sniffing allowed.

Turning, she stared at the television, which was usually on and blaring when they were home. Light from the adjoining dining room reflected off the dusty screen, highlighting the words, "Wash me." Ellie grinned in spite of herself. The brats. In the time it had taken one of them to scrawl that message, he could have polished the glass.

Her smile slowly faded. The quiet inside the house seemed so loud that it echoed against her eardrums. Most mothers would probably take advantage of the reprieve to read a good book or take a luxurious bubble bath, but Ellie just felt lost. For two weeks straight, she hadn't had a second to call her own. Now she suddenly had twenty-four hours of emptiness stretching before her.

It was always this way when Tucker had the boys. She never knew quite what to do with the time. She stared at the dog hair on the mauve carpet and briefly considered hauling out her old Kirby, but like an alcoholic tempted by drink, she shoved the thought away. Instead, she stepped to the entertainment center and punched on the stereo. Zach, her fourteen-year-old, kept the CD player filled with his favorite country-western disks. Garth Brooks would chase away the silence and lift her spirits in short order.

She cranked up the volume, grabbed the portable phone from the end table, and headed toward the kitchen. As she passed through the dining room, the first strains of "Every Breath You Take" by the Police thrummed in the air. She stopped dead in her tracks. In July of her sixteenth year, that had been the song blaring on the radio of Tucker's rattletrap Chevy when she lost her virginity. She hadn't listened to it since the divorce, and Zach surely hadn't put it in the player. He disdainfully called all songs from his parents' era "oldie moldies."

Ellie almost swung around to change the selection. But no, it wasn't a problem, she assured herself. Two years ago, she might have fallen apart if she'd listened to that song, but she could handle it now. A stroll down memory lane might even be good for her, proof at long last that she was completely and forever over Tucker Grant.

Continuing toward the kitchen, she let the music carry her back to that summer night nineteen years ago. The details came so clear in her mind that it might have happened yesterday. She could almost smell the breeze rolling in off the river, redolent with the perfume of wildflowers and the scent of pine. She and Tucker had climbed into the back where they could stretch out on the seat without the steering wheel and gearshift getting in their way. Heads bent, hands shaking with nerves, they'd shyly undressed, neither of them completely sure how to proceed once they got naked. Finally, Tucker had simply taken her in his arms. *Don't be scared, Ellie girl*, he'd whispered. *I'll love you forever—until the rivers stop flowing and the ocean goes dry.*

Snapped back to the present by the coldness of the worn kitchen linoleum under her bare feet, Ellie sighed and shook her head. Talk about a sappy line. She was surprised she hadn't giggled. Back then, of course, it had seemed terribly romantic, just the sort of thing a young girl yearned to hear.

Determined not to think about Tucker a second longer, Ellie advanced across the floor. Halloween was only a month away. She would put this time to good use by making sugar cookies for her sons—great big round ones, decorated to look like jack-o'-lanterns. In the morning, she'd go up to the attic and dig out the Halloween decorations. By tomorrow night, the house would be cheery and bright with pumpkins and witches hanging at the windows, and she'd welcome the boys at the door with a big smile and a plate of treats for them to devour. They'd love that.

Images flashed through her mind of holiday baking sprees when her boys had been much younger, their faces smeared with icing, their pudgy fingers gooey and coated with multicolored sprinkles. The kitchen had fared no better than their faces, unfortunately, and afterward she'd always felt compelled to scrub the floor on her hands and knees.

Looking back on it now, Ellie wished with all her heart that she'd let the floor go and just enjoyed having cookies and milk with her sons. But no, before Sammy's death and the ensuing divorce, her priorities had been seriously skewed. She'd been caught up in the super-mom syndrome back then, convinced she had to be a perfect wife, mother, and homemaker, all while she pursued a career. She'd had no time to sit around on a winter afternoon, eating cookies with her precious little boys.

It had taken a tragedy to make her realize that nothing was more important than her kids. *Nothing*. These days, if it came to a choice between devoting time to her sons or scrubbing the floor, the floor lost every time. When the boys were grown, they wouldn't remember how clean her kitchen had been, but they'd have fond memories of this holiday season and the goodies she'd baked for them.

A cook who habitually washed up as she worked, Ellie stopped the sink drain and squeezed in dish soap. While the water ran, she lighted the candle on the windowsill that Kody had given her for Mother's Day, a misshapen lump of yellow wax he'd poured for her at school. He'd used one of Bucky's dog food cans as a mold, and the rings in the aluminum had left telltale lines. Every time she looked at it, she smiled.

Beyond the glass, the drizzly gray of afternoon had given way to the deeper shades of early evening. Still leafy from summer, hydrangea, lilac, and camellia bushes crowded the weathered board fence, creating a dense jungle of rain-drenched foliage that needed to be pruned back. Lending some bright relief from all the green, splashes of autumn orange decorated the drooping maple trees. Soon the grass would be hidden beneath a carpet of fallen leaves that would crunch cheerfully underfoot and turn the backyard into a colorful wonderland.

The wavering candlelight washed the windowpane with patterns of gold. As the flame licked its way down the wick, the sweet smell of vanilla wafted to Ellie's nostrils, reminding her of the task at hand. She wrenched off the faucet and turned from the sink. Studiously ignoring the range top, which only got washed when one of the boys decided to give it a few swipes, she climbed on the step stool to get the salt and vanilla from the spice cupboard above it. As she hopped down, she kept her gaze carefully averted from the stove's crusty burner plates. A vow was a vow. No matter how filthy they got, she would never scrub them, so why drive herself crazy noticing the buildup?

Singing along with Bonnie Tyler, she belted out the refrain of "Total Eclipse of the Heart" as she measured ingredients. She was about to soften some butter in the microwave when the portable phone on the counter rang. She jumped and then stared at it, knowing before she answered that it was probably Marvin calling. *Great.* She had grown very fond of him over the last few months, and most of the time she was glad of his company, but she didn't want to have him over when the boys weren't there. Whenever she was alone with him, he grew amorous, and it was becoming increasingly difficult to fend him off.

What to do, what to do? The phone jangled again, the sound urgent and demanding. She considered not answering. Only what if it wasn't Marvin? There was always a possibility that one of the boys might call.

On the fourth ring, she groaned and pressed the talk button. "Hello."

"Ellie?"

That deep, silky tenor was one she would have recognized anywhere. *Tucker.* Her hand tightened over the phone as an image of him took shape in her mind. Tawny hair, hazel eyes sharp with intelligence, and sun-burnished features, every chiseled plane of which had once been engraved on her heart. Now just thinking about him filled her with resentment.

She pictured him in a sunshine yellow kitchen with fake butcher-block counters. He'd be leaning against the wall, she decided, his booted feet crossed at the ankles, his rangy, well-muscled body showcased in a wash-worn flannel work shirt and faded denim jeans that hugged his long, powerfully roped legs like a second skin.

"Hi," she said stiffly. He so seldom called that she had to grope for something else to say. She opted for a note of humor. "If you're about to tell me the state has screwed up the child support again, I'll jump off a tall building. I just dropped a hundred and sixty bucks on football cleats and basketball shoes."

She hoped he would offer to kick in a little extra this month to cover the expense just so she could turn him down. He'd argued against her moving to Springfield, predicting that the cost of living would be much higher in the Eugene area and she would come to regret the decision. *In your face*, she wanted to say. *I'm doing just fine over here. I love my job. I just got a raise. I have a fabulous new boyfriend. I don't need your help, thanks very much.*

Instead of offering her money, he said, "No, it's nothing like that, Ellie."

His tone was taut and oddly expressionless. After being married to him for thirteen years, she knew when he was upset. Alarm raised goose bumps on her skin. "What's wrong?"

"I don't know how to say this."

Oh, God. Memories sped through her mind, all splashed with crimson. Her vocal cords felt like overstretched rubber as she struggled to speak. "What happened?" She braced a hand on the counter, feeling as if her knees might buckle. "It's one of the boys, isn't it? Who's hurt? Tucker, answer me."

"No, no, it's nothing like that. As far as I know, they're both all right."

"As far as you know?" Her heart was pounding so hard that it pained her. She pressed a fist over the spot. "Something's wrong. I hear it in your voice."

"They've taken off."

For a moment, the words circled in her mind, making no sense. "What do you mean, they've taken off?"

"Exactly what I said. I just got home, and the little snots are gone."

She stared stupidly at the roses on the faded hunter green wallpaper. "Gone? This is your weekend. You're supposed to be watching them."

"I worked today."

"So? I have a job, too. Have I ever called to tell you the kids were gone?"

"That isn't fair. Zach's fourteen, for Pete's sake, and the old lady next door is always available in case of emergency. You leave them alone on Saturday all the time while you're working."

"I also call to check on them. If they don't answer the phone, I hightail it home to see what's wrong."

"I was way out past Wickiup Reservoir, overseeing a team of stream surveyors. I tried to call home on my cell phone and couldn't get out."

Ellie knew the cell phone reception wasn't as good in Central Oregon as it was in the valley. There were fewer towers over there, and the mountainous terrain sometimes interfered with the signals. Knowing that and admitting it were two different things. She wasn't obligated to give Tucker Grant a fair shake. When the shoe had been on the other foot, had he been fair to her?

She pushed a shank of blond hair from her eyes. She

was shaking so hard that the strands shivered back down over her forehead the instant she withdrew her hand. "Where do you think they went?"

His voice turned gravelly. "According to the note they left, they're somewhere in the Baxter Wilderness Area."

Ellie knew the place. While they were still married, they'd taken the boys camping there several times each summer. "*Somewhere* in the area? I'm not following. That's a long way from Bend. How did they get there?"

"I think they rode their bicycles." He paused as if the next words came hard. "Ellie, they've run away."

"They've *what?*"

She heard a rustle of paper come over the line. "The note is in Zach's handwriting, but Kody signed it as well."

Iridescent hues of blue and pink shimmered in the froth of dishwater suds. The scent of vanilla from the candle suddenly made her feel nauseated.

"Ellie, are you still there?"

She nodded and then realized he couldn't see her. "Yes. I'm here. I'm, uh, just trying to assimilate this. Are you *sure* they've run away, Tucker? Maybe they just got bored while you were gone and—"

"No. I wish that were the case, but it isn't. They've definitely run away."

"Why? Did something happen to upset them?"

"Nothing that I'm aware of."

This was so unlike her sons she felt sure there had to be an explanation.

"My guess is that they left shortly after I did this morning," Tucker went on. "All that's in the dishwasher are two cereal bowls. I don't think they had lunch here. It would also take them quite a while to reach Baxter on bicycles. At least five or six hours, depending on how often they stopped to rest. They had to leave here fairly early to get there before dark."

Panic clawed at the edges of her mind. She held it at bay by trying to concentrate on absolutes instead of possibilities. "Did they take camping gear?"

"Yes. All that's left in the garage is mine."

She pictured her boys pedaling along the shoulder of that busy road, and her self-control took another hard hit. She caught the inside of her cheek between her teeth.

"Ellie, don't," he said softly, as if he knew exactly what she was thinking. "They've done this expressly to scare the bejesus out of us."

"And they've succeeded. Highway 97 is the most dangerous road in Oregon."

"Ah, now, it's not that bad."

Ellie remembered another time when he'd pooh-poohed her concerns, and she'd ended up standing over her child's grave. "I've warned them a *hundred* times not to ride their bikes in heavy traffic." Pain bunched in her temples.

"I'm sure they're both fine. If anything happened, someone would contact me."

"They don't carry ID."

"No, but the bicycles are licensed. The cops could easily trace them back to me. They're fine, Ellie. We need to keep our heads."

That was true. Panic would accomplish nothing. She took a deep breath. "Right." Kody's face flashed through her mind, and she wished she'd never let him out of her sight. "We'd, um, better call someone. We need to find them as quickly as we can."

"I can find them, Ellie. You know that."

She made a small sound of agreement. Tucker's reputation as a tracker was well known in Deschutes County. Search-and-rescue teams frequently called upon him to help locate lost hikers.

"I'll gather my gear and head up there as soon as we get off the phone," he said. "By first light, I'll be on their trail. Riding bicycles, they weren't able to take the dog with them. Bucky can help sniff them out. They'll be fine for the night."

"In a wilderness area?"

"They have warm sleeping bags, and they ransacked my cupboards and fridge, so they shouldn't go hungry. Even if they run low on food, they both know how to catch fish with whatever they have on hand, and I've taught them damned near everything I know about the edible plant life in that area."

"There are cougars and bears out there, Tucker. They're just little boys."

"Not so little anymore. Zach's fourteen, and Kody's eleven. I know grown men with less wilderness savvy. No worries, Ellie, I promise."

"I can't believe they've done something so harebrained."

"Yeah, well, they have. As for finding them quickly, I'll have them home tomorrow night, guaranteed." He released another weary sigh. "You know, Ellie, getting them back isn't the primary worry. We have to figure out what the hell we're going to do once we get them home."

"Shaking them silly sounds highly appealing at the moment." She stared bewilderedly at the half-mixed cookie dough, remembering all her grand plans for a cheery welcome-home party. How many kids got home-made cookies, just because? She lived with ring around the toilet, dirty grout, and dust bunnies under her furniture, and this was the thanks she got? "I can't believe they've done this. What earthly reason do they have?"

She heard the rustle of paper again. "They've made a couple of demands."

"What kind of demands?"

He hesitated before answering. "They refuse to come home until we agree to get back together."

"What?"

"You heard me. They want us back together again, no discussion, no bargains. It's that or nothing. They've made it very clear they won't settle for less."

In the background, Kim Carnes belted out the lyrics of "Bette Davis Eyes." Now Ellie understood why Zach had put that particular CD in the player. He knew she usually turned on the stereo while they were gone, and he'd been hoping to soften her up with old favorites from her and Tucker's dating days.

How long had he and Kody been planning this, anyway?